D0878238

THE

HIGHLANDER'S
VOW

A Novel of Loch Moigh

Barbara Longley

Montlake
Romance

This is a work of fiction. Names, characters, organizations, places, events, and incidents are either products of the author's imagination or are used fictitiously.

Text copyright © 2016 Barbara Longley

All rights reserved.

No part of this book may be reproduced, or stored in a retrieval system, or transmitted in any form or by any means, electronic, mechanical, photocopying, recording, or otherwise, without express written permission of the publisher.

Published by Montlake Romance, Seattle

www.apub.com

Amazon, the Amazon logo, and Montlake Romance are trademarks of Amazon.com, Inc., or its affiliates.

ISBN-13: 9781503934887
ISBN-10: 1503934888

Cover design by Jason Blackburn

Cover illustration by Dana Ashton France

Printed in the United States of America

THE
HIGHLANDER'S
VOW

Also by Barbara Longley

Love from the Heartland series, set in Perfect, Indiana

Far from Perfect

The Difference a Day Makes

A Change of Heart

The Twisted Road to You

The Novels of Loch Moigh

True to the Highlander

The Highlander's Bargain

The Highlander's Folly

This book is dedicated to my readers. Thank you!

CHAPTER ONE

Scotland, 1443

Weary of travel and sore from sitting upon her palfrey's saddle-clad back, Sky Elizabeth shifted yet again, trying to ease her discomfort. She shivered against the damp chill, and her gaze strayed to the keep looming against the distant horizon. The sight of Kildrummy Castle, soon to be her home, brought her no joy, and her heart grew heavy at the thought of her betrothed.

Sir Oliver of clan Erskine did not want her any more than she wanted him, and thanks to her accursed fae gifts, Sky could not pretend otherwise. He could not hide his true feelings behind good manners or honeyed words. Faced with naught but a life of loneliness amidst strangers, 'twas duty alone that compelled her forward.

"Just think, Sky." Helen, her younger sister, nudged her mount ahead so the two of them rode abreast. "You'll be a bride within a fortnight. I envy you. Your betrothed is young and quite pleasing to look upon."

Her sister's dreamy-eyed expression served only to deepen Sky's misery. "I'll gladly trade places with you, Helen. *You* may marry the earl of Mar's grandson, and *I* shall remain at Loch Moigh." *For the rest of my days.*

A lump rose to her throat. Indeed, had it not been for the passing of her grandsire, the old earl of Fife, following so closely upon the loss of her great-uncle, she would already be Oliver's wife. She'd been granted a reprieve, and now 'twas at an end. "I am nearly one and twenty, well past the age most ladies of noble birth marry. 'Twould please me well enough to remain unwed."

"Nay, you dinna . . ." Helen studied her for an instant and frowned. "Och, you do mean it. Do you no' yearn for bairns of your own?"

Like her, Helen had a trace of fae blood running through her veins, and she too could discern truth from lie. With the exception of her younger brother Thomas, all of Sky's siblings, including her foster brother, Hunter, were "gifted," as her mother would say.

"Nay." Sky shook her head. "I want to become a healer and a midwife like cousin Erin and Ma, only without the additional burdens of a husband and bairns."

Quick and sharp, a yearning cut through Sky's heart, and just as quickly she closed herself off from the unwanted emotion. She could not hope for bairns, not if it meant they'd be burdened with the same fae traits she carried. Hiding her gifts took a heavy toll. 'Twas exhausting, and the price of being such an oddity carried far too great a risk.

Only ensconced within the bosom of her clan and kin did she feel safe. At Loch Moigh she could be her true self, and that was where she wished to remain.

"Hmm." Helen frowned. "Mayhap you and Oliver will come to care for one another with time, aye? And you can practice your healing arts with the Erskine clan as well as you can with ours."

"Mayhap." She doubted time would have any effect on how she and Oliver felt for one another, and she kent well enough she could only practice her healing arts if her husband granted his permission for her to do so. She would soon become the future countess of Mar, and 'twas not considered seemly for a countess to attend the births of commoners, or to act as a village wisewoman, setting broken bones and tending the sick.

Sky turned her attention to the surrounding hills, already showing hints of green from the early spring rains. This late in the afternoon, and with the sun hidden behind heavy clouds, the Grampian Mountains appeared a dark bluish-gray. How fitting. The day she arrived at her new home *should* be dull, gray and dismal.

Blinking against the sting in her eyes, she looked to her da and ma, who rode at the head of their party. David, the elder of her twin brothers and heir to the earldom, took his place behind their parents. Sky's sister rode beside her, and their entire party was flanked by a score of MacKintosh guards.

"We shall arrive before nightfall," Helen said. "'Tis certain Owain regrets 'twas he Da entrusted with the clan's well-being whilst we are away. He so loves travel and adventure."

"Aye, that he does, and when he canna find adventure, he's sure to stir up mischief for his own amusement." Sky shook her head, remembering some of her brother's antics from the past. "For certes, 'tis why Da chose to leave him behind to look after things at home. Owain needs to settle down and take his responsibilities more seriously, and with no one else at Moigh Hall *but* him, he'll be forced to shoulder the burden of looking after the clan. I trow he'll have no time for aught else."

Their youngest sibling, Sarah, had also remained at home, so their granddam would have company. And Thomas, her youngest brother, was fostering with Hunter, who was now the baron DúnConnell. 'Twas too close to the birth of their second bairn for Lady Meghan to travel, and they'd not be attending the wedding.

A wave of sadness engulfed her. Of all her siblings, 'twas the twins she'd miss most, for they embodied all the qualities she lacked. Her brothers were bold and fearless, whilst she lurked in the periphery, watching their antics and longing to have but a small portion of their audacity.

Nay. 'Twas not in her nature to be adventurous or daring. *She* was the dutiful daughter, the proper lady, demure and acquiescent. Safety and security meant far more to her than adventure. Glancing once again toward Kildrummy, the keep's Snow Tower growing ever larger, she contemplated the merits of a sudden declaration to take vows and don the veil at the nearest abbey.

All too quickly the distance between her kin and the portcullis of Kildrummy Castle disappeared. Once through the barbican, they were met by a festive gathering, led by Lord Robert, the earl of Mar, his lady wife and Oliver, Sky's betrothed.

Several guests in residence for the wedding filled the inner bailey, and Sky's senses were assaulted by a myriad of emotions: curiosity, excitement, resentment and . . . jealousy? Searching the faces around her, she sought the source of the resentment and envy, for those powerful emotions emanated from a single individual.

"My lady." Oliver reached up to help her from her mount as a stable lad took the reins. "Welcome to Kildrummy Castle."

Placing her hands on his shoulders, she slid off her mare's back and into his arms. *This is when my heart should flutter, yet I feel naught.* And from Oliver? Resignation. Peering into his blue eyes, she searched for the merest ember of warmth and found only indifference. "My thanks, Sir Oliver."

"How was your journey, my lady?" He took her hand and placed it within the crook of his elbow. "Did you encounter any difficulties along the way?"

"Nay. Our journey was quite uneventful." Her parents were busy exchanging pleasantries with the earl, and her brother and sister stayed close beside them. Having similar fae abilities as she, her siblings must also be suffering the onslaught of feelings swirling through the air.

She and Oliver were alone at the outer edge of the throng. Now was the time to beg him to release her from a bleak future devoid of love— or even the slightest wisp of affection. Sky cast a glance his way, racking her brain for some legitimate reason why they should not wed—and failed. Not for the first time she cursed her rank. Duty and obligation to her kin and clan weighed heavily upon her, a burden she could not be free of without causing an outright feud between the Erskines and MacKintosh.

Once again a surge of jealousy reached her. Sky surveyed the people milling about and met the glare of a young woman. "Who might that lady be, my lord?" She tilted her head in the direction of the flaxen-haired lass standing by a portly older man. By the look of the two, they were kin to one another.

"Hmm?" Oliver followed her line of sight. "Ah, that is Lady Alice, the daughter of baron Lumsden, who stands beside her. They are our nearest neighbors to the east."

Sky sensed Oliver's pulse quickening as his gaze lingered upon the lass. He couldn't hide his desire for Alice, nor could he mask the warmth filling his eyes. No wonder Lady Alice suffered envy and resentment toward her. *The two are in love.*

Sky gasped at the revelation. She now had a way out of her unwanted marriage. All she need do was arrange time alone with Oliver, and she could talk him into approaching their parents together. Once they convinced all involved that there would be no animosity over yet another broken betrothal between their clans—her father and the earl of Mar's daughter being the first more than a score of years past—Oliver would be free to marry Alice.

She'd be free to return to Moigh Hall, her true home. Her heart's desire to continue learning the healing arts could finally be realized. She'd remain in the service of her beloved kin and clan. Aye, 'twas the perfect solution. Surely her betrothed would be as relieved as she to find himself free of the unwanted union.

Damnation! Sky poured water from the ewer into the basin and washed her face. Nearly a se'nnight had passed since she'd arrived at Kildrummy Castle, and not once had she been able to arrange time alone with her betrothed. What with all the feasting and entertainments, and Oliver's obvious avoidance of her, she'd not had a single opportunity to convince him to release her from their marriage contract.

Time was slipping through her fingers. They were to be wed three days hence. She had to act. Determination stiffened her spine. She'd hunt him down this very day and bring him to ground if need be.

Helen sat up in the large bed they shared, stretched and yawned. "You're up and dressed early this morn. Have you somewhere to be? Do you mean to attend mass?"

"I am up early every day, Helen. I wish to see the hunting party off." The earl of Mar, her da, brother and several other guests planned to hunt wild boar, which gave her an excuse to wander the keep in search of Oliver. He planned to remain behind, claiming he cared naught for such sport, as he preferred to hunt with falcons.

"I'm going back to sleep then. After last eve's entertainments, I trow none of the other ladies will be afoot yet." Sighing, her sister flopped back onto the down mattress.

"As you will." Sky cleaned her teeth, brushed and braided her hair and set out for the great hall. The large chamber held a goodly number intending to go on the hunt, along with a few of the ladies wishing them well. Food had been laid out, and many were breaking their fast. She joined her family where they sat at the far end of the high table. "Good morn." Sky took a place beside her brother and reached for a piece of the thick black bread and a slice of cheese.

Her mother reached across the table and patted Sky's arm. "Good morning. Where's Helen?"

"Still abed. She'd sleep every morning away if allowed. 'Tis no' a good habit, Ma. You should speak to her." Scanning the great hall, she searched for Oliver.

"If you're looking for your betrothed, he's not here," her mother said. "We haven't seen him yet this morning."

Nodding, Sky took a bite of her bread and cheese. *Today. I will find him, and he will listen to me.* Her breath caught in her throat, and her heart pounded with trepidation.

Her mother's brow rose. "Is everything all right, Sky?"

"Aye. I had hoped to catch Oliver here is all. I thought he might be willing to take me riding. We've had so little privacy, and with most of the men off hunting, 'twould be the perfect time for the two of us to spend a few hours together." Clamping down on her roiling emotions, she turned to her brother and da. "I hope the hunt goes well."

"As do I." Her brother rubbed his stomach. "I do so enjoy roasted boar."

Her da slapped David's back. "We're certain to feast on the morrow from today's hunt. The gamekeeper and villagers have been complaining about the destruction wrought in the fields and woods by a sounder and their young. 'Tis likely we'll take a few by day's end."

"Be careful," her mother said, studying her husband and son. "I don't want you returning to the keep gored by filthy tusks."

"Och, do you no' ken by now what a canny hunter you've wed? This past score of years, have I ever let a boar get the better of me?" Her da placed his hand over her mother's, his eyes shining with love. "David and I will return to you unscathed, *mo leannan.* I'll no' let aught happen to our lad."

"Nor will I let aught happen to *Da.*" David's mouth quirked up. "Dinna fash, Ma. We're MacKintosh."

"Even the MacKintosh are vulnerable to a wild boar's wrath," her mother murmured, her expression tight with concern.

"Have you *seen* aught, *mo céile?*" her da asked.

When something threatened their clan, she or her mother oft had visions of the impending danger. Her mother shook her head just as the earl of Mar stood and gave the signal for those wishing to hunt to gather at the stables. The men filtered out, leaving those few ladies who had come to see them off. Sky picked at her meal, her thoughts upon the conversation she meant to have with Oliver.

"There's something in the air. I sense it, but I can't quite tease out what it means." Her mother propped her elbows on the table and rested her chin on her fists. Even after all these years, her speech and mannerisms still set her apart, foreign.

Her mother, Lady True, as she was called by their clan, as well as Lady Erin and Hunter's wife, Lady Meghan, had all come to the MacKintosh clan from the future. Sky shuddered at the thought of being so unwillingly displaced. Another *adventure* she wished to avoid. "Och, with so many about, such unsettling feelings are bound to occur. The very air is rife with rivalries, envy and gossip."

"Hmm. Speaking of envy, don't think I haven't picked up on a certain lass's resentment toward you."

"Wheesht." Sky searched the hall for any who might be listening. "I am aware as well, but I sense no ill intent. 'Tis only jealousy," she said, leaning close and lowering her voice to barely a whisper. "I'm no' concerned." Should she share her plan with her mother? Nay. Not until she'd had a chance to sort things out with Oliver.

What if he wouldn't agree to release her? One of the bits of gossip she'd gleaned whilst here was that Lady Alice's father, like so many other minor barons, was near to impoverished in these trying times. Alice's dowry was scant, while Sky came to the union rich with land and a nice fat purse, not to mention the alliance their union would secure between the Erskine and MacKintosh clans. "All will be well," she murmured, trying to convince herself.

True's eyes grew bright. "I will miss you so much, Sky. I . . . I can't believe my firstborn, my baby girl, is leaving the nest." She clasped Sky's hands.

"I will miss you as well." Sky's chest tightened and she studied her mother's features, memorizing every beloved detail. "Come, let us retire to the ladies' solar and sit with the others for a bit of gossip. 'Twill keep our minds off the sorrow of parting, at least for a bit."

"I know you don't feel anything for Oliver." Her mother's grip tightened on Sky's hands. "I don't like the way things are done in this time at all. Everything is so political. Heartless. If your father and I hadn't handfasted while your grandsire was away ransoming King James, you'd—"

"If you and Da hadn't wed, I would no' have been born, and we would no' be having this discussion." Sky squeezed her ma's hands and then released her. She rose and smoothed the skirt of her gown. "Let us speak no more on the subject. A few hours with a needle and thread will calm us both."

Like her mother, Sky had taken well to sewing, beading and embroidery. Next to the healing arts, they'd become her favorite pastimes. Following the countess of Mar and the other ladies, she and her mother made their way to the solar. Sky found the basket holding her things and settled into her latest project, a wee garment for Hunter and Meghan's new bairn. 'Twould be a lass this time. Hunter's fae abilities had made it possible for him to discern as much. Sky bent her head over her task and stitched away the minutes.

Glancing out the narrow window, Sky gauged the hours that had already passed. Hadn't she vowed to find Oliver? Yet here she sat, whiling away the day. Biting her bottom lip, she put her things back into her basket. A strange restlessness took hold, and a sense of urgency unfurled within her. "If you will excuse me, my lady," she said, bowing slightly to the countess of Mar. "I wish to stretch my legs for a bit."

"You have my leave, Lady Sky." The countess barely lifted her head from the tapestry before her. "We will expect you for the midday meal."

"For certes." Sky's mother had left earlier, intending to roust Helen. After tucking her basket into a corner, she left for the great hall. Mayhap one of the servants could tell her where she might find Oliver.

As she neared the stairs, she heard muffled voices coming from the earl's solar. Sensing a woman's anger, Sky moved closer. Her skin turned to gooseflesh, and her heart rose to her throat. She recognized that voice and the bitterness assailing her from behind the heavy oak door. *Lady Alice.* Tilting her head, she strained to hear what was being said, willing all of her fae gifts to aid her.

"I mean what I say, Oliver. If you wed the MacKintosh lass, 'twill be the end of us. From that wretched day forward, I will have naught to do with you, for you will have proven yourself faithless where I am concerned."

"Now, now, my love, if you would but listen, you would—"

"I *have* listened, and I believed all the sweet words and promises you plied me with. We grew up together, Oliver. I have loved you for as long as I can remember, and you *said* you loved me. You led me to believe that I would be your wife, and now I find I have been deceived. You have played me false," she wailed. "I am ruined!"

"Nay. You dinna understand." Oliver's tone hardened. "My grandsire holds the title of Mar, but no' the lands or even this keep."

"What? How can this be? Is the property no' entailed to the title?"

"Nay. Alexander Stewart took the earldom and estates by force and—"

"Aye. All ken the story, my lord," Alice snapped. "Alexander, the bastard son of the Wolf of Badenoch, murdered the countess of Mar's husband, laid siege to Kildrummy and forced the countess to marry him. He stole the title and the estates. 'Twas long before our time, and your grandsire holds the title now. What has that to do with—"

"Be patient. Alexander traded the earldom of Mar and all *our* lands away to King James in exchange for a more appealing title—one that none could claim he'd taken illegally. My line are kin to the original holders of Mar, which is why my grandsire was able to reclaim the title, but King James has refused to grant us back the estates. Grandsire has petitioned the court to have the properties returned to us, but—"

"Why am I just now hearing of this?" Alice asked accusingly.

"None but our family are privy to the truth of the matter. Indeed, you must say naught about this to *anyone*."

"Surely your family holds other titles and properties not associated with the earldom of Mar. Lord Robert is laird to the Erskine clan, is he no'?"

"Aye, we have another holding, but the land is scant and poor. I will inherit very little, and because of my grandsire's persistence in his suit against the throne, our king is threatening to strip us of even the title of Mar. Our clan's very future is in jeopardy. Do you no' see, *mùirninn*? I must marry the MacKintosh lass.

"Lady Sky brings both land and wealth to the union, and once we are wed, all that comes to me. Indeed, Grandsire feigned insult against the MacKintosh clan all those years ago for the broken betrothal between Malcolm and my mother. Even then Grandsire sought to gain from the situation. His sole purpose in agreeing to a union between myself and Lady Sky is to gain a portion of what the MacKintosh hold."

A chill coursed through Sky, but his words didn't surprise her. 'Twas the way things were done amongst the nobility, the way nobles advanced their standing and wealth. Only merchants and villeins could wed at will.

"I'm marrying Lady Sky for us, Alice. You must see 'tis so."

"For us?" Alice bit out. "How will your lady wife bring *me* aught but heartbreak?"

"Be at ease. I shall not be wed to her for long."

"What mean you to do, Oliver?"

Sky covered her mouth, suppressing the cry threatening to alert the two of her presence. Waves of shock and fear weakened her knees as Oliver's intent overwhelmed her. She could scarce draw a breath and had to force herself to stay and hear the rest.

"Think, Alice. Lady Sky shall fall prey to an unfortunate accident or a mysterious illness. Be patient, my dearest. Another year is all I ask, and then we shall be wed and live out the rest of our days in comfort."

All the blood left Sky's head, and spots danced before her eyes. Oliver intended to kill her. Dear God, how had she become embroiled in such a heinous plot? She inched away as quietly as she could. The door behind her opened, and she fled, praying the two conspirators hadn't seen her.

She ran to the chamber she shared with her sister, hoping her ma and Helen were still within. Her mother would ken what to do. Sky threw open the door and nearly tumbled through in her haste, only to find the room empty. Mayhap Helen and Ma were out gathering the first shoots of some healing herb or another. Her da and brother would be in the forest hunting. Pacing, she bit her lip. *Think.*

Oliver would have to wed her first in order to claim her dowry, and that would never happen. Not now. She could wait until this eve to reveal what she'd learned to her family, but . . . nay. The thought of staying in this place even another moment sickened her.

What if Oliver realized she'd uncovered his plans? The door had opened behind her as she'd left the earl's solar. Had he caught sight of her as she fled? If he was ruthless enough to murder her, surely he was ruthless enough to force her into marrying him—like Alexander Stewart had done long ago with poor Isabel, the countess of Mar. Mayhap the Erskines would hold her family hostage at Kildrummy, threatening to do them harm to gain her compliance.

Panic overwhelmed her. She couldn't allow anything to happen to her family. She needed to find her da and brother before the Erskines had time to conspire against them any further. She'd tell her sire everything. They'd gather their guards and leave for home immediately before the Erskines had time to act. Aye, haste was of the upmost importance.

Grabbing her cloak from its peg, she struggled to bring her panic under control. Once she found her da and brother, all would be well. 'Twas a sound plan. Sky raced out of the chamber and down the stairs.

Dread stole her breath. What kind of accident had Oliver planned for her? Would he push her down a steep stairwell like the one she now trod, or send her plummeting over a parapet? Did he mean to poison her? She hurried across the great hall and out the door. Lifting her hem, she ran to the stables.

"Good morn to you, my lady." The stable lad's eyes widened at her breathless state. "Do ye wish to ride?"

"Aye. Bridle my mare, and be quick about it. No need for the saddle." The lad disappeared into the shadows of the stable, and Sky paced again. Her mind turned over every possible way her betrothed could do away with her. The lad returned, leading her horse. She took the reins from him and tossed them over her mount's head. "Help me up," she commanded, gripping her mare's mane.

He cupped his hands. "Aye, my lady."

One of her father's guards hurried up to her. "Lady Sky, where might ye be off to in such a hurry?"

"I need to find my father and brother." Her horse pranced beneath her, and she tightened the bit.

"Wait but a moment, and I'll accompany you," the guard said.

"Nay. Follow as soon as you can." She turned to the stable lad. "Which way did the hunting party set out?" He pointed. "Catch up with me," she told the guard. "The trail will be easy enough to follow." With that, she kicked her mare into a gallop and set out to find her kin—and safety.

Once past the heavily trodden ground near the curtain walls, Sky found the newly churned earth caused by the hunting party. She slowed her pace to a canter and followed. She'd been riding but half a league when the trail cut into the forest. Glancing over her shoulder, she saw two MacKintosh guards riding after her, the one she'd spoken to at the stables and another. Some of her tension eased.

Pausing until the guards were closer, Sky nodded to them and nudged her mare onto the trail into the wood at a gallop. The need to find her da rode her hard, as if Oliver, rather than MacKintosh guards, gained ground behind her. Keeping her eyes on the signs left by the hunters, she raced on.

Movement from a clearing ahead caught her eye. Shimmering pale pink and green light rose from the very earth, and she was heading straight for it at a gallop. An unfamiliar energy and the scent of impending rain filled the air. "By the Holy Mother, nay!"

With all her might, she pulled the reins to turn her mount away. Her mare's ears flattened, and the whites of her eyes showed. Her sweet, good-natured palfrey planted her hooves, bunched her haunches beneath her and bucked. Without pommel or cantle to grip, Sky flew through the air—straight for the wavering light.

She tried to twist away, but a powerful force gripped her, drawing her into a gyre of punishing pressure pushing and tearing at her from all sides. Wood and sky disappeared. Utter darkness broken by eerie flashes of light flew by. Sky screamed, closed her eyes and curled into a ball. *Saints preserve me!* She kent well what held her. Hadn't she sat at her mother's knee throughout her childhood, listening to the terrible tales told by her kin of falling through time?

Just when she could bear no more, she thudded to an abrupt halt upon soft dirt. The smell of fresh dung filled her nostrils. She became aware of pounding hoofbeats drawing near, and the cries and gasps from a crowd filled her senses. She opened her eyes a crack, only to find the large, sharp hooves of a war horse cantering straight for her. Had she survived the excruciating force, only to be trampled to death by a destrier?

Covering her head and curling into a ball again, Sky closed her eyes. She waited for the pain of being trampled. Instead, the air around her stirred as the horse leaped over her. She dared to open her eyes again. Peeking out from between her arms, she saw a knight in full armor with a jousting lance gripped in his hand. Shouts and screams from the spectators assaulted her ears, but she couldn't tear her eyes from the knight.

He turned his mount, gestured to the knight opposing him and spurred his destrier toward her once more. Scrambling up to standing, she panicked. War horses thundered at her from opposite directions, hemming her in and too close for her to make a dash for it. Besides, where would she run to if she could escape? *Bloody hell!* She'd landed in the midst of a jousting tournament, and she was trapped between the contestants. Did they not see her at all?

She pressed her arms tight against her sides and tried to make herself as small as possible, hoping to avoid the clash between the two. The first knight dropped his lance, leaned over and snatched her up by the waist. The spectators let out a roar. Confusion swirled through her, as he settled her on his lap.

He bent his helmeted head close and whispered into her ear, "You are safe with me, my lady. You have my word. Be at ease."

Truth. Powerful emotions pulsed from him, and all she could manage was a weak nod. She sensed so much more than simple sincerity. Loss. Regret. Excitement. Disoriented, she placed her hands on his arm and turned her attention to her surroundings.

Never had she seen a jousting arena such as this one. Where was the keep of the noble who must be sponsoring the tournament? And what of the villagers sitting on the benches surrounding the field? Only a few were dressed properly. Where had she been taken to . . . and when?

Looking out beyond the field, she gasped. She was in a village surrounded by forest. The buildings appeared . . . false somehow. The fronts didn't match the rears. The thoroughfare teemed with people in a variety of garments. The smells of roasting meat and sweets filled the air, and more cheering erupted from the crowd as new jousters cantered onto the grounds.

She studied the gauntleted hand of the knight who held her. "If you please, sir, I must speak with your liege lord immediately. 'Tis of the utmost importance." He chuckled low in his throat, and the deep, rich timbre of his voice both calmed and stirred her.

"I have no overlord, so I'll have to do. I know what has happened to you, for the same happened to me a decade ago. I recognized the shimmering lights." He guided his mount out of the arena.

"What the hell, Struan?" an older man cried and grabbed the reins of the knight's destrier. Peering intently at her, he continued to address the knight. "If I hadn't seen it with my own eyes . . . You and Michael did a great job of shielding her and making the whole thing look like part of the show."

"We need to head for the RVs, Gene," her knight said.

Arvees? She had no idea what that might mean.

The older man, dressed in a tunic and hose, peered up at her. "Who might you be?" He began leading the horse across the park beyond the jousting arena.

Blinking against the tears filling her eyes, Sky straightened her posture, though every inch of her was shaking. "I am Lady Sky Elizabeth of clan MacKintosh, and the earl of Fife's eldest daughter." Swallowing against the tightness in her throat, she asked, "If you please, could you tell me where I am?"

Her knight removed his gauntlets and helmet. "You're in Sterling at the—"

"Stirling? Why, 'tis where our young King James resides. Take me to him at once, and all will be put to rights." Again the deep timbre of the knight's chuckle caused her heart to flutter like the wings of a wee hummingbird.

"As I was about to say, this is the New York Renaissance Faire in Sterling."

"*New* York?" Exhausted and confused, she closed her eyes against the throbbing pain in her head. "What has befallen the old town of York that you must now call it new? Though I've ne'er been to the walled city myself, I am well educated, sir. I ken York is near the border between Scotia and England."

To add to her misery, sweat trickled down the back of her neck, and the heavy velvet of her gown stuck to her skin under the heat of the blazing sun. The knight must be miserable in this heat clad as he was in armor.

"Ah . . . not exactly." He shifted behind her. "I'm afraid you are far, far from your home and your time. This is the year of our Lord 2014."

"Nay!" she cried. "I willna hear it." Tears spilled down her cheeks. "I have gone from one terror to the next this day . . . and . . ." She lifted her cloak and peered at the dung clinging to her side. Her gown was ruined. Why something so trivial should affect her so, she could not fathom, but the sight of the burgundy velvet covered in horse shite was more than she could bear. "And this is my favorite gown," she cried. "I chose to wear it for luck, and see you what has befallen me?"

Her knight chuckled again. "You blame the gown?"

"Nay! Do you think me simpleminded?" She turned to glare at him. Stunned, her glare turned to a wide-eyed stare. Why, he so resembled a younger version of her aunt Elaine's husband, a Sutherland, that the two could be brothers. Brilliant blue eyes, blond hair and strong chiseled features, a fine, straight nose—never before had she thought of a man as beautiful, but he was, in a rugged, masculine way. Her face heating, she turned back around.

"You view the straits I find myself in as a source of amusement, sir? I assure you, I dinna." Ire stiffened her spine. For certes she'd lost her wits, one moment crying over a gown, the next gawking at the lad's comely face, then filled with indignation. She needed a good long nap.

She studied the older man who continued to lead the knight's destrier. His thick hair was completely white, as was the mustache he wore curled up at the ends in a most peculiar manner. How did it stay fixed as it was? He led them through a gate, which opened up to a large wood dotted with large . . . *trucks and trailers.*

Her cousin Robley had drawn her pictures of such after his sojourn to the future, and he'd also explained their use. They approached a grouping of trailers and trucks arranged in a semicircle under a stand of oak trees.

The knight lifted her down to the ground before he dismounted. Then he and the older man busied themselves with removing his armor, until the knight wore naught but a short tunic and hose. He was every bit as finely formed as she'd suspected, with broad shoulders, muscled arms and chest, and . . . Good Lord, the thin hose he wore did little to conceal his . . . assets. He caught her staring. Her cheeks burning, she averted her gaze.

Her thoughts spun out of control, flitting to one thing then the next. Every one of her family members who had traveled through time had done so for a specific purpose. Had she been sent here for a reason as well? Was her situation an accident or the caprice of some faerie?

Anger burned within her. More than anything, she needed to expose Oliver's plot and Lord Robert's deceit. With her disappearance, the Erskines would lay claim to her dowry anyway, accusing her kin of secreting her away, thereby once again breaking a marriage contract. Especially if Oliver suspected she'd overheard his plans for her. Aye, the Erskines would accuse her kin of some treachery to hide their own. Her clan would suspect the Erskines were behind her disappearance, and the entire tangle would surely lead to war.

She'd landed at a fair, like the one where Robley had met Lady Erin. Her mother had also been at exactly the same kind of place when Madame Giselle had sent her through time. Even Lady Meghan had been at a fair such as this when Hunter had snatched her away from her father and brought her back to the fifteenth century.

Hope flickered to life. Was it possible she'd find Madame Giselle here in this very place? If so, she could go to her and beg the fae princess to send her home. "Pray, tell me. Might this gathering include fortune-tellers and the Romany who read cards and such for coin?"

"Of course. There are several wagons and tents throughout the festival where fortune-tellers are stationed." Her knight leaned close again. "Why? Do you wish to have your fortune told? I can assure you, they're all frauds. They put on a show just like the rest of us."

Her hopes soared. "Have you heard tell of an old crone known as Madame Giselle? She's oft found at fairs like this in your era, and—"

"*My* era? How would you know the name of a fortune-teller frequenting Renaissance fairs in *my era?*"

Her knight's tone held an edge, and Sky focused her energy, trying to interpret what that edge might mean. His shock and confusion came through clearly, but he also now held a wariness toward her. Nay, 'twas distrust tinged with resentment. Why would he resent her? She'd done naught to him. "We have much to discuss, sir."

"Indeed."

CHAPTER TWO

Struan stood in the middle of their campsite in his T-shirt, a pair of medieval-style hose and leather boots. His gut churned. He had no idea what to make of the young woman he'd held on his lap a scant few moments ago.

When he'd seen the lights shimmering in the middle of the arena, memories of the day he'd been taken from his dying father's side tore at his heart. For a second, he'd been overwhelmed by an urge to jump from Brutus's back and run into the portal himself. Good thing he'd come to his senses just as quickly. Where would the shimmering portal have sent him? And to when?

He'd read the history books and knew the outcome of the horrific battle he'd fought so many centuries ago. If the portal took him back to 1333, to the very day he'd dragged himself into the shimmering lights, he could not have altered the outcome. Worse, he would have died—as had his father, the fourth earl of Sutherland. Nope. He had no reason to go back.

Realization slammed into him. Today was the anniversary of his fall through time, July 19. Was it mere coincidence that this woman appeared as he had on this very date, and in the midst of a modern-day Renaissance festival?

Whatever the reason, he knew what it was like to be yanked from one's place in time. He understood firsthand the confusion, fear and panic, and he couldn't resist lending her his aid. Where would he be today if the Gordon family hadn't done the same for him? Pay it forward, right?

"Your camper or mine, Gene?" he asked his foster father. Struan glanced at their guest, only to find her checking him out. When their eyes met, her face flushed and she averted her gaze. Heat of an entirely different nature curled through him.

"Mine," Gene answered. "Marjorie will have lunch ready."

"If you please," Sky said as she took off her cloak, draped it over the small table set under a large oak and busied herself with flicking at the drying bits of manure clinging to her gown, "I have told you who I am, but I've yet to learn who the two of you might be."

"My apologies, my lady." Gene bowed. "I am Eugene Gordon, and this is our foster son, Struan Sutherland. The other jouster who was on the field with Struan is my son, Michael. You'll meet my wife, Marjorie, in a minute. We also have an older son and two daughters, but they're at home looking after things for us while we're on the road."

Her eyes widened. "I am well acquainted with both clans. Our clan oft engaged in commerce with the Gordons, and I claim kinship with yours, Sir Struan. Indeed, my aunts are both wed to Sutherlands, one to the earl himself, and the other to his younger brother." She studied him. "Who are your kin within the Sutherland clan? I only ask because you bear such a strong likeness to the earl and his brothers."

Great. What the hell is going on here? She'd fallen through time on the anniversary of his own journey to this century, practically at his feet, and she had ties to the Sutherlands, his family by blood. Far too close to home to be coincidence.

21

He said nothing. He had no desire to discuss his origins with her. She was of noble birth, while he was the bastard son of an earl, reviled and spurned by those whose lineage was pure and unsullied. Indeed, his father's legitimate offspring, along with the countess of Sutherland, had certainly made Struan's life a living hell. If it hadn't been for his da, Struan wouldn't have survived his youth, of that he was certain.

The intensity of her scrutiny had him gritting his teeth—it was as if she looked beneath the surface for something deeper than words. Gene's RV door opened, and the woman who'd taken him in, fed, housed and loved him like a son, stepped out. She wore her shoulder-length silver hair in a French braid today, and the laugh lines around her blue eyes creased in welcome.

"Do you plan to stand out here in this heat all day? I've made lunch. Come in and bring your friend with you."

"I fear I am no' fit to enter your . . ." Sky's expression clouded with confusion as she viewed the fifth-wheel camper. "I'm covered in filth."

"Oh my. Hold on. We'll clean you up a bit first." Marjorie disappeared.

"This"—Struan pointed to the trailer—"is technically a camper trailer, a fifth wheel. We live in them while we're on the road. We call them campers or RVs for short, although—"

"Like the Romany?" she asked, turning her big, gorgeous eyes up to him.

What color were they? Kind of an earthy bluish-green with flecks of brown. Her lashes were dark and thick, and so was her lustrous chestnut hair. She was a pretty little thing, no doubt about it. And she certainly had made a luscious armful as he held her on his lap. He couldn't help but notice her curves, the fullness of her breasts. Distracting.

"You and your kin are wanderers?" she persisted, her brow raised in question.

Or was it annoyance? Her persistence brought him out of the stupor ogling her had put him in. "Something like that." He walked away from her to take care of Brutus. What was her story? Struan removed his gelding's bridle, replacing it with a halter and lead, attaching the line to the front of the horse trailer. Brutus had enough slack to graze and to reach the buckets of water Struan had placed there earlier.

Marjorie reappeared with a scrub brush and a bowl of water in her hands. She also had a towel draped over her arm. "Thank heavens for OxiClean," she said. "This will take out the stain and eliminate the odor." Marjorie set the bowl on the small picnic table where they sometimes took their breaks. "Is someone going to introduce us?" Marjorie looked at her husband, and then at him.

"Sky, this is Marjorie. Marjorie, this is Lady Sky Elizabeth, the earl of Fife's eldest daughter," Struan said, repeating what she'd told them. "She . . . appeared the same way I did a decade ago. Only she did so in the middle of my jousting match with Michael—in front of an audience. Practically under Brutus's hooves."

Marjorie's expression turned to shock. The towel slid off her arm. "Oh my."

"'Tis a pleasure to meet you." Sky's posture straightened, and her chin lifted a regal notch. "I am most grateful to you for your hospitality."

"Oh my," Marjorie repeated.

Sky's hands trembled. Though she presented herself as composed, regal, she had to be terrified. Out of her element, no way to prove who she was, no means of support and not knowing a soul, how could she not be? At least language wasn't a barrier.

He picked up the towel Marjorie had dropped and placed it on the table next to the bowl and scrub brush. His heart went out to Sky Elizabeth, along with a bit of admiration and respect as well. As frightened as she was, she still managed to comport herself like a proper lady at court.

"Here comes Michael." Struan gestured toward his foster brother cantering his horse toward their campsite.

"Come here, you poor thing." Marjorie clucked like a mother hen and set to work cleaning the stained gown. "See? Good as new, just a little damp."

"My thanks," Sky murmured. "How shall I address you, missus?"

"Call all of us by our given names. We're informal in this time." Marjorie gave Sky's gown a final pat with the towel. "What would you like to be called?"

"You may call me by my given name as well." She smiled shyly.

Struan's pulse quickened at the sight of her sweet smile. Clenching his jaw, he turned to Michael, whose attention was fixed on their guest. "Michael, this is Sky Elizabeth."

"Can't believe it." Michael dismounted and led his horse to the trailer where Brutus was tied. "Are we some kind of magnets for time-travelers or something?" He glanced over his shoulder at Sky.

"Best have this conversation inside," Gene said. He gestured toward his RV. "Let's have lunch, and we'll talk."

Michael had only been seven years old when Struan had fallen into the Gordons' midst, wounded in battle and heartsick from the loss of his father. It had been Michael who had helped Struan get over his fear of the unknown. The lad had a compassionate heart and a gentle, good-natured humor. "I think it's you, Michael," he teased. "That big heart of yours acts as a beacon through the centuries."

"I hope not." Michael's grin belied his objection. "Or we're going to have to start up a nonprofit organization to shelter displaced time-travelers."

Once he and Gene helped Michael out of his armor, they headed for the camper. Struan grabbed Sky's cloak from the table and followed her up the narrow metal steps and inside. "Are you hungry, lass?" He'd worked hard to eliminate his Scottish burr and to become American in every way, but her presence brought out the Scottish Highlander in him.

She nodded and looked around in wonder. "Why, 'tis so much cooler within than without, and we are no' even underground." She held up her hand and wiggled her fingers. "I feel a breeze. How is this possible?" She turned to him for an explanation.

"It's called air-conditioning, and it's one of the many technological wonders of this age." Struan hung up her cloak in the closet before helping himself to a beer from the fridge. "Would you like something to drink, Sky?"

"Aye, I find I'm most parched." She stood awkwardly in the middle of the living room space.

"Sit." Marjorie patted the seat of the booth-like dining area. "Would you like a soda, a beer or a cup of coffee?"

Sky sat down and scooted over. "Oh. My cousin's wife oft speaks of coffee. I would very much like to try some."

"Wait." Struan frowned. "When are you from?"

Sky clasped her hands together in her lap. "Early spring in the year of our Lord 1443."

"How would your cousin's wife know about coffee?" The fine hairs on the back of his neck stood on end. "And how do you know about a fortune-teller who frequents Renaissance festivals in the twenty-first century?"

"'Tis a very long and strange tale, sir, but my family has . . . we—"

"Wait. Save it until after we've eaten." Struan snorted. Already overwhelmed with everything that had happened, he wasn't sure he wanted to hear what she had to say just yet. "Better doctor the coffee up for her, Ma. Remember my first cup?"

"I do. In fact, I believe there might still be a few spatter stains from when you spit it out all over the wall." She chuckled.

"Mmm. I smell chili and I'm starving." Gene drew his wife in for a quick kiss, smacking her bottom before letting her go. "I'll fix Sky's coffee, while you get lunch on the table."

Sky's face turned a dusky rose at the obvious display of affection between his parents. Her blush was an enticing sight, to be sure.

Gene handed Sky a mug of coffee with lots of cream and sugar. "Try this."

Struan leaned against the kitchen counter, took a swallow of his beer and watched. In fact, his entire family watched.

Sky's gaze went from him to the others, her cheeks coloring again. "Am I to have spectators?" she asked, eying the contents of her mug. "I trow 'tis harmless enough, or my cousin would no' miss it so." She took a tentative sip, and her lips pursed. "'Tis so very sweet . . . and bitter at the same time." She set the mug down.

Struan laughed. "Just wait till you taste the chili."

"Is chili sweet as well?" Sky asked.

"Salty. You'll find the food in this time takes some getting used to. It's either far too salty, far too sweet or too spicy."

Marjorie handed him a bowl of chili with grated cheddar cheese and sour cream on top, just the way he liked it. There wasn't enough room at the table for all of them to sit, so Struan stayed where he was, using the counter as his table. Michael slid in next to Sky. His ma and Gene finished serving, and then they all settled into their meal of chili and cornbread.

Poor lass. Sky tried so hard to mask her expression of distaste as she took that first spoonful of the spicy, salty chili. She covered her mouth and coughed. Struan went to the fridge and grabbed a bottle of water. He unscrewed the top and placed it on the table in front of her.

"Has this been boiled?" she rasped out, eyeing the bottle. "My mother is from this era, and she taught us about germs and such causing illness."

"It's pure," Struan assured her. He'd buy her a turkey leg and an ear of roasted corn from the fair before his next jousting match. "Your mother is from—"

"Aye." Sky took a long drink of water. "Och, 'tis good, like the water from a Scottish spring."

"She really likes to drop the bombs, doesn't she?" Michael laughed.

"Bombs?" Sky frowned. "I dinna ken your meaning, sir."

"Michael. Call me Michael."

Sky pushed the bowl of chili away. "I'm sorry. It's no' that I don't appreciate the meal, but . . ."

"Don't you worry about it." Marjorie split a piece of cornbread, buttered both sides and poured honey over the pieces. "Try this. Can't have you starving to death your very first day here."

Sky took a taste and smiled, her eyes half closing with pleasure. "Mmm. 'Tis most pleasing."

Struan sucked in a long breath and concentrated on his meal. Sky Elizabeth was far too beautiful for his peace of mind.

"If you wish, I'll speak of what happened this day." Her voice hitched. "And tell you how I came to be here."

"Please do," Michael said. "We can't wait to hear what you have to say."

"All right." She began her tale, sharing with them her betrothed's plan to murder her for her dowry, and ending with her ride through the woods in search of her father and brother. Struan's family was enraptured. "I came to a clearing and saw the shimmering lights. My mare threw me, and I was powerless to escape the force gripping me. Then I landed in the dirt in the middle of your jousting field."

"Incredible." Michael stared at her.

"I assure you, sir, I speak naught but the truth."

Marjorie began gathering dirty dishes. "Oh, we believe you. Struan came to us the same way. We were working at a fair in Kentucky. That one is themed on the days of Robert the Bruce, which might be why Struan ended up there since it's closer to his time. We were enjoying a nice campfire after the fair closed, when the air right next to us shimmered and wavered. Then Struan fell to the ground out of thin air."

Gene nodded. "The boy was filthy. He was also wounded and feverish. We cleaned him up, changed his clothes and used our older son's insurance card to get him treated at a hospital. We told the doctor he'd accidentally been wounded during one of our performances, and that he didn't tell us about his wound until an infection had set in." He turned to glance fondly Struan's way. "They patched him up, kept him overnight and gave us a prescription for antibiotics. We brought him home, and Struan told us his story. He's been with us ever since. As far as we're concerned, he's our son."

Sky turned to him, her eyes filled with empathy. "From whence do you come, sir?"

Struan's chest tightened under her perusal. What was it about her that made him feel so exposed? "The year of our Lord 1333. My father and I were fighting the English at Halidon Hill," he said, reverting to speech patterns and the burr he'd worked so hard to eliminate. "We were in a bog whilst the English held the high ground. My da had already fallen with a mortal wound, and I was injured as well. I saw the wavering lights—soft greens and pinks."

A choked sound escaped from deep in his throat. "Young fool that I was, I believed 'twas the doorway to heaven. I thought I'd already died, so I dragged myself through, expecting paradise, or at the very least, purgatory."

"How old were you, Struan?" Sky asked, her tone filled with compassion.

"Ten and four."

"Nay!" She gasped. "'Tis far too young. You would still have been but a squire. Were you forced to fight alongside your father in that ill-fated battle?"

He shook his head. "I wanted to fight." A bastard aspiring to knighthood, trying to prove himself worthy of the father he adored. How impossible that dream had been for him. Still, his da had trained him alongside his half brothers, and his brothers' hatred toward him had become an advantage. He'd had to train harder, become better skilled in order to survive. "Naïve as I was, I believed I could protect my da."

"Who was he?" Her expression sharpened. "Who was your father to the Sutherland clan?"

"No one of import." He had no intentions of exposing himself once again to the kind of ridicule he'd suffered as a youth. He turned away, but not before he glimpsed the look of disappointment she couldn't hide. What exactly had disappointed her? Was it that he claimed no rank and refused to admit his link to the earl of Sutherland from her time, or was it because he hadn't really answered her question?

"I think it only fair to tell you of my kin, odd though they may be." She bit her lip. "And to reveal things about myself I'd rather no'. Once you hear my tale, you may wish to send me away." Sky shrugged. "If that be the case, I'll understand."

What could possibly be so bad that they would turn her loose in a world she knew nothing about? "Wait. I need to get a folding chair. I have a feeling I'm going to need to sit."

"Aye, 'twould be best." Her gaze met his.

The disappointment he'd caught a minute ago still lingered in her expression, and the thought that he'd somehow let her down caused a slight wrench to his heart. He strode to the storage area, grabbed a folding chair from the closet and set it beside the table. "Anyone want anything before I sit?"

"Here," his ma said, handing him a stack of dirty dishes. "Take these to the sink, and bring back a couple of beers for me and Gene."

"One for me too," Michael said, turning to Sky. "I'm not legal, but my folks let me have a beer now and then, so long as I'm with them."

"Legal?" Her brow creased.

Michael nodded. "I suspect the proverbial plot is about to thicken. Do you want a beer, Sky?"

"Och, aye."

Struan set cold longnecks in front of everyone before taking his seat. "All right. Tell us what is so terrible that you think we'd vote you off the island."

She blinked. "Vote me off . . . Are we on an island then?"

"It's an expression." Michael twisted the cap off her Blue Moon for her. "We're not going to send you away. Relax."

"You canna say for certain without first hearing my tale." Her lips thinned, and doubt clouded her expression. "Have you heard of the *Tuatha Dé Danann?*"

"Sure. Mythical beings, faeries." Gene nodded. "What about them?"

"They are no' a myth. Madame Giselle, the fortune-teller I mentioned earlier, is the daughter of their high king. Her true name is Áine, and she loves to meddle in the affairs of her mortal progeny. Many years ago, Giselle sent my mother from her century to the past to save the life of my foster brother. A few years later, my cousin Robley made a bargain with Giselle to visit the future in exchange for stealing an item from the fae realm that she coveted. He came to your time, stayed a while, and then he was sent back to us by a fae warrior charged with enforcing fae laws. Haldor, the warrior, also sent the woman who is now my cousin Robley's wife back to our time. 'Tis complicated. Then—"

"Wait. Too many names to follow, but . . ." Struan's ears rang from the blood rushing through his veins. "You're telling us that it's possible to . . . Your cousin came here . . . and then returned?"

"As did Erin, his wife." She nodded. "My foster brother also came to your time and returned to ours. He too brought a woman home with him." Her eyes widened. "Och, I must contact Meghan's kin. You said 'tis the year 2014, aye? According to Meghan, 'twas 2011 when Hunter brought her home with him to our time. Her family will want to hear she's well, and—"

"Why your clan?" He frowned. "What connection do you have with the fae?" Goose bumps rose on his forearms and at the back of his neck. How was all this, including him and the Gordons, connected?

Sky paled. "I . . . some of us carry fae blood. My foster brother is Áine's direct descendant many generations past. Haldor, the fae warrior, claims kinship with Lady Erin. My mother also carries fae blood, but we dinna ken the source. Mayhap we ne'er will." Her eyes met his for a moment. "So you see, I too have fae blood, and with that blood comes certain *abilities*." She squared her shoulders, looking as if she were bracing herself for the impact of their reaction.

"No shit." Michael's eyes went wide. "Do you mind if I ask you a personal question?"

"Nay, I dinna mind." Sky rubbed her temples and closed her eyes.

"What are your fae abilities?"

Her eyes opened and sought his, even though it had been Michael who asked the question. Struan couldn't take the intensity of her stare and shot up, heading for the fridge and another beer.

"Like my mother, I have the ability to discern whether or not someone speaks truth or falsehood. I can read people's emotions, and occasionally I'll have a vision of things to come. Though that happens only when those I love are being threatened or are in some kind of danger."

"Damn," Michael blurted.

"Watch your mouth, Michael," Marjorie scolded. "Too many foul words are polluting the air in here."

"Sorry, Mom, but . . . This explains so much. I think we must have *Tuatha Dé Danann* genes too." Michael raked his fingers through his shaggy brown hair. "Isn't that how we started working at Renaissance festivals in the first place, Dad? Your sister Marilyn was a psychic, and she started out as a fortune-teller at the fair in Virginia. Right?"

"It's true," Gene said.

"And don't you have some ability?" Michael persisted. "You knew Aunt Marilyn was sick before she went to the doctor."

Gene nodded. "Occasionally I get flashes of things I shouldn't have any way of knowing."

"That's why we're magnets for time-travelers," Michael exclaimed. "Oh, man. This is epic. It explains why I'm so intuitive. I pick up on emotions too, only probably not as well as you do, Sky."

"'Tis likely. The MacKintosh are no' the only Scottish clan to claim fae ancestry." She shifted. "When my cousin came to your time, he landed in a place called Minnesota. Do you ken where that realm might be? 'Tis also my mother's homeland."

"Of course we know where Minnesota is," Marjorie told her. "It's smack-dab in the middle of North America and right on the Canadian border."

"Is that near here?" Sky's tone was hopeful. "Robley met another time-traveler there, Connor McGladrey, and 'tis his daughter Meghan who is now my foster brother's wife. 'Twas just by chance that—"

"By chance?" Struan barked out a strangled laugh. He stared out the small window above the kitchen sink. He couldn't take it all in, but one thing he knew for certain, none of this was by chance. Was this woman meant to return him to his century? He'd always known he should've died at Halidon Hill. He'd been living on borrowed time ever since. Was his time coming to an end? "None of this is by chance, lass."

"I agree," Michael said, his tone filled with excitement.

"This is the anniversary of the day you came to us, Struan," Marjorie added. "It's July 19."

Silence descended, and a shiver of dread crept down his spine. "Tell us the stories of each of your family members who have time-traveled, Sky. I'm interested to hear about the others who have experienced what I have." He doubted he'd gain anything from the tales she had to tell, but he needed time to process what she'd revealed.

"If you wish." Sky gave them the historical accounting for each of her relatives who had time-traveled.

"That's a lot to process," Struan said once she'd finished. Truth be told, he just couldn't take in any more. Thank heavens it was almost time for their last jousting performance of the afternoon. "We need to get ready for our next show." Struan nodded toward the wall clock.

"Right." Gene pushed himself up from the table. "We'll come up with something you can do to earn a living while you're here, Sky. With your abilities, maybe you can work the fairs as a fortune-teller."

"I canna tell anyone's future, only whether or no' they speak the truth." A look of utter confusion and fatigue settled over Sky's features.

Struan recalled feeling the same way. He'd understood English well enough, but many of the words his new family had used held no meaning for him back then. "You look as if you're about to fall asleep sitting up. Ma will show you where you can rest, and we'll talk later."

"My thanks. I am exhausted." Sky yawned and covered her mouth. "'Tis been a most trying day, and I am grateful to have . . ." She frowned. "*Made your acquaintance* does no' sound right for the occasion. I'm glad to have fallen in with folk who are so accepting, and . . ." She yawned again.

Gene smiled down at her. "We understand what you're trying to say. You're welcome here."

Struan spared her a nod and left the trailer. Now he knew the source of her look of disappointment. She'd sensed the lie he'd told about his father being no one of importance to the Sutherlands. So what? It wasn't her business anyway. A twinge of guilt shot through him. She'd revealed her fae abilities to them, taking what she believed to be a great risk. Yet he hid the truth of his origins from her.

"Time to get back into the can," he muttered, heading for his armor. Performing at the fairs helped keep him in shape, but he far preferred his true calling, and longed to return to their farm in Virginia where he had his forge.

There he created medieval home decor, and the armor and weaponry that kept the Renaissance and medieval reenactors and theaters all over the world supplied. He also dabbled in gold- and silversmithing, creating Celtic brooches, pendants, rings, belt buckles and bracelets.

"What do you make of Sky's sudden appearance on the anniversary of *your* arrival here?" Michael asked as he tightened the cinch on his horse's saddle.

"I have no idea what to make of it or of her." Struan's jaw tightened. "I don't really want to think about it right now."

"Can't say as I blame you, son. It's spooky as hell if you ask me." Gene helped him into his armor. "Promise me you'll stay here with us," he said, his voice gruff. "Don't want to lose you."

"I promise." Struan's throat closed up and his eyes stung. "You heard what she had to say about the treachery of her time. My century was even worse because of the constant conflict with the English and the Bruce's recent death. I have no interest in returning to the past. None."

CHAPTER THREE

I have so much to do," Sky said, rubbing her aching temples. "I must search this fair for Madame Giselle, and I need to find a way to Minnesota to seek out the McGladreys. How am I to manage?"

Marjorie set about cleaning up from the meal they'd just shared. Sky guessed the woman to be in her fifties, though she still moved like a much younger woman. She wore a long skirt of linen and a loose chemise-type blouse with short sleeves. Sky envied her. The garments looked soft and light. Much cooler and more comfortable than the heavy velvet she wore.

"Nothing has to be done today," Marjorie said. "Once I'm finished here, we'll get you settled for a nap. In the meantime, tell me a little about yourself, Sky."

She'd been far more forthcoming with the Gordons than she'd ever been with strangers before, but her truth was all she had to offer in exchange for their hospitality and help. For certes, at her ma's insistence, she had a few gold coins sewn into hiding places in her gown, but she'd need them once she returned to her own time. She didn't ken whether or not such coins would do her any good in this century anyway. She'd seen the paper currency Robley had taken with him to the future. "'Twould be my pleasure. Ask any question you wish, and I shall answer as best I can."

The older woman smiled warmly. "For starters, tell me more about your family. How many brothers and sisters do you have, and how old are you?"

"I'll be one and twenty this coming autumn. I have one older foster brother and three younger brothers. Two of them are twins." Her voice broke. "I also have two younger sisters, many cousins, and . . ." She swallowed against the lump forming in her throat.

"We live on an island in the middle of Loch Moigh. 'Tis quite lovely, my home." When had the tears started? Her chest ached. She longed for the gently rolling hills of home, with her clan's kine and sheep dotting the fields. How sorely she already missed the loch, sparkling like the rarest sapphire under a blue sky.

"I must get back to my time. I need to prevent a war between the Erskines and my clan. At the very least, I must prevent Oliver from stealing my dowry. With my disappearance, the Erskines will surely claim my kin took me away, thus breaking yet another marriage contract." Her hands curled into fists. "Those deceitful, ruthless curs."

"Of course you must return, and if such a thing is possible, we'll help you find the way." Marjorie folded the cloth she'd used to wipe the counters and placed it over a small rack. "Let's get you out of that gown and into bed."

"You are most kind to offer such hospitality." Sky swiped at her cheeks and sniffed. Marjorie handed her a soft piece of something she assumed was meant to wipe her nose.

"If I suddenly appeared in your time and in your country, what would you do?" Marjorie asked.

Sky let out a strangled laugh. "You ken from the tales of my family we've oft dealt with that very thing. We would take you in, of course. You would be safe and well protected."

"Exactly. Things happen as they should, as they are meant to." Marjorie canted her head and peered into Sky's eyes. "You've come to us because we are the kind of people who will take you in and make sure you're safe as well."

"I . . . I hope I can repay you somehow. I'm no' able to tell fortunes, but I sew, embroider, bead and I can spin, weave and felt wool. Mayhap we will find a way for such skills to contribute to your family's coffers. I'm also a healer like my mother, and my cousin has been teaching me midwifery."

She stood up and began to unlace her gown. "This velvet is very heavy, and 'tis so warm here. I fear I'm no' used to such heat."

"As far as adding to our *coffers* goes, I'm certain you'll find your way. Struan certainly has. He's a blacksmith, and he makes Renaissance home decor, armor, weapons and jewelry, which he sells online and at the fairs we visit throughout the year."

Marjorie's eyes sparkled, and the lines at the corners of her blue eyes creased. "Tomorrow we'll go shopping for more appropriate clothing. There's an outlet mall not too far from here. You and I will take one of the trucks and make a day of it."

Sky could no longer think straight, much less decipher Marjorie's meaning. "Outlet mall?"

"You'll see." Marjorie's eyes lit with excitement.

She helped Sky out of her things until all Sky wore was her chemise and the *sgian dubh* she always kept strapped to her calf.

"Let me show you to the bathroom . . . er . . . I think you'd call it the garderobe, and then I'll take you back to Michael's room. Ours is at the very front of the trailer and his is in the back. You'll have plenty of privacy, and you can sleep for as long as you like."

Sky nodded and followed along through the narrow passage toward the rear, stopping at a door midway. Too tired to be impressed by the garderobe, she closed the door to the tiny chamber and used everything the way Marjorie had instructed. Then she washed her face and hands and followed the older woman to a small chamber at the very end of the camper. A narrow bed came out from the wall, with another cot fastened to the wall above it. Michael's things were strewn everywhere.

Marjorie gathered armloads of clothing, books and other items Sky couldn't identify. She transferred the clothing to a large basket placed in the corner, and then she set the rest of the items on a small chest of drawers. "Teenagers," she huffed.

"How old is Michael?"

"Seventeen, and Struan is twenty-four." Marjorie began stripping the linens from the bed.

"My twin brothers are but a year older than Michael," Sky said. "I can make up the bed, Marjorie. I don't wish to put you to any trouble, or to take the lad's bed from him."

"It's no trouble. You're our guest, and Michael can always bunk with Struan in his camper. He's over there all the time anyway. Wait right here."

Sky nodded again. Her parents hadn't raised her to be pampered. Though they had servants, Sky had been taught early on how to do for herself. Her mother had insisted upon it. When Marjorie returned with fresh linens, Sky took them from her. "Let me make the bed. You've already done so much for me."

"If you insist." Marjorie moved to the sliding door separating the chamber from the rest of their wagon. "Get some sleep, Sky, and don't worry. You are safe with us."

"My thanks, Marjorie." Sky's eyes burned, as she sensed the warmth and sincerity emanating from her new friend. Marjorie closed the door behind her, and Sky was left alone to ponder all that had happened to her in the span of a single day. Nay, not even a full day yet. At least she'd escaped Oliver's ruthless, greedy plot. She made the bed, settled herself onto the comfortable pallet and covered her eyes with her arm.

Her knight had lied to her about his father being no one of import to the Sutherlands. Why? Was it simply because his lineage had no bearing on his life in this century? Mayhap thinking about his kin caused him grief, and he didn't wish to speak of those he'd lost.

She turned onto her side, pulled up the covers and shut her eyes. She had no right to pry, and certainly no reason to suffer disappointment at his response. Yet she had. She'd sensed his wariness and resentment toward her easily enough. Indeed, 'twas those very reactions that had prompted her to reveal so much about herself. Surely he kent she was no threat to him. 'Twas no fault of hers she happened to land in the middle of his jousting match.

Sighing, she tried to fall asleep, but her mind would give her no peace. Struan's image filled her thoughts. His deep blue eyes shone with keen intelligence, and his thick blond hair fell almost to his shoulders. Broad shoulders, narrow hips, and so very powerful, he stole her breath.

Once again she was struck by his resemblance to the Sutherlands who were kin to her. When she'd been a wee lass of seven or eight, she'd been completely besotted with her aunt Elaine's husband, Dylan. In her childish way, she'd believed her uncle to be the strongest and most comely man in all of Scotland, and she'd staunchly defended him against any who disagreed—much to everyone's amusement.

Struan could be her uncle Dylan's brother, so close in features, coloring, height and build were the two. Mayhap her attraction to Struan was naught but an echo of her infatuation with her uncle. Aye, that must be it.

Sky rose up and punched the pillow a few times, wondering what the casing held. Sadly, not goose down as she was accustomed. Settling herself once again, she yawned. On the morrow, she'd search for Madame Giselle, and then she'd find a way to journey to Minnesota so she could talk with Connor McGladrey and his wife, Katherine.

Meghan had said many times that her father had made an extensive study of the *Tuatha Dé Danann* and their ways, especially after Robley's appearance in their midst. He'd collected all the lore there was to be found on the subject. If anyone could help her unravel things, 'twould be Connor.

Plus, the McGladreys would be overjoyed to hear news of their daughter. Thinking of Meghan, she wondered whether or not she'd given birth to her bairn yet—in her century, that is. In this one, all her kin would have been long dead. She couldn't bear thinking about that, and turned her mind to her plans for the morrow. Sleep finally came to her, and she gladly succumbed.

Sky awoke to the sound of voices. For a few glorious moments, she imagined herself at Loch Moigh, safe in her own chamber and in her own bed, but she kent better. Her stomach rumbled. Delicious smells filled the small chamber, including what she now recognized as coffee. Mayhap she'd try it again, only with less sweetness this time.

How long had she slept? She climbed out of the narrow cot. Sunlight slipped through the slats of the single window's odd shutter. Moving to the window, Sky studied the covering. A string hung to one side, and she tugged on it to see what would happen. The bottom edge of the shutter rose, letting in more light and giving her a glimpse of the surrounding wood.

She turned back to the chamber and searched for her gown. Had Marjorie taken it? She couldn't remember, but 'twas nowhere to be found. Male laughter drifted back from the front of the trailer, and her stomach growled again. Snatching a blanket from the cot, she wrapped it about herself like a cloak. She managed to slide the door open whilst holding the makeshift cloak in place as she made her way to the garderobe. Bathroom. In this time, 'twas called a bathroom.

"Morning, princess," Struan called out. "We were beginning to worry. You've been asleep since yesterday afternoon."

That long? "Good morn," Sky mumbled, slipping into the tiny garderobe and closing the door behind her. Embarrassment heated her face. She had no brush, no way to clean her teeth and no garments to don. How could she face the Gordons thus? How could she face Struan? Mayhap she'd wait within the privy until she heard the men leave for the lists. Did Michael, Struan and Gene even train as the men did in her time? Were there even such things as lists in the twenty-first-century Renaissance fairs?

A light knock on the door made her jump, and the blanket around her shoulders fell to the floor. "Aye?"

"I have clean clothes for you, and I thought you might like to take a shower," Marjorie said through the thin door. "I also brought you a toothbrush."

Take a shower? Sky opened the door. "My thanks."

Marjorie joined her in the small bit of space until there was hardly any room for either of them to move. "Let me show you how to use the shower, and then I'll leave you be." She hung the garments over hooks on the back of the door and set two thick folded cloths and the toothbrush on the edge of the basin. She patted the cloths. "Clean towels." Then she opened a drawer and pointed. "Toothpaste, a hairbrush and a wide-toothed comb you're welcome to use."

Sky nodded, eyeing the contents of the drawer and the things Marjorie had set on the edge of the basin. She watched carefully as Marjorie demonstrated how to make warm water spray out of the fixture within the curtained stall. She held her hand under the spray. "'Tis perfect."

"It's tight in here, but at least you'll be able to bathe. We should have enough water in the tank, but you might want to be quick." Marjorie turned off the water. "I know the skirt and blouse will be way too large for you, but I have a belt we can use until we can buy clothes that fit." She backed out of the garderobe. "When you're ready, come join us for breakfast." She leaned over and picked up the blanket Sky had dropped before leaving.

Sky hurried through her ablutions, dried herself and brushed her teeth with the sweet, minty paste Marjorie had shown her. The ends of her hair had gotten wet in the shower, and she unbraided it to dry. She pulled the comb through the tangles until her hair hung smooth and free to her waist. She had to clutch the front of the skirt to keep it on, and the shoulders of the blouse kept slipping off. 'Twas the best she could do for now.

Tidying up after herself, she gathered her chemise, her dagger and sheath, and hung up the towel to dry. She returned to the small chamber, and after she made her bed, she folded her chemise and placed it at the end of the cot. She bunched the waist of the skirt in one hand and made her way to the front of the Gordons' camper. The moment she stepped into the kitchen area, the short sleeves of the borrowed blouse once again slipped down her shoulders.

Michael took one look at her and choked on his food. He coughed, and his face turned scarlet. Gene slapped the lad's back.

"Good morn," she said, sliding the flimsy fabric back into place on one shoulder, only to have the other side slip farther down her arm. "I fear these borrowed garments are—"

"They certainly *are*." Struan stood abruptly and moved to the counter. "I have things to do," he said, filling a container with coffee. "You can have my place at the table, Sky."

With that, he left in a rush without even so much as a glance her way. She sensed his agitation. Sky's face heated. Did she look so ridiculous she gave offense?

Marjorie slid out from her place and snatched something from the padded bench behind the table. "This will help." She wrapped a leather belt around Sky's waist, fastened it, and then tugged the bottom of the blouse down under the leather until the top tightened enough to stay in place. "Right after breakfast, we'll head for the mall." She stood back to study her handiwork. "It'll have to do. At least with the belt, you don't have to hold the skirt up in front of you."

"Did Struan leave for the lists?" she asked as she took her place at the table. His sudden departure shouldn't upset her, but it did. Like his wariness and resentment toward her, she felt compelled to uncover the cause.

"He might be meeting friends for a bit of training." Gene shrugged. "But I suspect he's fighting a battle of an entirely different nature."

Sky puzzled over what that might mean. Surely her presence was a painful reminder of his past, and that was what Gene referred to.

Michael cleared his throat. "A minute ago, with your hair all wavy and hanging down around your shoulders, and with the sun from the window hitting you just right, you looked just like one of those old paintings of a beautiful medieval lady."

"From what I ken, I am a *medieval* lady, lad." But hardly beautiful. Her stomach growled audibly. "Am I no'?"

"That you are, and by the sounds of it, a hungry one besides." Gene handed her a clean plate. "Dig in."

Michael handed her a platter with sausages and eggs. Sky filled her plate, took a piece of the toasted bread from another platter and broke her fast. "Mmm, this is delicious," she mumbled through a mouthful. "I thought I might try coffee again, only not quite so sweet this time."

"I'll get some for you, and you can fix it yourself." Michael hurried to the counter and poured some of the dark liquid into an earthenware mug. He returned and placed the steaming cup before her. "Sugar," he said, sliding a small, lidded bowl close. "And here's the cream. Add a little of each and taste it before adding more."

She did as he suggested until the coffee was exactly right. "Ah, I find I do like coffee after all. My mother never cared much for it, but Erin and Meghan are always going on about how much they miss their morning coffee." She took another sip.

"It must have been strange for your family," Gene said, propping his elbows on the table. "Having all those experiences with faeries, time travel and such."

"I suppose, but it never felt strange to me, since one of the time-travelers is my mother. I've never kent any different. I've no' seen any of the fae myself, and I'm glad for it. Speaking of my mother, I believe I might have kin in Minnesota, for she had many cousins, aunties and uncles. She's Anishinaabe. Have you heard of her people?"

"Can't say as I have," Gene remarked.

"I think they're the same as the Chippewa, right?" Michael scraped up the last bit of egg on his plate, using a corner of his toast, and then he stuffed the whole thing into his mouth.

"Aye." Sky grinned. "My mother is also half Scottish, MacConnell like my foster brother, Hunter."

She finished her meal and helped Marjorie clean up the kitchen while Michael and Gene left to ready their destriers for the morning's jousting matches.

Marjorie wiped her hands on a bit of linen. Then she took a set of keys from a small hook. "Time to shop. Are you ready?"

"For the truck or for the outlet mall?" she asked.

Marjorie chuckled. "Both."

"I dinna ken." She shrugged. "I have no idea what an outlet mall might be, and I have only the vaguest notion of trucks and their uses."

"You're about to find out about both. Come with me."

Sky followed Marjorie out of the trailer. Already the morning held the promise of the day's heat to come. Hazy sunlight filtered through the thick canopy of leaves above them, and the air was still and moist against her skin. Not a leaf or a blade of grass stirred.

A fresh breeze always blew across the loch at home. Her heart wrenched. Mayhap she'd have time yet this day to search the fair for Madame Giselle.

"Climb in. You can put your foot on the running board there," Marjorie said, opening the door to the truck.

Once the two of them had climbed in and she'd settled back against the cushioned seats, Sky studied the interior. Everything was so foreign to her. A vibrating rumble started up, and she gripped the edges of her seat. Marjorie leaned over and drew a belt across Sky's chest and lap, fastening it beside her. She had to be strapped in for this? Eyeing the campsite, she began to have doubts about riding anywhere in a truck.

"Now, Sky, when we get to the mall, I want you to pay attention to how the young women are dressed. It's going to seem strange to you, but I'm sure you'll get used to it."

The truck began to move, and she tightened her grip on the seat. "How is it possible for this wagon to move without something pulling it forward?"

"It's propelled forward by something called a combustion engine, and it's fueled by gasoline."

She nodded, though she hadn't understood a single word. What good would it do to ask more questions, when they'd only lead to more answers she couldn't understand? Instead, she focused on the road ahead and continued to grip the edges of her seat. They followed a trail of flattened grass and hard-packed earth that led out of the forest to a large area covered with more cars and trucks. Marjorie followed large signs with the word EXIT printed upon them, and soon they joined a vast river of cars and trucks hurtling along at a dizzying speed.

"Are you all right, Sky?"

"I am, though 'tis passing strange to travel thus." The changing landscape flew by.

"I can imagine. Before you know it, you'll be driving yourself."

"Think you?" Sky's eyes went wide as she considered the possibilities. Could she drive a truck? Did she even want to attempt such a feat? Excitement thrummed through her. Aye, she did.

"Of course. That reminds me, we'll have to get Ethan, my oldest, started on procuring identification for you, like he did for Struan. Once you have a birth certificate, you can learn how to drive and we'll help you get your license."

Soon Marjorie turned onto a smaller road, and they came to a cluster of buildings—large, flat-topped structures with glass fronts. People walked along outside of the buildings, sometimes stopping in front of one or another, and then entering. What the structures held was a mystery. "Is this the outlet mall you spoke of?"

"It is." Marjorie found a place between two other vehicles, drove into the spot and did something that caused the truck's rumbling to cease. "Remember to pay attention to how the young women of this time dress. You'll want to fit in."

Sky surveyed the people walking along before her. Shocking! The women were scarcely clad at all. The legs, midriffs, shoulders and arms of many of the lasses were completely bare. "I can't dress like that! Why, they're practically naked."

Marjorie clucked. "We'll find things you can wear that are somewhere in the middle of what you're accustomed to and today's styles." She climbed out of the truck, slung the strap of her bag high on her shoulder and waited for Sky to get out.

She hesitated, visualizing her father's reaction should he catch her dressed in such an immodest manner. His face would turn purple, and his tirade would raise the slate roof of their hall. Sighing, she climbed out. She couldn't wear her velvet gown in this heat, and the skirt and chemise Marjorie had loaned her were far too large. "How shall I pay for—"

"You don't have to worry about that. Struan is paying."

"He is?" Her brow rose.

"He says since he's a Sutherland, he's the closest thing to kin you have here. He sees it as his duty to look after you." Marjorie led her toward the buildings. "We'll have to get some underthings first, so you can try on everything else. Normally we'd wash your new clothes before you wear them, but under the circumstances that's not possible."

"Why would Struan view me as kin just because he's a Sutherland?" She'd asked about his sire, but he'd told her naught. Still, there were many Sutherlands, and only the earl's family were kin to her by marriage.

"I don't know that he does, but you did mention your aunts are married to Sutherlands. He said the closest thing *to* kin. Besides, you landed at his feet."

"Och, nay. 'Twas more like at his mount's hooves. Mayhap the horse should take responsibility for me, if that be Struan's logic."

"You don't want his help?"

"In purchasing clothing? Nay, 'tis far too personal a gift for one who is no' a male relative," she muttered, "but I have little choice in the matter." She'd give him one of her gold coins. He already resented her, and for whatever reason, he'd become agitated by the sight of her earlier. It must gall him to see himself as the only male kin she had here, therefore his responsibility.

Her eyes stung. She'd always been surrounded by a large and loving family. She'd never doubted her place or her worth. Being dependent upon a man who clearly wished she hadn't dropped into his life chafed. "Marjorie, where is my gown? I could no' find it this morn."

"It's hanging in the closet. Why? Did you want to wear that heavy thing today?"

"Nay. I have a few coins sewn into the hem and bodice. I shall repay Struan for his generosity once we return."

"Ah. I see." She gestured toward one of the many doors. "There's the underwear store. We'll start there and work our way down to the shoe store."

Hours later, and dressed in what Marjorie had referred to as khaki capris and a T-shirt, Sky tugged at the uncomfortable undergarment she wore beneath her soft shirt. A bra, Marjorie had told her, was an absolute necessity. *I think not.* And as soon as she could, she meant to take it off and put it away. She did like the panties, though, and the sandals. The shoes cushioned her feet in a most amazing manner.

Sky shifted her hold on the bags she carried. They had purchased jeans, capris, blouses, T-shirts, shorts, skirts and even a scanty garment called a sundress, which seemed more like a chemise to her. She had two sets of garments solely for sleep, and she now had a pair of sandals and another pair of sturdier shoes Marjorie called "sneakers." Were they truly meant for sneaking about?

"Here we are," Marjorie said, unlocking the truck. "Even though it's only been a couple of hours since we had lunch, I'm starving. Shopping is hard work."

"Indeed," Sky said, stowing her bags in the space behind where she'd sit. They'd had their midday meal earlier in a *restaurant*, and Sky had eaten her very first cheeseburger and fries. Her mother oft spoke of missing bacon cheeseburgers and extra crispy fries, and now Sky understood what she'd been talking about. Far too salty and greasy for her tastes.

"Gene is grilling tonight." Marjorie added the bags she carried to the pile. "Good thing, too, because I'm beat. We're going to stop at a grocery store on the way back and pick up a few side dishes."

"Och, aye?" She tried to respond appropriately, but without having any idea what Marjorie meant, 'twas far too taxing. She already had a headache from trying so hard to keep up with all she'd experienced this day.

Marjorie chuckled. "You don't have any idea what I'm talking about, do you?"

"Nay." Sky climbed into the truck and sighed. Never had it felt so wonderful to simply sit. Only during their clan's harvests did she feel this tired, and that was only physical. The exhaustion she suffered in this time affected her mind as well as her body. Mayhap she still suffered fatigue from her journey through time as well. 'Twas only yesterday, after all. "Might I remain in the truck when next we stop?"

"Of course." Marjorie patted Sky's arm. "I imagine this is all a bit overwhelming for you."

"Aye, for certes." Sky leaned her head back and closed her eyes. "Overwhelming, confusing, disconcerting . . . and I miss my kin so terribly much." A lump rose to her throat, and her eyes filled. "'Twould no' be so bad if I kent for certain I'll return home, but—"

"Things will work out, Sky. You'll see."

Sky nodded, wishing with all her might that she had Marjorie's certainty about her future. The next thing she kent, Marjorie was nudging her awake.

"We're here."

Stretching, Sky scanned her surroundings. Gene stood before a contraption spewing smoke from the top. She climbed out to find the air redolent with the delicious smell of roasting meat.

Struan sat at the table with an ale in his hand. Immediately she sensed his agitation toward her. She sighed. "Marjorie, if you please, I'd like to have my *sgian dubh* returned to me."

"Oh, of course." She fished around in her bag. "I couldn't let her wear it strapped to her calf while she tried on clothes, you see," Marjorie said, aiming her comments at her husband. "So I kept the blade sheathed and in my purse."

She handed Sky her wee dagger just as Michael opened the door of the camper and started down the stairs. "Wow, Sky. Looking good." He grinned. "I like your new outfit."

"You are most kind, Michael," she said, tucking the dagger into the waist of her capris. She turned back to the truck and grabbed a few of the bags holding the day's purchases.

"Let me help you with those," Struan said.

His deep voice startled her. "If you wish," she muttered. He stood so close, his warmth touched her skin. And his scent, uniquely masculine and delectable, filled her senses. Her heart took flight. His hands touched hers as he took the bags, and a shock arced through her, heating her blood. Their eyes met and held for a moment, until once again his disquiet hit her full force.

"My thanks." She clasped her hands together, embarrassment singeing her from within.

"Michael, get the rest would you? Ma has groceries in the back," Struan called.

Sky followed Struan into the camper. He set the bags down on the table. "Want a beer or a glass of wine, Sky? We're going to eat soon."

"Aye, wine would be most welcome." 'Twould also help calm her nerves. She opened the closet door, found her gown and ran her fingers along the hem until she located one of the hidden coins. Her ma always said women needed to be prepared for anything. You never knew when you might find yourself in a circumstance where you'd need coin to stay at an inn or send word home for help. Carefully, Sky picked at the threads with her *sgian dubh*.

"What are you doing?" Struan approached, his brow furrowed.

"You'll see." Sky drew out a coin, straightened and handed it to him. "Here, I trow this will cover what I owe for the garments Marjorie and I purchased." She met his gaze. "I dinna wish to be indebted to you, Struan. Despite what you might believe, 'tis no fault of mine that I landed in the midst of your life or the Gordons'. I am no more content than you about my intrusion, and I mean to find a way home. In the meantime, I canna deny that I need your help."

The furrow between his brows deepened, and his mouth tightened. He glared at the gold in his palm as if it offended him.

"If you would be so kind, help me find a way to reach Minnesota, and then—"

"I'll do no such thing," he snapped, looking as shocked as she at his outburst.

"Hey, what's going on?" Michael entered the camper, his arms full of the foodstuffs Marjorie had bought for their supper. Concern shadowed his features as he looked from her to Struan and then back again.

"Nothing." Struan's eyes bored into hers, his roiling emotions far too numerous for her to decipher. "There's a glass of wine on the counter for you, princess. Dinner will be ready soon." With that he turned abruptly and strode out of the camper.

Sky blinked against the sting in her eyes. "I dinna understand him. He's no' at all like my father, uncles or brothers. Nor is he at all like the Sutherlands I call kin."

"Aw, now . . . don't let Struan upset you," Michael pleaded, setting the bags down on the counter. "I think he's just all stirred up about the past right now. The day he came to us, his dad lay dying right beside him. Your appearance is probably a painful reminder. It's not you, Sky. Don't let him make you feel unwelcome."

"Think you that's why he resents me so?"

"Uh . . . Hmm. Can't really say." He gave her an awkward hug. "It's a bitch, isn't it?"

She couldn't help smiling at the open, utterly good-hearted lad. "Of what do you speak, lad?"

"Being able to sense what others feel about you." His face colored.

"Oh." She studied him, sensing his gifts. "Aye, 'tis oft a *bitch*, but just as oft a blessing."

"Not when it comes to girls," he muttered.

"Och, Michael. You're a comely lad, and soon enough you'll grow into those long legs and arms. You'll fill out, and the lasses will swoon at your feet."

"You really think so?"

"Aye. Dinna doubt it." She patted his cheek, warmth for the lad who reminded her so much of her brothers filling her heart.

CHAPTER FOUR

The Monday morning sun had just begun its ascent, painting the eastern horizon in orange, soft pinks and varying shades of deep blue. Dew covered the grass of their campsite, and already the soles and sides of Struan's leather boots were damp. He paused for a moment to watch the sunrise, glad to be alive and in the moment.

He opened the storage compartment at the front of the horse trailer and hefted his saddle into its place. Then he loaded Michael's saddle and their tack. He couldn't wait to hit the road. He had orders waiting to be filled, and he was never happier or more content than when he worked in his forge.

He grunted. Contentment would not come so easily now that Sky had fallen into his life. Why had he snapped at her last evening, refusing her request to help her get to the McGladreys? It would be far easier and better for his peace of mind to hand her off to them. Struan could wash his hands of her, and passing her to the McGladreys made sense. Didn't it? She was related to them by marriage, after all.

Ah, but she was also related to him by marriage. Struan's sire had been the fourth earl of Sutherland, and Sky's aunt was wed to the sixth. Plus, Sky had appeared in *his* path, not Connor McGladrey's, and that had to mean something. Her fate and his were somehow inextricably tied. No matter what, he couldn't escape whatever fate Sky brought to him until he knew what it held. Only then could he take evasive action.

Once he figured out which direction he needed to turn, he'd pat Sky on the head and send her wherever it was she wanted to go. Why did that thought twist his gut into a tight knot? Some remnant of his father's lessons on chivalry, honor and responsibility, no doubt.

"Where has everyone gone?"

Struan's heart kicked against his ribcage at the sound of her voice, as if she'd caught him in the act of . . . something. Could she sense his thoughts about her? "Good morning to you, too." He glanced at Sky over his shoulder. "They're gassing up the trucks and checking the air pressure in the tires." She nodded like she might have a clue what he was talking about. Poor lass.

As if yesterday's capris and T-shirt hadn't worked on his nerves hard enough, today she wore snug denim shorts and a silky sleeveless top that divided his attention between her bare legs and the fullness of her breasts. A surge of heat flooded his system—especially in the region south of his belt. *Get a grip.* By today's standards, her shorts weren't even all that short. They came almost to her knees, and he'd certainly been around women who wore far less. He hadn't reacted to them the way he did with Sky.

Turning away, he stacked the breastplates, pauldrons and plackarts of their armor and placed them on the racks he'd designed especially for their horse trailer. "They're also picking up bagels, cream cheese and coffee for breakfast. We'll eat on the road."

"On the road? But . . . I . . . I thought to search the fair for Madame Giselle this morn. Can you tell me—"

"Look around you. The gates are locked up tight, and there's no one inside the fairgrounds. The fair is closed. And that's how it will remain until next weekend." Glancing at her over his shoulder, he added, "Besides, I asked around yesterday afternoon. There are no fortune-tellers at this fair going by the name of Madame Giselle. Your faerie isn't here." Her face fell at that bit of news, and he regretted putting it out there the way he had. "Sorry, princess, I—"

"Why do you call me *princess*?" she bit out. "You ken well enough I am no such thing."

"You carry yourself like royalty." He shrugged, turning back to stow the greaves and cuisses. "I mean it as a compliment."

"Nay. You dinna. Do you forget I am a truthsayer, sir?" She made a snorting noise. "Though your words sound pleasant enough, your intent is most disparaging." With that revelation, she turned on her heel and strode back into his parents' camper, slamming the flimsy aluminum door behind her.

Damn, he *had* forgotten. Guilt swamped him. She got under his skin on far too many levels and for far too many reasons to count. None of them were her fault. He blew out a breath and stared blindly into the surrounding woods. He should apologize, and he would, just not right this minute. He wanted to have everything ready to go by the time his family returned. Struan went back to packing up their gear, his mind in turmoil. Again.

Michael pulled Struan's pickup into the campsite first. By that time, Struan had the horses fed, watered and ready to load. He patted Brutus's neck as the gelding snuffled at his pockets in search of a treat.

Michael climbed out of the truck, holding a cardboard tray full of covered cups of coffee. He handed one to Struan. "Where's Sky?"

Struan gestured toward the camper.

"Still?"

"She's up and dressed. We . . . had words earlier. I guess she objects to being called *princess*."

Michael's expression turned accusatory. "It's not about what you call her, Struan. It's—"

"I know, and you're right. My intent is *most* disparaging. I can't seem to help myself. She just gets to me for some reason." Her sudden appearance, her very presence churned up too much from his past and scared the shit out of him about his future—or the possible lack thereof. He couldn't admit that to Michael though. "I know I behaved badly, and I swear I'll apologize."

Michael scrutinized him. "You'd better, or else."

"Or else what?" He tousled Michael's hair. "You'll kick my butt?"

"That's right." Michael grinned before heading for the trailer.

Michael would do his best to smooth Sky's ruffled feathers. Another pang of guilt hit him. *He* should be the one to soothe her injured feelings, since he'd been the one to wound her in the first place. Should he follow his brother into the trailer, tell Sky he was sorry? He stood in the middle of their campsite, indecision immobilizing him.

Gene pulled in next, followed by Marjorie. Gene climbed out and frowned at him. "What's got your boxers in a bunch?"

"Just thinking." He'd apologize to Sky while they were on the road. "Everything's ready to go here."

Marjorie set a large paper bag on the hood of their pickup. "Good. Where's Michael with that coffee?"

"Inside with Sky."

His ma's sharp gaze settled on him for an uncomfortable second, before she nodded and headed for the trailer herself. Sighing, Struan imagined Michael would fill her in on all his transgressions. He'd get an earful from her later, he was sure.

The next half hour was spent readying everything for departure. Sky pitched in where she could, surprising him, adding to his load of guilt. With broom in hand, she was currently sweeping out Gene and Marjorie's trailer. In his experience, women of noble birth were accustomed to having servants take care of such things like that for them.

Sky was a paradox, proud and regal, yet willing to undertake even the most menial of tasks.

"I'll take the horse trailer," Struan said. "Sky, you can ride with me."

"I'd rather travel with Michael or Gene and Marjorie." Her delicate hands tightened around the broom handle.

He'd only added to her fear and uncertainty with his bad attitude. "I can't blame you, but I think we need to talk."

Michael came up beside her. "It's OK, Sky. Ride with Struan for now, and when we stop, if you want, you can switch." He patted her shoulder. "You two do need to talk."

She shrugged as if it didn't make any difference to her one way or the other. "Mayhap 'twould be good to come to some accord." She disappeared into the trailer, reemerging a few moments later sans the broom and with her coffee cup clutched in one hand.

"That's settled then," Marjorie said, shooting Struan her sternest *make nice* look. "Let's fix our bagels and head out."

Using the hood of the truck for their table, Marjorie flattened the paper bag for a tablecloth and laid out their breakfast. "Sky, we have veggie cream cheese or honey walnut. Which would you prefer?"

"I dinna ken. Choose for me, Marjorie, for I am unfamiliar with such fare."

"Honey walnut it is," Marjorie said, slathering the spread onto both sides of a split bagel. She wrapped it in a large napkin and handed it to Sky. "Struan, help her get settled in your truck," she commanded, "and I'll fix your bagel."

His stomach rumbling in anticipation, he did as he was told and helped Sky into her seat. "There's a holder for your coffee," he said, setting his own cup into one of the two spots between the seats.

"My thanks," she murmured.

Struan took his bagel from Marjorie. "I'll take up the rear, so we can keep Michael in the middle."

"Take it slow," Gene instructed Michael, as he helped himself to a couple of bagels. Gene helped Marjorie put away the extras, and then they climbed into their truck.

Soon they were bumping over the ruts in the hard-packed dirt trail leading out of the forest, and Sky was ignoring him. "I owe you an apology," he said. She didn't reply. He glanced at her. She wore a look of deep concentration, her brow furrowed. "Are you doing it now, Sky?"

Her eyes met his for a second. "Doing *it?*"

"Checking my apology for truth."

"Nay." She made a tsking sound. "I sensed the ambivalence in your *apology* the moment the words left your mouth. You spoke thus only because you feel you must."

"I meant it. The ambivalence—"

"Why do you carry such resentment toward me?" She glared, her hands forming a tight little nest around her napkin-wrapped breakfast. "What have I done to offend you, sir? Pray, tell me now, so that I might—"

"You've done naught to give offense, save bringing the past forward to haunt me," he snapped, reverting to the patterns of speech he'd worked so hard to suppress.

"We are no' even from the same century. I have naught to do with *your* past," she said, her voice hitching. "Your resentment is misplaced, sir. I want only to go h-home."

Tears slipped down her cheeks, and his heart dropped painfully to the pit of his stomach. "I'm sorry, Sky. I . . . I fear your sudden appearance in my life will somehow lead me to peril, and that is the source of the resentment and the ambivalence you sense." Partially, anyway. He couldn't give voice to the labyrinth of emotions she evoked. Not rational, any of it, but he couldn't seem to control associating her rank with what he'd suffered as a youth. Nor could he control his overwhelming attraction to her.

"Lead you to peril? How? Other than to helping me get to Minnesota, I have asked naught of you." She picked at the napkin holding her bagel. "Nor will I."

"I don't believe your sudden appearance in my life has anything to do with chance." He owed her an explanation, but he didn't care one bit for sharing his fears. Would she see him as weak? Struan's gut wrenched. "I should have died at Halidon Hill. My father did, along with too many of our clansmen to count."

"Och, Struan. Nay." She laid her hand on his forearm for a moment. "If you were meant to die that day, naught could have prevented you from doing so. That you were spared means your life still holds purpose."

Hearing his name fall from her lips, along with the gentleness of her touch, brought a lump to his throat. He stifled the impulse to twine their fingers together and grasp at the comfort she so freely offered.

"That's not how I see it, lass. I *was* dying. Grievously wounded and feverish, my life was slipping away bit by bit. Then the shimmering lights appeared, and I escaped fate's decree. Do ye no' see? I *was* meant to die that day. I'm living on borrowed time, and I fear that borrowed time is running out. I fear you are meant to take me back to the past, and it makes no difference whether it be Halidon Hill or Kildrummy. I cheated death once, and I ken well I will no' be so lucky the second time 'round." His voice broke. "And that, my lady, is at the root of my resentment toward you."

"What power do you believe I hold to take you anywhere?" Sky asked, her eyes clouded with confusion. "I assure you, I have no such intent or expectation. I—"

"You have my oath to protect you, my lady. That holds power enough."

"I remember no such oath. When did you swear fealty to me?"

"The moment you fell through time. Do you no' recall? I gave you my word that you would be safe."

"Ah, well then . . . I release you from your vow." She straightened her posture and lifted her chin. "There. Will you cease resenting me now?"

"If only it were that simple." He couldn't help smiling. How could one wee lass be so haughty, and yet so warm and generous of heart at the same time? "I believe there are forces beyond our ken at work here. Perhaps fate has caught up with me at last."

"Och, but 'tis naught but superstitious thinking on your part." She shook her head. "You can take the man out of the fourteenth century, but you canna take the fourteenth century out of the man," she muttered.

"What?"

"My cousin Robley's wife says that whenever she's vexed with him, only she says fifteenth century." She glanced at him through her lashes. "Robley is the cousin who came to this century by choice. He returned to us, which leads me to believe I will be able to return home as well. By whatever means, send me to the McGladreys in Minnesota, and you need no' worry over my presence any longer."

There was the knotting sensation in his gut again. "You don't need to go to Minnesota to talk to Connor McGladrey. Once we're in Virginia, we can look him up on the Internet, and then we can e-mail or phone him and arrange a time to Skype."

She rubbed her temples. "I've no bloody idea what you just said."

He grinned. "Once we're home, I'll show you. In the meantime, will you accept my apology? I'm truly sorry for my churlishness. I know none of this is your fault, and you certainly don't deserve my resentment."

"Aye, I will accept your apology." Up went her chin again. "Will you set aside your resentment once and for all?"

His feelings went so much deeper and were way more complicated than what he'd been willing to share, but those were his issues, not hers.

At least what he'd told her was the truth, just not all of the truth. "I'll do my best."

"Think you we might become friends, Struan?"

The vulnerability in her tone tore at him. He, more than anyone, knew what she was going through, and yet he'd offered her nothing but suspicion, defensiveness—and lust. "Aye, lass. I would like that."

She chuckled. "Are you aware of the way you slip in and out of the speech of our time and now?"

"Aye. I've worked hard to fit in here, but speaking to one such as yourself brings the old ways to the fore." He studied her for a second. "Are you able to shut off your fae abilities? Do you have any control?"

She nodded.

"I might not always be able to control my emotions. I want you to know that none of what I feel about the past has anything to do with you, and I can't always turn it off. If you would agree to allow me my privacy, that would help us to get along better."

"Oh." Her face turned pink. "I . . . Och, now 'tis my turn to apologize. I've been so frightened and confused, I fear I've relied upon my abilities to gauge my surroundings."

"Understandable under the circumstances."

"I too will do my best to . . . to . . ."

"Stay out of my head?" He shot her a grin.

"Aye." Her blush deepened, and she turned to stare out the window.

"Are you going to eat that bagel, or just hold it on your lap all morning?" Struan took a bite of his, eliciting a growl from his stomach. "Try it, Sky. I trow you'll find it most pleasing."

She took a hesitant nibble. Her features once again took on an intense look of concentration. Her brow rose slightly. "Aye, 'tis quite good. Sweet." Her next bite was much larger.

One bagel wasn't going to be enough for him, and he regretted not taking another before they'd left camp. He finished his bagel, keeping one eye on Sky, and the other on the road ahead. "You going to eat both halves? They are really big bagels."

She laughed, and her eyes sparkled. "You remind me of my younger brothers, always hovering over my trencher on the chance that I might leave some tasty morsel. 'Are you going to eat that?' seems to be a common question no matter the century. Are young men never full?"

"Never." The sound of her laughter made his insides do a slip-slide. "'Tis hard work being a man, even more so whilst young and still growing."

"I can only imagine." She handed him half her bagel and set the other half on the dashboard with only a few bites missing. "Will you tell me a bit about where we're going?"

"Aye. My family owns a thousand-acre farm that lies in a valley amongst the Appalachian Mountains of Virginia. 'Tis very much like Scotland there, with rolling hills, mountains, lochs, burns and thick forests." He glanced at her, pride swelling his chest. "A year past, I was able to purchase five hundred acres of land for myself from an old man whose farm abuts ours. My home lies just across the road from theirs."

"You're a laird then."

"Not in the way you mean it. I have no villeins or serfs. Anyone may own land in this time and place. We don't have overlords or nobility, and our leaders are elected. We have the freedom to become whatever we wish. I also own a business, so I'm a landowner and a merchant."

"And a knight." She smiled.

"Nay, lass." He shook his head. "I was never knighted. As you said yourself, I was but ten and four when I came here."

"Still, had you continued your training, you would have been knighted, surely."

"Mayhap, had I lived through Halidon Hill." Did his rank matter so much to her? Of course it did. She was an earl's legitimate daughter. His grip on the steering wheel tightened, the taunts and derision from his youth echoing through his mind. He forced his thoughts back to the present.

"We've a small, spring-fed loch on our land, and a burn that runs the entire length of the valley. 'Tis perfect for the kine my brother Ethan raises. He produces milk, which he sells to a nearby dairy. He also raises goats and sells the milk to a gourmet cheese-maker. Ethan used to perform at the fairs with me, but once Michael was old enough to take over the jousting and swordplay, Ethan took to farming full-time."

Sky nodded. "Sounds lovely."

"It is. I've a grand life here. I make a great living, and I have a wonderful family and good friends."

"And . . . is there a lady?" Sky asked, her attention fixed upon the side of the road.

Struan's heart pounded. "Nay." He glanced at her, inordinately pleased by the blush his answer brought to her cheeks.

"With your kin lost to you, will the Gordons make a match for you in their stead?"

"That's no' how things are done in the twenty-first century, Sky. If we meet someone who appeals to us, we ask them out on a date, get to know them without chaperones hovering about."

"Nay," she cried, her eyes wide.

"Aye," he assured her. "In this time, men and women wed for love, and they choose their partners on their own."

"Hmm." She cleared her throat. "I couldn't help but notice you call Marjorie Ma, but you call Gene by his given name. Why is that?"

"My mother died giving birth to me. Marjorie is the only woman ever to mother me or to claim me as her son, and so she is truly my ma. I kent my da. He raised me, trained me, and he died whilst we fought our enemies side by side. I love Gene like a father, and I have told him how I feel. But, out of respect for the man who sired me, Gene and I agreed that I should call him by his given name."

"You are very fortunate indeed to have found such a family."

"I am." He shifted, reached to the floor behind his seat and snatched up one of the science fiction books he loved to read. "It's an eight-hour drive to our home in Virginia. Do you read?"

"Aye, my mother taught all of us to read, write and how to tally sums and such. Why do you ask?"

Struan placed the book in her lap. "I thought you might like to read to pass the time."

"'Tis an odd-looking tome, to be sure." Frowning, she picked up the paperback and studied the cover. "What might this be about?"

"It's called science fiction, Sky. It's all make believe, a tale of adventure in another world." He grinned. "Give it a try, and if you don't care for this book, you can try another, or mayhap you'd prefer a magazine. The floor behind your seat holds quite a few books and magazines to choose from."

"Did the Gordons teach you to read?"

"Aye, and once they helped me get caught up to others my age, I went to high school and earned a diploma."

"Aye?" Her brow puckered. "Is that similar to attending Oxford in Britain?"

He chuckled. "Somewhat. One must have a diploma or a GED certificate in this age in order to seek employment. You must have a high school education in order to go on to a college like Oxford. Everyone here learns to read and write, and so much more. For the most part, it's a well-educated population."

"Ah."

One small word, yet it conveyed so much anxiety. Why had he brought up education and earning a living? He'd made her feel even more insecure than she already did. "Dinna fash. If need be, we'll help you to gain what you need to get a GED, and then you can decide what you want to do from there. You're a canny lass, and you'll learn quickly."

"Think you?"

"Aye."

She shrugged. "It matters no', for I intend to return to my kin as soon as may be arranged."

He nodded, once again his insides rebelling at the notion. "This is a grand place, and a good time in which to live, Sky. Most diseases that felled folk in the past are easily cured now. Very few women die in childbirth as they did in the past." What was he doing? Did he mean to comfort her, or was he trying to talk her into staying?

"I must go home, Struan." She glanced at him, her features clouded. "My disappearance will set off a clan war, and I canna bear the thought of any of my kin coming to harm. My da has no idea just how deceitful and ruthless the Erskines are. I must warn my family." She straightened. "I am already learned, and my cousin Erin brought back vaccinations with her when she returned to Robley. And since I have decided never to marry, I will no' face the risk of childbirth."

"Never marry?" His gaze flew to her. "Why not?"

"I dinna wish to burden any bairns with the fae abilities I carry," she said in a small voice.

Had she suffered stigma and suspicion because of her gifts? He knew well what happened to anyone thought to be a witch in the fourteenth century, and it didn't take much to cause an accusation, either. The fear of such a fate must have been a constant in her life. His heart wrenched, and protectiveness for her surged. Mentally, he renewed his oath to be her champion. "Your abilities aren't feared or scorned in this century like they are in the past. Wiccan practitioners, witches, are free to follow their beliefs in this age, and—"

"I'm no' a witch," she cried. "I'm part fae, and I dinna practice aught but the healing arts."

"I ken as much. I'm just trying to show you how different things are today. You have nothing to fear."

"Humph." She lifted the book from her lap. "I wouldst try this *science fiction* of yours now."

He nodded, his mind already shifting to his own dilemma. Sky Elizabeth had been open and honest with him, while he'd kept his secrets. He glanced sideways at her. She was so pretty he lost his breath every time he looked at her. He should tell her right now that he was the bastard son of Kenneth, the fourth earl of Sutherland, and therefore kin to her by marriage.

He opened his mouth to do so, and closed it again. Best think on it a while yet, examine the pros and cons, let her get to know him first and foremost as the man he'd fashioned himself to be in the present. He was a well-respected, successful artisan, a landowner and a highly skilled performer. Once he was certain she saw him in the light he preferred to cast upon himself, then certainly the circumstances of his illegitimate birth would not matter.

Why did her opinion matter so much? He ground his molars together. Clearly, he had more thinking to do before he did or said anything to Sky Elizabeth of clan MacKintosh, the earl of Fife's eldest daughter.

CHAPTER FIVE

S ky could make no sense of the book in her lap. Alien beings? Other
worlds and intergalactic intrigues? She had no idea what intergalactic meant, and she had enough difficulty with the one world in which
she found herself at present. Besides, Struan's words kept distracting her
from the incomprehensible story.

In this age, couples wed for love and chose their own mates. How
could that notion not send her thoughts to her own circumstance? Her
foster brother, Hunter, married for love, as had her cousin Robley and
her cousin Liam, and Liam's wife had been the daughter of their most
bitter enemy.

Indeed, her own parents had gone against the wishes of her grandsire and had handfasted whilst the earl was away, later taking their vows
before a priest. Yet Sky had been *bartered* away to a black-hearted knave
so despicable he'd already planned her murder, and they hadn't even
spoken their vows yet.

Soon enough, her twin brothers would be forced to wed ladies of
noble birth, and both lasses would be chosen by their father, who was
now himself the earl of Fife. Already the twins had received numerous

offers from earls and barons with marriageable daughters. And what of her dear sisters? Would they suffer a similar fate as hers, being given in marriage to men who would never care one whit for them? The thought of wee Sarah married to a man who cared naught for her, whilst congratulating himself for acquiring more land, more wealth, brought a sting to her eye.

'Twas not just. Whilst her parents had gone against the old earl's wishes, she and her siblings remained assets to be traded away for property, fortunes and alliances. The disparity, the utter iniquity existing within her own clan had never before occurred to her, yet now she could think of little else. She closed the book on her lap and stared out the window.

"Not to your liking, Sky?"

She shook her head. "I canna make any sense of the words."

"Would you like to try one of the magazines?" Struan reached back behind the seat.

"Nay." She shifted in her plush seat. Riding in a truck was far more comfortable than traveling on horseback. "In this century, a man may fashion his life to suit himself, aye?"

"Aye." He smiled her way. "If he's willing to work hard for what he wants."

Her insides fluttered. When he smiled, when his wide-set blue eyes weren't filled with resentment or haunted by the past, he was most charming. "What of the women? Can they too determine for themselves what their futures will hold?"

"They can. Women can be and do whatever they wish. Some even choose to be soldiers."

"Soldiers?" She canted her head, trying to imagine such a thing. "Och, the women of our era have oft fought alongside the men in defense of home and kin. 'Tis no' so different I suppose. Can women hold land as well, or does ownership revert to the husband should she wed?"

"Women may own property, and ownership does *not* revert to the husband should she marry." He glanced at her, his eyes twinkling in a most beguiling manner. "Why? Are you thinking of buying land? Just how many gold coins do you have sewn into that gown of yours?"

"No' so many as that." An answering smile broke free. "Och, 'tis but curiosity."

"If you could be or do anything you wanted, what would you do to earn your living in this century?"

"I am a healer like my mother and cousin, but Erin has told me about the miracles of your time. My skills are poor indeed in comparison. Hmm." She tapped her chin. "Mayhap I would choose to be an artisan. I do enjoy creating things of beauty, tapestries, clothing, beading, weaving and the like. "

"There you go," he said with a look of triumph. "We travel to Renaissance festivals all over, and I rent booths in most of them. Soon, I plan to quit jousting and focus solely on my business. Your wares would be a most welcome addition to what I already sell. Plus, there's always the Internet."

"There is that word again. What is this net you speak of? The only nets I ken are those used by our fisherman."

"Uh . . . hmm. Hard to explain. It's best to show you, and I'll teach you how to use my laptop."

"My thanks." Her thoughts returned to her family. What must it have been like for her mother? To come from an age where she could have been and done anything she wished, only to be thrust into a society where women had little say in what became of them?

She'd heard the tales all her life, how her mother had been a talented violinist attending a prestigious school with a job already awaiting her. Her mother still played her harp, but her precious violin had been shattered long ago by an enemy who had captured her to lure Sky's father into a trap. She sighed.

"Are you tired or just bored?"

"Neither." Sky glanced at Struan. "I've much to think on. 'Tis quite different here." Sliding her palms down the denim of her shorts, she continued. "Clothing, food, how you travel from one place to another and your society . . . I dinna ken what to make of it all. At home, my future was determined for me from the moment of my birth. You say in this era women decide for themselves. I canna imagine what it must be like to have such freedom."

She bit her lip, as a wave of conflicting emotions overtook her—bitterness, mixed with love and loyalty for her family. She chafed at the constraints her rank and duty placed upon her, yet with every fiber of her being, she missed her kin and wanted nothing more than to go home. The sting of tears burned her eyes. She blinked rapidly, trying to stem the flow.

"Oh no. Don't cry, princess."

She choked out a strangled laugh. "Still you insist upon calling me by a title I cannot claim."

"Aye, but without any disparagement. Surely you can sense that." Struan reached for her hand and gave it a squeeze.

At his touch, a quivering ensued low in her belly. "You asked me not to invade your privacy." She turned away lest he see her guilt. She hadn't closed herself off to him.

"Aye, but I dinna expect you have."

Chagrinned, she shrugged. "*Ceart go leor.*" *Right enough.*

"Och, *ceart go leor.*" He grinned. "I've no' heard that expression since coming to this century."

"I imagine no'." Sky looked his way, an eyebrow lifted. "Still, my name is no' *Princess.* 'Tis Sky Elizabeth."

"I ken your name well enough, lass," he said, his tone gruff.

A sudden awareness thrummed between them. There was no mistaking the desire emanating from Struan, nor could she ignore the answering heat pooling deep within her.

Nay, she could not allow herself to feel aught for Struan. She had no intention of staying in his time. Besides, he'd confessed his fears regarding her presence, and she had released him from his vow of fealty.

She would not—indeed, she could not—ask him for aught but help in contacting and reaching the McGladreys.

"Warm Springs," Sky read the sign at the edge of the town their caravan had just entered. They'd been in the realm of Virginia since late afternoon, and once she'd given up on the science fiction book, she'd entertained herself by reading the many signs they passed along their journey, whilst trying to make sense of them. "Are there really warm springs here?"

"Quite a few. This part of the Appalachian Mountains is called Bath County."

Sky searched the surrounding area as if she might see spirals of steam floating upward from one of the springs. All she saw were buildings lining the thoroughfare through the village.

"Once you're settled in, I'll take you to visit some of the hot springs in the area. I'm sure one of my sisters will have a swimsuit you can borrow."

"A *swimsuit*?" All that came to mind at his words were suits of armor, and surely that could not be what he meant.

He chuckled. "You'll see."

"Hmm, you say the same for much of what we discuss."

"And so you will." He glanced at her. "Thank you, Sky."

She sent him a questioning look. "For what?"

"For choosing to keep me company the entire trip." He grinned. "It's been nice, and I've enjoyed listening to you figure out the road signs along the way."

"You are most welcome." His words gladdened her. Mayhap they could be friends after all.

Soon they left the village of Warm Springs behind and continued along a narrow, twisting road through the mountains. Struan turned onto yet another road, this one wending its way down into a valley. "We're almost home," he said, his tone tinged with pride.

"Oh my." Sky surveyed their surroundings. "'Tis quite lovely." They were surrounded by magnificent vistas in every direction: thick woods and rolling mountains, with slopes covered in verdant greenery. The valley itself boasted such rich and fertile land, she could only stare in wonder.

"This is Gordon Hollow. Gene's family has lived on this land since the early eighteen hundreds. Somehow his ancestors managed to hold on to the family farm all these years, despite the Civil War, the Great Depression and all manner of hardships and upheavals."

Her heart wrenched. "I wonder if my kin still hold Moigh Hall after all these centuries."

"Moigh Hall would be nothing but a ruin now, lass. Very few castles from our era are still standing, much less owned by their clans or lairds." He studied her for a moment. "If you wish, we can also search for information about your kin while we're on the Internet."

"Is that what you did, Struan?" she asked. "Did you search this thing you call the Internet to see what became of your kin?"

Struan's jaw tightened, and his distress was obvious, even without her abilities. He nodded, but said naught.

"I'm sorry. I did no' mean to bring up unpleasant memories. Mayhap 'twould be best if I dinna look for answers about what became of my family, aye? 'Tis quite disheartening and confusing to think that all the people I love are long gone, though I was with them less than a se'nnight ago." She frowned. "And they are living their lives in the past at this very moment."

His Adam's apple moved. He cleared his throat and pointed. "There's Gene and Marjorie's house, and you can see mine a short distance down on the opposite side of the street. That other house, the one set well back from Gene's and surrounded by all the outbuildings, belongs to Ethan and his wife. They have a little boy who's about four months old now. My sister Lindsay just graduated from college, and she's home now."

He turned to her. "You'll like Lindsay. You two are close in age. My other sister, Courtney, is married and she and her husband, John, live in Lexington. They visit often, so you'll meet them soon."

Sky nodded, taking it all in. Such valuable land! The Gordons must be very wealthy indeed. "The kine are so very different in appearance from ours," she said, surveying the herd grazing peacefully alongside a burn. Hadn't Struan mentioned the burn, saying that it ran through their entire valley? "They're no' shaggy at all. Are the winters less harsh here than in our highlands?"

"Aye. Not nearly so brutal. The temperature rarely goes below freezing."

Gene and Marjorie pulled their truck into the short road leading to their home, while Michael continued on to the place Struan had indicated as his dwelling. He turned onto the narrow lane, and Struan followed, continuing to one of the three buildings near his neat cottage.

"Your stables?"

"Yep. Besides the two destriers, we have other horses we keep for riding the trails hereabouts, and for going after stray cattle. The horses board here, since Ethan's barn is full to capacity with the dairy cattle. Do you enjoy riding?"

"Very much." Sky scanned the buildings, settling upon a structure made of stone with a roof of some kind of metal. An attractive sign affixed above the wide double doors caught her eye. "Sutherland Forge," she read aloud. "Your smithy?" She couldn't help but pick up on the pride emanating from him.

"It is. I have one full-time employee, and I also take on paid apprentices who wish to learn the trade."

"Is an employee like a serf?"

"Not at all." He stopped the truck and turned off the engine. "Andrew works for a good wage, and he owes me nothing. I'm not his overlord, only his boss."

"Humph. Is no' a boss like a lord?"

He chuckled. "It's hard to explain. Andrew has chosen to work with me, and it doesn't have anything to do with being a tenant on my land or anything else."

Michael rapped on her window, just as Struan's phone rang. Sky had become accustomed to the sound. The Gordons used their phones to communicate whilst on the road. Another marvel, yet she had a vague recollection of seeing the like before when her cousin Robley and Erin were at Moigh Hall. Erin had shown them pictures on hers after she and Robley arrived from the future.

She unbuckled her seat belt and opened the door. "You must be glad to be home, Michael."

"I am, but I like traveling for the fairs. It's fun, and I have a bunch of friends around my age who do the same with their folks." Michael held out his hand and helped her step down from the truck. "You can take a look around while Struan and I take care of the horses."

"That was Ma," Struan said. "She wants us at their house for dinner in half an hour. I guess Lindsay has prepared a feast for our return." He winked at her. "And to welcome the newest time-traveler into our midst."

"She kens about me already?"

"Yep." Struan held up his phone. "Ma keeps in touch with all of us on a daily basis. After supper, if you're not too tired, we'll start our search for Connor McGladrey." He turned to Michael. "Let's get the horses taken care of so we can get going. I'm starving."

Sky left them to wander around as Struan and Michael unloaded the destriers and led them to the stable. She slipped her feet out of her sandals to feel the land beneath her feet. The grass was the greenest and softest she'd ever beheld. The sun nearing the tops of the western ridges cast golden streaks of light over the peaks. Truly this place was beautiful and so tranquil.

She inhaled deeply. The air was redolent with the sweet scent of grass, pine and clover. The occasional lowing of the Gordons' kine and the sounds of birds as they called to their mates, exhorting them to return to their nests for the evening, cast a sense of peaceful well-being over the land.

She stopped walking to stare into the deep shadows of the forest behind Struan's cottage. No enemies lurked in those cool depths, nor did any rival clan hide behind the hills. There were no reavers awaiting nightfall to steal the Gordons' kine or burn their fields. No clan feuds or political intrigues marred the serenity of this place and time. She shouldn't be envious of these good people, but she was, and greatly so.

"Sky."

"Och." She jumped, her heart pounding at the sound of Struan's voice. "I did no' hear you approach."

"You were deep in thought, and I didn't wish to intrude. It's time for supper. Would you like to walk, or would you prefer we take the truck to Gene's?"

"Let's walk. 'Twould be good to stretch my legs." Slipping her feet back into her sandals, she searched the toft surrounding Struan's cottage. "Where is Michael?"

"He went on ahead." Struan reached for her hand and placed it in the crook of his elbow. "Come, my lady. Supper awaits, and Lindsay is an amazing cook."

"The Gordons dinna keep a cook?" She frowned. "They seem wealthy enough, I trow."

He chuckled. "That's not how things work today, and Lindsay just finished culinary college. She's what we call a chef, someone who cooks as their profession. My sister wants to start her own restaurant eventually, but for now, she works at a nearby resort. We get a lot of tourists here because of the hot springs."

She nodded, and her stomach rumbled. It had been quite some time since their midday meal. "There is so much to learn."

Struan patted her hand. "Aye, that there is."

They continued on to Gene and Marjorie's abode in companionable silence. Sky savored the moment, feeling close to her new friend, feeling safe. The gathering twilight combined with the surrounding peaks to cast shadows upon the road. One minute they were bathed in sunlight, and the next they walked in the coolness of dusk. It seemed the very air was filled with magic. "This is a special place," she murmured.

"It is," he said with a smile. "Three Gordon brothers came to the United States from Scotland at the turn of the century, hoping to make a better life for themselves. The Jacobite uprising had pretty much decimated the clans in Scotland, and those who remained lived in abject poverty."

"Jacobite uprising?" Sky frowned. "I ken naught of such an uprising."

"You wouldn't. The Stewarts lost the throne, and Scotland was ruled by the English. The uprising occurred in the mid-seventeen hundreds, and the Gordon brothers came to this land as lads in 1790."

"Ah."

"Each of the brothers worked hard in the growing cities hereabouts, and they lived like paupers until they had the funds to purchase land. Once they each owned their adjoining parcels, they swore to always keep it in the family. Eventually their land merged into one large farm, and the bulk of it now belongs to Gene. There are more Gordons, descendants of the three brothers in the area, who also own tracts of the original property."

"You are very fortunate to live here, Struan." She averted her gaze, not wanting him to glimpse the envy she felt so keenly.

"What were you thinking about a moment ago, Sky? You seemed to be searching the forest for something."

"Aye." She huffed out a breath. "I was searching the shadows for reavers from a rival clan intending to steal the Gordons' kine, and me without my dirk."

Struan laughed, and she joined him. "'Tis all so very different. I remember when I went to court for the first time. The very air was fetid with strife and intrigue. I could scarce draw a breath." She surveyed their surroundings. "The sense of peace, the very goodness of this place is quite foreign to me. As much as I love my home, we're always fending off one enemy or another. If rival clans or brigands aren't harrying our borders, they're harassing the borders of our neighbors and allies, and my clan is called to offer aid. When my foster brother inherited his title, his clan had been under attack for a decade from a neighboring clan, the MacKenzies, whose laird was determined to destroy the MacConnells for the sole purpose of stealing their holdings."

"Aye." Struan patted her hand. "You've no idea how long it took me to trust my surroundings. I too searched the shadows for enemies. You'll get used to the peace."

Would she? Not likely. She wouldn't be here long enough to get used to anything.

"Here we are." Struan opened the front door to the Gordons' home and ushered her inside. Unfamiliar delicious smells filled the hall. "Oh yeah. Italian." Struan put his hands on Sky's shoulders and guided her toward the sound of voices and the wonderful smells. "You're going to enjoy this."

"There you two are," Marjorie cried. She hurried toward them and took Sky's wrist to tug her forward. "Lindsay, Ethan, Carol, this is Sky Elizabeth, the eldest daughter of the earl of Fife, come to us from 1443. Sky, this is the rest of the family." Marjorie left Sky to lift the rosy-cheeked, chubby bairn perched upon Carol's hip. "And this is our first grandson. His name is Gene, after his granddad, of course." She bounced the bairn in her arms, eliciting a grin from the wee lad.

Sky's face heated from all the attention turned her way. "I'm pleased to meet all of you." Ethan was tall and lanky like his da. He had thick brown hair, brown eyes and an angular face. His wife, Carol, a fair-haired lass with wide gray eyes, was tall and lanky like her husband. Lindsay more closely resembled Marjorie, who was rounded and diminutive. "It smells wonderful in here," Sky said, sniffing the air.

They were in a large room that served as the kitchen on one half, with an adjacent dining hall. A cozy hearth took up the end of the great room, though no fire burned at present. A large, rough-hewn table with benches on either side had already been set for the meal.

"I hope you're hungry, Sky," Lindsay said. "I made lasagna Bolognese, a Caesar salad with homemade dressing, and of course, my famous roasted garlic and rosemary bread."

"I understood naught but the words *rosemary, bread* and *garlic*," Sky said. "I am starving, and Struan tells me you are a chef, which I take to mean a most excellent cook. 'Tis certain this will be a meal to be remembered."

A flurry of activity, accompanied by good-hearted banter and teasing, went on around her as the Gordons put food on the table and took their places. Michael patted the bench beside him, and Sky suffered a pang of longing for her brothers. They oft gestured to her in the very same manner. She took her place beside him, and Lindsay sat on her other side.

"Your hair is so thick and gorgeous." Lindsay filled Sky's bowl with the greens she called a Caesar salad. "Without a hair dryer, it must've taken forever to dry after you washed it."

"Aye, though in the winter, sitting near the hearth helps."

"Ever thought about cutting it?" Carol asked. "I'm a beautician. I have a shop in the back of our house, and lots of the locals come to me for haircuts and colors."

"Colors?" Sky shook her head. "I'm no' familiar with the word *beautician*." A basket came her way, and the wonderful fragrance of garlic and rosemary wafted up to her. Neatly sliced bread filled the basket. She took a piece and found it was filled with bits of roasted garlic and herbs. Her mouth watered.

"Sure. I can turn your hair any color you want it to be." Carol grinned. "Even blue."

"*Blue?*" Sky blinked. "Why would anyone do such a thing?"

Carol laughed. "You'd be surprised."

"Here." Lindsay placed a dollop of butter on a small plate. "I imagine our place settings are unfamiliar to you."

"Nay. Marjorie took me to a restaurant my first full day here, and she taught me how everything is used. I've had several meals since." She buttered her piece of bread and took a taste. "Mmm." 'Twas so fine and savory, she wanted to stuff the entire thing into her mouth at once. 'Twould be impolite for certes. She chewed and swallowed. "Truly, 'tis the very best bread I have ever tasted in my entire life," she gushed.

"I like her," Lindsay said with a laugh. "Let's keep her."

"You haven't heard her story yet," Struan said.

His sympathetic gaze met and held hers, and her pulse quickened. "Let us no' speak of it now. No' whilst we have such a wonderful feast laid out before us."

"That's right," Ethan agreed. "She hasn't even tasted the lasagna yet."

Michael placed a serving of lasagna upon her plate. Sky inhaled the wonderful scent and cut a piece with the edge of her fork. "It smells so good." She looked up to find she once again had an audience. Their faces were so expectant she couldn't help but laugh.

"I made it as unsalted as I possibly could. I remember how it was for Struan when he first arrived."

Sky took a taste, and delicious flavors burst in her mouth. "Mmm, mmm." Her eyes went wide. Never had she tasted anything so divine. "You are truly gifted, Lindsay," she muttered, taking another bite. "You must teach me how to make this, so that when I return to my home, I can share it with my kin."

"I don't think you have the tomatoes to make the sauce."

"Och, can I no' bring seeds back with me?" She peered around the table. "My cousin's wife brought us apple seeds from your era, and she taught us how to improve our orchards by grafting."

That prompted a lively discussion about changing history and the like, and Sky only half listened. She gobbled her meal until she could hold no more. Och, would they think her a glutton? Her cheeks heating, she stacked her dishes and pushed them away. The men got up and began to clear the table.

"Michael, I'll finish clearing the table and load the dishwasher," Struan said. "Go get your laptop so we can find Connor McGladrey for Sky."

"OK," Michael said, setting his pile of dishes on the counter.

Michael left, and Gene turned to her. "Go ahead and tell the others your story while Struan and I clean up. I know they're eager to hear the tale."

"If it pleases you," she said, gauging the interest of those remaining at the table.

"We're *dying* to hear what happened," Lindsay assured her.

"All right then." Sky took a sip of her wine before sharing her tale of woe.

Michael slipped back into the room before she'd finished, and he carried a slender rectangular object in his hands. Sky's curiosity piqued, she rushed through the rest of the story, ending with how she'd landed in a fresh pile of dung in the midst of Struan's jousting match. Anticipation sent her heart racing. "That is the laptop?"

"Yep." He slid back into his place beside her and opened the laptop to reveal rows of letters, numbers and unfamiliar symbols. He touched one, and the thing chimed and came to life.

"What does this laptop do?"

"Well . . . that's not an easy question to answer." Michael frowned. "Right now we're going to do a Google search." He glanced at her. "What can you tell me about the McGladreys?"

"They live in the realm of Minnesota in a place with a name that has to do with apples." She straightened, pleased that she remembered so much. "Connor McGladrey owns what my cousin Robley called a *fencing club* there. They teach swordplay."

Gene and Marjorie came to stand behind her. Marjorie laid a hand on Sky's shoulder for a moment. "We're going outside to the patio for a bit. Carol, Ethan and the baby are heading home. Lindsay, do you want to join us outside?"

"No, I want to see what the search brings up," Lindsay told them.

Sky bid Carol and Ethan good night before turning back to the laptop.

"You've given me enough information to do a search." Michael's fingers flew over the letters. "Huh. Minnesota Fencing Club, Twin Cities Fencing Club and the University of Minnesota Fencing Club. This is going to be a cinch. There are only three to choose from in the entire state." He clicked on the first. "Here you are, Sky. The Minnesota Fencing Club in Minneapolis," he said. "Apple . . . *apolis*. Get it?" He grinned and pointed. "Look. They teach medieval combat classes. I'll bet this is the one."

She gasped. "This *Internet*, 'tis some sort of wizardry, surely."

"Nope." Struan came to stand behind her. "It's technology. Click on the staff contact page, Michael."

He did, and there it was, Connor McGladrey's name. "Och, Struan, what do I do now?"

"Scoot over, Michael. I'll compose the e-mail for Sky."

"OK."

Struan sat down. "Tell me what you want to say, and I'll type the words."

"Hmm. My name and clan, for certes, and tell him I'm Robley and Erin's cousin, and that I've come from the fifteenth century with news of their daughter, Meghan." She sucked in a much-needed breath. "Tell him I seek—"

"Let's keep it simple. I think this is enough to catch his attention. I'll add my cell phone number and introduce myself. We can tell him the rest when he calls."

"Think you he'll call yet this eve?" She gripped the edge of the table, barely able to contain herself. "Is that no' a phone number there on the laptop? Can we no' call him *now*?"

"They give lessons in the evening. It says on the contact page that e-mails are answered only when classes aren't being held. Connor will call tomorrow morning." Struan shut off the laptop, stood up and stretched.

"Be patient, Sky," Lindsay told her. "I'm sure you'll hear from Connor tomorrow, and if not, then we can call. In the meantime, let me show you where you're staying for as long as you're here." She rose from her place. "Michael already put your things in the room, which is right next to mine. We share a bathroom."

Sky's gaze flew to Struan. "My thanks. You spoke truly. This Internet is most miraculous." She looked from one to the next. "I am grateful to all of you for the help and hospitality you have so freely offered. If there is aught I can do—"

"Get a good night's rest, and I'll take you riding tomorrow afternoon." Struan reached out a hand to help her up. "Do you want to join us, Lindsay?"

"Wouldn't miss it, and I just happen to be off tomorrow. Good night, you two," she said to Michael and Struan. "I'm taking my newest friend from the past to her room, and then I'm heading to mine."

Sky's mind spun from all that had happened in just a few days. Everything she'd learned, the new things she'd experienced overwhelmed her. She followed Lindsay up a flight of stairs at the front of their cottage and down a corridor.

"This was Struan's room before he moved into his own place. It's kind of masculine, but it's comfortable," she said, opening the door. "Michael's bedroom is the one across the hall. Whatever you do, don't open his door. It smells like a boy's locker room. My mom and dad's is the door at the end of the corridor."

"What is a locker room?" Sky asked, bewildered yet again.

"Trust me. You don't want to know." Lindsay gestured for Sky to enter.

A bed, flanked by two identical chests with drawers, took up one side of the room. Sky was drawn to a framed likeness of Struan. She walked across the room and lifted the frame.

"That's Struan's senior picture. Practically every girl in school had a mad crush on my brother," she said with a chuckle. "A deadly combination, blue eyes, wavy golden hair and dimples."

"Aye, he is quite a comely lad." Was that a pang of jealousy tweaking at her? Sky placed the image back in its place.

"The bathroom is off the hall between my bedroom and this one. There are clean towels and everything you're going to need. Just look under the sink if you don't see what you want on the counter."

Sky nodded. "My thanks, Lindsay."

"Let me show you how to work the lights and stuff, and I'll leave you to get settled. Your bags are in the closet there." She pointed to a door.

Lindsay showed her how to turn on the lamps, and then she left. Sky moved to the open window and looked out at the moon rising in the gathering darkness before pushing the pane closed. The temperature had dropped considerably. She wrapped her arms around herself and shivered before turning back to the task of getting ready for bed.

Tomorrow, she'd talk with Connor McGladrey, and hopefully he would have information that she would find useful. If not, then at least she'd be able to put his family's mind at ease about their daughter. Surely they'd be glad to hear of their grandbabies . . . who would be long dead by now. She rubbed her temples. "Och, 'tis far too disturbing to think of such things." Tomorrow would soon be here, and mayhap she'd be a step closer to finding a way home.

She readied herself for sleep, images of Struan's sparkling eyes and dimpled smile dancing through her mind. If only she'd been given in marriage to a lad such as he. How very different her future would've been.

Regret stole her breath, and her chest tightened. She had no claim to any future save that which awaited her in the past.

CHAPTER SIX

A mug of coffee and peanut butter toast in hand, Struan strode along the path toward his forge. His leather work boots crunched against the ground limestone path, a sound so familiar it seemed to him a "welcome home." *Home. His* home. He breathed in deep, taking in a lungful of the clear mountain air.

Andrew and their apprentice wouldn't arrive until eight or eight thirty, which was fine. It wasn't even seven yet. Having the shop to himself for a while suited him just fine. He savored the early morning peace and quiet. With no distractions, he could think better and get things organized. By the time Brian and Andrew showed up, he'd be ready to begin the actual physical work for the day.

His mind strayed to Sky. He grinned at the memory of the way she'd inhaled her lasagna last night. Judging by her blush and the way she avoided eye contact, she'd hoped no one noticed. Gordon Hollow was yet another unfamiliar place, and she'd had so much to contend with the past few days. He certainly remembered what it had been like for him, facing new and unfamiliar surroundings, people and things every day. Protectiveness for Sky rushed to the forefront, and in its wake, anger at the fool who had meant to do her harm.

Struan stacked his toast on top of his coffee mug, and then he slid open the barnlike double doors to his shop and flipped on the overhead lights. Setting his breakfast on the old metal desk in the corner, he noticed the pair of medieval-style candlesticks sitting on the shelf, ready to be shipped.

His customers would go nuts over authentic, handcrafted tapestries, should Sky decide to make them. He could fashion frames, looms for weaving or whatever else she might need. All it would take was a bit of research.

She'd be far better off in the twenty-first century, blending in with their worldwide community of medieval and Renaissance reenactors and making a living doing what she loved to do. Sure, she'd miss her family, but she'd adjust. He and the Gordons would become her kin and clan.

His phone rang, snapping him out of his reverie. He pulled it out of his pocket, taking note of the unfamiliar area code. "Hello?"

"Who *are* you?" an angry male voice demanded, a slight lilt to his words.

"Struan Sutherland, and I'm guessing you're Connor McGladrey."

"I am. Explain the e-mail in my inbox this morning, and if this is some kind of prank, you *will* be sorry."

"It's no prank." Struan hooked his foot around a leg of his desk chair, pulled it out and took a seat. "Sky Elizabeth of clan MacKintosh appeared out of thin air in the middle of the jousting field at the New York Renaissance Faire on Saturday. She's from 1443, and she's kin to you. Her brother is married to your daughter, Meghan."

"The devil you say!" Connor exclaimed, his voice breaking.

"It's true, and there's more. Way more." Struan raked a hand through his hair and told Connor the rest of Sky's story as concisely as possible. "She believes you might be able to help her get home somehow, and she wants to give you news of your daughter."

"Where are you?"

"Warm Springs, Virginia. Do you have a pen and paper handy?"

"I do."

Struan gave him their location, the closest airport and directions to Gordon Hollow from Warm Springs. "I take it you plan to come here, then?"

"Humph. My wife and I will book a flight for today if we can. Expect us this evening or tomorrow at the latest."

Struan opened his mouth to suggest a nearby bed-and-breakfast where they could stay, but Connor had already ended the call. Ah well, he'd let them stay in his camper if needed. He had an outlet he could plug it into for electricity, and they could use the guest bathroom in his house. He set his phone on the desk and scrubbed his face with both hands. The McGladreys would come, and maybe they'd take Sky away with them when they left.

What if she did manage to find a way to return to the past, and Oliver got to her somehow? He had no illusions about what would happen then. The Erskines would force the wedding, and Oliver would move ahead with his nefarious plan to do away with Sky. Tales of men and women who had met with suspicious accidents, mystery illnesses, or had been locked away to starve to death abounded in the Middle Ages. He growled low in his throat, itching to get his hands around the Erskine lordling's cowardly throat.

"Hey, Struan." Andrew strode through the doors. "How was Sterling?"

"Eventful." Struan shuffled the papers on his desk. "I didn't hear you drive up."

"Irene needed the car today, so I rode my horse. I put her out to pasture with your herd." He took a heavy leather apron from its post and tied it on. "Eventful? How so?"

He'd long ago shared his origins with Andrew. Not only were they coworkers, but good friends. They'd met while performing at the local

Renaissance fair when he was about Michael's age, and Struan had made Andrew's first suit of armor for him. They'd been fast friends ever since.

Andrew took things in stride. He was as solid and steady as the mountains surrounding them, and Struan trusted him. "We have a new addition to the Gordon clan." Andrew's eyes widened slightly as Struan told the tale, the only outward reaction to Struan's news.

Finally, one side of his friend's mouth turned up. "Is she pretty?"

Struan huffed out a laugh. "Very."

"Good." Andrew moved to light the coals waiting in the pit. Once that was done, he opened the back door and turned on the fan.

They could utilize a more modern method for tempering their steel, using superheated melted salt, but he found the red-hot liquid to be much more dangerous, and he preferred the old methods. After all, those tried-and-true methods were how he learned his craft. He'd rigged a sluice sink next to the pit for the liquid cooling process, though. One of his many modern-day concessions. Struan flashed him a puzzled look. "What does her beauty have to do with anything?"

"Since she escaped her evil fiancé, she's single, yeah?" Andrew returned his look with one that suggested Struan was completely dense. "We both know the selection of young single females hereabouts is pretty thin. I'm always on the lookout for potential wife material for you." He turned on the hood vent above the burning coals.

"I'm only twenty-four." Struan scowled. "Just because you recently tied the knot doesn't mean I have to."

"Trust me. You'd be a much happier man. It's not like you're the womanizing type. I don't know if you realize this, but you're not very outgoing. Wouldn't you like to have someone to share your life with?"

"Someday." But he'd choose a modern-day woman. Someone who wouldn't care about his origins. He needed to be with a woman who would accept and love him for who he'd become, not judge him for where he'd come from.

"What are you going to work on today?" Andrew hit the foot peddle for the bellows, causing sparks to rise above the heating fire pit.

"I'm going to start etching the bearing sword for the Society for Creative Anachronism's new King of Atlantia. I'd like to get that piece done this week. I thought I'd use the acid method for this one, intaglio, rather than engraving. It'll give it a nicer, more antique-looking finish."

"Mmm. Those folks from SCA . . . makes me wonder."

He waited, but Andrew didn't elaborate. "You going to tell me what you wonder about the SCA group?"

"Well, you came here from the fourteenth century, right? Now you tell me about this daughter of an earl who dropped into the middle of your jousting tournament from the fifteenth century. SCA is this huge organization that has divided North America and Europe into kingdoms. The members all play medieval and Renaissance lords and ladies, alewives, archers, swordsmen, et cetera. You all hang out on the fringes of mainstream society—with the ren fests and the SCA events and gatherings. Doesn't it make *you* wonder? Just how many of the SCA and ren fest folks are displaced time-travelers like you and Sky, do you suppose?"

"I have wondered." Even more so since Sky mentioned how the faerie calling herself Madame Giselle liked to hang out at the modern-day Renaissance festivals and meddle in the lives of humans. "Maybe I ought to start a Facebook page or a Yahoo group for displaced time-travelers like myself. What do you think?"

"I think you might be surprised by how many join."

"After this weekend?" Struan grinned and shook his head. "Not so much. Sky told us about her family's history with time travel, and she also mentioned this guy in Minnesota who's from thirteenth-century Ireland. He owns a fencing club where they teach medieval combat. He and his wife are on their way here, by the way." The sound of a motorcycle pulling into his driveway echoed inside the stone walls. "Don't say anything about this to Brian."

"I wouldn't." Andrew shot him another *how dense can you be* look, and set a sword into the glowing coals for its final tempering. "Apprentices come and go. You and I are here to stay, not to mention we're friends. Your secrets are safe with me."

"Thanks." Struan gave him an appreciative nod as he reached for the long ceremonial broadsword. He'd etch the blade with the Latin phrase for the pretend king of the SCA's pretend realm. Once the broadsword lay on a workbench, he headed to the storeroom for the waxy coating he'd apply to protect the steel from the acid.

"Morning. I brought doughnuts," Brian called as he walked into the forge, a bag in one hand and his helmet tucked under his other arm. "Old-fashioned cake, glazed."

"Oh man, I wish you'd stop bringing that shit here." Andrew snatched the bag from their apprentice and took out a doughnut. "These are deadly, like cigarettes," he said around a mouthful.

Brian shrugged. "I'm not forcing you to eat them."

"I know." Andrew grabbed another doughnut and tossed the sack on the desk. "I have two weaknesses: my wife and sweets."

"Only two?" Struan chuckled. "Brian, after you pack the candlesticks for shipment, I want you to start water-cutting the rapiers for that Shakespeare theater order."

"Great," he said with a wide grin. "You're going to let me do them without hovering behind me this time?"

"Yep. You're ready." He set waxy material for his project at the edge of the coal pit to melt. Then he dug through a bin for a decent brush, so he could coat the blade.

The three of them settled into their work, and as always, a deep sense of peace and purpose filled Struan. He was a lucky man. He'd been snatched out of hell and placed in paradise. He spent the next hour or so transferring the pattern for the Latin phrase down the sword's blade and began scraping the wax away from the letters. The acid would eat away at the blade to etch the phrase into the steel.

The sounds of Brian in the back, cutting blades from the roll of steel, and the hiss of heated metal being plunged into the cooling sluice provided a pleasant din. This was the life he was meant to live. He even loved the smells of metal-tinged steam and the coal fire burning away in the pit.

By midafternoon, his natural optimism had returned. Everything would work out. Like him, fate had plucked Sky out of a dangerous situation and placed her exactly where she needed to be to keep her safe. If he was lucky, her appearance had to mean she was meant to live the rest of her life in this century, and he wouldn't be called upon to *do* anything other than help her adjust. Now *that* he could get behind.

And the McGladreys? Struan would go to Minnesota with Sky if need be, and once her efforts to get home failed, he'd be there to bring her back to Gordon Hollow to stay. She'd soon make a life for herself.

What if she didn't want to return with him? What then? He frowned.

"Hey, Struan, are you about ready to head for the trails?" Lindsay stood at the entrance to his forge, with Sky beside her. She wore jeans and a short-sleeved cotton blouse with elastic around the bottom, emphasizing the curve of her waist. The front was embroidered, and a tie held it together just below the hollow of her delicate throat. After thinking about her all day, seeing her in the flesh sent his heart thudding. "Sure. Just give me ten minutes to close things up here."

"Hey, Lindsay, how's the new job going?" Andrew came to stand beside Struan, his eyes riveted on Sky.

"It's going really well. When are you and Irene going to come eat at the restaurant where I work?"

"We thought we'd treat my folks to dinner there for my mom's birthday," Andrew said. "It's August 5, a Tuesday. Do you work on Tuesdays?"

"My schedule rotates, but I'll trade with someone if I have to. I'll have a cake ready for your mom."

"That would be great." Andrew took a step forward. "You must be Sky."

Brian wandered up to the front of the forge, shoving his safety visor up. "Hey, Lindsay." His expression took on that *I adore you from afar* look he always got whenever Lindsay was around. His sister spared him a cursory nod.

Struan stifled the urge to snort. "Sky, this is Andrew. He works with me full-time, and this is Brian, our apprentice, who is also the local farrier." Struan gestured toward the men. "Andrew, Brian, this is Sky MacKintosh. She's visiting us from Scotland." True enough. "She's related to the Gordons." Lindsay grinned, and Sky's brow rose a fraction at his flimsy explanation for her presence.

"'Tis a pleasure to meet you both," Sky murmured.

His knees went a little weak at the appearance of her shy smile. She was so pretty, with those big hazel eyes, and all that lustrous hair . . . not to mention those curves. Lord, she was a temptation. "I just need to clean up here."

"OK," Lindsay said. "Sky and I will bring in the horses from the pasture while we wait."

"If you wouldn't mind, bring in my mare with the rest," Andrew said. "I put her out when I got here this morning."

"I ride," Brian added, his tone hopeful.

"Oh? Good for you." Lindsay turned toward the doors. "Come on, Sky. Let's go lure the horses in with a bucket of grain." With that, she walked away, Sky trailing after her.

"Why don't you just ask Lindsay out?" Struan frowned at Brian. "The moon-eyes and not-so-subtle hints aren't going to get you anywhere with her."

"She might say no," Brian muttered, his shoulders slumping.

"She might say yes." Struan started putting away the tools on his workbench. "You'll never know if you don't give it a shot. Lindsay is a strong, confident woman. She's attracted to men who are equally confident. Step it up if you want her to notice you."

"Augh." Brian removed his safety visor. "I've always *been* strong and confident when it comes to women, only not with your sister. She kind of sucks all the wind right out of my sails, if you know what I mean."

"Really? I never would have guessed," Andrew teased. He untied his apron, took it off and hung it on its hook. "I'll help you, Struan, so you can go riding with that pretty little Scottish lass. Remember what I said earlier. Slim pickings around here in the single women department."

Struan scowled at his friend. "I'm not getting involved with Sky. She's not going to be here for long." If she had her way, that is.

Once the three of them closed the shop for the day, Brian took off on his motorcycle, still dejected. Struan had offered him advice, and it wouldn't be on him if Brian chose not to take heed. He and Andrew walked together toward his stables.

"Did you ever think maybe Sky came through time to land at your feet due to some cosmic matchmaking scheme?" Andrew asked.

"No, I didn't, and anyway, she's in no position to start something. Having been displaced myself, I know how confusing and overwhelming everything is for her. She's in a vulnerable place. I feel a proprietary sense of . . . protectiveness where Sky is concerned, but that's all."

"Right," Andrew said again, glancing askance at him. "Proprietary like a big brother?"

"Doesn't matter. Like I said, I'm looking after her only because she needs me." Given the way his blood rushed at the sight of her, the way he wanted to taste her sweetness, touch her? Nope. Not a brotherly feeling in the least.

Lindsay and Sky had the horses bridled and in the corral by the time they arrived. He and Andrew helped them saddle the horses, and Struan led the gelding Sky favored to the mounting block. "Up you go, princess."

"It's Sky." She huffed out an exasperated breath.

"All right. Have it your way." Struan winked. "Up you go, Princess Sky." He didn't wait for her to step up onto the mounting block; instead, he placed his hands around her waist and lifted her. Mostly he'd just wanted an excuse to put his hands on her. The color rising to her cheeks was an unexpected bonus. He brought the reins over the gelding's neck and placed them in her hands. "How are you? Did you sleep well last night?"

"I fare well enough, and I'm well rested." Her expression clouded, belying her words.

He searched her face for some hint of what might be troubling her, and it took a minute before he remembered how anxious she'd been about reaching the McGladreys. Getting lost in her the way he did, he forgot everything except the magnetic pull she exerted on him. "I spoke with Connor this morning, lass. He and his wife will be here this evening or tomorrow morning at the latest."

Her face lit up. "Truly?"

"Truly. I wouldn't lie to you." He patted her denim-clad knee before heading for his mount. Guilt nipped at him, and he hoped she hadn't caught a whiff of his half-truth. He had lied to her already. In fact, more than once if you counted omission.

"See you tomorrow," Andrew said, turning his horse toward the path that would take him home. "Nice meeting you, Sky."

"And you," she called back.

He, Lindsay and Sky took to the trail heading into the forest behind his house. The way was wide enough to ride two abreast. Lindsay took the lead, with Sky riding beside her. Struan took up the rear, brooding over his unworthy lack of openness and honesty where Sky was concerned.

"You're awfully quiet, Struan." Lindsay glanced back at him. "I figured you'd be bragging about our valley by now. Something bothering you?"

"Just thinking." He nudged his horse into a trot to close the gap between them. "I'd always thought I was the only one in the world to have passed through the centuries the way I did. Guess I'm not so special after all. Sky's stories about her time-traveling kin, Connor McGladrey's experience, it's all . . . we're connected somehow, by our common experience if nothing else."

"It is a lot to take in, and not just for you, but for all of us." Lindsay peered over her shoulder at him. "Michael thinks we have fae genes, like Sky's family, and that's why we're part of this bizarre circle. What do you think, Sky?"

"'Tis possible, but our meeting could as easily be naught but fae capriciousness or even an accident. No matter where I landed, wouldn't those around me see my sudden appearance as an act of fate?"

Struan grunted. "You already know how I feel about all this being a random encounter. There are too many coincidences for me to believe your coming to us is mere chance. I don't have fae blood running through my veins. I don't know any faeries to bargain with for such a trip. So why did I come through time, and why am I part of all this?"

"Because shit happens?" Lindsay laughed. "Who knows?"

Struan grunted. The trail narrowed, and they were forced to ride single file. He glanced ahead at Sky. Once again she studied the shadows in the forest, her posture stiff with tension, and her expression anxious. Was that her dirk tucked into the back of her jeans? "Sky."

"Aye?" She twisted around in her saddle to look at him.

"There are no brigands, reavers or cutthroats in our wood, lass. I give you my word; we will not be ambushed today." Her answering smile stole the air from his lungs. Or . . . the wind from his sails, as Brian had said? He drew a breath, just to prove to himself that he still could. They came to the end of the forest and continued on through a hay field of clover, alfalfa and timothy grass to the bridge across the stream.

"So, what do you think of Gordon Hollow, Sky?" Lindsay asked.

"'Tis a wonderful place. You are most fortunate to live here and in this time."

Was that a hint of sadness or regret in her tone? Struan studied her, remembering the turbulence of his own past, the plots and counterplots and his half siblings' attempts to do away with him. Back then, moments when he could let down his guard and just *be* had been few and far between, and all of them had happened while with his father or the blacksmith to whom he'd been apprenticed.

"You're welcome to stay, you know," Lindsay told her. "If you're not able to return to your time, that is."

"I must return. I *will* find a way."

"But if you can't, just know that you have a place with us," Lindsay added. The three of them crossed the bridge and the trail widened, transforming into a narrow gravel road again.

"I am most grateful to you for your kindness, but let us speak no more of such matters. 'Tis a fine day, and the way ahead is clear. I've a mind to let this fine animal have a canter. May I?"

"Of course," Struan said. "We'll join you."

Sky leaned forward and kicked the gelding's sides. The gelding took off at a gallop, rather than a canter. Struan and his sister urged their mounts to catch up, as Sky's laughter drifting back taunted them to race with her. She surged ahead, widening the gap between them. Heaven help him, she sat her horse as if born riding.

The tie holding her braid came loose and fell to the ground, and her hair began to unravel. Sky flew like the wind. Joy and exhilaration fairly pulsed from her as she rode with wild abandon. Fearless. Magnificent. Never had he seen such a compelling sight.

He lost a little piece of his heart, maybe not the first bit she'd stolen. Struan kicked his mount's sides, narrowing the space separating them. When Sky saw he was gaining ground, she cast him a look of challenge, leaned low over her horse's neck and sped up, triggering a primitive response.

He was in pursuit; *she* was his quarry.

The need to dominate, to prove himself better, faster, stronger, able to protect and provide, overrode all common sense. Once Struan reached her side, he reached out and snatched her from the saddle, bringing her to sit across his lap. She squealed and wrapped her arms tightly around his neck. Pulling back on the bit, he slowed his mount to a smooth canter, and then to a walk.

The exhilaration of the chase gripped him. Satisfaction at the outcome thrummed through his veins, and before he knew what he intended, he leaned close to claim his prize. His mouth took hers in a scorching kiss.

What began as yet another primitive urge to demonstrate his supremacy, soon turned to his utter defeat. She smote him where he sat, for he had no defenses against the softness of her lips, her taste or her unique intoxicating scent. Her breasts pressed against his chest nearly obliterated his restraint. He deepened the kiss, his tongue plundering her sweetness.

At the sound of approaching hoofbeats, Struan forced himself to break the contact. Breathless, he peered into Sky's hazel eyes, inordinately pleased by the befuddled awe suffusing her beautiful features. He tucked an errant strand of her hair behind her ear, needing to feel the silken texture between his fingers. He couldn't tear his eyes from her.

Somehow she'd managed to rob him of the ability to muster a single sensible thought. It was a good thing their woods weren't filled with brigands, because should any attack at the moment, they'd find him as helpless and as blind as a newborn kitten.

Lindsay rode up beside them, catching Sky's riderless horse by the reins. "Well, isn't this an interesting turn of events." She chortled. "What have you to say for yourself, Struan?"

CHAPTER SEVEN

Dazed, Sky struggled to catch her breath while Struan continued to hold her on his lap. She'd been kissed. Thoroughly. By the saints, she'd kissed him back . . . with equal fervor! 'Twas her first, and her wits had scattered like goose down caught in the wind. She pressed her fingers against her still-tingling lips, lips that had just been pressed against Struan's.

To make matters worse, she couldn't ignore the evidence of his aroused state against her bottom, or the answering throb between her thighs. Did he suspect? Her face burned. How could he not be aware of how he affected her? She couldn't bear to look at him—or at Lindsay. How would she face his parents? "Och," she stammered, "mayhap you'd best put me *back* on the gelding."

Struan loosened his hold. "I'm sorry. I . . . I got caught up in . . . hmm—"

"An overload of testosterone?" Lindsay offered, her tone smug.

Was that amusement Sky sensed? She found nothing amusing about what had just happened. Never before had she been so swept away or behaved in such an unladylike manner. Struan brought his horse alongside hers, supporting her weight while she put her foot in the stirrup and transferred herself to the saddle. Her insides still fluttered, and his hands upon her waist sent her blood rushing again. "I did no' mean to—"

"Entirely my fault." Color crept up his neck and he too struggled to regain his breath. He kept his gaze fixed upon the trail. "This way leads to a ford in the stream." He pointed. "We'll cross there. Then the trail takes us back to my place." He nudged his horse into a trot and took the lead, putting a little distance between them.

Lindsay came to ride beside her. Sky's face flushed. "I dinna ken what came over me."

"My brother chased you," Lindsay quipped. "You were caught."

"He . . . Struan . . . *kissed* me."

"From where I sat, it looked like you kissed him back."

"Aye." Chagrined, she glanced ahead to where Struan rode. "I did." Even to her own ears, she still sounded breathless.

Lindsay grinned. "Don't be embarrassed about what happened. It was just a kiss."

Just a kiss? Sky frowned. "Is such a thing taken so lightly in this age?"

"Much more lightly than in your era, I'm sure. Relax, Sky. It's a beautiful day. Let's enjoy it. I understand what my brother meant. He got caught up in the excitement of the chase is all. Believe me, he's as embarrassed about the whole thing as you are."

"Think you?" Sky's gaze shot to Struan again, taking in the masterful way he sat his horse, the broadness of his shoulders . . . his very fine backside. A fresh wave of heat shot through her.

"I know so." Lindsay gestured toward the ley spread out before them. "My brothers, sister and I used to tear through this valley on horseback all the time when we were younger. We also spent endless hours splashing around in the stream, catching crayfish in the shallows and grasshoppers and fireflies in the tall grass. I'm very lucky to have grown up here."

Grateful for the change in subject, Sky's thoughts went back to the carefree years of her youth. "My siblings and I oft raced our horses through the hills surrounding Moigh Hall as well. 'Twas my favorite sport."

She caught movement at the edge of the forest beyond the kine grazing peacefully in the pasture. Three deer and their fawns left the forest, most likely searching for more tender fodder. "Do your kin hunt these woods?"

"Sometimes, and we also fish." She pointed to a gap between two hills. "We have a small lake through that pass. If you'd like, I'll take you swimming there on my next day off. Our lake is so clean, you can see clear to the bottom. It's beautiful, one of my favorite places."

"I would like that." Sky smiled. "I can tell you're quite attached to your valley."

"Absolutely. I can't imagine living anywhere else." She surveyed their surroundings and sighed. "I've traveled all over with my family, but I've never found a place that calls to me the way home does. I want to open a restaurant right here in Warm Springs, something that will appeal to tourists and the locals."

"I feel the same about Loch Moigh. I wanted to remain at home and become a healer like my mother and cousin, but young women of my rank are no' so free to choose." The searing sensation of Struan's embrace, his mouth on hers, came back to her in a flood of longing. 'Twas frivolous to desire things she would never have—like a husband who would love her despite her oddities. 'Twas not to be.

If only she'd been born in a different time. Duty to her rank, clan and her father's title had been deeply ingrained, and she hadn't the will to act against the expectations placed upon her by virtue of her nobility. Her only hope was that after the Erskines' treachery, she'd be allowed to remain unwed. Mayhap she'd follow her granddam's example and hie herself off to an abbey to avoid marriage altogether. Of course, her granddam had her grandsire to come after her, whilst Sky had no one.

Soon, Struan's cottage came into view. A car had been parked in front, and Michael stood with an unfamiliar couple. Struan kicked his gelding into a canter, and Sky followed. It had to be the McGladreys. By the time she reached them, Struan had already dismounted. He turned to help her. "I can manage," she muttered, but his hands were already on her waist.

Struan lifted her down before she could stop him, and once again her insides tumbled at his touch. She did her best to quell the sensations and focused upon the couple. Struan took her by the elbow and led her to them.

"Welcome," he said. "I'm Struan. This is Sky Elizabeth and my sister Lindsay. You must be the McGladreys."

"Aye, I'm Connor, and this is my wife, Katherine." Connor reached out, and he and Struan clasped hands for a moment.

"Nice meeting you." Lindsay gathered the reins of their mounts and led them toward the stables. "I know you have things to talk about, so I'll take care of the horses."

"Thanks, Lindsay," Struan called after her.

Sky couldn't help but notice Meghan's resemblance to her parents. Meg's hair was red like her da's, though his was now threaded with silver, and she strongly resembled Katherine in her features. Connor and his wife studied Sky with a mixture of hope and wariness.

"I assure you," Sky began, "Meghan is content. She's well settled and has two bairns, or at least that's how many she and my brother had at the time I—"

"Oh God," Katherine cried out, tears springing to her eyes. Connor put his arm around his wife's shoulders, his own eyes bright.

"Let's go inside where we can talk." Struan opened his front door. "Where are you staying while you're here?"

"We've not yet made arrangements. Our primary goal when we set out was to hear news of our daughter," Connor rasped out. "I was there when she was taken from us."

"You're welcome to stay in my camper. I have an outlet so you can connect to electricity, but I don't have a way to hook up the camper to a water source." Struan turned to Michael. "Do Ma and Da know the McGladreys are here?"

"Yep. Mom already invited them to dinner. They stopped at our house first, and I brought them here."

"Good." Struan ushered all of them inside. "Whiskey or ale?"

"I believe a dram or two of whiskey would serve," Connor said, his voice hoarse. "Katherine?"

"Yes, thank you." Katherine ran her fingertips under her eyes. "Whiskey would be most welcome."

"Do you have wine?" Sky asked.

"No wine, sorry."

"Ale then, if you please."

Struan and Michael left to fetch their libations, and Sky studied the chamber. Struan's cottage boasted a floor of wooden planks that shone with some sort of polish. A jewel-toned floor rug covered the area where comfortable seating had been arranged in a U shape. One wall of his small living room, as the Gordons referred to such a chamber, held a variety of swords, shields and daggers. Struan's cozy home so reflected his personality, she had to smile. Hopefully she'd have the chance to explore the rest soon.

Another wall held pictures, and she moved closer to take a look. Many of the framed images were of Struan and the Gordons at various Renaissance fairs. Some were taken on the inside of the Gordons' home with the family grouped together. One frame held what must be a wedding picture of Ethan and Carol. Carol held a bouquet of flowers and wore a long white gown and veil. Ethan stood proud and tall beside her, with Struan and Michael beaming by his side. Struan's contentment with this time and place came through so strongly, she couldn't help but feel a bit envious.

"So, you're related to our daughter?" Katherine came to stand beside her. "She's truly OK?"

Sky bit her lip and nodded, nearly overcome with the strong emotions coming from Meghan's mother. "Aye, she married my foster brother, the baron DúnConnell. He is the man who took her from you. Hunter believed the battle he saw was real, and that he was snatching away a young knight who would surely have been killed."

"I figured that much the day it happened," Connor rasped out. "I can't fault him for his actions. Under the circumstances, I would have done the same."

"Hunter and Meghan have a fine, braw lad, whom they named Connor, after you," she told them. "Erin and Robley also named one of their sons Connor. We view you as kin to us."

Katherine brought her trembling hand to her mouth for a moment, struggling to contain her emotions. "You said bairns," she managed to whisper.

"Aye. The day I left, Meghan was due to give birth at any time. Erin is with her, my lady, and she's very skilled at midwifery. She saved my mother's life when my twin brothers were born. Your daughter is in good hands."

"I have grandchildren I might never get to hold," she choked out. "I might never even see them."

Connor turned his wife into his arms. "Someday, my love. We'll find a way."

"Think you 'tis possible to come and go at will?" Sky's eyes widened. She'd been so disappointed not to find Madame Giselle at the fair, and now her hopes soared once again.

"It may be." Connor led his wife to the couch. "We've been doing a lot of research since the day Meghan disappeared."

Struan and Michael returned and handed out their drinks. "Let's all sit," Struan suggested.

Once they were all settled, Connor asked her to tell them everything that had happened that day, and Sky repeated her story, leaving nothing out. Mayhap the tale held some clue she didn't see.

"Were there any fae involved in your coming here?" Connor asked. "Did you have any contact with one of the ancient ones before you came forward through time? Was the one called Madame Giselle anywhere in the vicinity?"

"Nay. As I said, I was riding through the forest, and I came across the wavering lights in a clearing. My mount balked and threw me, and I tumbled through."

The McGladreys exchanged a knowing look. Connor set his whiskey down and rose to his feet. "I'll be right back. I left something in the car you need to see." He strode across the room and out the front door.

"This is a beautiful valley," Katherine commented. "And your home is very nice, Struan."

"Thanks. I like it."

Sky watched the door for Connor's return whilst Katherine, Struan and Michael spoke of inconsequential matters. What could he have to show her? She'd felt his excitement and anticipation. Even without her gifts, his tension was a tangible force in the small cottage.

Connor returned carrying a tube of some sort and a leather satchel. "Do you have a place where I can lay out a couple of maps?"

"Sure. In the kitchen." Struan got up and led them into a chamber resembling the Gordons' eating hall, only without the hearth. One end was for cooking and held his pantry cabinets, and the other end was where a trestle table and several chairs stood. Like the Gordons', Struan's eating area also had sliding doors leading outside to what they referred to as a *patio*.

Michael hurried over to the table and cleared the surface, while Connor set the satchel on one of the chairs. He removed a cap from one end of the tube and removed a roll of some material akin to parchment.

"Do you have something we can put at the corners to hold these maps down?"

"Sure, we can use coffee mugs." Struan went to one of his cabinets and started handing mugs to Michael.

Once the maps were laid out flat, Sky drew closer to take a look. One was of Scotland, the other of Ireland. Both had clusters of red dots in specific areas, and the areas were scattered over both maps. "What do these red spots mean?"

"Since Meghan's disappearance, Katherine and I have traveled to Ireland and Scotland looking into local legends and tales—stories about people who have vanished, or folks who have suddenly appeared decades after having gone missing." Connor reached into his satchel and pulled out a laptop. "I've scanned a lot of the stories if you want to read them."

Struan had gone pale, and his eyes were riveted upon a particular place on the map of Scotland. "What . . . uh . . . I don't know what to make of this." He touched a spot with several red dots. "This is near Berwick where I fought at Halidon Hill in 1333. This . . . this has to be where I came through to this century."

Struan's eyes sought hers, and the disquiet, the deep fear she sensed caused a lump to rise in her throat. She wanted to put her arms around him, comfort him, but 'twas not her place.

"*You* are from the past as well?" Conner frowned. "Why did you not say so when you called?"

Struan shook his head, his expression dazed. "It didn't seem relevant at the time."

"Sit, laddie," Connor commanded, pulling out a chair. "You look about to drop. Michael, fetch your brother's whiskey for him, and bring ours as well, if you would."

"Sure." Michael scurried off toward the living room.

"I'll have your tale before we leave, boyo." Connor shot Struan a determined look. "I noticed the building behind the house. *You're* Sutherland Forge, I take it?"

Struan nodded.

Connor slapped Struan's shoulder, sending him pitching forward in his chair. "I've a few of your swords. Ordered them online, I did, and fine weapons they are, too. Do you wield a blade as well as you forge one, I wonder?"

Struan recovered himself, and rubbed his forehead as if it pained him. "Well enough."

"We'll have a go to test your mettle before my wife and I leave."

Struan's eyes narrowed, and Sky sensed the mixture of anticipation and dread coursing through him. Why dread? He engaged in swordplay for the fairs, and she'd seen the lists with the quintain behind the Gordons' house. Surely training with Connor was no cause for concern.

Michael returned with his hands full of glasses, and Sky helped him get the drinks to their rightful owners. Then she took a seat and pointed to a place on the map of Scotland. A dozen dots were so close in proximity they nearly formed an island of red. "This is very near Castle Kildrummy. 'Tis certain this is the clearing in the wood where I came through. If there are so many stories, surely the Erskines ken the tales well enough."

"Aye. Most likely." Connor pulled out a chair and sat. He thrummed with excitement. "There are two kinds of time travel stories. Those in which a mortal has come into contact with one of the *Tuatha Dé Danann* and disappeared, and those in which no contact took place. In the latter, some hapless soul stumbled across a spot where a portal opened, and they were taken to a different place and time.

"Katherine and I have searched for some kind of pattern, maybe a specific time of year when the occurrences happened, but we can't find any rhyme or reason for when a passageway opens or closes." He looked around the table at each of them.

"In my case, I followed one of the ancient ones through time. In your mother's case, Sky, she was sent to the past by Madame Giselle, who also provided Robley with the means to travel back and forth at will with the use of uncut diamonds." His eyes met hers. "I suspect you happened upon one of the gates just as it opened, as did you, Struan."

"Madame Giselle was responsible for sending my brother to the fair where you and your daughter were putting on an exhibition," Sky added. "She chose Meghan for Hunter, because of her strength and her fighting skills."

"I had wondered, and now I know for certain." Connor's expression hardened for a moment. "We know the fae travel through time, and to do so, they open these . . . corridors through the centuries. We believe a number of their passageways have been abandoned or forgotten. They've been left in an active state, and unfortunately, the unsuspecting wander right into them."

"Are there any of these dot clusters in the US?" Michael asked.

"I couldn't say. We haven't been able to find any stories here involving sudden disappearances, appearances or reappearances other than those involving Sky's kin, and they are fairly recent. It's entirely possible that the people who are indigenous to this land have legends of such, but the stories have most likely been lost. We couldn't find anything on the Internet, in books of folklore or any hint of such in our visits to museums and history centers."

Sky's heart stuttered. The implications were overwhelming. "You believe I can go back, don't you?"

"I do." Connor tensed. "What's more, I believe anyone can travel back and forth once they discover the key to when the portals open and close." He glanced at his wife. "We hoped to find a way to bring our daughter back home. That's why we began the research. Robley told us that Madame Giselle instructed him to keep his heart and mind fixed upon the time and place he wished to go, and that doing so would get him there."

"Och, but it didn't," Sky cried. "Not exactly. Robley meant to arrive on the exact day my mother left, and at the exact same fair in New York where she worked. Instead, he landed in Minnesota and at a different fair."

"Aye, but he said he believed your mother's birthplace was also fixed in his mind, since she'd told him so many stories about her life there." Connor shook his head. "Until now, we had no idea what time or place our girl had been taken to. Thanks to you, now we know."

Katherine tossed back her whiskey in a single gulp and slammed the tumbler down on the table. "When you go back, Sky, we're going with you."

"What?" Struan shot up from his chair. "Are you crazy?"

"Nay, you canna risk such a thing." Sky looked from Connor to Katherine. "Your son's in Minnesota. You have grandchildren here, and extended family. What of your fencing club?"

"You can't go back alone, Sky. If your betrothed suspects you know of his plans, you'll be in danger." Connor's jaw tightened. "If you are to prevent a clan war, you must try to return to the very spot and time from which you left, but as you pointed out with Robley's case, you can't count on ending up exactly when and where you wish. We can only hope to get to your kin before they fall into the earl of Mar's clutches. If possible, we need to go back to the moments *before* you disappeared to avert disaster altogether.

"Should something go wrong, you'll need protection, which is where I come in." Connor reached for his wife's hand. "I will guard you, and in exchange, you will take us to our daughter. We'll bring the maps with us, and if we cannot locate Madame Giselle to beg her aid in returning home, then we'll seek another portal and camp there until the way opens."

"I wanna go too," Michael cried. "This would be the adventure of a lifetime."

"Absolutely not, Michael," Struan shouted. "What the hell are you all thinking?" He glared. "There are no guarantees that you'll be able to go where you want to go, much less that you'd be able to return. I won't allow it."

"In my time, I was heir to a chiefdom, laddie, and you'll not be telling me what I can and cannot do." Connor glared back.

"I meant that for my brother," Struan gritted out. His chest worked like the bellows in his fire pit, as if breathing had become a struggle, and the muscles at his clenched jaw twitched.

Struan growled deep in his throat, strode to the patio doors, shoved open the screening and stomped out.

Sensing the internal battle waging within him, Sky started after him. Surely he realized his parents would never allow Michael to go anywhere. So what had stirred him into such a state?

"Don't, Sky," Michael warned. "When Struan gets like this, we've all learned it's best to leave him alone until he's cooled down and worked things out for himself." His phone chimed from his back pocket. Michael pulled it out and checked his text messages. "Mom says it's time to head home for dinner. Dad's grilling." He grinned the grin of a hungry adolescent. "He's a gourmet griller."

She and the McGladreys followed Michael out the front door and down Struan's driveway. Katherine walked beside her. "We'll talk more about our plans tomorrow morning, Sky. There are things we must do to prepare, and we brought along a few things for you to help the process along."

"Aye, we'll talk tomorrow. Will you stay the night in Struan's camper?"

"Perhaps, if we're still welcome. If not, we'll find a nearby hotel."

"Och, I dinna believe Struan to be the kind of man to rescind his welcome," Sky said. "My sudden appearance in his life has been difficult for him, and I'm sure the thought of his brother's wish to accompany us was too much for him to bear. Like Michael said, once he's worked things out for himself, I'm sure he'll be fine."

Katherine's expression smoothed. "I'm sure you're right."

All the way to the Gordons', Sky scanned the valley for any sign of Struan. Mayhap he walked through the forest, hidden from her view. She still longed to comfort him, and 'twas difficult to keep from setting out to find him.

Gene was outside his garage with his grill as the four of them walked up the driveway.

"Glad you could stay for supper," he greeted them, waving a pair of tongs in the air.

"Thank you for inviting us." Connor put his arm around Katherine's shoulders. "I'm afraid we've upset Struan. He took off on foot."

"Oh?" Gene looked to Michael, who launched into a brief description of what had transpired.

"Ah, well, you're not going anywhere, son, so don't even think about it."

"I know, Dad. I was just saying it would be the experience of a lifetime. Epic."

"You know what would really be *epic*?" Gene flashed a pointed look Michael's way. "Seeing you graduate from high school next spring, and then packing you off to college to get a four-year degree. Now that would be the experience of a lifetime, for your mother and me, anyway."

Michael let out a purely put-upon groan and skulked off into the house.

Gene turned to the McGladreys. "These steaks will be done in a few minutes. Go on in. It's just us tonight. Lindsay is out with friends, and Ethan and his family had plans for the evening."

All through supper, Sky watched the door, hoping Struan would return. He didn't, and concern for him gnawed at her like a hound with a bone.

"Do you know of a hotel nearby where we might stay the night?" Katherine asked.

Marjorie waved their request away. "You're not staying at a hotel. We have room here, and you're welcome to stay."

"We don't wish to trouble you." Connor leaned back in his chair. "Struan offered us the use of his trailer, but . . . after the way we upset him, my wife and I think it would be best if we stayed in town."

"Oh." Marjorie's eyes clouded with concern. "Struan can sometimes be a bit reactive, but he'll be himself again once he's had time to work through whatever's bothering him. If you'd prefer to stay in town, there's the Inn at Gristmill Square. It's a lovely historic bed-and-breakfast." She slid her chair back and rose from her place. "The owners are good friends of ours. Let me give them a call and see if they have a room open."

Marjorie left the kitchen to make the call, and Sky began to clear the table. "If you will teach me how to put the dishes in yon contraption, Gene, I'd like to clean up this eve."

"I'll help." Katherine joined her. "Gene, you sit and keep my husband company. I can show Sky how to load the dishwasher."

She and Katherine worked side by side and made quick work of cleaning the Gordons' kitchen. All the while Sky's mind went over the day's happenings, especially Struan's kiss. Where was he, and what had upset him so? Was it the daunting realization that traveling through the centuries at will might be possible? Mayhap like her, he both feared and longed to go back to prevent the disaster befalling his father and clan. That would explain his sudden burst of anger, followed by his equally sudden departure. After all, he believed her presence in his life signaled the approaching end of his. He had naught to fear. She would not allow him to leave his valley or his family.

CHAPTER EIGHT

Struan strode through the woods, kicking at anything in his path. He'd been tromping for at least an hour, ever since his abrupt departure from his kitchen, leaving the McGladreys, Sky and his brother behind. Yet, he still hadn't regained control over himself. His life had been perfect, dammit. He'd been happy, content. And then *she* had to fall into his path, churning up the past and unsettling his equilibrium.

Oh, he'd known. Two minutes after his tirade, he'd known his tantrum had nothing to do with his brother's ridiculous declaration about going to the fifteenth century. Nope. His parents would never allow Michael to go anywhere. His fit had been entirely "Sky centered," and that just made no sense at all. In fact, his reaction made him all the angrier.

For God's sake, he'd chased her down on horseback today—like some medieval hunter in hot pursuit of his next meal. Worse, he'd snatched her from her horse and kissed her like some hormone-driven madman, his raging hard-on poking into her sweet rounded derrière.

He groaned and scrubbed his face with both hands, hoping to wipe out the images behind his eyes. What must she think of him? What the hell had he been thinking?

Who was he kidding? There hadn't been any thinking at all, and that was the problem. His hands fisted, Struan dropped them to his sides. He didn't need this entanglement. He didn't *want* to want her. He should be leaping for joy that the McGladreys were going to take her off his hands. So . . . why wasn't he leaping for joy? Why did he feel as if something deep inside was being ripped asunder?

His stomach grumbled with hunger. Also *her* fault. If it weren't for Sky Elizabeth, the eldest daughter of the earl of Fife, he'd be sitting at his ma's table right now, enjoying a hearty meal with his family, instead of tromping through the woods by himself.

He stopped walking and stared at the pine needles cushioning the path beneath his feet. Hadn't it been just this morning that he'd convinced himself Sky would be better off staying in Gordon Hollow, making him and the Gordons her kin and clan? Now he couldn't be rid of her fast enough. He should probably sort through his feelings.

One thing was certain: he did *not* like this roiling ache in his gut or the all-consuming need to hold Sky in his arms. He didn't like the way she wreaked havoc on his peace of mind and threatened his perfect life with her tale of treachery and woe. If she was stupid enough to go back to that dung heap of trouble awaiting her in the fifteenth century, so be it. Not. His. Problem.

"Dammit, dammit, dammit," he shouted, throwing his head back to glare at the canopy of pine boughs overhead. Then he shook himself, turned around and started back down the path toward home. He'd make a sandwich, open a bag of chips, some salsa and have a few beers while sitting in front of his TV.

If Connor and his wife showed up for the camper, he'd get them all hooked up, show them where the guest bathroom was located, and once they were settled, he'd hide out in his basement rec room with his food and his bad mood.

By the time his place came into view, the McGladreys were walking up his drive toward their car. A part of him wanted to hide until they were gone. Another part, the more mature portion, suffered a twinge of embarrassment at his childish outburst. Striding out of the forest, he waved and called out to them to wait as he jogged toward them.

"Are you leaving?" he asked. Dumb question. Obviously they were leaving, since the two of them were about to climb into the sedan.

"We are." Connor rested his forearms on the top of the open door. "Marjorie was able to find a room for us at a B&B near town."

Struan gestured toward his camper. "You don't have to leave. My camper is—"

"Listen, boyo, I understand why you reacted the way you did, but we didn't come here to upset you. We came to help *Sky*, and because her presence here means there's a slim possibility we might see our daughter again." Connor fixed him with a hard stare. "Rest assured, we will not be takin' young Michael with us."

"I know." Could he feel any smaller? "I apologize for making you feel unwelcome. I . . . all this has stirred up a lot of—"

"The Gordons told us a little about your history during dinner." Connor and Katherine shared another one of those annoying *we're sharing something you don't know* looks. "I carry unpleasant memories as well, as does Sky. You're not the first or the only to suffer being ripped from your life and time, and this isn't about you."

Ouch. Is that what they thought? Did they believe he suffered grief for having come through time to a life that was a hundred and fifty percent better than the one he'd left behind?

Connor continued to glare. "Sky wants to do right by her kin, and we mean to help her in any way we're able."

"I want to help her too."

"Good." Connor grinned, a wicked glint lighting his eyes. "I'll meet you in the lists tomorrow morning at the crack of dawn. If I'm to go back to the fifteenth century, it's best I keep my combat skills in peak form."

Me and my big mouth. Struan nodded. "Did you bring equipment, or do I need to loan you some of mine?"

"I'll need a broadsword and a buckler shield." He climbed into the car. "We'll talk more tomorrow morning. Sky is going to need some practical help on your end. My wife and I need to prepare for our time away from home. That will take us a week or so. Until tomorrow." Connor shut the door and started the car.

Struan swallowed against the hollow ache rising up in a choke hold around his throat. He was being propelled in a direction he didn't want to go, and the only way he could rebel was by digging in his heels deeper into the here and now. The McGladreys' car wended its way along the road out of Gordon Hollow, and Struan stood still until he couldn't see them anymore. Finally, he turned to head into his empty house, his appetite gone.

Struan reached out and hit the button on his buzzing alarm clock. Only 5:00 a.m., too early to be up. Yawning, he got up, reached for the sweatpants at the end of his bed and pulled them on. He stretched, walked to his dresser and chose a T-shirt from a drawer. The coffeemaker in his kitchen gurgled away, filling the glass carafe on the burner. As he tugged on the T-shirt, he inhaled the smell of fresh coffee.

Athletic shoes or leather boots? He stared into his closet while trying to decide which would be best for his bout with Connor. Even with blunted blades, accidents happened. He stuffed his sock-covered feet into a pair of leather boots that reached his knees. Yawning again, he made his way to the kitchen for a much-needed mug of coffee. He took a few fortifying sips before heading downstairs to gather the gear they would need.

His *armory* was located in a windowless storage room behind his laundry facilities. He shivered, no doubt his body's reaction to getting up way too early after a mostly sleepless night. He hadn't done this early morning routine since the days he'd trained with his father and his half brothers. When he trained with Andrew or Michael, they usually did so in the afternoon after the forge had been shut down for the day.

Struan opened the door to the walk-in closet and flipped the switch for the overhead lights. He surveyed his inventory: poleax, war club, a few swords and shields in various sizes. Why did he stock an armory, anyway? Was it a holdover from his life in the fourteenth century, or had he been preparing for some unforeseen primitive twenty-first-century enemy? Did he think the Society for Creative Anachronism would one day rise up and take over the world? They *had* already demarcated their realms and chosen their kings and queens, after all.

Funny. Everything he'd stored in the room had to do with medieval warfare, yet he had no desire to return to the past. Connor had volunteered to go with Sky to her century. He would protect her. Right. One old man protecting two females against an entire Erskine garrison. *That* would turn out well. Guns. Cannons and matchlock rifles were in existence back then. McGladrey should forget about fighting fair, upsetting the time continuum and all that, and just bring a couple of modern-day handguns and a shitload of ammo. Done.

He huffed out a guilt-laden breath and selected his very best leather brigandine, rather than a heavier chain mail haubergeon. He wanted to protect his back and chest—just in case Connor became a little too enthusiastic in his efforts to slice and dice his sorry hide. Next he chose two broadswords with leather-wrapped grips, nicely rounded pommels and broad cross guards—fashioned by his own hand, of course. The blades on the swords were as yet unsharpened, and if he had his way, they'd never need a cutting edge. Finally he picked out two buckler shields.

With his gear in his arms, he returned to his kitchen and dumped the load on the table with a clatter. He hadn't eaten since lunchtime yesterday, and he couldn't train on an empty stomach. He fixed himself a big bowl of oatmeal in the microwave, adding brown sugar, mashed banana and milk. While he ate his meal, he mentally went over the art of swordsmanship.

Be the first to strike, lad, and whilst you're about it, hit fast and hard. Attack where your opponent's weapon just moved away from. Remember, where your head goes, the rest of you will follow. His father's litany echoed through his skull, until Connor pulled into his driveway. Struan shoveled the last spoonful of his breakfast into his mouth and shot up. He put his bowl in the sink, grabbed the gear and headed out the front door.

"Good morning," Connor called out as he stretched out his hamstrings. "Are you ready to be bested by a master?"

"Humph." Struan walked down the front steps. He handed a sword and shield to Connor. "Drive, or walk to the field?"

"We'll be jogging." Connor wore cutoff sweats, a T-shirt and athletic shoes, of course.

"Do you want to borrow a hauberk, or—"

"No need. You'll not be getting close enough to touch me."

Struan rolled his eyes. The guy had to be in his fifties, while *he* was in his twenties. Who did Connor think he was kidding? Struan slid the heavy steel-enforced leather brigandine over his T-shirt and fastened the laces. "Let's go, *old man*. I have work to do today."

Connor barked out a laugh and jogged down the driveway with the borrowed sword gripped in his right hand and the shield in his left. Struan followed. He was in decent shape, though he trained sporadically, but he didn't jog on a regular basis.

He glanced at Connor. The old guy seemed unaffected, while Struan already huffed and puffed. Great. Good thing the field behind the Gordons' place wasn't too far away. A mile at best, unless they crossed through a field. Might be a good idea to do something to improve his stamina.

By the time they reached the training field, Struan was gasping for breath and sweat dripped down his face. Leaning over with his palms on his knees, he glanced at Connor, who still breathed easily and had hardly broken a sweat. Struan straightened. Of course, *he* wore a heavy piece of protective equipment, while Connor wore only a T-shirt. That had to make a difference. Right?

Connor assumed a battle-ready pose. "I'll be needin' a shield like this one when I go. I haven't bothered with such for years, since swordplay in this time is for show and not to kill." He hefted the small shield. "They are effective at disabling an enemy's sword arm, after all. Come hither, boyo. Let's see what you've got."

His father's lessons echoed through Struan's mind: space and time, stance, hold the shield so it faces your opponent, cut and thrust. Connor beat him to the offensive, shortening the distance between them. He brought his sword down fast and hard, and Struan barely managed to block him. Connor then let loose a flurry of strikes and thrusts, driving Struan back. He defended himself as best he could, but turning the tide so he could take the offensive wasn't happening. They'd just begun, and already he was exhausted.

The one-sided battle raged on and on until his muscles burned and begged for mercy. Sweat poured down his face and into his eyes, causing a stinging blur, and he was forced to readjust his opinion about Connor's abilities.

Finally, Connor ended the match. Circling Struan, he clucked his tongue and shook his head. The guy hardly seemed winded. Embarrassed, Struan struggled to bring air into his lungs. "This *wasn't* my idea," he rasped out. "I'm rusty is all. I haven't really needed to—"

"You said you wanted to help Sky."

"From here, not . . . not . . ." He swallowed convulsively. "I've . . . the Gordons have given her shelter, fed her. I bought her clothes." He'd also been rude to her, blaming her for things that had nothing to do with her. Besides, she'd repaid him for the clothing, giving up one of her precious gold coins. She had no idea the thing was worth a fortune today. Plus, he'd sworn he'd keep her safe. Lord, he was tired of the load of guilt piling up on his shoulders. "I'll help her get to Scotland, but—"

"Come. Your family is expecting us. We'll discuss how you can help *from here* once Sky is present for the discussion. My wife is at the Gordons' already. I imagine we've had an audience."

Struan's gaze shot to the glass patio doors facing their training area. Heat crept up his neck to scorch his face, and it had nothing to do with physical exertion. Very likely Sky had witnessed his ignominious defeat. Connor put his hand on Struan's shoulder, turned him toward the house and forcefully started him moving toward the back door. He was really beginning to dislike the guy.

They entered the kitchen through the patio, and Struan stifled the groan rising in his throat. Sky, his ma and da, Katherine and Michael were sitting at the table, and judging by the way Sky avoided eye contact, she had indeed witnessed his utter humiliation at Connor's hand.

Struan busied himself with unlacing his brigandine and drawing it off. His T-shirt, soaked with sweat, clung to him. "Can I borrow a towel and a dry shirt, Gene?" he asked. He strode over to the kitchen sink and splashed cold water over his face and neck. A towel hit him in the chest when he turned back.

Michael smirked. "Dad went to get a shirt."

Struan nodded before drying himself, still avoiding looking Sky's way.

"Coffee?" Marjorie asked, her voice cheery.

"Sure," Struan said, pulling off his soaked T-shirt.

"Connor?" she offered.

"No. Never learned to like the stuff. I've had my morning tea, thank you."

Gene returned with a clean shirt. Struan slipped it on and took a seat at the table where his ma had set his coffee. Katherine had a folder in front of her, piquing his curiosity. "What do you have there?"

"We brought a few things for Sky just in case." She pushed the folder across the table toward Sky. "Connor and I believe it's best if we keep things as simple and above suspicion as possible, so Sky can travel with us to Scotland without difficulty. Inside, you'll find our daughter's official birth certificate, her social security card and a passport application," she said, her voice hitching. "We suggest you use Meghan's identity to get an ID card here in Virginia."

"Oh." Sky studied the folder. "I am most grateful to you both. I know this must be difficult for you."

"Since Connor and our sons witnessed what happened the day Meghan disappeared, we never reported Meghan missing. You shouldn't encounter any difficulty assuming her identity." Katherine's voice broke again. "I've also taken the liberty of filling out the passport application for you, since you wouldn't know our personal information—or Meghan's, for that matter. All you have to do is sign the document. Once you have the picture ID and a passport photo, you can send it in to be processed."

Connor covered his wife's hand with his. "We thought about having you come home with us, Sky, and getting an ID in Minnesota. But we fear if we did so, Meghan's driver's license would pop up in the system, and someone might suspect your request was fraudulent. We didn't want to take the risk. It's best you stay here. That's where you come in, Struan."

Connor leaned forward. "She'll need a local address to get the state ID, and you'll have to take her in and vouch for her. We're heading home later this morning. We'll be back in a week or so."

The McGladreys rose from the table, and once again Connor's intimidating gaze fixed upon Struan. "I suggest you start training a bit more seriously, because I'll expect a better showing when I return. We figure two weeks for the ID and another six for the passport. During the wait, I'm counting on you to train with me."

"Why?" Struan frowned. "Surely there's someone you can work with in Minnesota. Why not just stay at home until her passport arrives?"

Michael sat up straighter. "I'd like to train with you, Mr. McGladrey."

"You are welcome to join us, Michael. As to why here and not at home, it's because none of my present-day sparring partners understand the mentality of a medieval warrior. Though you've let yourself go soft, you lived with the mindset. You know what it means to face peril on a daily basis. I prefer to hone my skills with someone who understands the 'kill or be killed' environment in which we both managed to survive. And quite frankly, you need to get in shape, boyo." He arched an eyebrow, his expression mocking. "It's a sad day indeed when a young man in his prime is so easily driven into the dirt by an *old man* like myself." He huffed out a laugh. "Did I mention I'm a grandfather?"

Ire rose like bile up his throat, and his jaw clenched down on the hot retort he wanted to make.

"Thank you so much for your kind hospitality, Marjorie, Gene." Katherine smiled warmly. "It was lovely meeting all of you, and Gordon Hollow is absolutely idyllic."

"You're very welcome." Marjorie returned her smile.

"Plan to stay with us when you return," Gene said, shaking Connor's hand. "We have the room, and I'd very much like to hear more about the fourteenth century."

"We'll gladly take you up on your offer," Connor replied. "Walk with us to the car, Struan. I've a few more things to say to you before we leave."

"Great." Struan slid his chair back, so that it made an unpleasant scraping sound against the floor. He followed the McGladreys to their rental, widened his stance and crossed his arms in front of his chest, bracing himself to be ground into the dirt yet again, even if it was only metaphorically this time around.

Connor helped his wife into the car, circled around the hood and came to face him toe-to-toe. "Despite what you might think, laddie, heroes are *not* born; they're forged through trial and tempered by adversity in much the same way as your steel blades. When called upon, a hero rises above his fellows, while a common man chooses to remain . . . common. At some point in our lives, each of us is given the choice to either rise above or remain rooted to the ground."

"OK." Struan squirmed beneath the man's unwavering scrutiny. "Got it. To rise, or not to rise. *That* is the question."

Connor huffed out a laugh. "Think about it, and we'll talk more when I return."

He saluted him. "Will do." Then he crossed his arms in front of him again and tried really, really hard *not* to throw curses at the retreating rental car. Life was closing in around him, herding him closer and closer toward a ledge, and he couldn't help feeling like he was about to be shoved into the waiting abyss.

He surveyed the land, taking in the mountains sheltering their valley. The deep green of the pines and spruce covering the hills, and the pastures where Ethan's cattle grazed were as familiar to him as his own face. He caught sight of Andrew's truck near the forge.

Needing time to regroup, finish his coffee and spend a little time with his family, he turned to go back inside. His heart thumped against his sternum. Sky stood by the front door, watching him in that intense way she had about her. Had she heard Connor's cryptic speech? "So, what are your plans for today?"

"Lindsay is taking me shopping for a suit for swimming."

"A swimsuit."

Her chin lifted a notch. "That's what I said."

Every time she lifted her chin like that, the urge to drag her into his arms and ravish her sweet mouth slammed into him. The image that sprang to mind—Sky wearing nothing but a hot barely-there-bikini—really didn't help matters. "When do you want to apply for that state ID?"

"Mayhap 'twould be best to put off shopping and take care of the ID as soon as can be arranged."

"Mayhap." One side of his mouth quirked up. "While we're at the DMV, do you think you could speak with an American accent using more contemporary speech?"

"For certes . . . er . . . of course I can. I've been listening carefully and practicing in the privacy of my bedroom."

Her words came out so artificial and stilted he had to bite down on the urge to laugh. "Say as little as possible, and we'll be fine." He abandoned the idea of going back inside. He had coffee at his house, and Andrew would be waiting for him. "I have to take care of a few things at the forge. I'll come for you after lunch."

He started for the lane, considering whether or not he should take Connor's advice to get in shape and jog home. His sore muscles heartily objected to the notion. He'd get up early tomorrow morning and begin his jogging regimen, and he'd ask Andrew to train with him on a daily basis. If Connor wanted a worthy opponent, Struan intended to give him one.

"Struan."

"Hmm?" He turned back.

"I don't expect you to rise above your fellows." Her gorgeous eyes were filled with concern. "If you please, I'd much prefer it if you'd stay rooted here in Gordon Hollow."

With that, she marched back into the house, and Struan was left staring at air. And scowling. "Hmm. So she doesn't see me as the stuff of legends," he muttered under his breath. Damn if that didn't take more than just the wind out of his sails. It also took his pride. He growled low in his throat and strode down the street in his medieval boots.

He was still in stomp mode when he walked into his forge. "Andrew, we need to start knocking off a little early every afternoon, so we can practice our combat skills."

"Oh? Why is that?" Andrew spared him a glance. "No. Wait. Let me guess. The folks at the Society for Creative Anachronism have finally begun their global takeover. Am I right?"

"No." Struan scowled.

"For the sake of argument, if the SCA did start a coup, whose side would you be on?"

"Can we leave the SCA out of this?" he huffed. "I need to train harder because I just got my ass handed to me in the lists by a man in his fifties. He's a grandfather, for crying out loud!" Still scowling, he scanned the interior of his forge. "Where's Brian?"

"He had horses to shoe this morning. He'll be in as soon as he can." Andrew finished cutting the leather strips for wrapping the grips of their swords, and then he straightened. "You want to tell me what's going on besides the ass kicking?"

"It's complicated."

"I'm intelligent."

"Seems I've fallen in lust with the earl of Fife's eldest daughter."

"Ah, I see." Andrew nodded. "So we're done with the brotherly proprietary looking out for her thing?"

"I never said it was brotherly. That was you."

"Granted. What else?"

"Connor McGladrey is trying to coerce me into becoming a hero."

"Hmm?" Andrew cocked an eyebrow.

"I'm a bastard."

"Well, you've always been a moody sort, but we all have our moments. Don't be so hard on yourself."

Struan slanted a narrow-eyed look at him. "Not *that* kind of bastard." He launched into an explanation of everything that had happened since the McGladreys' arrival. "He hasn't said it outright, but Connor wants me to go back with them to protect Sky. I know he does. But, see, if I do go back, I'll have no chance with Sky. None." Not to mention his fears that the timer on his extended life was about to go *ding*.

"If you convinced her to stay, do you believe you'd have a chance with her?" Andrew asked. "Oh, wait. You said you're in lust. Just what kind of *chance* are we talking here?"

The kind of chance that had the eldest daughter of the earl of Fife falling willingly into his bed. "I had this stupid notion that once she got to know me, my origins wouldn't matter." He shrugged. "Where things between us were supposed to go from there is still a little hazy. I figured she'd settle into this century, and I'd have time to sort it all out."

He shook his head and heaved a frustration-laced breath. "But in her time? Sky's father, the *earl*, would never allow me anywhere near her. I'm not even a knight. I'm just a common blacksmith. Besides, I don't have the slightest desire to be in any time or place other than this one."

"I'd say you were an uncommonly excellent blacksmith, Struan. And wasn't your dad also an earl? Doesn't that count?"

"No. I'm illegitimate, and with the nobility that makes me persona non grata. Bastards are to be avoided like the black plague. Especially by eligible bachelorettes possessing large dowries, and I'm certain Sky Elizabeth falls into *that* lofty category." He didn't mention the fear, the panic and the overwhelming sense of foreboding the thought of stepping through time's portal caused him. "So you see, I'm a shit if I don't and screwed if I do."

"Have you considered talking her into staying here with you?"

"I've toyed with the notion, and I'm not above attempting to do just that." He sent Andrew a pointed look. "But what kind of an ass does that make me? Her family is going to suffer the fallout for her disappearance, and if she doesn't at least try to rectify the situation, she's going to suffer the guilt for the rest of her life. If I'm the one who talks her out of returning, eventually she's going to resent me."

"Hmm. Quite a dilemma you've found yourself in, my friend. I don't envy you."

"Heroes aren't born; they're forged through trial and tempered by adversity," Struan bit out.

"Sounds like something you'd see written on the front of a T-shirt." Andrew began wrapping a sword grip with leather.

"Sounds like coercion." Struan grabbed the bearing sword he was working on for the pretend SCA king and dropped it on the workbench. He had a few spots to finish cleaning up, and then he'd put it in the acid bath. "I never signed up to be anyone's hero. I don't *want* to be a hero. All the men I've thought of as legendary died violent deaths much too young." A chill traipsed down his spine.

"There is that. What are you going to do?"

"I don't know." Once again the hollow ache rose up to engulf him. "I really don't know."

"Alrighty then. I guess we'll be knocking off early to train."

"I guess so. Starting tomorrow though. I already took a beating today. There isn't a square inch of me that doesn't ache."

He was certain Sky had watched his very poor showing in the lists. Is that why she preferred he stay in Gordon Hollow? She probably didn't think he'd last a day in 1443. Come to think of it, she might be right.

"So . . . back to my earlier question. Say the SCA did attempt a world takeover." Andrew peered at him. "Which side would you be on?"

Struan huffed out a laugh, settled into his work, and the rest of the morning was spent weighing the pros and cons of an anachronistic takeover.

CHAPTER NINE

Sky buckled herself into the seat of Struan's truck, trying her best not to think about his kiss, or the way he'd snatched her from her horse and held her to him but a day ago. She already suffered enough torment—like worrying about whether or not her family was safe. She didn't need to add to her list. Still, think about it she did, and she couldn't seem to keep her eyes from him.

"Did you and Lindsay go shopping this morning?" Struan turned the key, and his truck roared to life.

"We did, and I now have a garment to wear when swimming." If you could call such a wee scrap of cloth a garment. Her face heated just thinking about being garbed thus in front of Struan. "While we were in Warm Springs, Lindsay pointed out the DMV. She said that's where one gets a license to drive."

"That's right." Struan glanced at her before backing the truck out of the Gordons' driveway.

"Might I get a license to drive whilst we're there?"

"Um, not today." He grinned. "That's not how it works."

The laugh lines at the corners of his eyes creased in a most charming manner. Struan was irresistible when he smiled and intriguing when brooding. He drew her in a way she'd never before experienced, and if she wasn't careful, she was likely to lose her heart. "How does getting one's license work then?"

"You have to take a class, study a manual, learn all the rules and laws first. Once you feel you're ready, you take a written test, and if you pass, you get a permit. With a permit, you can learn to drive, so long as a licensed driver is in the vehicle with you. Once you're very good at driving, then you have to pass another test—this one behind the wheel."

"Och, 'tis a lengthy process."

"Very."

Still, she was likely to be in Gordon Hollow for some time to come, and the thought of learning how to drive excited her. "I wish to get a license to drive before I leave. Where might I find a manual, so that I can begin studying the laws and such?"

"Why?"

"So that I will have accomplished something whilst here." Sky shrugged. "Something I can boast about to my brothers and sisters. They'll be envious. Especially Owain. He's the adventurous sort, and for once I'd like to best him."

"Michael just got his license a few months ago. He probably still has his drivers' manual and his notes from the class he took. I'm sure he'd be glad to pass all of it along to you. I'd be happy to teach you to drive, but I think we'll borrow Lindsay's car. It's smaller and easier to manage than a truck."

"I'd be most grateful to you. I'll ask Michael for his manual once we've returned." Anticipation brought a smile to her face. They reached the main road, and Struan turned away from Warm Springs. "Where are we going for this ID?" she asked.

"Lexington. In Warm Springs, everyone knows everyone, and I'm sure news that you're staying with us has already circulated. I don't want to draw attention, especially since we're using Meghan McGladrey's documents, when everyone will have heard your name is Sky."

He shifted in his seat. "It'll be early evening by the time we return. Do you want to stop for pizza?" His eyes met hers for an instant before returning to the road. "Pizza is similar to lasagna. Lots of melted cheese, tomato sauce, meat and vegetables. What do you think?"

"I enjoyed Lindsay's lasagna very much. I'd like that." *If we meet someone who appeals to us, we ask them out on a date, get to know them without chaperones hovering about.* That's what Struan had told her when she'd asked if the Gordons would arrange a marriage for him. Had he just asked her out on a date? She didn't want to ask, fearing he'd tell her 'twas just the circumstance and the hour of their return that compelled him to see that she was fed.

Nay, she'd rather imagine he'd asked her for a date, and that she appealed to him enough that he wished to spend more time with her. After all, once she returned home, she planned to convince her father to allow her to remain unwed. This might be her only chance to experience how men and women in this century courted. Her pulse quickened as she recalled the feel of Struan's lips against hers, his tongue plunging so intimately into her mouth. If only he would kiss her again.

The rest of their journey was spent in companionable silence, broken only by small talk about the view, the weather and Struan's family. He didn't bring up yesterday's kiss, so neither did she.

Sky studied his strong profile, the way the muscles in his forearms moved as he handled the massive truck so competently. She'd always longed for the breathless, heart-fluttering sensations Struan elicited, and now that she'd felt them firsthand, it only made things worse. Her heart was engaged. 'Twas unlikely she'd ever experience the same again once she returned to her own time—without Struan.

Was it wrong to want to experience a man's touch just once? Not any man's, but Struan's. He was the only man who had ever set her heart racing or caused this aching longing within. Her face flushed at the thought, and she turned to stare out the window lest he wonder at the cause.

Struan pulled his truck to the side of the road in front of a red brick building with white columns in front. "This is it." He reached to the backseat for the folder holding the documents Katherine had given her. "Don't forget. You're Meghan McGladrey. I guess we should start calling you that all the time now."

"'Twould be easier to continue calling me Sky and claim 'tis a sobriquet."

"Sure, but while we're here to get your ID, it's Meghan, and don't say any more than you have to." His blue eyes sparkled with amusement. "When you try to speak like Americans, it sounds more like a speech impediment than it does an accent."

Sky lifted her chin. "There is naught amiss . . . nothing wrong with my American accent."

"If you say so." He laughed as he climbed out of the truck and came around to her side.

He helped her to step to the ground, and she followed him along the paved pathway to the building and in through heavy glass doors. Struan led her to the space designated as the DMV. He took a scrap of paper from some sort of dispenser before ushering her toward a counter holding various forms.

"Here's an application for a state ID." He handed her a sheet of paper.

He stood next to her, close enough that she could detect his masculine scent and feel his warmth. Distracted by his nearness, she took the pen he offered and began filling out the information she'd studied from what the McGladreys had written down for her. Struan completed the lines where it called for her local address. Folder and application in hand, she took a seat and awaited her turn.

Struan sat next to her, leaned close and whispered, "Nervous?"

His breath against her skin caused a shiver of pleasure, and again she recalled his kiss. "No, not really," she replied in her best modern-day speech.

"That's the spirit, princess."

A number was called out by an older, silver-haired woman behind a different counter, and Struan rose. "That's us. I'll do most of the talking." They approached together. "My girlfriend has recently moved to Virginia and needs a picture ID." He took the application and documents from her and gave them to the clerk.

The clerk behind the counter studied the documents and Sky's application.

What if she could tell Sky wasn't Meghan McGladrey? "My wallet was stolen," she added, using the story she and Lindsay had concocted just in case. "And since I live here now, it makes sense to get a Virginia ID, rather than replace the one from Minnesota." Struan looked askance at her. She looked back, forcing a smile.

"Step around the counter to the camera." The woman gestured, her expression disinterested.

Sky did as she was told, her nerves calming. She hadn't been challenged or questioned. Her picture was taken, and then the woman told them the cost, and Struan handed her the paper currency to pay the fee.

The woman glanced at Sky. "It will take a week to ten days for your ID to arrive in the mail."

"Thanks," Struan said, taking the receipt and the copy of her application. He tucked them into the folder with the other documents as he led her back outside to his truck. "You lost your wallet, eh?"

"Lindsay suggested the tale in case I was asked why I didn't already have a picture ID."

"Ah, I see." One side of his mouth turned up. "Hungry?"

"I am." She studied his handsome features and manly form. Aye, she hungered all right, but for more than food. She hungered for the experiences her lot in life had thus far denied her. What would her father say if he learned she wished to lie with Struan, to give herself to a man who would never be her husband, simply because he sent her blood rushing?

Mayhap she would seduce Struan before returning to her own time. Smiling at the ridiculous notion, she climbed into the truck and buckled up for the journey back to Warm Springs. What did she ken of seduction?

"What are you smiling about?" Struan asked as he pulled his truck away from the curb.

"The prospect of pizza." Her smile grew. How shocked he would be if he learned of her desire to have her way with him.

By the time they'd finished their meal in the tiny restaurant and started out for Gordon Hollow, daylight was fading fast, and so was she. With the warm box of pizza leftovers on her lap, she struggled not to yawn. "I am most grateful for your help today, and for the pizza." She patted the box.

"You are most welcome."

All too soon he pulled into the Gordons' driveway and shut off the truck. He turned to face her, placing his arm across the back of her seat. "I promised to take you to a hot spring."

"Aye?" Another date? Her breath went shallow at the thought.

"Aye." His eyes sparkled in that beguiling way he had. "Tomorrow is Friday, and I'm leaving to work at the fair, but once I'm back, we'll visit a nearby hot spring."

"Am I no' to return to the fair with you?"

"There's really nothing for you to do there. Here you can ride, swim, explore . . . whatever you wish. You'd be bored to tears in New York, but it's up to you. Talk to Ma and Lindsay. See what they think."

She nodded, oddly stricken at the thought of being separated from her knight.

"Sky, about that kiss yesterday . . ."

"Aye?" she said to the box in her lap.

"I . . . it was . . ." He heaved a sigh that settled into the space between them. "If I had it all to do over, our first kiss would not have been so . . ."

"So impassioned? Rash?" She raised her gaze to his. He'd said *our first kiss*, as if he intended for there to be more. She sensed his uncertainty, and somehow she found his vulnerability bolstered her courage.

"Aye. That," he muttered, his tone tinged with self-deprecation. "I apologize."

"There's no need. You said if you had it to do over . . ." She could hardly believe her own daring. "How *would* you have kissed me for the first time?"

He undid his seat belt, leaned close and undid hers. Wrapping his arm around her shoulders, Struan moved closer still. "I would have been far more gentle." His knuckles skimmed her cheek, and he tucked an errant lock of hair behind her ear. "Mayhap just a brush of my lips across yours, my lady. Like this." His mouth touched hers for a brief instant, before he moved away.

'Twas all she could do to keep herself from following. "But . . . I rather liked the way you kissed me the first time," she whispered. With just that brief touch, sensations had streaked through her, lighting every nerve as if they were torches he alone could set aflame.

Struan chuckled low in his throat. He trailed kisses across her cheek and down the side of her neck, sending glowing embers of heat cascading through her. She sighed and tilted her head, encouraging him to continue. He took the lobe of her ear between his teeth and applied pressure, and a bolt of desire shot like an arrow to the very center of her core.

A rumbling came from deep in his chest, almost like a cat's purr, and once again Struan sought her mouth. This time his kiss was insistent, possessive. He held her face with both hands, deepening his assault upon her senses, demanding entrance. Gladly she opened to him, and he drew her tightly against his chest. She threaded her fingers into his thick hair, marveling at how soft it was against her skin.

Never had she imagined kissing could be so sensational, so inciting. She didn't want it to end. Sky ran her hands over his shoulders and down his arms, seeking bare skin. Sliding her hands up his short sleeves, she reveled over the feel of the bunched muscles of his upper arms and powerful shoulders. More. She needed more. What would it be like to feel his warmth and hardness against her from head to foot? A throbbing ache burgeoned deep within her, and she lost herself to overwhelming desire.

Sky could feel the pounding of his heart against hers. Lord help her, she wanted him, and if she were to be truthful with herself, she wanted more than a brief seduction with Struan. If she allowed herself the luxury, she could easily fall in love with him. Och, best not. 'Twould break her heart for certes when the time came to leave him.

Struan ended the kiss and pressed his forehead to hers. Several moments passed in silence as they both struggled to regain their composure. "You're going to be the death of me, lass," he murmured.

His words pierced her heart, chasing away all traces of lingering passion. "Nay! I will no' allow you to put your life at risk for my sake." She gripped his wrists and held him fast. "I willna'."

He straightened and peered intently into her eyes. Taking one of her hands in his, he pressed her palm against his chest. "Can you not feel the way my heart pounds for you? Do you not sense how I can scarce draw air to fill my lungs when you're near? That's what I meant. It's a figure of speech. I wasn't referring to—"

"Oh." Her face burned. He had no intention of returning to the past with her. She didn't want him to. Shouldn't she feel relieved? Instead, confusion and disappointment tightened her chest until it ached.

"We should go in, princess. I want to see my family before I head home."

She nodded mutely and retrieved the leftover pizza. At some point during their kiss, the box had slid from her lap to the floor. He came around the truck to help her out almost immediately. The intensity of his gaze held her captive.

"Nothing is written in stone, Sky."

"What mean you by that?"

He put his hands on her shoulders, drew her close and kissed her forehead. "Only that the future is unknown to us, and everything can change in an instant." He took the box from her and reached for her hand, twining the fingers together. "Come. Let us say goodnight to Gene and Marjorie."

Still puzzling over what he meant, she allowed him to lead her inside. The sound of the Gordons' TV came from the chamber they referred to as their "family room," and she and Struan headed in that direction. There they found Marjorie and Gene sitting close together on the couch, watching the flat screen, as they called the device that played movies and such.

Marjorie smiled a greeting. "How'd it go at the DMV?"

"It went well." Struan set the box on the low table in front of the couch and plopped down on the couch, tugging her with him. "Shoot. I left the folder in my truck."

Gene's eyes touched upon her hand in Struan's, and she freed herself. "I don't need any of the documents this eve." She pressed her hands together and tucked them between her knees.

"I see you stopped at Jason's Pizza and Subs." Gene pointed to their box. "What did you think, Sky?"

"'Twas very tasty, but no' nearly as delicious as Lindsay's lasagna."

"You'll get no argument from me on that. You ready to head out tomorrow, son?"

"I am. Are you coming, Ma?"

"I'm staying put this weekend. Carol and Ethan need a babysitter Saturday night, and Lindsay has to work. Besides, it's much more comfortable here than in a cramped camper trailer. You can fend for yourselves for this weekend."

"We'll only take our camper and the horse trailer then," Gene added. "There's room enough for the three of us with the bunk beds."

"See?" Struan flashed Sky a triumphant look. "You're much better off staying here."

"True enough." She didn't wish to be the only woman along, especially in such tight quarters given the way she reacted to Struan's nearness. Sky relaxed into the soft cushions and stared at the scenes unfolding on the TV. She had little interest, and her mind wandered. What had Struan been thinking when he'd remarked that things could change in an instant? She cast a sideways look at him, only to find him staring back. Her breath hitched, remembering the way he'd kissed her just moments ago.

Struan rose, stretched and sighed. "I should get going. I want to jog before we leave for New York, which means an early start. Mind if I take the pizza, Sky? There's nothing like cold leftover pizza for breakfast. Mmm-mm."

"Really?" Her eyes widened as she handed him the box.

"Really." He laughed. "Good night, all."

Gene and Marjorie wished him a good night, and he left. He'd only just gone, and already Sky felt bereft of his presence. "I should retire as well." She too rose from her place. "This has been a most productive day. I will have my picture ID within a fortnight."

"Good night, Sky." Marjorie's warm smile lit her eyes. "I'm glad you're staying this weekend. It'll be fun. You can help me watch little Gene."

"'Twould be my pleasure." She couldn't help but notice the way Gene scrutinized her. His expression unreadable, she reached out with her senses. Fear. Fear and sadness. Did he too see her presence in Struan's life as a harbinger of doom for his beloved foster son? She wished to ease his fears, but to do so would be a breach of privacy. If he wanted reassurance from her, let him be the first to bring it up.

Guilt weighed heavily upon her as she made her way upstairs to Struan's childhood bedroom. Though this era held far less political intrigue, the emotional turmoil, for her anyway, more than made up for the difference.

Sky awoke at the crack of dawn Tuesday morning to the annoying beep of the alarm clock. She reached out and shut it off the way Lindsay had demonstrated. Her blood thrummed with anticipation. Struan had returned last eve, and he'd promised to take her to a hot spring this morning. Their second date. He meant to take her to a place called the Jefferson Pools Hot Springs Spa early in the morning.

Though the weekend had passed pleasantly enough, she'd sorely missed Struan. Pushing the covers aside, she sat up in bed and stretched. A quick shower, and then she'd don her suit for swimming, wearing it beneath her jeans and top. She rose, grabbed the things she'd set out the night before and headed for the bathroom.

Quickly she showered and readied herself for the day. Struan had said they were to break their fast at a nearby resort afterwards, and she looked forward to the experience. She brushed her teeth and rinsed her mouth. Toothpaste was another item she'd miss, along with the tiny brush used to clean her teeth. Mayhap she'd take both home with her. She checked her reflection in the mirror above the basin.

Did Struan find her visage as pleasing as she found his? He'd said he could scarce draw breath when she was near, and she'd felt the pounding of his heart, so he must. In her eyes, he was the epitome of male perfection, despite the fact that Connor easily trounced him in the lists. Struan had been lax is all. Since then, she'd seen him training with Andrew and Michael every day.

She tidied up after herself and stopped in her room to grab the bag holding a towel, dry undergarments and Struan's old T-shirt to wear over her swimming garment. Then she checked the clock before hurrying downstairs and out the front door to wait.

The sun sent fingers of light reaching over the hills, and the day already held a haze of humidity and a hint of the searing heat to come. Another thing she was not used to. Fog hovered just above the treetops bordering the fields, and the grass before her sparkled with droplets of dew, like rare jewels reflecting the early morning light.

The sound of Struan's approaching truck brought a smile to her face. She hoisted the straps of the canvas bag to her shoulder, took a deep, pine-scented breath and walked toward the driveway just as he pulled in. He hopped out, and her insides fluttered at the sight of him.

"Good morning," he said, his blue eyes sparkling. The tight T-shirt he wore emphasized the sculpted muscles of his torso and the broadness of his shoulders. "Are you looking forward to the hot springs as much as I am?"

"I am." She nodded. He took her bag from her and opened the passenger door. Once she was settled, he placed her bag in the backseat next to his. She caught his scent, purely masculine, hot and slightly musky, and her blood heated. She wanted to lean close, take in his essence.

He climbed in and turned up the fan, sending a blast of cold air through the vents, and backed out of the driveway. "My friend manages the two bathhouses at the spa, and he's opening up one of the bathhouses for us before the facility opens. If we went during normal hours, you'd have to go to the women's bathhouse, and I'd have to go to the men's, because clothing is optional." He grinned at her. "Blake will meet us there to let us in, and we'll have an hour or so to ourselves before he returns to get the place ready for the first wave of guests."

"'Tis kind of your friend to do you this favor."

"We went to high school together, and I've done him a few favors myself over the years."

The road they were on wound around bends, up hills and down through the mountains. Occasionally the surrounding forest opened up to reveal spectacular vistas of rolling hills, which seemed to continue on forever. Sky wrapped her arms around herself, chilled by the blowing air.

"Sorry." Struan turned down the fan. "I showered, but I'm still overheated from my morning run."

"I really dinna mind the chill if you still need to cool yourself. I can close the vents on this side if need be."

"I'm good." He turned onto a gravel road. "We're close to the springs, princess." He sent her a boyish grin. "You're going to love this. The men's bathhouse is the oldest spa in the nation, harking back to 1761."

"Hmm, that hardly seems old, since I was born in the year of our Lord 1423," she murmured. 'Twas his boyish grin and his enthusiasm about sharing the experience with her that she loved.

"That's too weird to think about." He shot her a wry look. "That makes me, what, one hundred four years older than you, since I was born in 1319, but I've only been alive for twenty-four of those years."

She giggled. "If we go by the year of my birth, I'm nearly six hundred years old, yet I'm not quite one and twenty."

Struan turned onto a gravel road and drove for a short while, and signs for the Jefferson Pools Hot Springs Spa began to appear. Soon, a cluster of unimpressive buildings appeared, huddled together in the midst of a field. They turned onto a shorter lane leading right up to the complex. One of the structures was circular in shape with two tiered levels. Another was rectangular, resembling a cottage where someone might live, with a broad porch in front, and the last was also rounded, but with flat sides.

A lone car was parked in front of the cottage-like structure, and a young man stepped out as they drove near. He waved, and Struan waved back as he pulled his truck beside the other car.

Again she found herself awash in Struan's excitement. He grabbed their bags from the backseat and hopped out. She climbed down and circled around to where he stood with his friend. Blake's curiosity and speculation surged toward her.

"Blake, this is Sky MacKintosh. Sky, this is my friend Blake Johannes."

Struan's broad smile, his happiness, brought forth an answering smile. "'Tis a pleasure to make your acquaintance, Blake."

Blake leaned against his car with his arms folded in front of him. His brow lifted, and amusement filled his warm brown eyes. "'Tis a pleasure to make yours as well," he said in a teasing tone. "Where'd you find her, Struan? At one of those Renaissance festivals where you play medieval knight?"

"Exactly." Struan cocked an eyebrow. "She fell into my path, and I picked her right up and kept her. Finders keepers, losers weepers."

Finders keepers, losers weepers? What could he possibly mean by such a ridiculous statement?

"Mmm." Blake's studied her, his eyes lit with interest. "Might have to start hanging out at Renaissance festivals."

Struan grunted. "Good luck, buddy. You're not likely to find anyone there like Sky. She's one of a kind." He slung his arm around her shoulders and pulled her close to his side.

"Ah, well." Blake winked at her. "If you get tired of this lug, you come find me, Sky. OK?"

"Not going to happen," Struan said, tightening his hold around her shoulders. "Which pool do you want us to use?"

Blake pointed. "I've unlocked the women's bathhouse for you. Go on in and have a soak. I'll be back around nine."

"Thank you, Blake," Sky said. The air was redolent with the scent of rotten eggs. Sulfur, her mother had explained once. She'd smelled the same whilst she and her family traveled near a hot spring on their way to visit Aunt Elaine. Because of spring flooding, they'd been forced to take a more difficult route through a mountain pass on Sutherland land. She glanced at Struan. Mayhap now that they'd become closer, he'd be willing to share more about his kin.

Struan shook Blake's hand. "I owe you."

"You do," Blake quipped. "Since you already have yours, next time you're at a fair and a beautiful woman falls at your feet, toss her my way."

"I'll see what I can do." Struan laughed. "But don't hold your breath."

Blake grinned, circled around to the driver's side of his car and climbed in. Struan waited until his friend drove away before ushering her toward the women's bathhouse with his arm still around her shoulders.

They entered the large, round building, and Sky found the inside as in need of maintenance as the outside of the weathered complex. All around the inside wall, curtained stalls were set up for changing. The steaming water at the center was clear enough to see the stones at the bottom. And every few seconds, bubbles rose to burst through to the surface. The air inside was heavy with steamy, sulfur-tinged moisture.

"Go change, Sky." Struan released her and set their bags on the narrow planks edging the water. "I'll wait." He took off his shirt.

She would go into a stall to remove her outer garments, if she could only tear her eyes from him. He had a fine dusting of dark-blond hair on his sculpted chest, which narrowed into a path leading down to the waistband of his shorts. She had to force herself *not* to reach out and touch.

She raised her eyes and found him watching her intently. Did he stand a little straighter and flex his muscles for her benefit? *He did!* Their gazes met and held, and the ability to think deserted her.

"You plan to stand there ogling me all morning?" His gaze smoldered into hers.

"Well . . . I . . ." She frowned. She'd never before heard the word *ogling*, but 'twas clear enough what he meant. He'd caught her staring at his very fine form. Lifting her chin, she turned on her heel and strode to the nearest stall, pulling the curtain shut behind her. Holding her palms to her flaming cheeks, she realized she'd forgotten her bag.

"Do you need anything in this tote, princess?" Struan called out smugly.

"No," she snapped. But she did. She wanted the long T-shirt to wear over her suit. She bit her lip. If he could stand half-naked before her, surely she could walk out of the tiny stall in her swimming garment to fetch the T-shirt. Grumbling under her breath, she toed off her sneakers and slid out of her jeans, setting them on the wooden bench before lifting her blouse off over her head.

Not since she'd been a bairn, splashing about in Loch Moigh with her siblings, had she exposed herself so to anyone. Damnation, she was a MacKintosh. Straightening her posture, she swatted the curtain aside and forced herself to walk as if she hadn't a care in the world. Still, she couldn't look Struan's way, nor could she hide the color filling her cheeks.

His sudden intake of breath drew her attention. His eyes darkened, and his mouth opened slightly as if he meant to say something but forgot how to form the words. He stared, his gaze roaming slowly over her from head to toe. Sky moved to her bag, pulled out the white T-shirt with a sports logo printed across the front and tugged it over her head.

"Hey, that's mine," he rasped out.

"So? Lindsay said you left it behind. She gave it to me to use as a cover-up."

He grinned wolfishly. "It won't help."

"I dinna ken what you mean. Are we going to bathe in the pool, or do you plan on *ogling* me all morning?"

"I plan to get into the pool *and* ogle you simultaneously. The water is crystal clear, and I'm an oddity, a rare species of multitasking male."

Laughter burst forth, and her embarrassment evaporated. For certes, she planned to do the very same—look her fill and soak in the mineral water.

Struan climbed down one of the rickety ladders into the pool. "Should you slip and fall as you enter, I'll be right here to catch you, my lady." He flashed her a boyish grin.

Her pulse raced. Was he inviting her to fall into his arms? "Such chivalry," she muttered. For all her thoughts of seducing Struan, she lacked the courage, or mayhap the skill. The importance of her virtue and rank had been hammered into her since she'd been a bairn, after all.

Carefully, she stepped on the first rung of the ladder and descended into the hot water. At the bottom rung, she pushed herself off to float on her back. "Och, 'tis like bathwater." The occasional bubble rose from the stones beneath to tickle her backside.

Struan swam to her and stretched out to float by her side. "Relaxing, isn't it? Just what I need for my aching muscles."

"I have noticed you've been at the lists every day. What compels you so? There is no need, since you will no' be returning to the past with me and the McGladreys."

"I'm competitive. I want to be in better shape once Connor returns." He grunted. "I can't stand the idea that a man in his fifties beat me so easily. My da would never have let me hear the end of such a defeat."

He'd given her the perfect opening. "Tell me about your sire. Did you have siblings?"

"My da was a good man and strong. We were close." His voice wavered a bit. "I had two half brothers and a half sister. I never knew my mother. She died in childbirth with me."

"I am sorry you lost your mother, Struan." Sky stopped floating and turned toward him whilst treading water. "Who was your sire to the Sutherlands? I only ask because, as I mentioned before, you resemble the earl of Sutherland who is kin to me most remarkably, and his brothers as well. If you were to stand amongst the Sutherlands of my time, anyone who saw you together would believe you to be another brother."

"What difference does it make who my father was, or my half siblings for that matter?" he snapped. "They're all long gone, and who I am today has nothing to do with them."

She'd touched upon an open wound, and her heart turned over at the roiling emotions emanating from him. Her curiosity only grew stronger at his refusal to open up to her. What was it in his past that still plagued him so? "Talking about your kin might ease the ache. I sense a deep hurt within you whenever I bring them up. Mayhap—"

"Let it be, princess." He came toward her, and she soon found herself buoyed in his arms. "What do you think of the hot spring?"

"Very relaxing. Pleasant." She searched his face, looking for some clue as to why he hid his past from her. He didn't trust her, and that hurt.

He kissed her lightly. "Let the past stay in the past. You're with me in the here and now. Can't we just relax and have a good time?" He waggled his eyebrows. "I'm even willing to help you do just that."

"How so?" Best not press him. Mayhap at some point, he'd trust her enough to share his troubled past with her.

"Like this." He kissed her again, this time teasing her lower lip with his teeth. She sighed, mingling her breath with his. Tentatively, she touched her tongue to the seam of his mouth. He groaned, slanted her head and accepted her invitation, plunging his tongue in to tangle with hers. The evidence of his desire pressed against her belly, and need spiraled through her.

"You don't need the T-shirt," he whispered. "Now that it's wet, I can see right through it anyway."

She backed out of his arms and looked down. The fabric clung to her, and the cotton did little in the way of covering her. He chuckled deep in his throat, sending shivers down her spine.

"Here, let me help." Struan reached below the surface of the water and tugged the sodden fabric up. Sky raised her arms. He lifted the T-shirt over her head and tossed it to the ledge surrounding the pool, where it landed with a resounding splat. Then he pulled her close again. "Do you have any idea how breathtakingly beautiful you are?"

She shook her head. All she could do was stare at him, losing herself in the deep blue of his eyes. She studied his face, taking note of the darker blond stubble covering his cheeks and chin. Her perusal came to rest on his generous mouth.

"I'm having trouble treading water while wanting to kiss you like I do." He kicked harder, propelling them toward one of the many ladders. "Let's get out and dangle our feet in the pool."

"If you wish," she managed to reply.

"I do wish," he said, his voice hoarse. He placed her on the lowest rung of the ladder and followed her up.

As soon as they were out of the pool, Struan settled himself on the wooden slats and tugged her down beside him. Once again he held her close and his mouth sought hers, and she melted against him. His hand rose along her waist, brushing the bottom of her breast. A riot of sensual pleasure exploded within her, shooting downward toward the apex of her thighs.

Struan broke the kiss to peer intently at her. "What will you do if you can't get back, Sky?"

"I . . ." She cleared her throat, attempting to eliminate the quaver in her voice. "I *will* get back."

"But if you can't," he said, his mouth a heartbeat away from hers, "stay here. Stay in Gordon Hollow with me." He kissed her again, his tongue sliding around hers before he pulled back again. "Obviously there's something between us. If you stayed, we could get to know each other better and see where it leads, aye?"

Reading the hope and vulnerability in his request nearly broke her heart. She forced herself to move away from him and struggled to regain control over her passion. "I canna stay, Struan. I have a responsibility, an obligation to protect my family. How could I live with myself if my disappearance should lead to their demise?" She shook her head and wrapped her arms around herself.

"I wish things were different, but I must get back to my time. I have to at least attempt to avert disaster. What . . . what if Oliver forces my younger sister to become his ill-fated bride in my stead? She's already there in his keep. 'Twould be all too easy to force my father's compliance."

"Humph. Have you so little confidence in your father that you think him unable to defend his family without your help? You said yourself your ma and siblings sometimes have visions when your clan is in danger. Think you they have not already *been* warned?"

None of those possibilities had occurred to her, but even so, what if the Erskines imprisoned them whilst they were still at Kildrummy? What good would visions or fae abilities do her family then? "'Tis no' enough. So much could happen. If they're still with the Erskines, far from home and separated from our allies, they are vulnerable. How will visions help if they're already being held deep in the pit of our enemy's keep?"

Struan growled and raked his fingers through his damp hair. "OK, let's say you aren't able to find an open passage through time on your trip to Scotland. Then what? Do you plan to spend decades trying to get back? Will you waste the rest of your life in pursuit of that goal until you're old and gray?" His gaze bored into hers. "Fate brought you here, princess. Chances are good you'll remain here—that you're meant to live out the rest of your life in this era. Have you thought of that?"

"Nay, Struan." She shook her head. 'Twas no' fate that brought me here."

"We're going to have to agree to disagree on that point." He reached for her hand, gripping it tightly in his. "If it would put your mind at ease, we can research what became of your kin. Your sire is an earl. Surely we'll find plenty written about him and your family."

She shook her head again, and a tear slid down her cheek. "You dinna understand."

"Nay. 'Tis *you* who dinna understand," he snapped. "You refuse to see the obvious." He let go of her hand and shot up. Stomping over to where their bags sat upon the planks, he grabbed them both. "Let's change and go have breakfast. I'm starving."

He dropped her bag beside her and disappeared into one of the changing stalls. Swallowing against the tightness in her throat, Sky stared after him. Their morning together was ruined, and all the good feelings she'd held but a few moments ago were caught in an impasse between them.

Images flashed through her mind, her dear sister, gaunt, thirsting, being starved to death in the Erskines' dungeon. Her mother, in much the same state, weeping over the murder of her beloved husband. Though they weren't visions, they were possibilities. She kent well enough what could happen, and she had to intervene.

Struan couldn't understand the ties that bound her. Despite what he believed, she had no choice but to return.

CHAPTER TEN

Triumph flared as Struan drove Connor McGladrey back with yet another series of offensive blows. Inch by inch he gained ground against his nemesis. Connor grunted with effort, and sweat dripped down his face. Struan smirked. He'd finally reached the point where he'd forced Connor to break a sweat and retreat. He let loose a raucous laugh.

"Enough," Connor cried, dropping the tip of his sword into the hard-packed clay of the Gordons' lists. "Well done, laddie. You gave this *old man* a grand workout. You've come far since that first time we trained together."

"Thank you." Struan bowed slightly. The McGladreys had returned to Gordon Hollow three weeks ago, the same day Sky's picture ID had arrived in the mail. Since their return, Struan had spent all his spare time running, training and improving his skill. Grinding, but well worth the effort if for no other reason than to be able to claim a single victory over the master swordsman panting before him.

His respect for Connor had grown. Not only was the older man excellent at training, but Connor also proved himself to be fair, honorable and even humorous at times. "I'm grateful to you for teaching me a few new tricks," Struan conceded. Lucky for him, the animosity he'd suffered at the hands of his stepbrothers had forced him to become a fast learner. His skill had improved by leaps and bounds under Connor's brutal tutelage.

He waved toward Gene and Marjorie's house. "Let's go have some breakfast. Trouncing you has given me an appetite, and Lindsay said she's trying out a new recipe for baked French toast this morning. She wants taste testers." He lifted his nose into the air and sniffed. "Mmm. I can smell it from here."

"You just want to strut about the kitchen and crow over your victory," Connor teased, wiping the sweat from his eyes with his shirt sleeve.

"That's definitely a perk." Struan grinned. Sky sometimes watched him work out. Hopefully, she'd witnessed today's performance.

"Have you given any thought to coming with us to Scotland, laddie?"

And . . . here it is. His gut twisted. As he'd expected, Connor meant to pressure him into turning hero and joining them on their mission. "I've thought of nothing else."

"The odds of being able to travel to and from are in our favor, what with the map of portals Katherine and I have made. And don't forget, the MacKintosh have ties with the fae, especially to Áine. Sky says Áine has her own cottage near baron DúnConnell's keep, and she's a frequent visitor to our son-in-law's hall. I'm confident she'll aid us if need be."

Struan replied with a grunt of skepticism. "I want to read some of the histories you've gathered about folks disappearing and reappearing, especially those you collected about Scotland." Going back and forth through time couldn't be as easy as Connor wished to believe. Struan started out for the back patio doors, and Connor took up a position beside him.

"All right. I'll give them to you today. I could use another sword arm by my side, laddie. We don't know what we'll be facing once we reach the past, especially if we use the same portal in Scotland where Sky came through."

"Sure enough you'll be facing more peril than you bargained for," Struan grumbled. "That's just the way things were back then, and it makes no difference where you land. It's foolhardy to even attempt such a thing." He stopped walking. "What if you end up in the middle of a village market? Suddenly popping out of thin air is a sure way to be seen as a demon from hell. I see stakes and a large bonfire in your future."

"According to our research—"

"Damn your research," he bit out. "The only thing you can count on is a total lack of control over anything that happens once you step through that accursed wavering light show. You *should* be helping me talk Sky into staying where she is, not encouraging her to place herself in the hands of her enemy. Keeping her here is the best way to protect her."

"I'm disappointed, laddie," Connor told him.

"It's not about you." Struan glared. "I care about Sky, and going back to 1443 is *not* in her best interest." He did care about her, and unfortunately for him, the more time he spent with her, the deeper his feelings ran, making his decision all the more difficult. Plus, the more he felt for her, the more he wanted her. Which made no sense at all, since what drew him to her was also what drove him batty.

Her loyalty to her clan and kin, the way she loved her family uncon-ditionally—despite the fact they'd bartered her off to a black-hearted scumbag—her obstinacy, wit, quiet strength, even her willingness to sacrifice her own safety for the sake of others. The very qualities that had her stubbornly refusing to see the futility of her insane plan were the characteristics that called to him the most.

She embodied everything he'd ever hoped for in a woman, and letting her go would tear him apart. Yep. His desperation and indecision increased tenfold each day they waited for Sky's passport to arrive.

Struan started walking again. He wasn't about to tell Connor or Sky that he'd already done the research on her kin. The outcome of the feud that had indeed ensued between the Erskines and the MacKintosh clan was not good. A lot of blood was spilled, and innocent lives were lost. But Sky's return wouldn't guarantee things would turn out any better.

All the accounts he'd read dealt mostly with the earls and the men on either side who'd lost their lives. At least he knew the earl of Mar had been stripped of his title and evicted from Kildrummy. Unfortunately, too many common folk had lost their homes as well. Still, the best part was learning that Sky's betrothed hadn't survived.

Though he'd searched, Struan hadn't been able to find a single word written about Sky, and he didn't know what to make of that. Barely a line had been added alluding to the fact that it had been a second broken betrothal contract on the part of the MacKintosh that had caused the clash.

Struan suffered a spasm of guilt over yet another sin of omission against the woman who had laid siege to his heart. He shook it off. After all, Connor might have already done his own look-see through the history books, and nothing was stopping Sky from doing the same if she wished. It wasn't like he'd hidden all the computers and purposefully kept anything from her.

"You say you've thought of nothing else," Connor said, bringing Struan out of his own thoughts. "Am I correct in assuming you have not yet reached a decision?"

"As far as I'm concerned, heroism is like driving in the fast lane to an early grave, and I have no wish to exceed that particular speed limit," he muttered under his breath. They'd reached the patio doors, and the wonderful scent of bacon and egg-rich cinnamon French toast had his taste buds standing at attention. He and Connor set their weapons against the wall.

Struan reached for the sliding door. "Take it as I meant it. The thought of letting Sky go without me is torture; the thought of going back through time is torture. I'm beginning to develop a complex, so *don't* ask me again what I'm going to do. I won't know until I'm forced to make a decision." He slid the door open with a little too much muscle.

Connor clamped his hand on Struan's shoulder for an instant. "Fair enough. I'll not ask you again."

Struan entered the kitchen to find Sky helping Lindsay put breakfast on the table. When their gazes met and she smiled, the unmistakable pride shining from her eyes sent his heart soaring. She'd watched him defeat Connor, all right. He straightened his posture and grinned back. "Smells good in here. Are Gene and Michael joining us, or have they already left for the fair?"

"They left, but don't worry. I made two batches of French toast." Lindsay opened the oven door. "I fed them my first attempt at the pecan praline yumminess. Mom and Katherine will be down in a minute. Katherine is showing Mom her medieval clothing and they're swapping sewing tips."

The Morlandshire Renaissance Fair in Pennsylvania had begun, and knowing Sky's time in his century was limited, Struan had begged his way out of performing that weekend. Luckily, Andrew had stepped up to take his place, claiming he and his wife could use the extra money to take a vacation somewhere warm and sunny over the winter.

"Lindsay, do you have a printer here I might use?" Connor poured two mugs of coffee and handed one to Struan.

"Sure. It's in the corner of the family room. Help yourself."

"Thanks." Connor turned to him. "I'll print the stories for you right after breakfast."

"Good. I'll take a look at them later." Struan took a seat and glanced at Sky and Lindsay. "Speaking of later, are you two interested in riding this afternoon after I close up the forge?"

"I'd love to." Sky did that shy half-smile thing that never failed to send his pulse racing. She placed a platter of bacon and a bowl of fresh fruit on the table before sitting beside him.

"I can't." Lindsay b3rought the steaming pan of baked French toast and a pitcher of syrup to the table. "One of our cooks is sick, and I've been called in to work tonight."

"Oh, too bad." Struan stifled his glee. Lindsay's absence meant he'd be alone with Sky, and he knew exactly where he wanted to take her. In fact, he'd bring Connor's stories with them, and they could read through the collection together.

Today might be the day he'd finally convince her of the futility of attempting such a feat. The longer she stayed, the more determined he became to persuade her to make Gordon Hollow her permanent home. More than anything, he wanted to see where these feelings between them might lead.

At the peak of the trail leading to the Gordons' lake, Struan reined in his horse. He waited for Sky to ride up beside him. The section of trail they'd just passed through was too rocky and narrow to ride abreast, but once they reached the crest, the trail widened. Late afternoon sun hit the water, sparkling like gold dust across the surface of the spring-fed caldera below.

Varying shades of green and a cloudless blue sky framed the idyllic scene below. A hawk, its wings outstretched, called out as it caught a thermal draft and rode the wind. Struan's soul settled as it always did in this place.

"'Tis such a lovely view," Sky said softly. "And so tranquil."

"It is. This is one of my favorite places to be when I need to think or just to relax," he said. Large boulders surrounded the lakeshore, put there by some long-ago volcanic eruption. Struan nudged his mount forward down the well-worn trail to the area Gordons generations past had cleared for their recreational use.

Since there were no roads to accommodate trucks or cars, he, Gene, and Ethan had built a small split-rail paddock in the shade for the horses. Struan dismounted, handed his reins to Sky and walked to the paddock to slide open the rails of the makeshift gate. Once the horses were inside, he took out the blanket from his backpack and handed it to her. "Find a nice grassy spot to spread this out, and I'll remove the horses' bridles so they can graze."

She took the blanket from him. "We should have worn our suits for swimming under our clothes. 'Tis a lovely afternoon."

"Swimsuits." He glanced at her just in time to see the glint of amusement in her eyes.

"That's exactly what I said," she teased with another sexy smile.

A surge of heat hit him, and blood rushed to his groin. Oh, how he longed to get her naked, take that next step toward deepening their relationship. "Ever heard of skinny-dipping?"

"Nay. What does it mean?"

"It means we don't need swimsuits. We can swim naked."

Color rose to her cheeks, and she blinked a few times before turning and walking away without a word. He'd give his best suit of armor to hear what was going through her mind right now. Chuckling under his breath, he took off his gelding's bridle, then moved to do the same for Sky's mount.

Struan closed the gate and slung his backpack over a shoulder before heading for the stubborn woman to plead his case yet again. His breath caught at the sight of her. She leaned back on the blanket with her legs outstretched. Her skin was dappled with sunlight, and a smile lit her pretty face.

He sat beside her, and she turned to glance at him through her lashes. His beleaguered heart tripped and tumbled, and need played havoc with his senses. If he kept Connor's reports to himself, perhaps things between him and Sky would progress, and this would be the day that they made love for the first time.

The lake was secluded and surrounded by a thick forest of evergreens. The air smelled clean and sweet, piney. Making love with Sky here would create a memory to savor for the rest of their lives—for his life anyway.

On the other hand, if he presented her with yet more evidence supporting his belief that she was meant to stay in this century, they'd end up arguing. Struan shifted, trying to relieve the growing discomfort in his lap. *What to do? What to do? Keep my mouth shut, or press her to see things my way and ruin a perfect afternoon?*

He had to do the right thing, of course, and making her his when they weren't on the same page about the future definitely reeked of selfishness—especially if she somehow managed to make it home. She'd been raised in an era when a woman's virtue was all she owned. Taking her virginity would ruin her, and he couldn't bear the thought of causing her that kind of hurt.

Damn his chivalrous hide. He swallowed the regret and turned to her. "I brought along some of the research Connor printed off for me. I thought we could go through a few of the stories, see what we can learn."

Her brow rose, and she peered at him over her shoulder. "Doing so willna change my mind."

"I figured as much, but it might help you to prepare."

Sighing, she sat up. "All right. Let us see what the McGladreys have uncovered."

He sighed too, but for an altogether different reason. Sometimes, doing the right thing sucked. He pulled the papers out of his backpack, along with a couple bottles of water. He handed her a bottle and half the pile of Connor's research. For the next half hour, they both read, trading sheets back and forth until they'd read them all.

"You know what I'm noticing?" Struan bumped his shoulder against Sky's. "More often than not, decades pass between reported incidents where people disappear or appear. In this case"—he waved the paper he held—"nearly a century passed."

"Aye, but 'tis no' like anyone in these accounts went looking for open corridors through time." Sky waved her sheet of paper in response. "These are but records of folk who accidentally stumbled through time. They did so unawares, whilst I am purposefully seeking a way back. 'Tis a different matter altogether."

"Sure, sure," he said, doing his best to appear as if he were seriously considering her argument. "Still, you might get to the spot in Scotland, and nothing will happen. How long are you willing to wait?"

"Struan . . ." Her mouth tightened.

"All right, look." He took the stories from her hand and set the entire stack aside. "I admit it. I'm not going to stop trying to talk you into staying." The need to protect her had gone far beyond "want," and had slid into "imperative" some time ago, but he kept that to himself. "It's not safe to return, and above all, I want you to remain safe."

The moment the words were out, he made a decision. He would travel with her to Scotland, stay by her side and be there to support her when the inevitable letdown occurred. Reading through the tales of disappearances and reappearances only reinforced his beliefs. Despite what Connor thought, the odds were in *his* favor, not theirs. Portals didn't simply open or close because mortals wished them to. They'd go, wait and watch, and most likely nothing would happen. Then he'd bring Sky home to Gordon Hollow to stay.

"Life would be so much easier if you just gave in, Sky. What we have together is good, isn't it? If you stay, I believe things between us will only get better." She opened her mouth to respond, and before she could argue, he drew her close and kissed her. She was so very sweet and soft in his arms, his heart melted. Stretching out on the blanket, he brought her down on top of him.

"Struan . . ." She pushed herself away and sat up. "I must return. We've been over this a hundred times, and you canna distract me to your way of thinking with kisses."

A shame, that, because kissing her was his favorite distraction strategy thus far. "I can be every bit as obstinate, princess. I won't stop trying to convince you, because your future is at stake. So many things can go wrong. What about us? Don't we owe it to each other to see this thing through?"

"I . . . we," she stammered.

He folded his arms under his head and frowned up at her. "I? We?"

She stared out over the water. "Let's no' argue. 'Tis too fine a day."

"OK." He reached out and ran his hand down her bare arm. "What do you wish to do this fine afternoon? Skinny-dip?"

Her gaze darted to him and quickly returned to the lake. "I've something else in mind." She slid her hand into the back pocket of her shorts and drew something out. Taking his hand in hers, she placed whatever it was on his palm and closed his fingers over it. Struan sat up, opened his hand and stared at the small foil packet. His jaw dropped. "Do you have any idea what this is?"

"Aye, 'tis a condom." She studied the foil packet in her hands. "Lindsay explained what they are and how to use them."

His mind scattered in a dozen directions at once, the excitement, consternation and confusion making him dizzy. She wanted to have sex with him. Just as he wrapped his mind around *that* possibility, he wondered how she'd gotten her hands on a condom.

"You . . ." His voice came out an octave higher than usual. He cleared his throat. "You talked to my *sister* about having *sex* with me?" Blood that had been surging south suddenly changed direction and crept up to heat his face. "Wait. Lindsay has condoms? I didn't even know she was dating anyone. Who's she sleeping with? Not Brian, surely."

Sky giggled. "I found the box of condoms in the cabinet of the bathroom she and I share, and I asked her what they were. I did no' ask her about her personal life, nor did I share my intentions with her."

"And then you *stole* one?" His brow rose nearly to his hairline.

"Nay." Sky slid her hand into her back pocket again, a wicked glint in her eyes. She dropped two more condoms onto his lap. "I stole three."

"Woman . . ." Struan flopped back onto the blanket and scrubbed his hands over his face. "Augh, what were you thinking? If we do . . . this, you'll be ruined."

"I am thinking that once I return home, I will never wed. I refuse to be handed off again in barter for an alliance or political gain." Her voice hitched. "I dinna wish to go through life without ever having experienced—"

"Sky, this will change everything between us. If we make love, you're mine and I'm yours. I'm not a one-night-stand kind of guy." He gestured between them. "This *means* something to me. *You* mean something to me."

She nodded, and her chin quivered. "As you mean something to me. I'll never give my heart or my body to another."

Wait. Did that mean that she'd already given him her heart? Pressure banded his chest, and damn if his eyes didn't sting. He drew her down to lie beside him and wrapped her up in his arms. Her arms came around him, and the two of them stayed motionless and silent for several moments. He made a last-ditch effort to think, even though thinking was the last thing he wanted to do. Taking in the flowery scent of the shampoo she used, mixed with her own unique essence, her warmth and curves plastered against him, he struggled for control. For both their sakes, someone had to be rational.

"I want you," she whispered. "Don't you want me?"

He choked out a strangled laugh. "Do I want you?" He tilted his head down to peer into her hazel eyes. "No matter how oft I drink you in, you are a thirst within me that will never be quenched. That's how badly I want you," he croaked.

"Well then," she said, rising to support herself on her elbows. "Make love to me."

With that, her lips met his, and rational thought deserted him. He wanted to meld into her, fusing their bodies and souls. He gave up the struggle for control and held her against his heart. She'd offered him a free pass to paradise—who was he to refuse?

He took over, dominating her and deepening the kiss until they had to separate in order to take off their shirts. Desperate to feel her silky skin next to his, he brought her back into his arms, and discovered his erotic imaginings had not done her justice. Her bare skin against his sent him reeling. He unfastened her bra and drew it off. He rolled with her, so that he was now on top of her.

Struan raised himself to stare at the vision beneath him. She was the embodiment of perfection. Her generous breasts were crowned in dusky rose, and her beautiful eyes were hazed with desire. Color bloomed in her cheeks under his perusal. He leaned in and ran his tongue over one of her glorious nipples, and it hardened immediately. Sky gasped, and the sound went straight to his already throbbing member. "So lovely," he whispered, before taking the hardened bud between his teeth.

Sky's hips rose to press against him, inciting him further. "Sky, I want to look at you—all of you. May I?"

"Only if I might look at you as well," she whispered.

"Done. I'll even go first." Struan rolled to his back and stripped out of his clothes in record time. Sky's nervous giggle, her tentative touch running over his chest and lower, sent waves of desire pulsing through him. He drew a long, steadying breath. He needed to take things slow, be gentle. Her first time would hurt, and he wanted to bring her pleasure. Capturing her wandering hand, he pressed a kiss against her fingertips. "Now you."

Sky sat up and took off her shoes, her lower lip tucked between her lips, and an expression of consternation suffused her features. "I've never . . . this is no' as easy as I imagined. I'm embarrassed." That last part came out in a barely audible whisper.

"Don't be. You've no reason to be embarrassed." He ran a knuckle down her cheek. "You are a vision, princess. In my eyes you are beyond compare."

"Think you?" Her gaze met his for a fleeting moment before she turned away again.

The vulnerability he'd glimpsed and the telltale quiver in her voice brought his rational self front and center. He reached for her, brought her to his lap and brushed a kiss across her forehead. "We don't have to do this today, love. Mayhap you're not as ready for the next step as you might think, aye?" He undid the tie holding her braid and plied his fingers to the task of unraveling her lustrous hair.

"But I . . . I want to. 'Tis shyness—no' a change of heart that stays my hand." She shrugged one shoulder. "I made up my mind weeks ago that I would seduce you."

He laughed. "Did you?"

She nodded, and again her fleeting glance caused a wrench in his chest. "How did you intend to go about seducing me, my sweet?"

"Well . . . I hadn't gotten that far in my thinking." Color flooded her cheeks, and she bit her lower lip again. "You see, I rather counted on your cooperation to . . . to move things along."

"Ah, I see. How can it be construed as seduction if you meant for me to do all the work?"

"That hadn't occurred to me."

"Hmm, I've half a mind to thwart your plans. However, since I am such a generous man, I've an idea."

"Aye? And what might that be?" Her chin rose, and her natural assertiveness was once again firmly in place.

"I will lie here on this blanket, naked as the day I was born, and you have my permission to do with me as you will."

She shot him a wry grin. "How very generous you are."

"Don't forget chivalrous."

Laughing, Sky pushed him down. "Chivalrous indeed. I accept your terms, for they please me." She moved to sit by his side, her gaze roaming over him in a slow, hot glide. "I love the way your muscles sculpt your chest. You are without compare as well, the most comely man I've ever laid eyes upon."

"Have you seen scads of men naked?" He cocked a brow in question.

"Nay, other than my brothers when they were wee lads, you are the first."

Was it too much to wish he'd be her *only*? Her hands traced his pectorals, circling his nipples. She ran her fingertips downward, her touch feathery and light. Struan held his breath, and the muscles beneath his skin rippled at her touch. "Lord have mercy, you will be the death of me."

"Nay, I vow I willna."

Continuing her exploration, she ran her hand over him from balls to head, and he couldn't prevent himself from thrusting his hips against her palm. He groaned and shut his eyes. Sweet torture.

"I want to lie on top of you," she said before circling her tongue around his erect nipple.

"OK," he managed to rasp out. "Sounds like a good idea to me." Watching her get out of the rest of her clothes almost snapped the wee bit of control he clung to. She needed to be in charge if she was to overcome her shyness, and he wanted that for her. Sky draped her naked self over him. Her breasts pressed against his chest, and her pelvis was snug against his erection. "Now what?" he asked through his clenched jaw.

"I believe I'd like to kiss you."

"Sound thinking." He grinned. "A logical next step." Her kiss started out hesitant, but as he kissed her back, she grew bolder. Her tongue entered his mouth to touch the tip of his.

She lifted herself to stare down at him. "You *can* use your hands, Struan. If you were the one doing the seducing this day, I'd surely be using mine."

"Thank God," he said on a moan. He stroked and explored her curves, discovering every delectable feminine charm she possessed. Her thick hair blanketed the both of them, creating an intimate veil of privacy. Instinct took over, and he rolled them over so that they were side by side. "I want to touch you here," he whispered, pressing his hand against her mons. "May I?"

Her eyes filled with trust and desire, she nodded.

He took one of her nipples into his mouth and suckled as he dipped a finger into her slick heat. He circled her clit with his thumb while his fingers continued to tease and thrust. She writhed, lifting her hips and groaning. He increased the pressure and laved each of her breasts with his tongue, sucking, biting. She tensed in his arms, her breaths coming out in puffs, and then she spasmed around his fingers and clutched his shoulders.

Sky sighed and pulled his face to her for a kiss. Her tongue tangled with his for a moment, before she issued a command: "I want you inside of me, Struan."

He ached for the very same thing. His cock twitched and strained in response. He was as hard as granite as he searched the blanket for a condom. He found one and tore it open. Sky sat up and watched as he sheathed himself. "Your first time is going to be . . . uncomfortable, love."

"I ken as much. My mother was always open and honest in sharing information with us. She told me what to expect."

Her glorious hair cascaded around her shoulders, and spots of sunlight peeking through the leaves brought out the deep brownish-red highlights. Her lazy, satisfied smile pleased him to no end. He'd put that expression on her face. Struan drew her close and brought them both down to the blanket. He kissed and fondled her until once again she moved mindlessly against him, caught in the throes of renewed passion. Moving on top of her, he nudged her thighs apart with his knees. She opened herself to him, and his heart nearly burst. Taking himself in hand, he rubbed the head against her opening until she moaned. Slowly, in small increments, he entered her until he met with resistance.

"I don't want to hurt you," he said, helpless to keep himself from thrusting slightly.

"The pain will only last a few seconds." She ran her hands down his back to his buttocks. "Come to me, Struan."

He raised himself, watching her for any sign of distress, and gave a single strong thrust, seating himself fully inside her. She winced, but then her eyes met his, and her expression filled with wonder. He intended to give her a few seconds to recover, but she moved beneath him. "Starting the party without me, lass?"

With a slight smile, she nodded and rocked against him again. Her eyes closed and her mouth opened slightly. He'd never seen anything so erotic in his life. He leaned close to capture her moan in his mouth, and let nature take over. They fit perfectly, and the way she responded drove him mad. He tried to keep it slow and gentle, but she didn't see things his way and demanded more.

Capitulating to his lady's wishes, he surrendered, thrusting into her again and again until they both lost control and toppled over the edge. One more strong thrust, and he came. She cried out and gripped him to her as she followed him into that place of pure sensation and communion.

He collapsed, careful to support the bulk of his weight with his forearms. Raining kisses all over her beloved face, he knew he was forever altered. His heart was now bound to hers, and it always would be. Somehow, he had to find a way to keep her by his side and safe. Everything in him cried out that she was his.

He swallowed the lump rising in his throat as it occurred to him that he'd never shared with her the truth about his origins. In the here and now, being illegitimate made no difference, but being raised as she'd been, in an era where one's nobility meant the difference between being served or serving, would revealing the truth about his bastardy tear them apart?

"That was amazing, Struan," she said on a sigh. "I'm most content."

"As am I, lass." He rolled onto his back beside her and stared at the sky. The way he saw it, his best bet was to pray the portal through time wouldn't open. If his luck held, he'd bring her home to stay. That way, he'd never have to tell her anything about his past, because they'd be focused on creating their future. Struan slid his arm around her shoulders and tucked her against his side. "Want to go skinny-dipping?"

She snuggled close, throwing her arm around his waist. "Mayhap in a while. Right now all I want is this, lying here beside you with your arms around me." She turned toward him, rested her head on his shoulder and draped her knee over his thigh.

He had to swallow yet another lump as he tightened his hold on the woman who held his future in her wee soft hands. She had no idea the power she wielded over him. Sky Elizabeth, the earl of Fife's eldest daughter, would either destroy him or make him the happiest bastard ever born. *Och, well.* He grinned. At the moment, completely sated and with Sky snuggled against his side, he was a very happy bastard indeed.

Monday evening, Struan strolled up the Gordons' driveway toward Gene. He, Andrew and Michael had arrived home a couple of hours ago, and knowing his foster father's habits, Struan knew he'd find him puttering with the camper, making sure everything was in order. Sure enough, Gene was circling the RV, kicking the tires and checking latches and valves as he went.

Struan watched the man who'd taken him in, given him a home and a family. He had to swallow a few times before he could speak. "Da," Struan called, the word slipping from his mouth. "Do you have a few minutes?"

"*Da* am I now?" Gene straightened. "Must be serious. Hold on a sec." He disappeared into the camper, emerging seconds later with a couple bottles of beer. He handed one to Struan. "Let's go sit out back and watch the moon rise."

Following along behind him, Struan went over in his mind what he wanted to say. How would he explain to the man who'd given him the family he'd never had that he was about to break his promise? Gene took a seat at the glass-topped patio table, and Struan followed suit.

"What's put that crease in your forehead? Woman troubles?"

Struan shrugged. "That's one way to put it." He took a swallow of beer and looked out over the valley. "I went through Connor's research, and I've come to a conclusion."

"Oh? And what's that?" Gene's grip tightened around his beer bottle.

"I'm convinced they're going to be disappointed. I believe their trip to Scotland is going to be a waste of time. Portals through time don't open on demand. The incidents I read about are sporadic and decades apart, and there's no way of telling when or where a corridor will open."

Gene raised his eyes to meet Struan's. "Why do I hear a 'but' in there?"

"Hmm, because . . ." He swallowed hard a few times.

"It's pretty clear to us you've fallen hard for the girl, son. Your mom and I figured things were heading in a particular direction where Sky is concerned. If I were in your shoes, I wouldn't be able to let the woman I love go off on her own, either. I'd want to stick by her side."

"I promised you I wouldn't leave, and I'm breaking that promise."

"I don't see it like that. Things change. When you said you didn't intend to go anywhere, Sky had just arrived. The two of you hardly knew each other. In fact, you two seemed at loggerheads with each other. Now your heart's involved. Am I right? Do you love her?"

He nodded mutely, affection for Gene, Marjorie and his siblings stealing his voice. It took a few seconds for him to find it again. "I'm counting on the fact that we won't be able to leave this century, but just in case I'm also going prepared."

"We've been damn lucky to . . ." Gene's voice broke. "To have you in our lives for as long as we have. Whatever happens, your mom and I want you to know how much we love you."

"I love all of you, too. I'll be back, Da. If I'm right, we won't go anywhere. If Connor is right, I'll be able to find a way back, and I hope to bring Sky with me. There's no mention of her in the history books about the feud between her clan and Erskines. I'm convinced it's because she's meant to be here with us."

"I hope you're right, son." Gene gripped Struan's forearm for a second. "I surely hope you're right. We'll look after your place and the livestock, and I'm certain Andrew will take care of the forge while you're away."

"Thank you," he said. "Not just for looking after the livestock and my house for me, but for everything. If it hadn't been for you and Marjorie, who knows what would have become of me. I owe you my life."

"Naw, you don't owe us a thing. This is your home, son. You've always pulled your weight and made us proud." Gene took a long pull on his beer. His expression turned inward, pensive. "I . . . know it. In my old bones, I feel you'll be back."

"I hope you're right." The two of them continued to sit on the patio, sipping their beers in companionable silence, watching the moon climb the surrounding mountains to light the sky. Things would be OK. Gene often knew things, had feelings about the future. If his da said he'd be back, he'd be back.

Struan's heart took a sudden drop as realization dawned—Gene hadn't included Sky in his forecast for the future.

CHAPTER ELEVEN

S ky began the task of folding the laundry she'd washed and dried earlier. Soon, stacks of sorted clothing surrounded her in neat piles on the coffee table and couch of the Gordons' family room. 'Twas a way to earn her keep in some small way, and with Gene and Michael home from the past weekend's fair, there had been quite a bit of laundry to do this Tuesday morning.

What would her fifteenth-century clan think of washing machines and dryers? She imagined the head laundress's delight with such labor-saving devices. Still, Moigh Hall employed several servants who did laundry and naught else. 'Twas for the best that they didn't have washing machines, for she wouldn't want to see those servants out of jobs.

"Sky," Struan called from the front door. "Are you here?"

Her insides fluttered at the sound of his voice. "Aye, in the family room," she called back. It had been but a handful of days since she'd lain with him, and even thinking about that afternoon by the loch sent desire curling through her. She and Struan hadn't had much time alone together since, and oh how she longed to spend time with him again. Struan walked into the family room carrying a large box.

"What have you there?" she asked, jutting her chin toward the package.

"A present."

His lopsided smile weakened her knees. "For whom?"

"For you, of course."

"For me?" She flashed him a questioning look. "Whatever for? 'Tis no' my birthday or Christmas."

Just then, Lindsay entered the family room, her car keys dangling from her hand. "What's up?" She looked from Sky to the package Struan held in his arms. "What's that?"

He set the box down and took the garment out of Sky's hands. "Something I ordered for Sky weeks ago. UPS just dropped it off. Open it, princess. I've already cut the tape."

His expression filled with tenderness as he stared into her eyes, and the pure anticipation she sensed from him came through so strongly, she could almost feel the emotion against her skin.

"All right." She drew back the flaps of the box and lifted the wadded-up paper stuffed inside, dropping it on the floor. "Why, 'tis a tapestry loom!" She reached out and touched the polished wooden frame. "A very fine loom at that." Her eyes stung. 'Twas a generous and thoughtful gift, but one that spoke of a future, whilst she and Struan had none.

"Wow," Lindsay exclaimed, moving closer to take a look. "That's really nice. You know how to use this thing?" she asked.

"Och, aye. I've spent many hours at my tapestry loom at Moigh Hall, especially during the winter months. 'Twas too cold to leave the keep for any length of time. My mother, sisters, granddam and I spent most of our day in the ladies' solar, mending garments or working on a variety of projects."

"I also ordered skeins of woolen yarn." Struan's smile lit up the room. "That package should arrive any day."

Heedless of the fact that his sister stood but a short distance away, Sky threw herself at him. He caught her, holding her close as she trusted he would. Sky lifted her gaze to his. "'Tis a very fine gift indeed. I shall cherish this moment forever. Thank you."

She couldn't help but pick up on the pride and happiness coming from him, and a wave of longing swept through her. Lately, she'd been tempted to try to convince Struan to travel with her to the fifteenth century, but doing so wouldn't be right. He had a life and a family here, and the Gordons had been very kind to her. 'Twould be unfair to return their kindness by stealing away their son.

Besides, how could she take Struan from all that he loved in Gordon Hollow? Nay, she could not ask him to give up everything he'd built for himself here, nor could she agree to stay. A lump rose to clog her throat, and her eyes stung. She saw no way for the two of them to remain together, though she'd given him her heart. Damnation, but fate had dealt her a cruel hand.

"I've got to get back to work." He kissed her forehead. "I'll help you put this thing together later this evening."

"Until then," she said, reluctant to leave the safety and comfort of his arms. My, how she loved the way he smelled—clean, masculine with a hint of the metallic scent of his forge clinging to the cotton of his T-shirt. She let him go, unable to tear her gaze from him as he turned and walked away.

"So . . . what's going on between you and my brother?" Lindsay crossed her arms and fixed Sky with a *tell me or else* stare. "It's obvious the two of you are hot for each other. I practically need a cake knife to cut through the pheromones in here."

"Pheromones? I dinna ken the word." Sky focused upon the basket of clean clothes left to be sorted. "I'm very fond of Struan, as I'm quite fond of all of you."

"Fond, eh?" Lindsay snorted. "I couldn't help noticing there are fewer condoms in the box since you discovered them under the sink."

Sky averted her gaze and grabbed a sheet from the basket to fold. "I . . ." What could she say? *When it comes to your brother, I lose all sense of propriety?*

"You're going to break his heart, you know," Lindsay muttered, her voice gruff with emotion. "I didn't figure you for a love 'em and leave 'em sort of girl, and I know it's none of my business, but—"

"Och, I dinna wish to break anyone's heart," Sky said, meeting Lindsay's gaze. "For what 'tis worth, Struan already owns mine and always will. If I had my way, I'd ne'er part with him." She shook her head. "You must see I've no choice but to try to save my family. I could no' live with myself if I did no' try to intervene."

She blinked back the tears filling her eyes. "Think you this is easy for me? Struan is the only man to ever make me feel as I do, and for me there will never be another. I did no' mean to . . . to—"

"Fall in love? Oh, Sky, you must feel so torn," Lindsay said, her arms dropping to her sides. "I had no idea, and if my family were at risk, I'd want to do whatever I could to help, too. I didn't mean to make you cry. I'm sorry. Who knows? Maybe things will work out for you and my brother."

Sky nodded, though she didn't see how. "Mayhap." She swiped at her eyes. "About those missing condoms, I—"

"Don't worry about it. I'm sorry I even brought it up. You can have as many condoms as you need. It's not like I'm using them, anyway," Lindsay muttered, backing away. "I . . . I have to go. I'm meeting a friend for lunch."

"A friend?" Sky picked up on the half-truth and took a guess. "You're having lunch with Brian, aren't you?"

"Who told?" Lindsay's eyes narrowed. "Did he tell you that?"

"Nay." She studied her friend. "I guessed."

"Ah, the superpower thing," she said, a small smile lighting her face. "Brian finally got up the gumption to ask me out, and I said yes."

"That's good, aye?"

"Too early to say." She shrugged. "I'll catch you later."

Lindsay turned and walked away, leaving Sky with her thoughts. Sighing, she went back to her task, her gaze drifting again and again to

Struan's gift. She'd have to make it clear she didn't want him to return to the fifteenth century with her. Though he hadn't offered, he was an honorable man, and chivalrous. Oh, he'd argue, try to convince her to stay, but in the end, he'd capitulate and insist upon going with her. She'd have to be strong, firm in her resolve to refuse his help. Assurance that he remained safe in this time would be her only solace in the otherwise bleak landscape of her future.

Sipping what Marjorie referred to as sweet tea, Sky watched the sun's arc toward the western horizon. She'd spent all afternoon at her loom, as she had every afternoon for the past fortnight. The woolen yarn had arrived the day after Struan had given her the loom, and she hoped to give him a completed tapestry before she left. 'Twould be small, but he would have something to remember her by.

Had it only been a little over two months since she'd come to Gordon Hollow? Sometimes it seemed an age since she'd fallen into the Gordons' midst. She glanced at young Michael where he sat at the table with his nose buried in his schoolbooks. Homework, he'd called the mess spread out around him.

He lifted his gaze, a frown creasing his forehead. "What is it?"

"I was just thinking about how much I'll miss all of you when I go." She surveyed the valley. The hours of daylight were growing shorter as the season began to change from summer's glory to autumn's full ripeness. Ethan had been out in the fields every day, harvesting hay to feed his kine over the winter months to come. The air held less humidity, and though it was still September, the leaves on some of the trees had already changed from dark green to pale gold.

"We'll miss you, too." Michael frowned. "You will always be welcome here, Sky. You know, just in case."

"Thank you, lad. Mayhap someday we'll meet again."

"Yeah, maybe." He nodded. "You never know."

"Struan called," Connor said through the patio door. "He says we're to go to his house in half an hour. He's in Warm Springs picking up pizza for our supper."

"Me too?" Michael asked, his expression hopeful.

"He didn't say, laddie, but I can't imagine he'd turn you away."

"Great." Michael unfolded his lanky frame and stood up. He pulled out his phone and began texting. "I'll tell Struan to order one more pizza. So much better than the PB&J I was planning to make," he mumbled, his thumbs flying over the keyboard of his phone.

"I've a feeling we'll be making travel plans tonight, Sky," Connor said, rubbing his hands together. "Katherine is looking for inns near Kildrummy Castle as we speak."

Sky nodded. Connor and Michael left, and her gaze strayed once again to the valley spreading out before her. For a blessed moment, her mind emptied, and she stared out into the gathering twilight.

She shivered, and the edges of her line of sight narrowed and darkened. A deep foreboding crept down her spine. Rather than fight the sensation, she reached for the darkness, hoping for a vision, yearning for some hint of what was to come. She waited, her mind open, but the premonition refused to yield its secrets.

The feeling receded, leaving dread behind to plague her. Grabbing the glass of iced tea, she rose and took it to the sink in the Gordons' kitchen. She poured the remains down the drain, and a weight settled around her heart. She only hoped she could warn her family in time to avert the loss of innocent lives.

Michael's heavy footfalls thudded upon the front stairs, and she hastened to meet him. "Are you ready to head to Struan's house, lad?"

"Sure," he said, glancing back up the stairs as Connor and Katherine appeared.

"I just peeked into your room to see how much progress you've made on your tapestry, Sky," Katherine told her. "It's truly a work of art."

Warmth filled her at the words of praise. "Thank you. I had hoped to finish it before we left for Scotland, but now I'm not certain I'll have the time."

"We don't have to leave tomorrow. If you'd like, we can make our reservations for a week from now." Connor opened the front door, indicating she should precede him outside.

"I'd like that. I mean the tapestry to be a gift, and I would very much like to complete the piece."

The four of them walked down the lane, and with every step, her dread grew heavier, while the McGladreys' excitement became more vibrant. Twisting her hands together, Sky shored up her defenses for the argument to come. She had yet to discuss with Struan her wish that he remain in Gordon Hollow when she departed. With so little time left to them, why stir discord into the heady mix of their passion?

Speaking of Struan, there he was, standing by his parked truck with three pizza boxes in hand, waiting for them. Her breath caught at the sight of him, as it always did.

"Hey, Struan," Michael called out. "Need help with those?"

"It's *pizza*, not a piano. I think I can handle three boxes." Struan shot his younger brother a wry look. "You could open the door for me, though. Come on in, everybody." His eyes met and held hers for a heated moment before Connor drew his attention.

"Did Sky's passport arrive, laddie?" Connor placed his hands on Katherine's shoulders. "Don't keep us in suspense."

"It did." Struan led them into his house. "Let's eat while we talk."

The passport, legal, but not even in her name, meant she'd be leaving Gordon Hollow within a se'nnight. Her gaze fixed upon Struan, and her appetite vanished. She trailed after him toward the kitchen, her stomach in a knot. Michael gathered napkins and plates while Struan set the boxes on the table and flipped open the tops. Pizza-scented air filled the room. Normally, the smell would have her mouth watering. Not today.

"I brought a deluxe combo, a pepperoni and a five-cheese pizza." Struan headed for his fridge. "Pop, beer or water?" he asked.

"Let me help." Sky took glasses from Struan's cabinet and made herself useful, distributing the beverages before taking a seat at the table across from Struan.

"What kind of pizza do you want?" he asked her with an empty plate in hand.

Sky shrugged. "I'm no' hungry."

His wonderful bluer-than-blue eyes filled with concern, and she turned away. "I . . . I had a snack a short while ago."

"When?" Michael blurted around a mouthful of pizza. "I never saw you eat anything, and I've been with you since the minute I got home from school. Do you feel all right?"

Struan reached for her hand, giving it a squeeze. "Eat something. Everything is going to be fine."

"Think you?" she whispered. All eyes turned to her, and she had to fight the urge to bolt from the room. "I'll have a piece of the five-cheese," she muttered, hoping everyone's attention would turn elsewhere now that she'd agreed to eat.

"I found a great place to stay near the Kildrummy Castle ruins." Katherine lifted a piece of pepperoni pizza. "Connor and I figured we could take turns watching for the portal to open, and we'll make Kildrummy Inn our headquarters. This is off season, so we shouldn't have any difficulty getting rooms." She glanced at Sky. "Four-hour shifts around the clock between the three of us; that means we'll each have eight hours off in-between. I think we can manage that comfortably."

"I'm coming with you," Struan announced. "And I suggest we watch the portal in pairs, rather than alone."

"Nay, Struan," Sky managed to croak. "I dinna want you to leave Gordon Hollow on my account."

Struan huffed out a grunt. "It's not up to you, and all I'm saying is that I'll go with you to Scotland—not to the past. Honestly, I don't believe you'll be able to return." He set his elbows on the table, his gaze boring into hers. "Once you've had your go at trying to get back to the fifteenth century, I'll bring you home to Gordon Hollow. For good."

"Nay." She shook her head, her vision blurred by the tears gathering in her eyes. "I canna allow you to accompany us. I ken well your nature. If the portal does open, you'll insist upon going with us. Not because you want to, but to protect *me*."

"Safety in numbers," Connor said. "I could use Struan's help, and—"

"Nay! I canna bear even the thought of something happening to him," she cried.

"Wow. I'm touched by your utter lack of confidence in my piss-poor abilities to defend myself, princess."

"'Twas you who said returning to the past means your borrowed time is at an end, Struan," she reminded him. "Think you I've forgotten?"

"I've learned a lot since then, and like I've said more than once, I think you're all cracked when it comes to the whole going-back-to-the-past thing. It's not going to happen. If it makes you feel better, consider this an I-told-you-so trip for me. *If* by some miracle the portal should appear, I don't plan to risk going back. *That* should allay your fears."

"Struan . . . I—"

"It's OK," he said, his features softening. "Don't you get it? I'm concerned about you. I . . . ." He raked his fingers through his hair. "I've read the history books, love. The scholars don't mention your disappearance—or your reappearance for that matter. Other than a vague line about how a broken betrothal caused the feud, you aren't mentioned at all." His Adam's apple bobbed. "My gut tells me the lack of mention means you don't make it back to your time. I want to be with you on this trip, because you're bound to be disappointed. OK?"

"History can be changed. My mother, Lady Erin and the McGladreys' daughter have proven that to be so. I am determined to return. 'Tis my turn to change history." Tears traced down her cheeks, her heart already breaking. "Surely you ken the accounting you read was written by men—men who saw women as inconsequential. For certes, 'tis why my name is no' mentioned. To those who recorded details, only the battles mattered."

"Perhaps." Struan fixed her with a determined look. "But you can't prevent me from buying a plane ticket or booking a room at Kildrummy Inn. You may as well make peace with the fact that I'm still your sworn knight in a shiny metal can."

As much as she wished he'd stay in Gordon Hollow, Sky couldn't help the frisson of relief. She and Struan wouldn't be parted. Not yet, anyway. "If I canna return to my century, I'll agree to come back with you to Gordon Hollow for good—on one condition." She lifted her chin and met Struan's gaze with a look of determination equal to his.

"What's that?" He arched an eyebrow.

"That if the portal does open for us, you'll remain in the twenty-first century." She held her breath, awaiting his response.

"All I can promise is that I don't *want* to have anything to do with the fifteenth century. Bottom line though? Your safety is what matters most."

"You two could go back and forth about this for days and never come to an agreement." Michael reached for another slice of pizza, his jaw tightening. "If it comes down to a vote, I'm against you going back in time unless I get to come with you."

"You can't," Struan said, shooting his brother a determined look.

"Fine," Michael huffed. "Then let it go. You two can continue arguing all you want on the six-hour plane trip to Scotland. I pity the poor souls sitting near you."

Connor laughed. "He's right. Let it go for now. After supper, we'll make our reservations and buy the plane tickets."

"Stubborn man," Sky muttered.

"Humph." Struan shook his head. "Obstinate woman."

The meal continued, and once the table was cleared and the leftovers put away, Struan brought out his laptop. It wasn't until they'd purchased their airline tickets that reality caught up with her. "Will we truly fly through the air?"

"Yep," Michael said, his head bobbing. "Wish I were going too, just to watch your reaction when the plane rises above the clouds."

"I'll be right beside you." Struan wrapped his arm around her waist and drew her close. "Stay with me tonight," he whispered in her ear.

A shiver of pleasure raced through her, and she looked around to see if anyone noticed the exchange. The McGladreys and Michael were engaged in an animated conversation. She nodded.

"Good." He kissed her temple.

A throbbing, fluid ache unfurled low in her belly. "I dinna want any harm to come to you. I could no' bear it. Promise me that . . . that . . ." Her throat closed up, and she couldn't seem to force a word past the constriction.

"Everything is going to work out as it's meant to." He drew her closer. "You'll see."

Again the sense of foreboding hit her. If only she could interpret what it meant. Was it a warning? If so, was it meant for her . . . or for Struan? "Damn fate," she said on a sigh.

"You don't believe in fate," Struan murmured.

"I try hard *not* to believe fate exists, but if there is no such thing as predetermination, then how could there be visions and premonitions?" Aye, despite what she wished, fate did exist and was oft a cold, hard mistress.

She could have tried harder to convince Struan to stay in the present. Guilt bit at her conscience. Mayhap if she'd been more adamant she might have dissuaded him, but the truth was . . . Struan was her weakness. Did wanting him by her side for as long as she could have him make her a despicable person? Och, but she couldn't help but long for more with Struan than fate had allotted.

Sky stood back from the Gordons once they'd reached the airport. Gene and Marjorie each embraced Struan fiercely, admonishing him to be careful and to come home soon. Michael helped the McGladreys unload their baggage, and then he wheeled her borrowed suitcase to her.

"I'm going to miss you, Sky." His face reddened.

"We're all going to miss her, son," Gene called.

"I shall miss all of you as well," she answered, her voice hitching. Her heart swelled with affection for the Gordons, and especially for the serious young man standing before her, his shoulders slumped.

Michael blew a breath. "Is it all right if I give you a hug?"

"Of course." Sky walked into his awkward embrace and patted his back. "Remember what I told you, lad. In a few years the lasses will be falling at your feet." She stepped back and smiled at him, her eyes stinging. He nodded, his eyes bright as well. Thank heavens she'd already said her good-byes to Lindsay and the others, or she'd break down altogether.

The Gordons drove off, and Sky stood with Katherine as Connor and Struan checked their bags with the attendant behind a steel counter. One of Struan's pieces of luggage had been made specifically to carry weapons. He'd explained he sometimes went to trade gatherings, or fairs that were too far from Gordon Hollow to drive, so he'd had the case custom made to hold long swords, small shields and even a crossbow and arrows.

Her case, once her gown and cloak were packed, could barely hold enough clothing and toiletries to last a few days, so she'd also stuffed as much as she could into her new rucksack.

"Are you nervous about flying?" Katherine leaned close to ask.

"Aye." She held out her hands. "Look. My hands are already shaking, and we've no' yet gone through security."

Struan and Connor had explained to her in detail what to expect once they arrived at the international airport. She kept her passport, state ID and boarding pass tucked into the outside pocket of her rucksack, which Struan assured her she could keep with her on the plane. Their flight would leave at six. Struan had insisted they leave no later, so she could see the ground from the air. He'd even arranged for her to have a seat next to a window.

"Once we get through the checkpoint, we'll find a bar. A glass of wine will help settle your nerves." Katherine patted Sky's shoulder. "I brought sleeping pills just in case. After you've gotten over the initial shock, you'll want to rest. It's a long flight, and doing so will help with the jet lag."

Sky nodded, doubting she'd sleep a wink during the six-hour flight. She'd watched planes taking off, and her hands weren't shaking with excitement. Nay. 'Twas terror at the prospect of leaving the ground in such an impossible manner that held her in its grip.

"All set. The bags are checked, and now we go through security." Struan hoisted his own rucksack on his shoulder. "Let's go."

He reached out to her, and she placed her hand in his, sweaty palm and all. They walked inside the large glass-and-steel building, and her breathing grew shallow. The place was teeming with people bustling about, dragging wheeled cases along behind them. A roped-off area formed a maze where people stood in a long line. Struan guided her into place behind Connor and Katherine.

"Breathe." Struan placed his hands on her shoulders and massaged the tight muscles in her neck. "You're going to be fine."

"If you say so," she grumbled, unconvinced.

"Where are your boarding pass and passport?"

"In the pocket of my rucksack."

He fished the documents out for her and placed them in her hand. "When we get to that guy in uniform there, you'll hand these to him. He'll check them, and then we'll walk through a metal detector, while our backpacks go through an X-ray machine. Did you pack a book or something to keep you busy during the flight in case you can't sleep?"

"I won't be able to sleep, and yes, I brought a book." She twisted around to glance at him. "Katherine said a few glasses of wine would help settle my nerves." Struan's chuckle vibrated through her, and she wanted to curl herself around him. Could he hold her in his lap during their journey? "She said we'd look for a bar once we're through this line."

"Sure. We'll get something to eat, too." He gave her shoulders another squeeze.

Sky handed her boarding pass and passport to the man in uniform. He smiled at her, checked her documents and wished her—nay, he wished Meghan McGladrey—a good trip. A blur of activity ensued, involving the taking off of her shoes and entering a frightening space where she placed her bare feet on yellow footprints and raised her arms whilst strangers wearing plastic gloves glared at her.

When she finally had her shoes back on and her rucksack once again on her shoulders, thinking coherently was beyond her. Too much. Too many people. Her anxiety spiked to a new high. Spots danced before her eyes. She swayed on her feet, and sweat beaded her forehead.

"Shite," Struan muttered, wrapping his arm around her waist. "Wait up, Connor. Sky needs to sit a minute." He led her to a cold metal bench and helped her down. "Lean forward," he ordered, rubbing her back. "Take deep breaths."

"I'm *trying* to," she muttered. Breathing was the problem. She couldn't get enough air into her lungs.

"Is everything all right here? Should I call for EMTs?" a stranger's voice asked.

All Sky could see of the stranger were a pair of heavy black shoes and navy-blue pants. She shook her head.

"It's just an attack of nerves," Struan answered for her. "She's afraid of flying." He continued to rub her back.

Afraid of flying? If only her distress were that simple. She feared going back to her own time as much as she feared not being able to go back. If they didn't arrive at exactly the right time, and the wheels of war were already in motion, what good would her reappearance do then? God in heaven, what was she to do? No matter the outcome, her heart would remain with Struan, and she'd be left an empty husk for the rest of her life. She swiped at the tears dampening her cheeks.

"Hey, now." Struan drew her into his arms and cradled her head against his shoulder. "Don't cry. It's going to be all right. Flying is safer than driving, and you mastered that skill easily enough. Right?" He dropped a kiss on her forehead. "Driving a car doesn't frighten you, does it?"

She let out a strangled laugh. Best not let on her fit had as much or more to do with churning emotions than it did with the prospect of flying. She sucked in a huge gulp of much-needed air and straightened out of his arms. "You're right. Of course you're right. I'm better now."

Connor and Katherine peered at her, their concern obvious. "I'm fine. Really. Let's find a place where I might have a glass of wine, and then I'll be ready to be hurtled through the sky." She shuddered at the thought.

Three glasses of wine and a meal later, Sky found herself strapped into a chair next to a small window, listening to instructions on what to do should the plane go down whilst flying over the Atlantic—not something she wished to dwell upon. Her rucksack was tucked under the chair in front of her, and Struan sat beside her. When the plane began to move, it creaked and rattled. She reached for Struan with both hands. He chuckled low in his throat, disentangled himself from her grip and put his arm around her.

"I've changed my mind. I don't wish to fly." She unbuckled her seat belt. "Surely there are ships that make the journey, aye?"

"Shhh. It'll be OK. I've flown many times," Struan reassured her whilst re-buckling her seat belt. "I'm still here, aren't I?"

"Where are Katherine and Connor?" She tried to peer over the seat in front of her.

"Three rows up."

BARBARA LONGLEY

The airplane picked up speed, and her gaze shot to the window. Struan held one of her hands. She gripped the armrest with the other and pressed herself back into the seat. "Och, saints preserve us, this . . . sucks."

Struan laughed again, and she glared his way. Faster and faster the plane rolled down the runway. She closed her eyes. Her world upended. She held her breath, as up and up the front of the plane rose, and the wheels left the ground with a frightening grinding sound. Her ears filled with pressure.

"Here," Struan said. "Chew on this. It'll make your ears pop."

She opened one eye a crack. He held a piece of something in front of her mouth. "What is it?"

"Gum. Chew, but don't swallow."

She opened her mouth, and he placed the gum on her tongue. She chewed, and a burst of minty flavor filled her mouth. Her ears did pop, but they also filled again with more pressure. Sky risked a peek out the window, and gasped. The buildings, roads and fields beneath had turned to miniatures. She leaned closer, practically pressing her forehead to the glass—or was it plastic? Amazement temporarily pushed her fear aside.

Struan brought her hand to his lips and kissed her knuckles. "Pretty cool, right?"

"Indeed," she murmured. Her gaze riveted upon the view outside the small window, she gasped again once they rose above the clouds. "Why, it looks like another world altogether!" She grinned. "It's as if we could walk upon the clouds, or reach out and touch them. I've always wondered what they're made of. Do you ken?"

"Clouds are made of water droplets, and when they become too heavy, the water falls to the earth as rain, sleet or snow."

"What holds the water droplets together so that they form clouds, and why are they white?"

"Um, light reflects off the surface . . . It's complicated. Once we're home, I'll buy you a book about clouds and such, and you can read all about it for yourself."

Sky leaned back and turned to face Struan. "You really believe I won't be able to return to my time, don't you?" Her heart filled with love and longing for him, and for a moment, she too wished he might be right.

"I do." He lifted the armrest between them and hugged her close. "You and I . . . we're meant to be together, at least that's what I hope. You fell into *my* path, into *my* life, and I don't think I'm meant to let you go."

Her heart melted, and with everything she had, she wished he was right. Wrapping her arm around his waist, Sky laid her cheek upon his shoulder. The warmth radiating from him seeped into her, calming her frazzled nerves, and she no longer feared flying.

"It's not too late to change your mind, love. We can visit Scotland, do some sightseeing and then go home." He ran his hand up and down her arm. "What do you say?"

"Hmm." Truly, she wanted nothing more than to do exactly what he suggested, but deep in her bones, she sensed 'twas not to be. "We will at least try for the portal first."

"All right. Can we agree on a time frame? How about a week?"

"Two."

"Ten days."

"Done." She snuggled closer and yawned. "Ten days, and if the portal does no' open, I will return with you to Gordon Hollow, and you will buy me a book about clouds." For right now, it sounded like a fine bargain, and when she wished to try another portal? Well, they'd face that argument then, not now.

Struan tightened his hold. "Try to sleep. Scotland is five hours ahead time wise, and we'd best get some rest while we can."

Engulfed in his strong arms and cocooned by the peace and contentment pulsing from him, she allowed herself to be lulled into believing he must be right. Even if that belief only lasted for a few hours, she'd grasp hold with both hands, wrapping herself in the promise of a happy future—a future with the man she loved by her side.

CHAPTER TWELVE

Struan stayed by Sky's side, keeping an eye on her as she walked around what remained of Kildrummy Castle. He hadn't set foot on Scottish soil since the day he'd dragged himself through the shimmering light, only to find himself transported to a different land and century. Superstitious much? Aye, that he was. All this time he'd avoided Scotland for fear he'd somehow be sent back to Halidon Hill.

"'Tis all so very different." Sky stepped over a pile of rubble that used to be part of the inner curtain wall. "To the east there," she said, gesturing, "'twas all a thick wood, and now there's naught but fields and rock."

"Do you think you can find the place where you went through?" Connor asked.

"Och, aye. The road is in the same place it's always been." Sky put her hand up to shield her eyes from the bright morning sun. "There's a copse of Scots pine and aspen." She pointed. "See you there? A half a league down the lane and over to the east. I'm certain 'tis the spot. 'Tis like an island in the midst of an ocean of heather, gorse and grass. Too out of place to be ignored, aye?"

She surveyed the castle ruins again, turned her back to the rubble and faced what was once the portcullis. "The stables were just there," she said, indicating the direction she meant, "and the outer curtain wall bordered the road. I rode out in that direction."

"All right," Connor said. "Let's go check it out."

The four of them piled into the rental car, with Katherine at the wheel. Struan slid across the backseat to sit closer to Sky, slinging his arm across the back of the seat rest. The car bumped along over the rocky ground toward the narrow lane. This time they turned away from the village of Alford and the Kildrummy Inn and headed north.

The island of trees Sky had pointed out looked as if they'd been herded into a tight knot in the middle of a pasture by some cosmic shepherd. Clouds moved across the sun to dim the afternoon light as he scanned the area. Sheep dotted the hills nearby, and the constant wind bent the grass so each blade bowed in homage toward the southeast.

"When's the last time you were here, laddie?" Connor slung his arm over the back of his wife's bucket seat and twisted around to peer at him.

"I was just thinking about that. July 19, 1333." He flashed Connor a wry look. "I've sold my swords, daggers and armor at fairs in England, Germany, Ireland and Belgium, but not here in Scotland." A rush of memories flooded his mind: His da, teaching him how to hold a sword, laughing at Struan's childish efforts to swing the weapon. He recalled the way his da would lift him upon his broad shoulders whilst striding through the village. He'd never doubted his father's affection for him. The earl never denied his paternity, nor had he ever forsaken Struan. It was his father who had arranged for Struan to apprentice with the very best blacksmith in the realm, ensuring that his bastard son would have a means of support. The backs of his eyes stung, and he turned to stare out the window. "Sutherland land is in the northwest. That's where I grew up."

Sky placed her hand over his where it rested on his thigh, and he turned his palm up to lace their fingers. "What about you, Connor?" he asked. "Have you been back to Ireland?"

"Several times." He nodded. "Most recently to research the stories I gave you."

"Does it bother you, going back to the place where you went through time?"

"No." He rubbed his hand over Katherine's shoulder as she drove. "I've taken my family to the very spot where I went through time. There's no trace of my passing, none that I can discern anyway." He grinned at Sky. "Perhaps you could sense something there that I can't, but it's not a spot that came up in our studies."

Sky had grown quiet beside him, and he glanced sideways at her. "Are you OK?"

"Aye. A wee bit nervous is all."

Tightening his grip on her hand, he settled back and reacquainted himself with the landscape of his country of origin. Somehow, he'd gotten Sky to promise she'd come home with him after ten days. What were the odds that this particular corridor would open within that short span of time? Zilch, that's what, and he couldn't wait to be on a plane, traveling home to Gordon Hollow with Sky by his side.

It would take her a few years to find her footing. She'd miss her family terribly, and he'd do his best to be there for her during those dark moments. His family had already accepted her as a member of their family, and he prayed that would ease the ache of missing her kin.

Aye, she'd need time to adjust, time to decide what to do with her life, and once she had things figured out, he'd ask her to marry him. His heart rate surged at the thought, and an exhilarating sense of rightness rushed through him.

They'd only known each other for a few months, but he already loved her like they'd been together a lifetime. He glanced at their twined fingers. Their hearts and souls were every bit as interwoven, and he was certain fate had brought them together for a reason.

Struan leaned forward and put his hand on the back of Connor's seat. "Have you ever wondered why it is that these portals seem to take people from Scotland and Ireland to different countries? I mean, why did the portal take us to the US and not just to Scotland or Ireland's past or future?"

"I imagine the fae have something to do with that." Connor peered over the seat at him again. "Perhaps something drew the *Tuatha Dé Danann* to North America. They may have had a connection with the indigenous people in the area centuries ago. If so, then the paths to North America were already established. No one can say for certain, but if an unwary soul went through the light with no destination in mind, the portals might revert to a default landing place, like the last spot visited by a faerie or something."

"Hmm. Maybe." Struan's gaze returned to the knot of trees drawing closer, and his mind wandered back to the topic of marrying Sky and starting a family of his own. Sky had said she didn't intend to have bairns because of her fae blood. Hopefully she'd change her mind once she was settled in the twenty-first century. She'd relax, see for herself that her gifts weren't feared or reviled. She'd be a great mom, and he hoped like hell she'd agree to have a couple of little ones with him. They'd live happily-ever-after in Gordon Hollow surrounded by family.

Warmth spread inside him at the scenario he'd created in his mind. Ten days. That's all. Ten. Short. Days. Two hundred and twenty-four hours, and the seconds were already ticking away. Not even a full two weeks stood between him and his idea of heaven. So . . . why did his chest tighten at the thought of spending a handful of those days waiting for nothing to happen?

Katherine pulled the car over to the side of the road and cut the engine. "We're going to have to walk from here," she told them. "There's no road, only a faint path. Makes you wonder why anyone would come to this spot, doesn't it?"

"It's likely the path has more to do with sheep and shepherds than it does with the place we're here to check out." Struan opened his car door and slid out. "Let's go take a look."

He walked through the field with Sky's hand in his, forcing himself to believe things would go his way. They entered the clearing, and the hairs on the back of his neck and on his forearms stood on end. "Weird." Unease prickled down his spine, and the all-too-familiar feeling of dread followed.

"What is?" Connor strode to the center and turned around. "Do you refer to the fact that the clearing forms a perfect circle, or to the way the trees seem to form a ring of protection around the perimeter?"

"Both." Struan scanned the ground. "Not even a seedling has crossed the tree line to sprout on the inside." He leveled a look at Connor. "Did your hackles rise the moment you stepped inside this place?"

Connor nodded. "I have goose bumps all over."

"So do I." Katherine ran her hands up and down her arms. "Why is that, do you suppose?"

"'Tis from the magic in this place." Sky held her hands palms up at waist level. "The clearing fair hums with the power of the ancients." She circled the outer edge. "This is it. *This* is where the shimmering lights appeared, and I tumbled through to the twenty-first century."

"That's good news indeed," Connor said, his grin wide. "Let's head back to Alford and gather provisions. We'll begin our watch this evening." He strode toward the path back to the car. "We'll want bottled water, jerky, nuts and dried fruit. May as well have lunch while we're in the village," he called out over his shoulder. "Katherine and I will take the first watch."

Katherine laughed. "Slow down, Connor." She hurried after her husband.

Struan stuffed his hands into the front pockets of his jeans. "Those two are excited."

"Aye, they're thinking of seeing their daughter again, and their grandchildren for the very first time. I canna imagine what it must have been like for Connor. He watched as Meghan was snatched away."

Sky crossed the clearing to join him. "I worry about what my own parents must be suffering right now, wondering what became of me. At least Connor was aware that his daughter had been taken through time. My parents don't even have that comfort. For all they ken, I've been murdered, or . . . or taken off against my will."

His gaze flew to her. Other than the blacksmith he apprenticed with, after Halidon Hill, no one was left who would mourn his loss, of that he was certain. His father's legitimate family wouldn't even have searched for his remains. He imagined his stepmother and half siblings celebrated his passing. Sky, on the other hand, had come from a large, loving family. Her parents were probably beside themselves with grief. He would be if she were lost to him.

He stopped walking and pulled her into his arms. "I'm sorry, love."

She bunched the front of his sweatshirt in her hands and let out a loud sigh against his chest. "I miss them so, and I'm frightened for them. It's a weight that never lifts from my heart."

He held her tight and propped his chin on top of her head. If only there was something that could be done that didn't involve going back through time . . . A few short beeps came from the rental car, and Struan snorted. "Even Connor's honking sounds impatient." He tilted Sky's chin up and kissed her. "Best get going before he comes after us."

His heart ached for Sky, and guilt knocked into him. He'd done his best to try to convince her to turn her back on the family she loved so fiercely. Glancing at the faerie ring behind them, he wondered what he'd decide if forced to make the choice between staying or going if he were in her shoes.

He loved the Gordons every bit as fiercely. If it were his family facing possible harm at the hands of a ruthless enemy, wouldn't he do whatever he could to get to them? Should the portal open, he might yet be faced with just such a difficult decision, one that meant he'd leave behind his family and the life he'd built for himself. Time travel offered no guarantees. How far would he go for love?

Plagued with restless energy, Struan paced around the outer edge of the faerie clearing. He glanced at Sky where she sat on the ground, huddled inside her blanket. Her face was barely visible in the predawn dimness, but he felt her eyes on him nonetheless. "I should've gone for a run yesterday. I'm not used to staying in one place for so many hours unless I'm asleep or working in my forge."

"You and Connor should take an hour or two to engage in sword-play between shifts."

He came to a stop in front of her. "Sky, it's been eight days. I don't think—"

"Dinna say it!" She turned her face away. "I ken what you think, and I dinna wish to hear the words spoken aloud."

The quiver in her voice went straight through him. His blanket lay on the ground beside hers. He sat down. Two more days, and all this would be behind them. "I'm sorry. I didn't mean to upset you."

She sniffed and swiped at her eyes with the edge of the blanket, and his heart turned inside out. "Aw, princess. I can't stand it when you cry." Struan scooted around, placed his legs on either side of her and encircled her in his arms. She leaned against him, and the soft sound of her crying nearly unhinged him. He stroked her hair and cradled her head in the crook of his neck. "Let it out. Have a good cry, and then you can tell me all about your family."

She put her hand on the back of his head and brought him down until their lips met. Her kiss, mixed with the salty taste of her tears, beseeched him for a distraction. He drew back. "You're upset. Maybe kissing right now isn't such a good idea."

"I am upset. For certes I've reason enough, but . . ." She drew him back until only their breaths separated them. "We both ken there's naught I can do to open the portal. I want you, Struan, and no' only because I seek diversion from my grief," she whispered against his lips. "I always want you."

Her palm slid under his clothes to stroke the bare skin of his belly, sending tendrils of heat unfurling through him. She nibbled the sensitive skin on his neck before continuing, "None of us ken how long we have here, and I'm no' referring to time travel. It's just that life is fleeting, and I dinna want to waste a single moment of my time with you."

Hard and wanting her, he spread his blanket out and drew her down with him to lie on the ground, using her blanket to cover them both. "You drive me crazy with wanting you, woman. All it takes is a touch or a look and I go up in flames." He fumbled with the fastening of her jeans, letting out a sigh of pleasure when he got the zipper down far enough to slide his hand inside to touch her. He kissed her, sliding a finger into her slick heat. "Let's get these off." He withdrew his hand from her and tugged at the denim.

"Wait," she said. "Shoes first, and take yours off as well."

"My shoes or my pants?" He nipped at her chin.

"Both."

Struan took out the condom he'd stashed in his wallet before he stripped, hyperaware that Sky was also removing every bit of her clothing. By the time he was bare and sheathed, he throbbed painfully. Pulling the cover up over their shoulders, he drew her close, reveling in the feel of her bare skin against his. He ran his hand over her chest, caressing a plump breast, teasing her hardened nipple with his thumb and moving on to the curve where her waist flared to meet her hip.

"You feel so good, Sky. I could stay like this forever, with you naked in my arms," he rasped out. "I'd be perfectly happy." He cupped the firm mounds of her bottom and pulled her tight against his erection, eliciting a sudden intake of breath from her.

She tangled her fingers in his hair and drew him to her for a scorching kiss, and he lost himself in her. Their lovemaking turned frantic, as if neither one of them could get enough of the other. Once the last shudder of her climax rocked through her, he followed, coming inside her in an explosion of pleasure.

Side by side they lay panting. He didn't want to let her go, didn't want to break the connection that made them one. Wrapping himself around her, he held her tight, breathed in her sighs and closed his eyes.

Full sunlight spilling over the tops of the trees, accompanied by raucous birdsong, woke him. Struan glanced down at Sky, sleeping peacefully with her cheek plastered to his chest. His full bladder prompted him to disentangle himself, carefully so as not to wake his sleeping princess. He slid out from under the cozy cocoon of blankets and naked woman, stood up, stretched and looked for his clothes. Right next to his briefs, the faintest hint of wavering pale pink and green light shimmered above the ground. "Ah, shite!"

"What?" Sky sat up and rubbed her eyes. "What is it?"

His insides caving in, all he could do was point.

Sky let out a startled cry and scrambled to gather her clothing. "Call Connor and Katherine."

He stood frozen to the spot, dread and indecision churning him into one big conflicted mess.

"Struan," Sky snapped. "Give me your phone if you willna call them yourself."

He reached for his jacket and drew out his phone, handing it to her. Numbness spread through him, and he had the odd sensation of somehow being outside his body and no longer in control of his limbs or his mind.

"For heaven's sake, get dressed!" Sky exhorted as she scrolled through his numbers in search of the McGladreys'.

"It's speed dial number four," he said, forcing his feet to obey his command to step into his briefs. Damn. Two more days. Had that been too much to hope for? Did being born a bastard mean he didn't deserve his happily-ever-after, that things would never go his way? Not fair. Since he'd had no choice in the matter of his birth, why should he have to suffer the consequences? There was no logical connection between his origins and the damned portal's appearance. He knew that, but being thwarted took him to a self-pity state of mind nonetheless.

He managed to get dressed, while vaguely aware of Sky's animated conversation with Connor. "Guess this means we'll miss the full Scottish breakfast at the Kildrummy Inn this morning," he muttered.

"*You* dinna have to miss a thing." Sky flashed him an indecipherable look. "Once Katherine and Connor arrive, you will take the car and return to the inn for the full Scottish breakfast. Then you're to return the rental car, catch a plane and go home to Gordon Hollow."

"Like hell," he snapped.

She fisted her wee hands upon her hips and gave him her haughtiest, chin-loftiest look to date. "You swore fealty to me, and so you are at my command. I *order* you to do exactly as I say. You *will* return to your home by day's end."

"Ha! Don't you remember freeing me from my vow, princess?"

"I . . ." Her brow creased. "Still, you belong in this century. You have a place in—"

"Damnation," he groaned, raking his fingers through his tangled hair. He strode around the accursed clearing, keeping a wary eye upon the growing strength of the wavering lights at the center. "My heart belongs with you whether you will it or not. Where you go—I go."

"Oh, Struan, no," she cried. "You canna' mean that."

"Aye, but I do." The feeling of being outside himself vanished, and determination coursed through his veins, lending him strength. He should've known. All along he should've realized—he had no choice in the matter and never had. He glowered at the light show at the center of the ring and swore under his breath. The sound of his fate, like metal doors slamming together, reverberated through his skull with deafening force.

Struan fastened the straps of his brigandine over the woolen tunic and linen undershirt he wore over soft deerskin trews and his very best knee-high leather boots. Plus, under that he wore a cotton T-shirt and briefs, with spares in his rucksack. He saw no reason to be uncomfortable just because he was returning to an uncomfortable era.

He shuddered at the thought of lice, fleas and all the other miseries awaiting them in medieval times. Soap, toothpaste, toothbrush, razor and a few other modern luxuries had been tucked deep inside his pack as well. "Connor, did you put a copy of the map of portals in my rucksack?"

"I did."

"Good." He sheathed his two swords and strapped them across his back. He'd already stowed daggers in both boots and another lay hidden in a specially designed place on the inside of his brigandine. His shield was fastened to his rucksack, which he planned to wear on his front, rather than awkwardly over the swords on his back. He glanced at Katherine and Sky, who were also preparing themselves, helping each other with their cloaks and gear. Seeing Sky once again in her velvet gown reminded him of the day she'd landed in the middle of the jousting field, and a bittersweet smile broke free at the memory. "Sky, tell us again what we must fix our minds upon as we go through."

By midafternoon, the time portal had grown to full strength. The lights now reached the height of a man, and Lord how he hated the undulating, freakish aura. He listened carefully as Sky recited once again the date, time and place they were all to focus on as they walked through. "Maybe we should hold hands, just to be on the safe side." He looked at each of them in turn, gauging their reaction to his suggestion.

"I agree," Katherine said, hooking her elbow through Sky's.

"Ready?" Connor's voice boomed.

The man's obvious excitement and broad smile annoyed Struan. How could Connor be so damned eager when he knew the inherent danger? Time travel was iffy at best. "No, but—"

"You dinna have to join us." Sky's gaze sought and held his. "I'd prefer that you stay here. Gene and Marjorie will never forgive me if aught happens to you."

He strode to her and reached for her hands. "And I'd never forgive myself if aught happened to *you*."

Connor gripped the hilt of the dagger at his waist and paced. "Let's *go!*"

"All right, all right. Take a breath why don't you." Struan held Sky's hand in his, and Katherine moved to her husband's side to take his. "I think it would be best if Connor and I link up, since our grips are the strongest," Struan told the group. "OK?"

"Right." Connor clasped Struan's forearm.

Struan gripped back with equal force. "Lead the way, princess." His heart hammering against his ribs, and with every cell in his body rebelling, urging him to run the other way, Struan followed Sky into the shimmering light.

The rending pressure, flashing lights and thick, unnatural darkness held him fast, and Struan was turned and twisted. He could no longer tell whether he was still connected to Connor and Sky. Too much was happening to interfere with his awareness. The force tore at him until he was mindless to anything but the pressure, fear and pain. This time, he was sure he would die.

"Ooof." He let out a grunt as he landed with a hard thud on top of his rucksack—his hands free. Panic swamped him as he scanned his surroundings. He was inside the ring still, but now the place was surrounded by a thick forest, and he saw no sign of the others. "Sky," he called out, pushing himself up. "Connor, Katherine," he shouted this time, his panic growing.

"I'm here," Sky called from a short distance away.

Struan forced himself up and staggered in her direction. A shrill whistle cut the air, startling him, and he swiveled around.

"Here, my lord," a man shouted, following with another shrill whistle. The sound of pounding hooves approaching sent a rush of adrenaline through Struan. Two guards stood just outside the clearing. Neither had their weapons raised, but their expressions were hard upon him.

Sky appeared from between two trees, walking unsteadily toward him. Struan widened his stance, keeping both hands in view so as not to provoke the men facing him. "Where are Connor and Katherine?" he hissed once she reached his side.

"No' . . . no' here. I . . . Katherine was torn from me. I dinna ken what became of them. Those are Erskine guards," she whispered.

"Of course they're Erskine guards." He grunted. "Of course Katherine was torn from you," he bit out. "Connor and I were also separated. No matter what the McGladreys fixed in their minds, their hearts were with their daughter." He could guess where the two had landed easily enough. Great. Judging by the guards keeping watch on the faerie ring, he and Sky had not managed to land in medieval Scotland prior to her disappearance. Oh, no. They'd fallen in the middle of the viper's nest, and protecting Sky fell squarely upon his shoulders.

"Well, well." A young noble in partial armor rode to the edge of the ring. His mount nickered and stepped toward them, but the lordling reined the mare in, bringing her to a halt. "Welcome home, Lady Sky. 'Tis good to have you back where you belong."

"My lord Oliver," she said, her chin lifting. "Pray, tell me, how long have I been away?"

Struan felt her trembling beside him, and he shifted, positioning himself between her and the three men facing them.

"Hmm, five days, I believe." Oliver looked to one of his guards as if he needed confirmation. The guard nodded.

"How . . ." Her voice quavered. "How did you—"

"Your father's men followed you on your ride, as you may recall. They saw what happened and dutifully reported the event to their liege lord. Thankfully, the entire conversation was overheard by one of our servants, who then shared the tale with me and my grandsire.

"My grandsire bid me set up a watch for your return, and I agreed to do so for no more than a fortnight." He sniffed, shifted in the saddle and peered around the clearing, his disdainful gaze touching briefly upon Struan. "I think it odd and most discourteous that your kin did no' deign to tell us what happened."

He leaned forward and rested his forearm on the horn of his saddle. "We could have told them yours is no' the only tale of such happenings here. Our clan stays well clear of this godforsaken clearing. My apologies for no' making you aware, my lady."

"My . . . my family is still here then?" Sky stepped forward.

Struan put his arm out to keep her back, and anger flickered in the lordling's eyes.

Oliver fixed his glare upon Struan. "Nay. Another insult against us. Your kin left without a word the very same night. I'll have word of your return sent to the earl of Fife immediately. In the meantime, we shall go ahead with the wedding as planned, and all will be forgiven. Once your family returns, they can toast our nuptials with us. Come to the keep, my lady." He gestured. "You look as if you could use a good rest and a meal."

"She's not going anywhere with you, *my lord.*" Struan pushed her behind him. "Nor will there be a wedding."

"Who are *you* to speak to *me* thus?" Oliver tensed, and the two guards flanking their lord drew their swords.

"He's a knight who agreed to protect and escort me home," Sky said, trying to get around him.

Struan shoved her back again. He took the shield from his rucksack and handed the pack to Sky. "The lady has decided she will not marry you, and if you have any honor at all, you'll let her return to her clan without a fuss."

"Without a . . . *fuss?*" Oliver let out a mirthless laugh. "Why the change of heart, my lady? We've been betrothed practically since birth. Need I remind you? 'Twas arranged by our grandsires to mend the rift between our clans caused by your father's unfortunate and most inconvenient marriage whilst contracted to wed my mother. Surely you dinna wish to cause another such rift." He scowled down his nose at Struan. "Where have you been these past five days, Lady Sky, and what is this knight to you?"

"Where I have been has naught to do with my decision. I will no' marry you, Oliver. I have indeed had a change of heart."

"Ah, I see." Oliver shrugged. "I trow a few days without food and water will make you more amenable to marriage, my lady—along with a good beating or two. If you starve to death, it is of little consequence to me. Fortunately for me, there are no MacKintosh here to tell your kin you've returned. I'll wait a suitable time before requesting your younger sister as your replacement. For certes your father will be only too happy to give her to me." He gestured to his guards. "Kill the knight, and take Lady Sky to a chamber. Keep her under guard with her door locked."

"Shite." Struan drew one of his swords. "Remind me to kick Connor's ass when we catch up to him, princess."

One of the guards rushed him; the other headed for Sky. Struan whipped his sword in a wide arc while retreating for a few much-needed seconds. He kept himself between their attackers and Sky, who now held her dagger at the ready. His maneuver gained him the time he needed to gather himself for a full-out offensive.

The first guard attacked. The moment the man's stance shifted, Struan swerved. He blocked the second guard's blow with his shield. Lunging low, he brought his blade up under the first man's reach, his sword finding its mark between his ribs. He pulled his blade free in the nick of time to defend himself against the remaining guard's assault.

Their swords met midstrike, and Struan moved close enough to jab the edge of his shield into the man's throat, sending his foe staggering back and gasping for breath. Taking advantage of his attacker's imbalance, Struan arced his sword through the air with all his might, severing the man's head from his shoulders in a single blow.

Bloodlust was upon him now, and he searched the clearing for any approaching threat. "Your men are poorly trained, Lord Asswipe. I wonder . . . are you able to acquit yourself any better?"

Oliver roared, his face distorted with rage. He dismounted, drew his sword and came at Struan in a mindless fury.

Perfect. Exactly what he'd hoped for. Struan rushed forward to meet him. The clash of their swords filled the air with the metallic ring of steel upon steel, and the vibration traveled all the way to his boots. "What kind of no-good"—he shoved Oliver back—"black-hearted, yellow-bellied coward preys on women? Who does that? Who schemes to murder his wife just to get his greedy hands on a wee bit of land and a few gold sovereigns?"

Oliver launched an offensive that had Struan struggling to regain the upper hand. For several long moments, all he could do was block his opponent's blows. He backed away, and Oliver lunged for him. Struan kicked at Oliver's kneecap while his leg was extended. Judging by the lord's resulting grunt, Struan had managed to cause some damage. He backed away in an effort to catch his breath, watching for a hint of his enemy's next move.

Adrenaline rushed through Struan's veins, and sweat dripped down his face. Never had his mind been so clear and alert. Never had he been more focused. *This* was the man who meant to kill the woman he loved.

Oliver came at him again in a flurry of offensive strikes. Struan parried, blocked and evaded, watching for just the right moment.

"Struan, we must leave at once." Sky had taken Oliver's horse by the reins. "Be quick. Can you no' hear? More guards are on the way."

"Humph. As you wish, my lady. I've no more time to play, *my lord.*" Struan swerved, feinted, and when Oliver brought his sword up to block his blow, Struan dipped, thrusting his blade into the man's black heart. "May you burn in hell." He pushed the hilt of his sword hard before drawing his blade out of the dying man's chest.

"Hurry." Sky motioned for him to come to her, their packs dangling over each shoulder. "We must be away quickly."

Struan wiped his blade clean across Oliver's velvet tunic, sheathed the weapon and ran to Sky. With the two packs and her heavy velvet gown, Sky was having trouble mounting. He fastened his shield to his pack before putting his hands around her waist. "Up you go," he said, tossing her onto the saddle. He put his foot in the stirrup and mounted behind her. "Where to?"

"This way," she said, turning the mare's head toward a narrow path shooting off the clearing. Struan kicked the animal's sides with his spurs, and the mare took off at a gallop. The two rucksacks bouncing against his and Sky's sides made it difficult to ride. After a couple of leagues stretched between them and the Erskines, Struan took the reins from Sky and brought the mare to a halt. The beast's sides were heaving from the double load she carried, and he didn't want to risk harming their only means of escape.

"We canna' stop. We need to—"

"We need to make a plan and get our gear better situated." Struan dismounted and reached to help Sky down. Once her feet were on the ground, he let her go and began pacing. He stopped to stare down the path toward Kildrummy. "I've done it this time." He waved toward the horse. "And now we can add horse thievery to the list, right under incurring the earl of Mar's wrath by killing his grandson."

"Nay, Struan. The mare belongs to me." Sky stroked the horse's neck, and the animal nudged her mistress, nickering softly in greeting. "She was a gift from my grandsire." She continued to pet the horse.

What the hell was she going on about? He stared at her, amazed by how calm she seemed. "I *killed* Oliver."

"You were magnificent." She kept her gaze on the mare.

"Are you talking to me or the horse?"

She glanced at him. "You, of course."

He basked in her praise for half a second before the fear and panic flickering through her eyes registered. The ramifications of his actions slammed into him again. He flexed and fisted his hands. "Maybe we were lucky and no one but the three dead men saw us." He paced to the other side of Sky and her horse. "What do you think?"

"I caught movement behind Oliver. 'Tis certain another guard was there, and he is the one who left to gather reinforcements. We were seen."

"Great." He groaned. "How is it you're so calm? They'll be after us soon."

"Struan, you did naught but defend the both of us. *We* were attacked. *We* did naught wrong, though I ken well the earl of Mar will retaliate." She sucked in a huge breath and let it out slowly. "The Erskines will believe we're headed straight for Moigh Hall."

"Aren't we?"

"Nay." She shook her head. "We're heading for Nair. There's an inn there oft used by my father and cousins whilst conducting business in the area. We'll stay there long enough for me to write a missive to King James about what has happened and to purchase another horse, so we don't overburden my mare." She glanced at him over her horse's bowed head. "I still have two gold coins sewn into my gown."

Struan reached under his brigandine to touch the hidden pouch inside. "I have the coin you gave me as well, plus some silver. We could live quite well for a year or longer on what we have. We could lay low somewhere."

"Aye, but we won't. A night or two in Nairn, and then we'll set out for Meikle Geddes. From there we'll have help. We can steal onto the island of Moigh late at night should the Erskines have spies lurking about." Sky began walking down the path, leading the mare. "We'll walk for a bit until my mare is rested."

"You amaze me, princess."

"As you amaze me, Struan." She smiled. "Thank you for saving my life. Had you no' been with me, I'd be locked away in a tower to be starved and beaten until I agreed to marry that . . . that . . . *asswipe*."

Struan laughed at the way his word came out of her mouth. Relief that the two of them remained alive, and so far unscathed, weakened his knees. His head pounded, either from their journey through time, or from the sudden loss of adrenaline pulsing through him. His stomach growled with hunger. "I could use a break and something to eat. How about you?"

"Aye." She jutted her chin toward a rocky outcropping in the distance. "There by those rocks, 'tis a place where we can make camp well hidden from view to anyone on the trail."

"Do you know this area?"

She nodded. "I've traveled this way many a time with my kin for various gatherings. The path we're on leads inland, and from there the road widens and will take us to the shores of Loch Ness. From there we'll continue southward toward Loch Moigh. But we'll travel west to the village of Nairn first."

"Here," he said, taking the rucksacks from her shoulders. "We'll hang these from the saddle horn for now, and then I'll figure a way to work the straps so that we can use them like saddlebags."

They walked along in silence, and everything that had happened replayed in his mind. "It's not over."

"Nay, and I pray we dinna cross paths with the Erskines as they ride toward Moigh Hall and we ride west toward Nairn. 'Tis best we travel under cover of darkness until we reach the inn I spoke of," she whispered, her breath hitching. "I should have listened to you, Struan."

His protective instincts surged, and he scanned the area for any possible threat. "What do you mean?"

"I had hoped to prevent a war between my clan and the Erskines," she sobbed. "Because of me, Oliver is dead, and the feud I meant to prevent will begin in earnest." She sniffed. "Only now, 'twill be worse. Because of my return, instead of a feud over a broken betrothal, now the Erskines' retaliation will be fueled by rage, a desire for vengeance and a thirst for blood."

"It'll be OK." He came around the horse and drew her into his arms. "Don't worry, love." After all, he'd do enough of that for the both of them. He'd killed Oliver, the earl of Mar's heir, and it wouldn't matter in the least that it had been a fair fight. It would be *his* blood the Erskines sought.

Struan's jaw clenched so tight it offset the pain throbbing between his temples. He'd known his fate all along. He'd felt it to his very soul— coming back would be the end of him.

CHAPTER THIRTEEN

Sky leaned against one of the boulders she and Struan had hidden behind to make their camp. She should be resting, since she and Struan planned to travel at night, but sleep would not come to her. She drew up her knees and watched Struan as he slept. Every now and then, he snored softly, and her insides melted. He appeared boyish and carefree in slumber, oblivious to the danger she'd put him in.

Guilt bit at her. Nothing had gone as she'd hoped. They hadn't arrived in the moments leading up to her disappearance as they'd intended. Nay, they'd fallen into Oliver's trap. Another worry inserted itself into her mind. Where were Katherine and Connor?

She'd been a fool—thinking herself so important—believing she *had* to come back because she alone could set things aright. Ashamed of her naïveté, hot tears spilled from her eyes. Struan would be hunted down by the earl of Mar and his men, and nothing but his death would appease the Erskines. "What have I done?" she whispered, laying her cheek on top of her knees.

Their only hope lay with getting word to King James, revealing all that had happened. The earl of Mar's persistence in pressing the king and court to return the estates once belonging to the earldom gave Sky an edge. Their young king would be gladdened to hear of any altercations involving the earl of Mar. 'Twould give young James another reason to strip away the Erskine laird's title.

Aye, once she and Struan were in Nairn, she'd write several missives, one to King James, another to their staunchest allies, the Sutherlands, and one to her brother, the baron of DúnConnell.

Glancing at Struan again, she bit her lip. Hers was not much in the way of a plan, but 'twas the best she could come up with at the moment. Once she and Struan were safely ensconced within the walls of Moigh Hall, she was certain her family would ken what to do to keep Struan safe until he returned home to Gordon Hollow.

She'd lose him, and no matter how her heart might break, helping him to return home was the right thing to do. She crawled to where he slept, lay down beside him and tried to rest. Even in slumber Struan reacted to her nearness. His arm came around her. He sighed as he pulled her to him and wrapped her in his warmth. The contented sound of her horse grazing, the stillness of the day, and with Struan pressed against her, sleep found her after all, and she dozed off.

"Time to rise, princess." Struan shook her gently. "We need to get moving."

She yawned and rubbed her eyes. "I'm awake."

Struan moved around their makeshift camp, gathering their things. "We can eat on the way."

Untangling her legs from her heavy gown and cloak, she rose and stretched her stiff limbs. "I'll be right back." She walked around to the other side of the rocky outcropping to relieve herself. By the time she returned, Struan had her horse saddled and bridled.

He handed her one of the many small bags of nuts and dried fruit they'd packed. "I'll walk for a bit," he said. "You ride."

"Nay, I'd prefer to walk as well. 'Twill ease my stiffness." Sky peered around the edge of the outcropping they hid behind.

"I've been watching." Struan took up the mare's reins. "No sign of Erskines on our trail."

"Good. I'm certain the earl and his garrison ride toward Moigh Hall as we speak."

"Won't they bury Oliver first, have a funeral befitting a noble?"

"Mayhap, but that doesn't mean the earl hasn't already sent men ahead to search for us. Let us be on our way." She took a handful of nuts and fruit and tossed it into her mouth as they started inland for Nairn. A gibbous moon, nearly full, seemed to sit upon the eastern horizon, too heavy to rise. "If it stays clear, we'll have light to travel by this night."

They trudged on through the night, taking turns riding, sometimes riding double, until they reached the road north. Exhaustion weighting her limbs, Sky yawned from her place on her horse's back. Struan led them to a wooden bridge spanning a small burn rushing toward River Ness.

"Stop here, Struan, and let my mare drink," she said. "Mayhap we could rest a bit behind that rise." She waved in the direction of the hillock bordering the road.

"All right, but only for a few hours." Struan scanned the area. "It's almost dawn." He glanced up at her. "How long will it take us to get to the inn from here?"

"A day's journey. Less if we push."

"We'll push. Once we're there, your mare will have grain and a good rest."

He reached up for her, and she accepted his help to dismount. They led the horse to the burn and let her drink her fill before walking to the far side of the hill to share a meal and rest.

Soon they'd reach the safety of the inn. With that goal in mind, she settled against Struan's warmth and fell into a fitful slumber, her dreams filled with battle cries and tributaries flowing red with blood.

Sky stood wearily beside Struan as he placed one of their coins on the polished wooden counter and slid it toward the innkeeper standing on the other side. She had to force her eyes to stay open.

"My wife and I require a chamber," Struan told the burly, aproned man.

The innkeeper's brow rose. He made a slight gesture with his hand, and two huge men materialized out of the shadowy depths of the taproom to block the front door. "Good eve to ye, Lady Sky," the innkeeper boomed.

Struan tensed beside her, nudging her with his shoulder and tipping his head toward the lads standing at the door.

"What?" Half-asleep on her feet, she'd been caught unawares. "Oh, good eve to you, Master Harold."

"I've kent ye since ye were a wee bairn, Lady Sky, and yer betrothed as well," he said, crossing his arms in front of him. "And this man claiming tae be yer husband is no' an Erskine. Are ye all right, lass?" Suspicion clouded his expression as he eyed Struan.

Sky's face filled with heat. She should have been a bit more specific with Struan about her family's association with the innkeeper and his family, or she should've stood well back with the hood of her cloak raised whilst he made arrangements. Struan glared at her.

Shaking off her weariness, she straightened. "I've . . . we . . . Struan and I eloped. He is my husband, and I am very well, Master Harold. My thanks for your concern." According to Oliver, she'd only been away for five days. Her disappearance and elopement within that time span, should the gossip have arrived this far, would now make sense.

She lifted her chin, daring the innkeeper to challenge her story. "I never wished to wed the earl of Mar's heir, for my heart was already given." She met Struan's gaze, smiling slightly as his glare turned to an expression of admiration. "We require room and board for two nights. On the morrow, I'll need several sheets of vellum, quills and ink as well. If you would be so good as to procure them for me, I would be most appreciative."

Master Harold threw his head back and laughed. "Writing tae your da, eh? Hope tae smooth things over with the earl afore you return home with yer new husband, do ye?" Harold eyed Struan's garments, assessing their worth. "Ye've the look of a Sutherland about ye, milord. Are ye blood kin tae the earl?" A speculative glint lighting his eyes, he took up the gold coin and made change, sliding the silver to Struan. "A nephew mayhap?"

"Aye," Struan said, taking up the change and stowing it in the leather pouch hanging at his belt.

How easily Struan agreed with Harold's assertion about his kinship with the Sutherlands. For the hundredth time, she wondered why he hadn't shared his origins with her. Was he blood kin to the earl of Sutherland's family? He surely held himself as if he were of noble blood. Regardless, his fine clothing, though dusty, along with the spurs on his boots and the rest of his gear, attested to his wealth and standing. Obviously he intended to encourage the deception, if indeed it truly was a deception after all.

"Now about that room?" Struan straightened. "My wife and I are weary from traveling. We'll want a bath, and a hot meal sent up as well."

"I'll see tae both anon." Harold made another slight hand gesture and the two men blocking the door melted back into the crowd filling the first-floor taproom. "Och, you're in for it now, Lady Sky." Harold shook his head. "As I recall, yer aunt Elaine eloped with a Sutherland as well, aye?" The innkeeper chuckled. "Ah, but I do love me job, I do. I'm always privy tae the juiciest bits of gossip."

Still chuckling, he moved out from behind the counter and started toward the stairs. "Come along, my lord, my lady. I've a room what befits yer station. 'Tis privacy ye'll be wanting, aye?" He winked at Struan. "What with being newly wedded and all."

Her face once again heating, Sky followed Struan and Harold up the stairs and down the long, narrow corridor to the very end by a single glass-paned window. "I trow you'll find this chamber tae yer liking." Harold took a ring of keys from under his apron and fit one into the lock. "I'll send the lads up with a tub and hot water, and my wife will be here shortly with yer supper."

Sighing, Sky entered the small chamber. A large bed stood against the wall, with a fleece mattress on top and blankets folded at the end. The room also held a few rolled pallets placed against the opposite wall, for any servants who might be traveling with their master. The hearth had been laid for a fire. Flint and steel to start the blaze rested in a mantelshelf built into the wall above.

"Why didn't you warn me you knew the innkeeper?"

"I did . . . in a way." She tested the mattress, finding it lumpy. The scent of mint wafted up from the bed, and thankfully, the mattress appeared to be free of vermin. "I told you my da and cousins oft stay here whilst conducting business." She stood. "And I did say I'd traveled this way many times. I had hoped you'd reckon—"

"No, I didn't *reckon* anything of the sort. Will Harold send word to the Erskines?"

"Nay. Though he loves a bit of gossip, he's no' one for spreading tales himself. Plus, he's loyal to the MacKintosh clan and to my da. He'd lose quite a bit of business should he do aught to incur the wrath of the MacKintosh laird."

She moved to the mantelshelf and took down the flint and steel. Leaning over the hearth, she struck them together, sending sparks into the waiting tinder. She blew gently, and the tinder ignited, catching fire to the larger twigs. "'Twill be wonderful to sleep in a warm chamber this eve, aye?" A neat pile of logs had been stacked against the wall by the hearth.

"Aye, and to eat a hot meal." Struan dropped their rucksacks on the bed.

They'd left her mare well tended in the livery nearby, and whilst there, Struan informed the owner they were in need of a good horse to purchase. Sky had no doubt there would be several palfreys to choose from on the morrow.

A light knock sounded on their door. "Enter," Struan called.

Harold's wife bustled in, carrying a tray with thick slices of dark bread, jam and a savory-smelling stew steaming from two wooden bowls. She set the meal on a small table standing in the corner, just as a line of servants followed their mistress inside, hauling a wooden tub, buckets of hot water and linens. Another brought two goblets and a flagon of wine.

"I hope you find the chamber to yer liking, my lady, my lord." The innkeeper's wife curtsied. "My man says ye've recently . . . er . . ."

"Eloped." Sky smiled warmly at the ruddy-cheeked matron. "'Tis true, Sally."

Struan came to stand beside her, draping his arm around her shoulders. Sky wrapped her arm around his waist. "This is my husband," she informed the curious matron, while wishing with all her heart she were speaking the truth. "Struan of clan Sutherland."

"Och, weel, me and mine wish ye all the best." Her head bobbed. "'That we do." Sally supervised as the servants made the bath ready, and then she shooed them out the door. "If ye should need aught else, just send word. We've a lad who waits in the corridor just for that purpose when we've nobles staying at the inn." She grinned. "Our youngest, he is. Our John likes tae make himself useful. He's a canny lad. Came up with the idea himself, he did." She dipped another curtsy before wishing them well again and taking her leave.

"I don't know what I want more right now—sleep, food or a bath." Struan scratched at three days of growth on his chin. "And a shave." He lifted the candle standing in the middle of the table and took it to the fire to light the wick, adding another log to the growing blaze as well.

"Let's eat. The water will keep well enough by the fire." Sky pulled out one of the two chairs by the table and poured wine into the goblets.

Struan placed the candleholder back on the table and took a seat. He reached for a slice of bread. "Do you think the Erskines will send word about what happened here to Nairn? They'll likely claim I murdered Oliver."

"If the earl of Mar was party to his grandson's plot against me, then nay. He'll ken my clan and I will refute anything he might spread about, and the word of a MacKintosh carries far more weight than that of an Erskine."

"I hope so." Struan tore into his meal as if he hadn't eaten in days. "This stew is wonderful, or maybe I'm just that grateful to fill my belly with something hot and easier to chew than jerky."

"Aye, 'tis one of the reasons my kin frequent this inn. They've a very fine cook."

Clean from her bath, and her hunger satisfied, Sky sat in front of the fire wearing naught but a T-shirt and the panties she'd brought with her. The undergarments she'd washed in the bathwater hung on pegs to dry, and she'd done her best to brush her gown clean. Contentment, along with the prospect of sleeping upon a bed, conspired against her until she could hardly keep her eyes open. She brushed her wet hair, holding it close to the hearth's heat to dry.

"I love your hair." Struan lifted her from the chair and sat down with her on his lap. "Have I ever told you that?"

"Nay, you've no' mentioned it." She leaned back against his chest and inhaled his clean scent.

"And your hazel eyes." He nibbled her neck. "You have the prettiest eyes I've ever beheld."

"Do I?" She smiled and tilted her head, encouraging him to keep nibbling. If only things could always be thus between them. Mayhap they would have been if she hadn't insisted upon returning. But then, if she hadn't, she'd miss her family, and she'd suffer the guilt of not attempting to intervene. Och, no matter what she did or which way she turned, there hadn't been a way out for her that led to happiness.

"Don't, princess." Struan tightened his arms around her. "I can feel you growing tense. Don't think about anything right now. Let's just enjoy the moment. We're warm, fed and clean. Plus, there's a bed awaiting our pleasure."

She giggled and twisted around to look at him. "The bed awaits our pleasure, does it?"

"Aye." Struan took advantage of her position, kissing her tenderly.

"Och, Struan." She turned and put her arms around his neck. "Do you wonder what life would have been like for us had I stayed in Gordon Hollow?"

Pain and longing radiated from him, and his wonderful mouth turned down. "Nay, I don't wonder. I know." His gaze bored into her. "You see, I had it all worked out. The damn portal was not supposed to open. We would've gone home, and I would've helped you figure out what you wanted to do with your life. Then, in a year of two, we'd marry. I had hoped we'd have a few bairns. I wanted to grow old together."

That he'd thought all that through, that he wished to marry and have bairns with her . . . Sky's mind reeled, and an ache spread like spilled wine from her heart to her soul. She swallowed a few times, and her eyes filled. "I . . . I've ruined everything."

He averted his gaze. "You did what you believed you had to do, and I respect and admire you for your loyalty." He set her off his lap and stood. "What happened to not thinking about anything other than the present? *I* had the forethought to bring a box of condoms with me, and we've never made love in the fifteenth century." He glanced at the bed. "Or on a fifteenth-century fleece mattress for that matter."

Turning back to her, he grinned and held out his hand. "Come, my lady. If it pleases you, let us give medieval sex a try."

She couldn't help it, a burst of laughter bubbled up, and she took his hand. "Aye, milord. Think you 'twill be somehow different?"

"Hmm." He drew her into his arms and rocked her back and forth while stroking her damp hair. "Let's find out."

He made love to her, his touch achingly tender. Sky sensed the desperation and sadness pouring from him, and she echoed the same. When they were both sated and Struan's breathing deepened with sleep, she lay awake, racking her brain for a better plan that led to her happiness as well as his. Naught came to her.

By the time Sky finished writing her letters, her hand was cramped and aching. She flexed her fingers. "My thanks for your help in copying these, Struan. We'll want proof of what I wrote should aught happen to the originals," she said, sealing the last vellum packet with hot wax. "Call for the lad in the corridor, if you would. All that remains is to address this last missive, and all will be ready." She dipped her quill into the ink again.

"You're most welcome, though I'm glad mine are the copies we're keeping. I'm no good at medieval penmanship." He shook his hand out. "I'm ready for an ale. What say you we head downstairs to put these missives directly into Master Harold's hands. The messengers will want their coins, aye?"

"What say I?" One side of her mouth quirked up.

"When in Rome." He shrugged.

She blinked. "What has Rome to do with us?"

"It's just an expression. 'Tis best I sound as I once did, to blend in."

"Ah." Sky stood and surveyed the results of their hours of labor. "A bite to eat, ale, and then we should head to the livery to choose a horse." She placed her hands at the small of her back and rubbed her spine. "I've been sitting for far too long."

Struan gathered the copies and stowed them in his rucksack. "Come, my lady, let us be about our business. The quicker we're done, the quicker we can put that fine bed to good use again."

"Och, do young men think of naught else but bed sport?" She laughed.

Struan opened the door and held out his arm for her to take. "Bed sport? Is that what we're to call what we do between the blankets, love?"

"What would you prefer I call our endeavors, my lord?" Sky gathered the messages and crossed the room to take his arm.

"Making *love*," Struan whispered into her ear before catching her earlobe between his teeth for an instant, sending a shiver down her spine. He snatched her cloak from its peg and draped it over his arm. "Come, let us be about our tasks."

"What do you suppose became of Katherine and Connor?" she asked. "I worry about them. Think you they're with the baron DúnConnell and their daughter?"

"I hope so, but there's no way of telling. I warned Connor oft enough about the unpredictability involved in our plans. I don't like to think it, but the McGladreys could have been sent anywhere and to any time. Perhaps they're in Ireland." Struan ushered her into the corridor and closed their chamber door behind them.

"My lady, my lord." A lad of about six or seven shot up from where he sat against the wall and gave them a slight bow. "If ye be needin' aught, I can fetch it for ye."

"Our thanks, lad, but we'll manage for now." Struan nodded. "Watch the door for us, if you would, and there'll be a coin in it for you when we return."

The lad straightened and puffed out his chest. "Aye, milord."

"This inn has an excellent reputation," Sky told him under her breath. "Our things are safe enough."

"For certes, but this will give the lad a task to do. Did you no' notice he's lame? He has a club foot."

Sky glanced back over her shoulder. The lad now sat with his back against their door, a serious expression on his young face. "I took no notice." Her heart swelled at Struan's thoughtfulness. Her knight was a good man, honorable and compassionate. Any woman would be fortunate indeed to be his wife. If only . . .

She bit her lip and choked back the tears. He'd seen to her safety and fought to protect her, even though he had no wish to be here in the past. The least she could do was to see that he returned safely to the future. Once home, she would take up her role as a healer to her clan. Somehow, the prospect didn't fill her with the sense of purpose it once did.

"Master Harold," Struan said, beckoning to the innkeeper. "We've several missives to send. Will you arrange for their post?" He took silver coins from the leather pouch he wore at his belt and handed them to the innkeeper. "Tell the riders we prefer they not take the main roads."

"Aye, milord. I'll see to it anon." Harold wiped his hands on a cloth slung over his shoulder before taking the coins and the letters. "Will ye be wanting yer midday meal in the hall, or shall I have it brought up to yer room?"

"Here would be fine." Struan took her elbow as he surveyed the great room packed tight with customers sitting at heavy wooden tables and benches. The place reeked with the stench of too many bodies pressed together in one space, along with the smell of stale beer, smoke from the hearth and whatever cooked in the kitchen.

"Take the table nearest the window. The air is fresher there, and it's just been cleared." Harold gestured. "I'll have food brought out to ye."

"And ale, if you would," Struan added.

"Aye, milord." Harold strode away, shouting orders as he went, sending two lads scurrying to do his bidding.

Sky took her place at the table, with Struan across from her. "We should leave on the morrow."

"Aye. Let's hope the livery master has a suitable horse for us. How long is the journey to Meikle Geddes from here?"

"A day's ride south, mayhap a day and a half, depending upon the weather or what we may encounter."

One of Harold's daughters came to the table, bearing a platter of bread, cheese and plump sausages. She also held two mugs of ale by the handles. She set the ales down before placing the platter at the center of the table. "Good day to ye, Lady Sky. 'Tis grand tae see ye again."

"And you, Moira. Last I heard, you and your good man had just had your first bairn. How is the lad?" Sky smiled at the young woman.

"Och, he's growing fast, and we've a wee lass now as well. They're with their granny whilst I help ma and da with the midday crowd. There's a passenger ship just come into port, so we're busier than usual." She shot Struan a curious look. "Enjoy yer meal, and if ye wish for aught else, I'll be about. Just wave." She curtsied and moved on to clear a nearby table.

Sky took a sausage and a piece of the thick brown bread and put them together. "Meikle Geddes is where my cousin Robley and his wife Erin live. I told you about them." She glanced at him. "Do you recall?"

"Umm-mm." He nodded, his mouth full. He chewed, swallowed and drank deep from his tankard. "Ahh, I have missed the ale from this era. There's nothing like it in the twenty-first century."

Sky laughed, and a rare burst of happiness warmed her. Despite his occasional bouts of angry brooding, Struan had a pleasant disposition and a quick wit. "You're an easy man to be with, Struan. You've a very pleasing nature."

"Aye, and I'm chivalrous." He sent her a pointed look.

"Chivalrous indeed."

"And let us no' forget my skill upon a medieval mattress." He winked and waggled his brow. "I'm most excellent at bed sport, aye?"

His boyish expression and twinkling eyes had her laughing again. "Och, Struan, if only . . ."

He sobered, and his expression closed. "If only what?"

"If only we had met under different circumstances, or . . . at a different point in time." Her throat tightened. "My kin and I will do everything we can to see that you return safely to Gordon Hollow."

"Without you?" Struan's gaze bored into hers. "Will you send me away, Sky, while you remain here? Am I so easily discarded?"

"How can you think that after everything we've been through together? I dinna wish to be parted from you at all . . . ever," she whispered, her heart pounding. "Will you stay here with me if I ask it of you?"

"I'd prefer it if *you* would return to Gordon Hollow with *me*. Think of all the advantages, princess—modern medicine, the freedom to choose your own path . . . a future together."

"I have a duty and an obligation to serve my clan. I'm—"

"I ken well enough who you are," he snapped. "If I agreed to stay, your father would never allow me to take you to wife. I'm a blacksmith. You, on the other hand—"

"You canna say what my father will or willna allow." She kept her voice low to avoid being overheard. A sudden wave of shame pulsed from him, and he turned his face away from her. "What is it you're hiding from me, Struan? Does it have aught to do with your ties to the Sutherlands? I can sense—"

"I'm nobody to the Sutherlands now or in the past," he hissed. "For God's sake, let it go." He grabbed a handful of food, gulped his ale down and rose. "I'm going to see the hostler about purchasing a horse. 'Twould be best if you remained here."

Stunned, she sat back and gripped the edge of the table. He'd once again gone from easygoing to brooding and angry. Whenever the Sutherland name was mentioned, he closed himself off from her and stomped away. If only he would share what plagued him, she might be able to ease his anguish.

Ah, but 'twas not only mention of the Sutherlands that upset him this time. Was it just yesterday he'd revealed his dreams for their future together? He'd asked her to return to Gordon Hollow with him, forsaking her family, her home and her proper place in time—as he'd done for her. Could she forsake all for Struan? She'd always been the dutiful daughter, the one who shied away from adventure and risk. Could she change her nature?

She blinked as the table and everything it held blurred before her. She couldn't think on it now. First they had to get to Moigh Hall in one piece, and then mayhap the answer would come to her.

CHAPTER FOURTEEN

S truan nudged his gelding into a trot and surveyed his surroundings as they approached Meikle Geddes's keep—one of the MacKintosh holdings. Sky had told him her cousin Robley and his family lived there. Though well fortified, the rectangular castle was small by fifteenth-century standards. Two towers, one on the east end, the other on the west, rose above the crenellated top. Narrow windows for archers dotted the various levels of the turrets. The land around the outer curtain wall had been cleared of any impediment, and the stronghold's catwalks were fully manned.

The heavy steel bars of the portcullis were down, and two guards, crossbows in hand, stood within the barbican above, watching as he and Sky rode closer. Were they expecting trouble?

Sky nudged her mare ahead. "Ho, the keep. 'Tis I, Sky Elizabeth, your liege lord's daughter and cousin to Lord Robley," she called, lowering the hood of her cloak. "And this is Sir Struan of clan Sutherland."

Struan didn't miss the way the two guards exchanged glances. He could only imagine what might be running through their minds, what with he and Sky unaccompanied by guards or a matron to protect her virtue. Had news of Sky's disappearance reached Meikle Geddes? The portcullis began its noisy ascent, and the guards called out their greetings and bid them enter.

He and Sky hadn't caught any sign of Erskine men as they'd traveled south from Nairn. Perhaps their enemy had already passed through, or perhaps he and Sky managed to evade the Erskines by taking less-traveled routes. Still, Struan kept a wary eye open, even as they rode through the hamlet bordering the narrow lane to the castle.

The MacKintosh holding was rich and fertile, with plentiful water, being situated by the river as it was. Perfect for raising kine, horses and crops. The hamlet they'd passed through reflected the care and prosperity of the clan. The cottages were well tended, and the villagers content.

Sky kicked her horse into a canter through the gate, and he followed upon her heels, staying a short distance behind to play the part of her guard, rather than her consort. They passed through the outer ward, continuing on to another gate leading to the inner bailey. He breathed easier than he had in days once he heard the gates lowered behind them. They were inside two tall stone walls guarded by a garrison of MacKintosh warriors. A lad of seven or eight ran from the stables to take the reins of their mounts. Struan dismounted and helped Sky from her horse.

"Is Lord Robley at home?" Sky asked the stable hand. She took her rucksack from the saddle and handed it to Struan.

"Aye, my lady." The lad grinned, exposing a gap where his two front teeth should have been. He bowed and led the horses away to be cared for.

Just as Struan set foot upon the bottom step to the heavy, steel-girded doors into the castle, a man's voice resounded through the air. "Sky! By the saints, lass. Can it truly be you?"

Sky gave a cry and ran toward the middle-aged man who had called out. Laughing and crying at the same time, she threw herself into his open arms, and he hugged her tight and spun her around. A younger version of the man stood by, a wide grin on his face.

The older man stopped midspin, his gaze catching upon Struan. His eyes widened as he stared. He set Sky down. "By God," he said, striding toward Struan. "If I did no' ken my cousin's offspring well, I'd swear this lad was one of Elaine and Dylan's brood."

"My lord." Struan tipped his head slightly.

"Robley, Will, this is Struan of clan Sutherland," Sky said. "Sir Struan, this is my cousin Robley and his eldest, Robert William, whom we call Will."

"Och." Robley clasped forearms briefly with Struan. "The resemblance to Dylan when he was a younger man . . . 'Tis quite remarkable," he said, flashing Sky a questioning look. "Do we have this young knight to thank for your return?"

"Aye," she said, her eyes misting. "He saved my life, Rob. I have so much to tell you. Is Erin here?"

"Nay." Will stepped forward. "Ma went to attend Lady Meghan for the birthing. She'll be there for a fortnight yet, along with Hannah." He glanced toward Struan. "Hannah is my younger sister. Meg and Hunter's bairn was born four days ago. We just received word this morn." Will held out his hand to Struan. "Welcome, Sir Struan. Our thanks to you for bringing Lady Sky home safe." They too clasped forearms for a brief moment.

"My, how you've matured, Will," Sky said, tousling his tawny blond hair. "Last I heard, you were on your way home for good to train under your da."

"Aye." He straightened his posture, a look of pride suffusing his features. "I'll be ten and seven soon, and I've earned my spurs. 'Tis time I learn what will be expected of me once I become seneschal to the earl. I'm helping Da, so we can both spend more time with the horses."

"Are your younger brothers home?"

"Nay, but they'll be returning with Ma for a visit."

Robley hadn't taken his eyes off him since they'd been introduced, and Struan desperately wished for a distraction. He'd had enough of the man's scrutiny.

"Last we heard, you'd . . . disappeared, lass," Robley said. "The MacKintosh guards who followed you into the wood at Kildrummy said you were in quite a state and wouldn't even wait for them to saddle their horses. They said you were in a hurry to find your da and brother."

"Can we move inside to your solar, Rob?" Sky scanned the bailey. "There is much to tell, and I would very much like to sit with a glass of wine whilst relating all that has happened." She shot her cousin a pointed look. "Though to you it has been less than a fortnight since I left, I have been gone for almost three months' time." She met her cousin's knowing gaze. "I've been on *quite* a journey."

"Ah, I see." Robley swept his arm toward the doors into the keep. "Will, lad, see to it that wine and something to eat are sent to my solar before you join us."

"Aye, Da." Will ran up the broad stone stairs and disappeared into the keep.

"You will join us, Sir Struan, for I would hear your accounting of what has transpired as well," Robley commanded. "Then you may billet with my garrison below the great hall."

Struan cringed inwardly. It had been a long time since he'd been ordered around by a noble or told where to lay his head, and already he resented being treated like an inferior. Stifling the growl rising in his throat, he followed, once again reminded of the gulf that separated him from the woman he loved—in this century, anyway.

He and Sky hadn't talked about the day he'd marched out of the inn, angry at her refusal to see things his way. Nothing had changed. The qualities that drew him to her still drove him nuts. Stubborn woman.

They went up a flight of narrow stone stairs and down a short corridor to the lord's solar. The chamber was well lit with a single glass-paned window against the southern wall. A table of oak, surrounded by four chairs with leather seats and carved oak armrests, took up most of the space.

"Sit." Robley gestured toward the table.

Struan pulled out one of the chairs for Sky before taking a place himself. How should he play this? Just how much should he reveal about himself? At least the MacKintosh were familiar with time travel. Robley himself had been to the twenty-first century.

"The day I disappeared," Sky began, twisting her hands together in her lap, "I overheard Oliver talking to his lover, the baron Lumsden's daughter. My *betrothed* revealed to her his plans to murder me within a year of our wedding so that the two of them could wed and live in comfort upon my dower lands and fortune. I feared they caught a glimpse of me as I fled from the door. 'Tis why I was in such a hurry to find Da."

"Bloody hell!" Robley strode to the window and stared out. "After your disappearance, your family stopped here on their way home to Moigh Hall. True said she'd sensed something sinister afoot all along, but she had no' been able to put her finger on what it might be." He turned back to face her. "'Twas she who insisted your family and guards leave Kildrummy under cover of darkness that very night. 'Tis also why you find my outer and inner gates closed at present."

"There is more to the tale, Rob," Sky said. "Oliver is dead. He had the faerie ring where I fell through time watched for my return. He meant to force me to go through with the wedding, and threatened to starve and beat me into compliance. He said none of my kin kent of my return, and so it made no difference to him if I died. He'd already planned to demand Helen's hand in my stead. Then, Oliver bade his guards to kill Struan, and—"

"Wait," Robley ordered, pulling out a chair and taking a seat. He fixed his stare upon Struan. "Who *are* you, and how is it you came to be with our lass?"

"Uh, that's a long story," Struan said. "She fell at my feet in the middle of a jousting match at a Renaissance fair in New York."

"Do you wish to tell the tale, Struan, or would you prefer that I continue?"

"You go ahead." Struan leaned back and folded his arms across his chest. "But first, I want to make something clear to your cousin. *I* am not accustomed to being ordered about or told where to sleep. I am my own man and have not sworn fealty to any *lord*."

Robley barked out a laugh just as the door to the solar opened, and Will came through, followed by servants bearing food and drink. Robley turned to one of the servants. "Have a chamber prepared for Sir Struan and another for Lady Sky. I trow that will suit you?" He arched a brow at Struan before turning back to the servant. "At opposite ends of the hall, mind. In fact, put Lady Sky in our wee Hannah's chamber. 'Tis next door to mine." He shot Struan a pointed look.

"Aye, milord," the young woman answered. "I'll see to it anon."

Struan didn't bother telling Robley his efforts were wasted. He and Sky had been sleeping together since that day by Gordon Lake. Still, he didn't wish to push things. He caught a glimpse of Sky and frowned at the expression of mortification darkening her lovely face. The servants set the repast on the table, curtsied and left, and Will took a seat at the table.

"Struan and I met in the twenty-first century at a fair like the one where you met Lady Erin," Sky began. "Struan had come to the twenty-first century himself but a decade before. He fought in the battle of Halidon Hill alongside his da when he crawled through a wavering light he saw in the bog."

"For certes?" Will leaned toward him. "Tell us what—"

"Later, lad." Robley shot his son an affectionate look. "Go on, Sky."

Sky took a swallow of her wine and continued. She told her cousins all that had transpired from the moment she'd fallen into the portal, to the present and their arrival at Meikle Geddes.

"The McGladreys helped us immensely, and Struan trained with Connor for weeks as we waited for my passport to arrive." Sky sat up a little straighter. "You should see Struan wield a sword, Rob. He oft defeats Connor whilst they train." She glanced at Struan through her lashes. "My champion makes defeating Connor appear effortless."

"Ah, I wouldn't say 'tis an *easy* feat to bring the man to his knees." Struan winked at her.

"By the saints!" Robley cried, letting out another laugh. "Did Connor and Katherine come with you? Are they here as well?"

"They walked through the portal with us, but we were separated." Struan shook his head. "There's no telling where they are now. I only hope the two of them remained together."

"Och, but I'd love to lay eyes upon them again. Mayhap they're with Meghan, aye? Surely their hearts led them to their daughter, no matter what they kept fixed in their minds."

"'Tis our hope," Sky agreed.

Then she shared what Struan had told her about his own journey to the future. The way she spoke about the Gordons warmed his heart, and a pang of longing to be home shot through him. He missed his kin and he missed his forge. The only thing Sky didn't touch upon was her relationship with him, and though he understood why, the slight still stung.

Did her loyalty extend only as far as blood kin? A knot formed in his stomach, but he forced himself to be rational. She'd said she didn't wish to part with him, and he'd planted the seed, suggesting that she return with him to Gordon Hollow. That discussion was not over by a long shot. No decisions had been made.

"Sky and I plan to continue on to Loch Moigh tomorrow, and I'd appreciate it if you'd lend us a few of your best guards to aid me in seeing to her safety," Struan said.

"Aye." Robley rubbed his chin, his expression pensive. "The Erskines may have already laid siege to Moigh Hall if that is their intent. To be safe, you should travel 'round to the south side of the loch under cover of the forest. Our clan keeps a few boats hidden there. Sky kens where they are. Wait for nightfall before crossing to the island.

"We've no' seen any Erskines passing through, but 'tis likely Lord Robert will have kept to the main road, especially if he's traveling with a large contingent of soldiers," Robley continued.

"If the two Erskine guards I fought are any indication, the earl of Mar's men are poorly trained. Lord Oliver was only slightly better."

"Three against one," Sky boasted on his behalf. "'Twas quite a feat. Struan managed to dispatch two guards and Oliver quickly enough for us to escape."

Her eyes shone with pride—and was that love he glimpsed in those hazel depths as they met his? He could only hope. Warmth surged through him, and with it, a fierce wave of possessiveness. She was his, and if he had any say in the matter, she would remain his. All he had to do was convince her to return to the future with him.

"I owe a great deal to Connor. He's an excellent trainer," Struan said. "I've never met a better swordsman."

"Nor have I." Rob looked from Sky to him and back again. "Humph. I'll travel with the two of you to Moigh Hall. Will, I'll leave you in command here. Keep the gates closed, and warn the villagers to scatter into the hills or to come within the walls of the keep should we catch even a glimpse of an Erskine. We'll take a score of my garrison with us, and I'll send word to a few of our allies yet this day."

"I've already dispatched missives to Stirling, DúnConnell and Sutherland. Word should have already reached our king and allies by now."

"Och, you're a braw canny lass and a credit to your clan." Rob beamed. "Your father would have alerted our neighbors to the south at any sign of trouble. Cousin Murray will send what men he can spare. The Erskines dinna stand a chance against us, and Lord Robert is a fool."

How likely was it that one of his da's direct descendants would travel to Moigh Hall? Struan's jaw clenched, and the taunts he'd suffered as a lad came back to him in a chokehold of misery. He glanced at Sky to find her studying him. Of course she'd sense his turmoil.

Would revealing his origins dim the light shining in her lovely eyes whenever she looked his way? He had hopes and dreams for his future, and they included having Sky by his side. He had no idea whether fate conspired with or against him. Helplessness to control the outcome or to alter the course of his life banded his chest and the familiar anger burned bright.

He lifted his goblet and took a long draught, feeling once again as if fate were hemming him in and pushing him toward a ledge he wished to avoid.

"Tell us about Halidon Hill, Sir Struan," Will begged. "I've heard the tales and read about it, but *you* were there."

"Aye," Robley added. "I'd very much like to hear the tale as well."

"If it pleases you," Sky said, rising from her place, "I'd like to wash off the dust from our travels. Would Erin mind if I borrowed something clean to wear?"

"Nay, help yourself, lass." Rob glanced at her. "Have our servants see to cleaning your garments whilst you're here, and they'll be ready for you before we depart on the morrow." He turned to Struan. "We're close enough in size, lad. I'll lend you something to wear so your clothing can be tended as well. In fact, let us take care of that anon." He rose. "What say you to a bit of swordplay before supper? Will and I would be glad to witness your skill for ourselves, and we can save the storytelling for later this eve whilst we sup."

Struan sighed. He was tired and not in the mood to show off, but he understood he was being tested. Robley had caught the heated look he'd shared with Sky, not to mention the way she sang his praises. Perhaps he was being given a chance to prove himself and to gain an ally. If so, he couldn't afford to pass it up.

After all, Robley had married a woman from the future, a lass with no land or political connections. Hopefully, the man would sympathize with Struan's plight. Too bad Sky wasn't Robley's daughter. Somehow he doubted Robley would have much sway with the earl of

Fife when it came to Sky's future with the bastard son of the fourth earl of Sutherland. Struan stood up and stretched. "If you wish."

Robley opened the solar door. "Let's find something suitable for you to wear before heading for the lists, and I'll arrange for a bath to be readied in your chamber."

"My thanks. If you don't mind, I'd like to fight you both at once. It's been a long few days, and I don't wish to expend too much more energy today."

"By God, you are a Sutherland through and through, and every bit as cocky." Robley laughed, cast him an incredulous look and laughed again. Will, on the other hand, kept his mouth shut and his eyes wide. "We shall see, lad. Dinna count on victory just yet."

Aye, it would be good to form alliances, make a name for himself with Sky's kin. The earl of Fife would then be much less inclined to remove Struan's head from his shoulders should he learn Struan had stolen his eldest daughter's virtue. Though to be fair, she'd seduced him, not the other way around—not that he wouldn't have gotten to the seduction part himself if given enough time.

Struan, Sky and the MacKintosh traveling with them had left their horses with a crofter half a league back and made their way through thick forest to a hill overlooking Loch Moigh. Struan lay flat on his belly and peered down at the village nestled beside the loch. Their worst fears had been realized. The village and the shores teemed with Erskines armed to the hilt. "Bloody hell, Lord Robert has a cannon."

"Humph." Robley peered down at the enemy now occupying the village. "'Tis unlikely to do him any good. Our island stronghold is out of range." He glanced at Struan. "Is it no'?"

"Hmm." He studied the island. "The keep is set far enough back. Maybe they'll manage to destroy a few of the fishing boats lining the shore, perhaps the outer curtain wall will suffer some damage, but the keep?" He shook his head. "Doubtful."

"Aye, and if we're lucky, the damn thing will explode in their faces. I've heard tell cannons are most unreliable." Robley put his hand on Struan's shoulder. "Come, let us continue on before it becomes too dark to find the boats. I dinna wish to spend the night in the forest. 'Twould be best not to be discovered by Lord Robert's scouts. Besides, even if we aren't discovered, we'd have to wait another day to make our way to the island."

He and Robley retreated to where the rest of their party waited, hidden in the shadows of the trees. Rob issued a silent order, and the guards formed a line with Sky safely ensconced at the midpoint. They crept along, careful not to make any noise that might alert enemy spies. By the time they reached the south shore and uncovered the boats hidden under the brush, the sun had sunk to the horizon.

"Clouds," Sky whispered, pointing to the north. Heavy, dark clouds were moving their way. "We'll have good cover, more if it rains."

"Aye," Robley agreed. "Sit. Eat something. As soon as darkness falls, we'll be off."

By the time the sun had disappeared, it was raining hard. Rob, Struan and Sky piled into the first boat, along with three of the MacKintosh guards. The rest of the men divided themselves amongst the remaining three, and they all shoved off from shore and headed for the island, keeping the darker outline of the castle in their sights to guide them. The way was slow, and they were careful not to make noise when slicing the oars through the water. For safety's sake, they kept a fair distance between each of the skiffs.

Sky's teeth were chattering by the time they landed, but there was nothing Struan could do. He had nothing to offer to shield her from the deluge. He helped her out of the boat and made sure she stood on firm ground before turning back to help drag the skiffs on shore.

"Come," Robley beckoned, "to the postern gate." He led them single file to an iron gate behind the castle. There, he called out to the guards manning the parapet, and the passageway was opened quickly.

"Welcome, Lord Robley." The guard bowed as they filed through into the outer ward. "Och, Lady Sky! 'Tis grand to have ye back, Lady Sky."

"'Tis good to be back, George," she said as she slipped through.

"Bad business afoot with the Erskines, aye? Best hie yourselves to the great hall anon. The lords are gathered within." George waited until the last man was through, and then the gate clanged closed behind them and the lock clicked into place.

The lords were gathered? What was he about to face once they entered Moigh Hall? Struan followed Sky along a narrow path leading past what must be the kitchen gardens. They stopped at a door at the rear of the keep. Robley sent his guards to the lower level to find a hot meal and a dry place to rest before ushering Struan and Sky past the kitchen and into the great hall.

A fire burned in the huge hearth nearest a long trestle table, and five men stood with bent heads, studying a map laid out before them. He recognized Connor immediately, and relief surged through him.

"Da!" Sky cried out.

A large man, broad-shouldered and fit, his hair streaked with silver, raised his head and let out a cry. He strode across the hall and had his daughter in a bear hug in an instant. "Och, my wee lass. We feared we'd ne'er lay eyes upon ye again."

Two younger men joined them, forming a huddle around her, shutting Struan out. They must be her twin brothers. What had she said their names were?

"Connor McGladrey!" Robley shouted. "'Tis good to see you again, my friend, and you as well, Dylan. How is it you're here, cousin?"

Connor and Robley embraced, slapping each other's backs vigorously, and then Rob did the same with the man he'd called Dylan . . . the man whose resemblance to Struan's da was so strong, it was like looking at his sire's ghost. Struan remained an outsider to yet another joyous reunion between Sky and her kin. His heart hammering inside his chest, his clothing dripping onto the rushes beneath his feet, he watched as tears of joy streamed down Sky's face.

He couldn't compete—not with this.

"Owain, lad," the earl rasped out, his own tears plain to see. "Fetch your ma." His eyes lit on Struan. He straightened, keeping Sky tucked against his side. "You must be Sir Struan. I'm the earl of Fife and laird to clan MacKintosh. Connor has had much to say about you, lad. We owe you a great debt of gratitude. You've protected Sky since the hour she entered your era, and now you've managed to see her safely home." His voice broke at that last part.

A strangled laugh burst out of Struan before he could contain it. "I'm also the reason you have Erskines squatting in your village right now, with a cannon aimed at your island." He tried to swallow, but his mouth had gone ash dry.

"Aye, and they're demanding we turn you over, since 'twas you who slayed the earl's heir." Malcolm clapped Struan's back a few times. "Dinna worry, lad. Connor also told us of the Erskines' plot. You're safe with us."

Struan nodded, too relieved to speak.

"By the saints," Dylan said, coming to stand beside the earl. "Connor did no' lie. You and I . . . 'tis bloody uncanny. Who are you to the Sutherlands? He also told us you fought at Halidon Hill against the English. My great-grandsire died at that battle. Did you fight under his command? Did you ken the earl of Sutherland? His given name was—"

"Kenneth Alexander." Struan raked his fingers through his dripping hair. "Aye, I kent him well enough. I fought by his side." A lump rose in his throat. "Your great-grandsire died in my arms."

Surveying the curious gazes riveted on him, he risked a glance at Sky. She'd been so honest and brave. Since the day she'd landed in the dirt in front of him, she'd been nothing but forthright, sharing things about herself she believed would put her at risk. And how had he repaid her? Time to come clean. He owed her his honesty. "The fourth earl of Sutherland was my sire."

"Why . . . that makes you my uncle. But . . ." Dylan's brow furrowed. "I dinna recall any mention of a Struan in our patents or in the family Bible. Were you kent by another name mayhap?"

"You won't find me on any of your *official* records." Struan shook his head. "I'm the earl's bastard."

Sky moved away from her sire, her eyes filled with hurt and betrayal. "Struan—"

"Sky Elizabeth," a woman called from the top of the stairs. "Oh, my dearest . . ." A petite woman hurried down the steps. Her hair was a darker shade of the same chestnut as Sky's, only with silver streaking her temples. No doubt this was Sky's mother, Lady True. The two were the same in height and build. Two younger women followed, their joyful squeals piercing his poor ears.

"Ma, Helen, Sarah!" Sky ran to meet them.

Once again the woman he loved was surrounded by her kin in a huddle of happiness—a huddle that excluded him.

Connor came to stand by Struan's side. He clasped Struan's shoulder for an instant. "I'm sorry. Katherine and I ended up at DúnConnell, and that left you alone to defend your lady. We did what we could by gathering forces and informing Hunter and the Sutherlands of what Sky had learned before she came to our century." He swept the hall with his gaze. "We all thought it prudent to prepare for the worst, whilst praying you and Sky would somehow make it to Moigh Hall." He squeezed Struan's shoulder. "You did well, Struan."

"Thanks." Struan couldn't tear his eyes from Sky. If only he were an accepted and welcome part of the reunion. More than anything, he longed to take her into his arms, hear her assurances his origins meant nothing to her. Ah, but he'd seen the hurt and betrayal in her eyes.

His jaw tightened. The earl was not likely to allow him to get close enough to Sky to have a meaningful conversation with her. He might not get the chance to beg for her forgiveness.

"Come. Stand by the fire before you catch a chill, lad." Dylan gestured toward the hearth. "You and I have much to discuss."

"Do we?" Struan glanced askance at the older man.

"Och, aye. We're kin, and you were at Halidon Hill. I wish to hear all about that day, and I'd very much like to hear about my great-grandsire."

"Though your great-grandsire was my sire, you'd be the first of his line—his legitimate line—to lower himself to engage in discourse with *me*. The countess and her brood were never civil where I was concerned." Why did it still sting? He was a grown man, with a life, family and friends of his own. Why did his childhood longing for acceptance and affection within his sire's household still haunt him?

Dylan's stare drove into him like a ploughshare. "I dinna hold you responsible for my ancestors' behavior, nor for the circumstance of your birth. Do *you* mean to hold me responsible for the actions of my predecessors? Ancestors, I might add, that I and my siblings never met?"

"Humph." Struan turned away, needing time to process. Dylan's reaction stunned him. All this time he'd feared returning to the past with Sky, feared revealing the circumstances of his birth . . . "Should I be surprised that all of you take the whole time travel thing so well?"

"We've had time to adjust." Dylan shrugged. "With so many of my kin touched by these strange circumstances, we've had little choice but to accept."

Dylan threw his arm around Struan's shoulders and turned him toward the table. "Come, lad . . . er . . . *uncle*," he said with a huff of irony. "Warm yourself by the fire, have an ale and fill your belly. The MacKintosh and Sutherlands have a battle to fight on the morrow, and this might our only chance to have speech with one another."

Struan cast a look over his shoulder in time to see the women hustle Sky up the stairs and out of his reach. Resigned, he allowed Dylan to lead him to the blazing heat of the hearth.

"I'm Owain, and this is my twin, David," the young man said, handing Struan a mug of thick, dark ale. "We're Sky's brothers."

"Glad to meet you." Seeing the two youths brought an ache to his heart. "I've a younger brother around the same age as you two. His name is Michael." His heart wrenched. "He's . . . my adoptive family is in the twenty-first century."

Malcolm approached, his expression intimidating. "Come, we've plans to discuss before we go to our rest."

Owain's eyes lit with excitement. "Will you join us on the morrow, Sir Struan?"

"Aye. I'd be more than happy to help you dispose of the refuse littering your shores." Struan studied the map spread out on the trestle table as Rob, Connor and Dylan joined them.

"Nay, lad," Sky's father said. "I think it best you leave for the western shore under cover of darkness yet this night. I'll send two of the baron DúnConnell's men with you." Laird MacKintosh stared at him, his expression hard. "From there, you will travel to my foster son's keep. There you will remain until Connor joins you. 'Tis my hope that Madame Giselle can be prevailed upon to aid you, Connor and Katherine in returning to your homes."

"Nope." Struan's heart pounded, and adrenaline pumped through his veins. He wasn't ready to leave Sky. Did the earl think he'd sneak away in the dark of night without even a word with her? "Not going to happen." He stared back, just as hard. Their gazes locked. Struan wasn't about to back down. "The Erskine heir meant to murder Sky, and I've no doubt Oliver's grandsire approved of his plan. I made a vow to protect your daughter, and I'm fighting tomorrow. Sky's enemies are *my* enemies."

"Let him fight, Malcolm." Robley placed his hand on the earl's shoulder. "According to Sky, he's earned the right."

"Humph." The earl turned his attention to the map and pointed. "Here is where Hunter and the earl of Sutherland's men are camped. At dawn, they'll move here." He slid his finger to the place where he and Robley had spied upon the Erskines from the top of the hill.

Struan nodded. "High ground. Always a good position to hold."

"Our cousin Murray's soldiers are already on the south side." The earl pointed again. "Just before daybreak, we'll land on the north shore, and at the signal, we'll converge upon the Erskines from all sides." He eyed Struan. "Do ye wish to borrow what armor we may find that suits you?"

"Nay. I prefer my brigandine. I can move more freely."

"Hmm, but you're also more vulnerable to the bite of blades and arrows." Malcolm sent him a pointed look.

For the next half hour, the seven of them debated the merits of armor versus hauberks and brigandines. That segued into a discussion of various weapons of war, and the cannon the Erskines had aimed toward the island.

Struan straightened where he sat. "I can attest to the fact that in this century, cannons are untrustworthy and prone to cause as much damage to those who fire them as to the target they're aimed upon. It'll be a few hundred years yet before the bugs are worked out."

Dylan frowned. "Bugs?"

"Flaws," Struan amended.

"Och, well, I'm off to bed." Owain yawned. "We'll be up before dawn, aye?"

"Aye." Rob nodded. "Struan, you're welcome to share my chamber. I'll have a pallet sent up anon."

"My thanks," Struan said, pushing himself from the table.

"Before you're off to your rest, I'd like a word, Sir Struan." Malcolm stood with his back to the hearth, his arms crossed in front of his broad chest, and his stance wide.

Rob's brow rose, and he caught Struan's eye, giving him a slight nod. "I trust you'll show the lad to my chamber once you've finished expressing the fullness of your gratitude, Malcolm."

The earl grunted by way of a response, and once again Struan's mouth went dry, as one by one the rest of their party wandered above stairs to their various chambers. Struan sat back down on the bench and faced the hearth with his back resting against the trestle table. He needed the support.

"I am indeed grateful to you and to the Gordons," the earl began. "'Tis my understanding that our daughter spent almost three months in your company." The earl's jaw muscle twitched. "The past handful of days the two of you have traveled the countryside . . . alone." His brow lowered in a most fierce fatherlike manner. "Now I must ask, what are you to Sky, and what is she to you?"

His ears rang with the rushing of his blood. Struan swallowed a few times, attempting to gather his wits. No use in lying. "I love your daughter, Laird, and I believe she loves me."

Malcolm's scowl deepened. "Be that as it may—"

"I've asked her to return to Gordon Hollow with me. I hope to marry her in a year or two, once she's—"

"That I will no' permit. Sky has a responsibility and an obligation to our clan. She is of noble—"

"So that's where she gets that asinine refrain she's forever spouting." He shot up. "It's just that kind of bullshit thinking that almost got her killed."

"Asinine refrain?" Malcolm took a step closer. "She is our daughter. Her mother and I love her more than you can imagine. We wish to see her well settled, happy . . . somewhere nearby—no' in the distant future."

"Is that why you traded her off to that scum, Oliver?" The earl hadn't said the words, but the implication was crystal clear. Being wed to a bastard and *well settled* were not a word match. His muscles tensed. "Sky told me the story about you and your Lady True. What's with the double standard? It was all right for you to marry a woman from the future, but—"

"The difference being, I was the heir to an earldom. Our clan did no' need a dowry, and she brought with her gifts enough that all kent she was worth more than gold. You, on the other hand—"

"*I* am a landowner with a thriving business. I can well support a wife and family." He wasn't about to touch the issue of his illegitimacy. "It may surprise you to know Sky has no intentions of allowing herself to be bartered off in marriage again. She won't sacrifice herself for the sake of the clan, so you can forget about handing her off to some stranger in exchange for thirty pieces of silver, a handful of dirt or an alliance that will be broken at the slightest provocation."

"You've . . . lain with her, haven't you?"

"*That*, my lord, is none of your business."

Several seconds of uncomfortable glaring ensued. Struan fisted his hands, ready to defend himself should the earl decide to attempt murder.

"Malcolm," a soft feminine voice called from the stairs. "Come to bed, *mo céile*. You know I can't sleep unless you're beside me." Lady True cast Struan a sympathetic look. "You've harassed the lad enough for one night. Let him go to his rest."

Malcolm cast his lady wife a tender look before turning back to glare at Struan. "Tomorrow we fight the Erskines. For this night, we'll set aside our . . . discussion, but rest assured—I am no' finished with you yet, and I willna grant you my permission to wed my daughter."

"'Course not," Struan muttered. "Didn't expect you would."

Malcolm turned on his heel and strode to the stairs. "Follow me. I'll show you where you are to sleep."

His heart heavy, Struan followed Malcolm up the narrow stairs. If he couldn't get close enough to Sky to talk to her, and with her da dead set against him, what hope did he have of convincing her to return home with him?

Responsibility and obligation. If there was one thing he knew about his lady, it was that honor and obligation to her clan were deeply engrained in her soul. Sky was loyal to a fault. What were the odds that she'd turn her back on all that obligation and duty business for his sake? Bone weary, he trod upon the corridor's medieval floorboards.

Malcolm stopped and nodded toward a door. "Here," he said, continuing on without another word.

Struan opened the heavy wooden door. A fire in the small hearth cast warm tendrils of dancing light around the chamber. Robley was already in bed, and a pallet and blanket had been laid out against the wall. Struan removed his clothing, hanging them on pegs in the wall. Hopefully they'd dry by morning. He settled himself upon the pallet and stared at the beamed ceiling.

"Dinna give up, lad," Rob said. "Erin and I faced much worse, and everything sorted itself out in the end."

"Malcolm is not about to give his daughter to the bastard son of a long-dead earl," he huffed out. "I have nothing to offer here but my sword."

"Och, but Sky comes with a nice bit of land and a tidy fortune." Robley grunted. "My cousin is motivated more by fear that you'll take Sky away from him than he is by the unfortunate circumstances of your birth. If she means that much to you, you might consider staying here."

"The twenty-first century has a lot more to offer, as you know. Besides, I already own a nice bit of land. I have a business, a nice savings account and a wonderful adoptive family."

"Och, well, you've much to think upon. Try to get some rest. We've a full day ahead of us on the morrow."

Struan continued to stare at the ceiling. Would he meet his end upon the battlefield tomorrow? Perhaps everything up to this point had been leading to yet another field and another fight, and this time he wouldn't be so lucky. Rest? Not bloody likely. His gut knotted, and his mind went round and round on the hamster wheel to nowhere inside his head.

He'd live or die; Sky would return to Gordon Hollow with him or she wouldn't. Everything could change in a heartbeat, and somehow he knew tomorrow would be the day that fate would reveal whether or not it was for or against him.

CHAPTER FIFTEEN

Sky awoke to the sound of booted feet traipsing down the passage-way outside her door, along with muffled male voices. She slipped out of bed, snatched up a gown and pulled it on over her night rail. Running out of her chamber in her bare feet, she caught a glimpse of Struan just as he reached the top of the stairs. "Hold, Struan, we must speak," she said, careful to keep her voice low.

He turned to face her, his expression unreadable in the predawn dimness. So much needed to be said, but she had no notion where to start. She hurried to catch up with him. "Do you mean to fight with my kinsmen this day?"

"I do, and don't try to argue me out of it." His expression was closed, but she felt his resolve as if it were a stone wall between them. "And *don't* worry about me," he added.

"I ken better than to try to talk sense into you, and I *will* worry whether you wish me to or no'." Oh, how she wished she could find a reason to keep him inside Moigh Hall and away from the danger awaiting him. "You've already done more than I have asked of you. 'Tis no' your fight. You need no' risk your life for—"

"Didn't you just say you wouldn't try to talk sense into me?" One side of his mouth turned up for an instant, and then the smile was gone. He reached out and tucked a strand of hair behind her ear.

Sky caught his hand and turned to kiss his palm. "Struan, why did you no' tell me who your father was, or—"

"That I'm a bastard?"

"Aye. That too."

He shrugged and stared at something over her head. "I didn't want to see . . ." He cleared his throat. "I wasn't certain how you'd react, and I didn't want to risk finding out. I suffered a great deal of ridicule as a child. I was reviled by my half siblings and by their dam. When you look at me, your eyes shine. If that light were to dim because—"

"Och, Struan, I dinna ken whether to shake sense into you or to hold you." Even in the half-light she could see his Adam's apple bob. She shook her head. "Why would you think something so beyond your control would affect how I look upon you? It grieves me to hear you say such a thing." She stepped closer. "Do you no' ken me at all?"

His chest rose and fell as if breathing were a chore. He cradled her face between his strong, callused hands and pressed his forehead to hers. "Aye. I ken you well enough, love. The problem lies with me, not with you."

Tears spilled down her cheeks as she gripped his wrists. "Promise me you'll come back to me unharmed, for you own my heart—today and always."

He crushed her to him, his mouth finding hers in a scorching kiss. Her heart beat wildly within her, and she pressed herself against him, memorizing every detail as a keepsake for all time.

"Struan, lad. 'Tis time. We must be off before the sun rises," Robley called up from the hall.

"You hold my heart as well, Sky." He set her away from him. "When this is over, we need to make some decisions." He wiped the tears from her cheeks with his thumbs. "*Don't* worry about me."

"I *will* worry. Stubborn man."

"Obstinate woman." He turned and strode down the stairs.

Sky sent up a prayer, nay, a desperate plea to the heavens to keep him safe. He loved her. She loved him. All that remained was overcoming the obstacles that stood between them. The most difficult of which was her sire's disapproval. Even without her gifts, she could see it in the way her da looked at Struan.

Never in her life had she considered defying her sire. He was the earl and laird of clan MacKintosh. No one defied him. How could she do so now? There was so much to consider. Between the two of them, who was to be wrenched from everything they held dear? She had her family, clan, wealth and standing in her century. Struan had land and a family he cared deeply about in the twenty-first century.

Her stomach churned. What if the obstacles proved too great, and they could not come to an accord? Mayhap 'twould be better for his sake if she refused him and sent him home to Gordon Hollow without her. Torn between her love for Struan and her love for her family, she returned to her chamber to prepare herself for the long day ahead.

Sky washed her hands in the bucket of hot water and scanned the great hall. All but a score of her clansmen had departed for the mainland before dawn. She and the women in the keep had been at their labors ever since. Old men from the village, taking refuge on the island, carried in barrels and broad planks, setting them up as makeshift tables where they could lay the wounded to be tended. Her sisters and a few servants were busy washing down every available surface with a mixture of boiled water and vinegar. The acrid scent tickled the inside of Sky's nose. She sneezed.

"Bless you," her mother said, glancing at her. True was busy sterilizing needles and silk thread. Jars of herbs, unguents, healing salves and tinctures were lined up along the high table, like soldiers awaiting their orders.

It had been months since Sky had practiced the healing arts, and this time, doing so held a far greater weight. She couldn't shake her fear for Struan. Had she been given the chance, she might have slipped a sleeping draught into his morning ale, preventing him from going off to battle.

Don't try to argue me out of it. Och, she kent well enough trying to talk sense to the man was a wasted effort. His head was every bit as thick as her sire's. Even believing he would meet his end in her century, he had marched off with sword in hand, ready to lend himself to a cause not his own. Her heart swelled and ached all at the same time. "Stubborn man," she muttered under her breath.

She snatched up the baskets she'd gathered and moved to the dais to join her mother. There, Sky cut clean strips of linen to be used as bandages, rolling each one before tucking them into the row of waiting baskets. A fire burned in both hearths, with large cauldrons of water set upon iron hooks to boil. Cook had more cauldrons going in the kitchen, and there were those whose job it would be to keep the cauldrons filled and boiling until the last man had been tended. They would need all the sterilized water for bathing wounds, cleaning their needles, knives and hands.

"Sky," her mother said, glancing at her. "I'm afraid I caught your father attempting to intimidate Struan last night."

Sky groaned. "Da told Struan he'd no' permit me to wed him, didn't he?"

"He did indeed." Her mother sighed. "I hope you understand Malcolm is motivated by fear of losing you again. It's not prejudice against Struan's lack of status. We grieved your loss deeply. Your disappearance was extremely hard on all of us."

Pressure squeezed her chest. If she chose to return to the future with Struan, she'd cause so much more pain to her kin. "When I overheard

Oliver telling his mistress of his plans, I vowed to return home and continue my training with Erin as a midwife. I vowed I'd never wed." She kept her gaze on the strips of linen before her.

"Oh, my dear. You're so young yet. Just because—"

"I canna face another betrothal with some stranger, a noble who sees me as naught but a purse and a bit of ground. I willna agree to another betrothal contract. If I canna alter Da's mind where Struan is concerned, I will hold to my vow."

Sky studied the row of baskets before her. "Och, so much has been left unsettled. Struan has asked me to return to Gordon Hollow with him, and I have asked him to remain here with me. We are at yet another impasse."

Could she leave her family behind? She'd always believed her rank obligated her to sacrifice her own happiness for the good of the clan. After spending time in the twenty-first century, witnessing for herself how everyone had the freedom to choose their own path, she wasn't sure she could fit back into the confines of her role in her century.

"Another impasse?" Her mother flashed her a questioning look.

"Aye, Struan tried his best to convince me 'twas folly to attempt returning to this century. He may have had it aright." She glanced at her ma. "He believes he escaped death at Halidon Hill, and that he's been living on borrowed time ever since. He fears he's meant to die here." Her voice hitched. "Yet, to protect *me*, he came anyway, and now he's off fighting the Erskines." She shook her head. "If aught happens to him, how will I bear it?"

Her mother's arms came around her, and Sky succumbed to the fear and grief that had plagued her since the day she rode out of Kildrummy to find her da and brother. "I've made e-everything w-worse," she sobbed. "And now S-Struan's life is at r-risk. The Erskines willna c-cease in their pursuit of vengeance until they have spilled his *blood*."

"Hush, now. Regardless of the choices you've made, we would still be at war with the earl of Mar. When I learned you had fallen through time, I knew at the very least you were safe from whatever evil we sensed at Kildrummy." She patted Sky's shoulder. "Though I missed you terribly, I know you're brave and resourceful. I trusted you would find your way no matter where you landed."

"I-I was fortunate. I fell into a kind and compassionate family willing to aid me."

"The day you disappeared, Helen was the one to unravel the mystery permeating the keep. She intuited your life was at risk and alerted us. She felt the threat growing stronger that day, most likely around the same time you heard Oliver telling his lover of his plans. I had already discussed my fears with Malcolm, and when Helen came to us, we agreed to gather everyone and leave before the wedding took place." Her mother lifted Sky's chin to peer into her eyes. "So you see? Either way we'd be at war."

"Why did you no' tell me?" Sky cried.

"I would have, but you disappeared. The chaos that ensued gave us the perfect opportunity to slip away. I almost wonder if Madame Giselle had anything to do with the portal opening when it did."

"I dinna believe so." She shared what the McGladreys had learned, and how the ring at Kildrummy had been responsible for comings and goings throughout the centuries. A loud booming resounded from the mainland, and Sky flinched.

"The Erskines' cannon no doubt," her mother bit out. "Best ready ourselves. It won't be long before the wounded begin trickling to the island. Once you're done with the bandages, best begin brewing the medicinal tea. Mind, you'll want to mix equal parts red willow bark with the antiseptic and antibiotic herbs. I'll help." She reached for her earthenware jars and rose from her place.

"Sarah," her mother called out, "go tell cook to gather several clean ewers for tea. Helen," she continued. "Go and fetch the *uisge-beatha* from the buttery. The men will appreciate the numbing effects of the strong spirits, and we'll use it to disinfect their wounds."

As her mother predicted, it wasn't long before the villagers began ferrying the wounded from the mainland, whilst the cannon continued to fire. Did a single ball make it to land upon their island? Sky shook her head and immersed herself in tending gashes, broken bones and pulling arrows from torn flesh.

The young lad currently stretched out before her writhed in agony. He'd suffered a wound far beyond her skills to fix. His torso had been sliced from side to side, and his entrails were severed clean through. All she could do was to stay by his side and make him as comfortable as possible until death took him far from the pain. His moans pierced her heart. Too young. His life had been wasted by a senseless desire for vengeance. She was not given to hatred, but in that moment, she truly hated the earl of Mar.

By midafternoon, her back ached and fatigue blurred her vision. Sky blinked against the burn in her weary eyes, straightened and rolled her shoulders to ease some of the tightness. They'd lost eight good lads, and saved a score. Each time more wounded were brought into the keep, she searched their agonized faces for Struan, heaving a sigh of relief each time she didn't find him amongst the suffering.

Mayhap he'd survive the day after all, or mayhap he lay dead somewhere upon the mainland. That didn't bear thinking upon, and she moved to wash her hands in one of the many buckets the servants kept filled with clean water.

"Sky," Connor shouted from the doors, his voice filling the great hall.

Gasping, she whipped around to see him stagger under the weight of the man he carried over his shoulders. She recognized Struan's boots and trews.

"Nay," she cried, hurrying toward him, her heart clawing its way up her throat. "How bad?" she asked, leading Connor to an empty table that had just been scrubbed down.

"He has a gash across one shoulder, not too deep, and an arrow lodged in his thigh." Connor laid Struan down as gently as possible. "I'm most concerned about a blow he took to the head. He's been out cold since he fell, and we've not been able to rouse him."

His expression filled with concern, he met her gaze. "I broke the shaft, but the arrowhead is still embedded in his leg. I didn't want to risk taking it out, in case I caused more harm than good." He stepped back and ran his sleeve across his forehead. "I fear the steel has pierced the bone. Could just be the tip, or it might be to the marrow."

Sky's weariness dissipated, and her blood rushed. She kent the danger well enough. If the arrow went through the bone to the marrow, he could easily develop a blood infection, one well beyond their fifteenth-century skills to treat. That he hadn't responded to Connor's attempts to rouse him to consciousness also knotted her stomach. She reached out and gripped the forearm of a passing servant. "Anne, bring me cold water from the well below the great hall, and gather enough fresh linen to make a compress."

"Aye, Lady Sky," Anne said before running off to do her bidding.

"Connor, help me lift him to sitting, so I can get some of this tea into him." Sky poured medicinal brew into a mug and held it ready, as Connor put his arms around Struan's shoulders and raised him. Struan showed no sign of awareness as Sky held a mug to his lips. "Drink, *mo rún*," she pleaded with his still form. "'Twill reduce the swelling and ease your pain." He didn't respond, and she lowered his jaw, tilted his head back slightly and poured a trickle of the liquid down his throat. He swallowed reflexively.

She managed to get a goodly amount of the healing tea down his throat, with an equal amount spilling down his chin. Connor helped her lay him back down. "Fetch my ma if you would." Her eyes met Connor's for an instant before she turned her full attention to Struan.

Her heart skipped a beat as she examined the swelling at the back of his skull. Erin had explained the danger of blood clots and the grave risks involved in brain injuries. Fear for him clogged her throat, as she struggled to rise above the panic. What good would she be to him if she couldn't control her emotions? He needed all her wits and a steady hand.

Anne hurried to her side, a pail filled with the icy water from the depths of their stronghold. She also clutched a pile of linen to her chest. "Here, my lady," she said, placing the pail on the table. "What else would ye have me do?"

"Soak the linen in the cold water and wrap his head. Don't wring out the cloth. We want to soak his head in the cold to reduce the swelling, aye? The compress should be changed oft," she ordered.

"Aye, my lady."

With that task taken care of, Sky cut off Struan's sleeve and began cleaning the gash running down his arm. Connor had it aright. Other than a short length at the top of his shoulder, the wound was not too deep. Only one section would need to be sewn. She poured a stream of *uisge-beatha* into the torn flesh and took up a clean needle and a strand of silk. Her hands shook as she tried to thread the needle. She drew a long breath, let it out and tried again, finally getting the thread through the eye. Bending over Struan, she began stitching together the edges of the deepest part of the injury.

"Sky," her mother said, coming to stand by her side. "What do you need me to do?"

"See to the arrowhead in his thigh, and tell me he's going to be . . ." Her voice broke along with her heart. "Tell me Struan will wake, that he'll recover." *Tell me I'm not to blame for this, and that I won't lose the only man I will ever love.* She had to stop what she was doing to wipe away the tears blurring her vision.

Her mother hugged Sky's shoulders briefly, before setting her knife to Struan's trews to get to the metal wedged into his thigh.

Silently Sky, her mother and Anne toiled over Struan, until they'd done everything they could. Sky stepped back and glanced around the hall. She called out for help to take Struan upstairs, and four men hurried forward to do her bidding, Connor amongst them. "Take him to Robley's chamber and lay him upon the bed." Two positioned themselves at his legs, and two moved to his shoulders. "Careful! Support his head and neck," she admonished as they lifted him.

Just then, a bell chimed from the village kirk, signaling the battle was over and pealing out the news that the MacKintosh had prevailed. A cheer rose up within the hall, but she barely took notice. Sky turned to Anne. "Fetch fresh water from the well, and bring it to Lord Robley's chamber."

"I will see to it anon." Anne snatched the rope handle of the pail and was off.

Sky hurried to follow the men carrying Struan, easing her way in front of them once they reached the corridor so she could open the door. She rushed to the bed, threw back the covers and gathered the pillows into a pile to support him. "The tea. I forgot the tea." She strode back to the door. "Undress him and lay him so that his back is propped." She nearly ran into her sister in her haste to return to the great hall for the tea.

"Och, you nearly spilled it, Sky," Helen scolded, bringing the pitcher she carried close to her chest. "I've brought a potion Ma brewed especially for your knight." She handed her the earthenware jug. "How can I help?"

Sky shook her head. "Unless you can wake him, there's naught to do but continue with the cold compresses and pour whatever Ma made for him down his throat. I can manage. Go below and help with whoever might yet come to the hall to have their wounds tended."

"If that is your wish." Helen narrowed her eyes, her gaze unfocused. "'Twill be all right, sister. I feel what is to come will bring you great upheaval, a wrenching of your very being, but 'twill be all right in the end."

"Helen, speak plainly." Sky tensed, and her poor heart pounded against her ribs. Her sister's words could mean anything. "Will Struan recover?" She asked only what she dared to voice. The rest she only thought. *Will he and I find a future together?* Mayhap Helen would hear that as well.

"I ken no' what is to be, Sky. I . . . 'tis only an impression. I get these . . . premonitions, a certainty about the future, but nothing is clear to me beyond the sense, the vibration, of what will be." She reached out and grasped Sky's arm. "Mayhap 'twould have been better if I had said naught. I meant only to offer comfort."

"I ken as much, and I'm grateful." Sky slung her arm around her sister and hugged her. "Go. Help Ma and Sarah. I'll be with Struan if anyone needs me." With that, she turned back to Rob's chamber with the potion her mother had concocted. She took a sniff of the contents, separating what she detected, tracing the source to the herbs her mother had used. Willow, the usual antiseptics and . . . hellebore.

Och, aye. 'Twould slow his heart, which might aid in reducing the swelling in his skull. 'Twould also help prevent fluid from settling in his lungs, which oft happened with those who were bedridden. By the time she returned, the men had Struan undressed and under the covers. "My thanks," she said. "If you see Anne on her way here, ask her to bring a clean mug. I need to give Struan the medicine Ma made for him."

With nods of agreement, all but Connor departed. He stood at the end of the bed and watched Struan. "I pushed him to come with us," he said, meeting her gaze, his expression tortured. "I'll never forgive myself if—"

"Say no more, Connor. None of what has happened is your fault."

"Nor is it yours, lass."

Wasn't it? Anne arrived with cold water, a mug and an oiled cloth to place beneath Struan to keep the mattress dry. "My thanks," Sky said. "Come back every hour, or send someone else. I'll want to keep the cold compress going throughout the night, and for that, I'll need the water changed frequently."

"Aye, I'll fetch something for ye to eat as well. Ye canna labor thus without feedin' yerself, my lady."

She nodded absently, all her attention focused upon Struan's far-too-still form. "Connor, you dinna have to stay. I'll be fine."

He lifted a chair from the corner of the chamber and moved it to the side of the bed for her. "Send for me if you need anything." He took the ewer from her hands and set it upon the chest against the wall near the bed. "Anything at all."

"I will." She turned to remove the linen wrapped around Struan's head, dropping the cloth in the fresh water. If only he'd taken the blow during the winter. She could pack snow into oiled cloth to lay under his head. She reached out to brush the wet hair from his brow, barely taking note of the chamber door closing behind Connor as he left.

Images ran through her mind, memories of afternoon rides through the tranquil valley with Struan, the first time they'd made love by the loch, even their many arguments. Her eyes stung from weariness and grief. Dammit, she hadn't had nearly enough time with him. She heaved a shuddering breath and reached for his hand. His fingers curled around hers. Dare she hope 'twas more than reflex? Leaning close, she whispered, "Come back to me, my love."

"I've brought yer supper, my lady," Anne announced from the door.

Wearily, Sky rose, reluctant to break the contact with Struan. "Leave it on the table. I'll eat once I put a fresh compress on his head and get some of this medicine down his throat."

"Do ye need help?" Anne asked.

"Aye, if you would, prop him up by the shoulders." Anne held him forward, and once again Sky managed to get a goodly amount of the fluid into him. She drew the linen out of the icy water and wrapped his head once more. "He'll be fine for now. Go and have your own supper, and come back within the hour with fresh water."

Anne curtsied and left, and Sky moved to the window to peer outside. The sun had begun to set, and she guessed the hour to be half past Vespers. She moved to the table and stared at the steaming stew. She had no appetite, but the night would be long, and she'd need sustenance. She sat, tore off a chunk of bread and used it to scoop the stew. For Struan's sake, she forced herself to eat every last morsel before she returned to his side. Taking a seat, she reached once again for the comfort of his hand in hers.

The door opened softly behind her, and the rattle of metal filled her ears. She turned to find her da standing at the threshold, still clad in his armor. His face was streaked with dirt and sweat, and his armor was spattered with blood. "*Mo inghean*, daughter, how fares your young knight?"

Her da had always seemed so large to her. Invincible. His eyes were full of compassion and love, and she unraveled under his gaze. A sob rose up her throat, and tears filled her eyes. All she could do was shake her head. Her da tore off his gauntlets, tossed them on the floor and strode to her side. He lifted her from her place and hugged her as best he could. "Och, lass, dinna greet so. He breathes. Where there's breath, there's hope."

"Truly?" She clung to the man who had protected and loved her since the day she was born.

"Aye, truly. I've seen lads who slept for days after such a blow to the head wake to take up their lives once more, and they had no' the benefit of you and your ma's gifts for healing." He patted her back. "Wheesht now, and let me look upon your man so that I might see for myself how he fares."

"*Now* you call him *mine*? You forbade him to wed me, Da." Her words were tinged with bitterness.

"Aye, I did, but the lad caught me unawares. He claimed he'd asked you to return to Gordon Hollow with him, and I . . . well, I reacted from the heart and not from the head." He kissed her forehead. "You are my firstborn, Sky Elizabeth. I'll ne'er forget how I felt, holding you for the very first time. 'Twas but a few moments after your birth, and you were such a wee thing. And sae lovely, my poor heart was full to bursting."

"And now?" She peered up into his eyes.

"And now? It still melts my heart to look at you, lass, I love you that much. No sire could be more proud than I. You've grown into a fine, canny lass, with a braw and compassionate heart. I want only the best for you."

"I meant have you softened toward Struan."

"Aye, I kent as much." He sighed. "He acquitted himself well this day. I'll no' deny he's a fine, honorable lad and good with a sword." He brought her to his side and moved to study Struan's still form. "The lad's color is good. He's breathing well." He drew down the cover to look at the gash down his shoulder, neatly stitched by her hand.

"Did I ever tell you about the time your ma stitched me up with our clan's colors?" He slanted her a grin. "I'd ne'er seen the like. I looked like her latest embroidery project."

She smiled back, her eyes misting. "Aye, you've told the tale a time or two, and how she would no' speak to you for days, because you went off without a word to fight Black Hugh and the Comyn clan after they attacked Meikle Geddes."

"I did what had to be done." He grunted.

"And came back gravely wounded and near death," she retorted. "Where Struan lives, there are no enemies lying in wait to take what is his. Gordon Hollow is the most peaceful, fertile and wholesome place I've ever been. You canna imagine what 'tis like to live with no' worry about intrigues and feuds. To live so free from constraint, or—"

"Obligation?" He tensed. "Nay, I canna fathom such a thing, nor do I wish to. Like my sire before me, and his before him, my life belongs to our clan. Our people depend upon us to defend them and to see to their welfare. In exchange, we have been granted a life of privilege." He scrubbed his face with both hands. "I did no' come here to give you a lecture. See to your lad, and we'll talk more once he wakes. Mayhap we can come to some accord, for I'll no' lose you again, lass."

She didn't ken what to say or how to respond. Not that it mattered. Her da was already on his way out the door.

"If you need aught, send word." With that he was gone.

"Time for more tea and a fresh compress," she muttered to herself. 'Twas true. Struan's color was good, and his breathing and pulse were steady. Mayhap he'd wake on the morrow, and all would be well.

Her family and servants trickled in and out of the chamber throughout the long night, offering aid and comfort, bringing more of the healing potion and fresh cold water for his compresses. Weariness pressed in upon her. A few hours before dawn, she succumbed. Crawling onto the bed atop the covers, she scooted next to Struan should he wake, and lay down. Finally, she fell into a fitful sleep, her dreams filled with the booming of a cannon and images of blood and torn flesh passing before her eyes.

"My lady, you must be up," Anne said, shaking Sky's shoulder. "Lord Robley and Sir Connor wish to speak with ye as soon as you may be ready."

Sky opened her eyes a slit and sought the source of the disturbance. Groaning, she stretched and pushed herself up to sitting. She glanced at Struan, her heart dropping at the sight of his unchanged state. Still, but breathing. "You've brought fresh well water?"

"Aye, 'tis right here," Anne said.

Sky climbed off the bed and stretched again. "Put a fresh compress 'round his head, whilst I go clean up a bit." She longed to visit the bathing room and soak in a hot bath, but she couldn't bear being away from Struan for that long.

"I'll see tae the compress, Lady Sky, and yer ma is brewing a fresh potion for the lad as we speak. Go now, and take as long as need be. I'm tae fetch Lord Robley and Sir Connor when ye are ready, and I'll bring food tae break yer fast as well."

"I am grateful to you, Anne. You've been an enormous help."

Anne beamed at the praise and bobbed her head. Sky left to visit the garderobe, then continued on to her chamber. She glanced down at her blood-spattered apron. A good wash and fresh clothes would surely renew her spirits, and then she'd resume tending Struan.

Washed, changed and her hair brushed and braided, Sky returned to Robley's chamber. She opened the door and walked inside to find Rob and Connor already within. Rob rose from where he sat at the table. Connor was pouring tea down Struan's throat.

"Is that the medicine Ma steeped this morn?" she asked.

"It is," Connor said, continuing with his task. "Sit, lass. Your mother, Robley and I have been talking."

"Aye?" Her knees weakened at his tone, and she dropped into the chair beside the bed.

"Aye." Rob came to her side and rested a hand on her shoulder. "We are all in agreement. Struan's condition is . . . unchanged, and we believe his best chances for recovery lie in the future."

Her throat closed, and she nodded mutely. The same thought had flitted through her mind during the long night.

"There are two possible portals between Moigh Hall and DúnConnell." Connor set the mug aside and carefully laid Struan back down. "We propose to stop at each, and if neither opens during the night we camp there, we'll continue on to your brother's keep. My wife is a doctor, Sky. She'll know what to do. We're hoping Madame Giselle will be at DúnConnell, and that she'll aid us in getting the lad to the twenty-first century—preferably near a hospital. If we find a portal along the way, I'll take him through. If not, Katherine and I will travel with him together."

Her poor heart would surely cease beating. "I fear the journey through time will kill him." She twisted her hands together. "Besides, you ken what happened when the four of us went through, clasping hands as we did. We were parted. How do you mean to stay with him? How can he fix his mind and heart on any destination in his current state?"

"We managed to keep our backpacks, aye?" Connor looked to Rob, who nodded encouragement. "Your cousin and I have come up with a solution. We'll lash Struan to my back. We've already talked to the tanner, and he's fashioning the straps now."

"Sky, it's Struan's best hope." Robley squeezed her shoulder. "A wagon and food are being prepared for the journey. We mean to leave within the hour."

She shot up. "I've much to do before we leave. Herbs for his healing tea, salve for his wounds, fresh linen for bandages. I must bid my family farewell."

Connor shook his head. "Sky—"

"Dinna think to stop me. Someone must tend to him along the way."

"Your sire forbids it, lass." Robley lifted Struan's rucksack and hoisted it over his shoulder. "I'll send servants up to see that Struan is washed, dressed and ready to go."

Sky fisted her hands at her side. "I'm going with you, and if you leave without me, I'll find a way to follow, so you'd best await me at the ferry." With that, she stomped out of the chamber and strode toward her da's solar. She threw the door open only to find the room empty. Mayhap he was with their garrison, praising their men for a job well done. He might be in the village, seeing to burying the dead and assessing damage to the cottages.

Hurrying down the corridor, she headed for the stairs to the hall, taking the stairs as fast as she dared. There she found her mother and sisters sitting at the high table.

"Come, Sky, break your fast." Her mother filled a bowl with porridge from a pot at the center of the table.

"I've no time." She gripped the fabric of her gown in her hands. "Robley and Connor mean to take Struan away, and I'm going with them. I fear Struan willna survive without a healer along to look after him." She blinked against the sting in her eyes.

"Ah, I suspected you might." Her ma lifted a canvas sack from the floor, and her worry and sadness washed over Sky. "I've prepared bundles of the best herbs to use for him, and there's a small copper pot within for steeping.

Stunned, Sky stared at the sack and then at her mother. "Where are Da and the twins?"

"I'm not certain. I know the three of them spent some time beneath the keep, talking to our garrison." Placing the sack upon the table, her mother stepped down from the dais and walked toward her. "Don't worry about your father, Sky. I'll deal with him."

Helen lifted a pack from the floor beside her and set it upon the table next to the one her ma had prepared. "Sarah and I packed a few things for you too."

"You . . . you kent I would go with Struan, even though Da has forbidden me from doing so?" Her gaze went to each of them. She was overwhelmed by gratitude and love. Her mother and sisters stared back, their expressions and emotions a heady mix of pride, sadness and strength. Humbled, she rushed forward, hugging each of them in turn.

"Sky, whatever you decide, know that we love you, and this will always be your home," her mother whispered in her ear. "Follow your heart, and never forget who you are."

Stepping back, Sky swiped at her eyes and nodded. "I dinna ken what—"

"If you should decide to come home, travel on to your brother's keep with Hunter's guards, and return with Robley and Erin when they journey home. I ken they won't mind stopping here first," her mother rasped out. "Go. Gather what you must from your chamber, and be quick. We won't let Robley and Connor leave without you."

One more fierce hug for her mother, and Sky ran upstairs. All she needed was the rucksack she'd brought with her from the future. It held her passport and state ID, along with other sundries she'd need . . . just in case. Slipping the straps over her shoulders as she went, she strode down the corridor to Struan's chamber. Connor was tugging boots onto Struan's feet.

"I'm ready," she announced, lifting her chin. "Ma has prepared what I need to look after Struan. We'll grab it on our way to the ferry."

Robley winked at her. "Your da is going to kill me, but truth be told, I'm gladdened by the news that you'll look after the lad."

She held the door open as the two men lifted Struan and carried him through the door. Connor carried his pack and Struan's on his broad shoulders. Following them down the corridor, her heart wrenched at the thought of not saying good-bye to her da and brothers.

An hour later, she laid a sheepskin, fleece side up, on top of a bed of hay in the bed of the wagon that would carry Struan. She arranged the bundles and packs around the outer edges, so that they might buffer him from jostling too much. "All is in readiness. Lay him down, and I'll ride with him in back. Tie my mare to a lead." She lifted a thick woolen blanket and oiled canvas to cover him, and glanced at the sky. The day was gray, the early morning air damp and chilly.

"Sky!" her da shouted. "What goes on here?"

She sucked in a breath and blood rushed to her face. The earl of Fife strode down the center of the village, flanked by Owain and David, and all three wore identical scowls.

"Tell me you dinna mean to leave Moigh Hall," her sire demanded, his arms crossed in front of his chest.

Shaking, she straightened and lifted her chin. "Aye, I do mean to leave. Connor will take Struan back to . . . to his *home*, and I mean to see that he's able to make the journey."

"You'll return to us?" David asked, reaching for her hand. "Once he's sent back, you'll come home?"

She shrugged helplessly. "I . . . I dinna ken. Oh, Da, what am I to do? I dinna wish to leave all of you, but . . . I love him." She peered into her sire's eyes, noting the gray hair at his temples and the new lines etched into his beloved face. "Dinna force me to defy you. Give me your blessing."

"Och, lass." She found herself in a fierce hug. "Is your mind made up then? Will you return to Struan's valley with him?"

"My mind, like my heart, is torn." She held on tight.

"Well, then," he said. "I'll hold on to the hope you'll come home to us anon." He stepped back and glared at the warriors who would travel with them, and then he sent Robley and Connor a hard stare. "Be on the watch for any stray Erskines, and guard my daughter's life well." Her da clasped Connor's forearm, and then Robley's. "Safe journey."

Everyone mounted as Sky hugged her brothers. She climbed onto the wagon and took her place at Struan's head. One of their guards took up the reins and started the wagon moving up the hill. She looked over the land and the village. Finally, her eyes rested upon the island. Home. Tears fell from her eyes. Now she kent what Struan had gone through when he faced the decision to travel with her to her century. Her decision would not be made until she had to make it, and she had no idea what she would do.

She must have dozed, for she woke to a chilly drizzle falling upon her face. She drew her cloak closer around her, then reached for the water skin filled with Struan's medicinal tea. Sky went up on her knees and turned toward him. His cheeks were flushed. She lifted one of his eyelids to find his eye bloodshot and glassy. Her stomach knotted as she pressed her cheek against his forehead. He was burning with fever.

"Robley, Connor," she shouted. "Make haste and dinna stop unless absolutely necessary. We must travel to DúnConnell straightaway."

Robley rode back to the wagon. "What is it, lass?"

"Struan is feverish," she said, her voice breaking. "Katherine brought medicines from the future back with her for Meghan and Hunter, anti-biotics she called them. I canna fight a blood infection with medicinal teas. Struan's only hope is to get to my brother's keep as quickly as may be." She met his gaze. "I'll do what I can with what I have, but . . . let us pray we get there in time."

CHAPTER SIXTEEN

S truan was underwater. He struggled to rise to the surface, tried like hell to move his feet and arms. Muffled voices were his only reward for all the hard work. He hadn't broken through. Were there others here with him in the murky depths? Must be the lake at Gordon Hollow.

But . . . if that were true, why wasn't anyone helping him? He inhaled, and his lungs didn't fill with water. Not a lake after all. Where was he, and what was the thick, dense heaviness pressing in on him from all sides?

Wait. Rest.

He floated for a bit, until he regained some of his energy, then he ordered his eyes to open. His heavy lids paid him no heed. Frustration and helplessness coiled through him. Concentrating, he poured all his will into the effort, and managed only the merest slit. His hand, resting upon a white blanket, was the only thing visible in his line of sight. A syringe had been stuck into a vein on the back, with a plastic tube connected to the end, stretching upward. The whole apparatus was taped in place. Damn, he hated IVs. He struggled, following the tube with his gaze, taking note of a bag of liquid and a plastic apparatus that dripped another liquid at intervals. Hospital. Struggling to pull his thoughts together, he tried to remember how and when he'd gotten there.

He'd been in a hospital before. Was this . . . then? He managed to catch a glimpse of his other hand; one finger had been encased in plastic, with yet another tube leading to some kind of monitor. Images began trickling into his awareness—people's faces, a battle fought upon the shores of a lake. The battle . . . he'd been surrounded and fighting desperately for his life when an arrow hit his thigh. He went down on one knee, his sword arm burning like the fires of hell, when a man called out to him, and then everything went black.

He remembered a medieval village, an unfamiliar place overlooking a lake. In the middle of the lake, an island, and on the island . . . a castle. Perhaps all of what he saw in his head had been a dream, and he was finally waking. He blinked. Concentrating made his head ache with dull persistence.

Surely the Gordons would come any minute now, and . . . The memory of a beautiful woman popped into his head. *Sky.* Focusing upon her image brought a wrenching ache to his heart. *Great.* Now his head *and* his heart hurt. Was he dying? He closed his eyes again. Too much. Thinking had worn him out. A door opened, and the muffled sounds returned, only this time, they weren't so muffled.

"His vital signs are good. The infection has responded well to the antibiotic drip," a woman's voice said.

He recognized that voice, but the name floated out of his grasp, disappearing into the cloud of confusion binding him.

"What about the swelling in his head?" a man asked. His words had a slight lilt.

"That's gone down too. He could wake at any time," the woman said.

Struan forced his eyes open a crack, hoping a visual would help him remember who they were.

"Katherine, his eyes are open again," the man said.

"It doesn't necessarily mean he's conscious. I've explained this already."

"Aye, I remember, but he seems to be following us this time."

Struan tried to talk. He opened his mouth slightly, but his tongue had turned to old shoe leather. Nothing worked. Since that was a bust, he exerted a monumental amount of energy and lifted his hand.

The woman, Katherine, gasped. "Struan, are you with us again?"

He nodded slightly.

"Push the nurse's button, Connor. Oh, Struan, we've been so worried about you."

He needed water, something to make his tongue work again. So many questions. He looked around him. A curtain had been drawn around the narrow bed he lay in, and there weren't any chairs for visitors. Katherine and Connor, the McGladreys—he remembered now—stood by his side and peered down at him, their faces wearing identical expressions of relief. Connor pressed a button at the end of a cord near Struan's head, and Katherine fussed with his pillows and blankets.

A nurse opened the door and popped around the end of the curtain. "Did you need something?"

A Scottish accent. So . . . he was in Scotland?

"Yes," Katherine answered, all businesslike. "Struan is awake. Please inform his doctor."

The nurse glanced at him with an expression of doubt. He stared back, raising his eyebrows slightly. Her eyes widened, and she moved closer, dragging a machine with her. She wrapped a blood pressure cuff around his arm and pumped it full of air, while checking the monitor and the IV drips.

"Water," Struan managed to eke out of his rusty throat.

"I'll get some for you just as soon as I'm done with your blood pressure, Mr. Sutherland." The nurse waited until the machine beeped, took a gander, and removed the cuff. "I'll page your doctor."

He nodded. The nurse raised his bed so that he was in a sitting position, and then she left.

"What happened?" he rasped, looking to Connor and Katherine for answers.

"You took a blow to the head whilst fighting the Erskines. You've been comatose ever since. We all thought it best to bring you back to . . ." He peered around the curtain for a second. "Well, back to *now*. You're at the Inverurie Hospital in Aberdeenshire, Scotland. We—"

"I hear our patient is awake," a male voice intoned. He pushed back the curtain, pen and clipboard in hand, and beamed at Struan. "You're a very lucky lad. Whoever did your triage care did everything exactly right, though I must say the stitches are a bit . . . unorthodox." He laughed as if he'd told a joke.

Stitches? That explained the tugging sensation on his right shoulder.

"I'm Dr. Hamilton." The doctor looked like he might be in his midfifties. He was on the stocky side, with graying hair, bushy brows and a mustache to match. He lifted Struan's eyelid, flashed a light in his eye, and repeated the process on the other side. "Headache?"

"Aye."

"Do you recognize these fine folks who brought you here three days ago?"

"Three days?" Struan's gaze shot to Connor.

Just then, the nurse returned with a plastic pitcher and a cup with a straw in it. Everyone shifted, and the wheeled tray was moved over his lap. She poured water for him and bent the straw so he could drink. Lifting it to his lips, she advised him to sip slowly. He drew in a mouthful, swished it around his mouth and swallowed. He took another couple of drinks before nodding to her and laying his back down on the pillow to answer Dr. Hamilton's question.

"I recognize the McGladreys." Where was Sky? His throat tightened. Perhaps she'd stayed behind. Surely her sire would have forbidden her from coming with him to the twenty-first century again, and she was nothing if not bound by duty and obligation. He closed his eyes. Weariness and grief sat squarely upon his chest, and he was far too weak to bear the weight of either. He listened as the doctor ordered some blood work, and the nurse hustled off to do Dr. Hamilton's bidding.

"Do you know what date it is?" the doctor asked.

Struan heaved a sigh. "No, but then, I don't know how long I've been unconscious either, so it's hard to calculate."

"Well if you've the wits to figure out why you can't say, that's a good sign." Dr. Hamilton put him through a series of questions, had him count and recite the alphabet, touch his nose with one eye closed, then the other, until finally he seemed satisfied. "I want to keep you here a couple more days to be certain the blood infection is completely eradicated, and we'll want to do a few neurological tests to make sure you're well on the mend." He straightened. "We'll know more once the tests are completed, but all signs point to a full recovery."

"Thank you, Dr. Hamilton." Katherine crossed the narrow space to shake his hand. "We appreciate the care he's been given."

So many questions swirled around in Struan's sore brain; it made the room spin just to think about them. He waited until the doctor left before turning to Connor and Katherine. "This isn't a private room, is it?"

"No, it's not, but your roommate is sound asleep." Katherine perched on the edge of his bed. "Or perhaps he's in a coma as you were."

"Who took care of me? Who did the excellent triage nursing the doctor mentioned?"

"Sky," Connor said, his expression solemn. "From the moment I brought you to Moigh Hall, she was by your side. She kept cold compresses on your head, dosed you with all kinds of medicinal teas and stitched up your shoulder. You had a gash there and an arrow in your thigh bone."

"I want to see the stitches." He tried to raise his hand to his shoulder, but he could only reach halfway because of everything hooked up to him.

"Here, I'll help." Katherine came to his aid. She untied his hospital gown and slid the sleeve down.

Struan twisted his head to get a look. Scarlet thread in a neat pattern ran a good four inches down his shoulder. "Silk embroidery thread."

"Indeed." Connor grinned. "Very neatly done, too. You probably won't have much of a scar."

His eyes stung. Closing them, he laid his head back on the pillow. He just didn't have the heart to talk anymore, and he couldn't muster the courage to ask the question burning a hole in his heart and mind. Sky wasn't here at the hospital with Connor and Katherine. Didn't that say it all? "I'm so tired. Thank you so much for everything you've done and for getting me back to . . . I know we have lots to talk about, but all I want to do right now is sleep."

Katherine fixed his hospital gown and brushed his hair out of his face. "Sleep, Struan. We'll be back tomorrow, and by then you will have eaten disgusting hospital food and gained a little bit more strength. We'll talk then." She patted his cheek. "Is there anything you want us to bring you?"

Yes. Bring Sky. He shook his head, his eyes still closed. The McGladreys left, and a few tears leaked out of the corners of his eyes. Did he dare travel through one of Connor's portals again? What if he took the trip and ended up somewhere else, or at the wrong time, like when Sky was only five, or seventy-five? If he'd lost the love of his life to the past, how could he face the future?

Struan forced another spoonful of the disgusting, watery oatmeal into his mouth. It had no flavor at all, and it was slimy. Once the stuff was in his mouth, he forced himself to chew and swallow. He needed his strength, and truth be told, he'd eaten worse whilst living in the fourteenth century. At least the porridge, if you could call it that, didn't have any bugs or wormy things floating in the soupy mess.

A plump middle-aged woman in scrubs pushed his curtain back. She carried a small tray with a syringe, a few vials and a length of rubber to tie off his arm. "I've come to take blood," she announced as if he hadn't the wits to deduce that much on his own.

"Again?" he grumbled. "If you keep taking my blood, how am I to recover?"

"A strapping lad such as yourself?" She gave him a once-over. "You shouldn't have any difficulty." She tied off his arm, placed it upon the wheeled tray and swabbed the crook of his elbow. She gave his veins a few taps and reached for the syringe.

"I hate needles," he muttered.

"Who doesn't?" She shot him a wry look. "This'll sting a bit."

Perhaps the sting would take his mind off his other pains, especially the gaping wound to his heart. He turned his face away from the proceedings while the woman filled the vials with his blood.

"All done," she said cheerily, taping a bit of gauze on his pricked skin. "Dr. Hamilton will be by to see you this morning around half ten."

He nodded his acknowledgement. She left, taking his blood with her, and a young man, also in scrubs, took her place. Struan frowned. "I'm out of blood."

The young man grinned and leaned a cane against the frame of the bed. "My name is Ronald, and I'm here to get you out of bed. We're going to take a stroll down the hall." He held up a folded hospital gown. "Even though they begged me not to, I brought this so you don't give the nurses a show."

"Great." Getting out of bed would be good. He'd have to ask the McGladreys how long he'd been comatose. Judging by how weak he'd become, it had been a while.

The orderly helped him put the extra gown on like a robe, threading the IV tubes through the sleeves. Struan sat with his bare legs dangling over the side of the cot, while Ronald put slipper-socks on his cold, bare feet.

"Ready?" Ronald asked, handing him the cane. He wheeled the stand holding the IV bags next to him. "You have the cane and the wheeled IV stand for support, and I'll be right beside you."

"Ready," Struan said. He clenched his jaw and pushed himself up to standing. The room began to spin, and stars flickered before his eyes. He sat back down. "Not ready. Give me a minute."

"Dizzy?"

"Aye. The room is spinning, and I'm seeing stars."

"Take it slow," Ronald suggested. "You've been flat on your back and comatose for several days, no' to mention the infection."

"And they keep taking my blood. There's hardly any left to pump," Struan grumbled, leaning over. "That's bound to weaken a man. Plus, today is the first day in I don't know how long that I've eaten."

"I'm sure your blood sugar is low." The orderly opened the top of a plastic container of juice sitting on his tray. "Here, drink this, and then we'll try again."

Struan finished the apple juice in two swallows, took a deep breath, and then another. "Let's go." This time, he rose slowly and remained stationary for a few seconds while he worked on regaining his balance.

The orderly took him by the elbow. "Hold on to the IV stand and the cane. Small steps now."

Struan managed to shuffle his way to the door and out into the hall. His thigh hurt where the arrow had pierced him, and he leaned heavily on the cane. He continued to shuffle along the hall and around the corner. Sweat broke out on his brow. "You wouldn't know it to look at me now, but I run, fight with a broadsword and joust at Renaissance fairs. Now I'm hobbling about like an octogenarian."

"My granny is eighty-three." Ronald grinned. "I hate to tell you this, but she gets about better than you."

"Thanks. I feel so much better." Determination lent him strength he didn't have, and he insisted on making another round. At the end of a hall, he stopped to lean against the door of a restroom. "I think I've had enough. Give me a minute before you help me back to my room."

"Want me to fetch a wheelchair?" Ron asked.

Struan shook his head, his limbs rubbery. "I just need a minute." He took a few deep breaths and waited until the shakiness receded. "All right. Back to bed." He pushed himself off the door and leaned on the cane. He gripped the IV frame with his other hand, rolling it along the tiled floor at a snail's pace.

Ron hovered close. "Someone will be by after lunch to help you take another walk."

Sweating, all he could manage was putting one foot in front of the other. Finally, they reached the door to his room. Ron opened it, and Struan dragged himself across the threshold. He almost fell to the floor when he saw who waited for him.

Sky stood staring at his empty bed with her arms wrapped around her midriff and her shoulders slumped forward. Her hair was loose and flowing down her back. His insides turned into a jumble of emotions, relief being the strongest. "Sky," he croaked.

She turned and burst into tears.

Struan's knees gave out, and Ron caught him before he collapsed in an undignified heap on the floor. His eyes never left Sky's as she hurried to his side. She put his arm around her shoulders to support him. Between the orderly and Sky, they managed to get him back to his bed.

Ronald arranged the pillows behind him so he could sit. "If I can, I'll take you for your next walk." He looked between the two of them. "Looks like you two could use a few minutes." He tugged the curtain around his space.

"Thanks," Struan called out, his gaze still fixed on Sky.

Ron chuckled, nodded to him and left.

"You're . . . here," Struan whispered. "I thought"—he swallowed a couple of times—"I thought you stayed . . . behind." He patted the bed and scooted over to give her room.

Tears coursed down her cheeks, and she shook her head. Sky stretched out on the edge of the narrow hospital bed next to him. Sighing, she put her arm around him and laid her head on his shoulder. He held her as she wept and ran his hands up and down her back while breathing her in.

Once her tears were spent, she sat up. "When I saw your bed empty, I feared you'd . . . you'd . . ."

"Died? Nah, I just took a walk." He cleared his throat in an effort to dislodge the boulder there. "When the McGladreys were here yesterday, and you weren't, I assumed you'd—"

"Katherine wouldn't let me come with them yesterday, but I was here both days before that. She said I'd exhausted myself and ordered me to rest. She gave me a sleeping pill. I slept and slept, all through that afternoon and that night."

"You're here," he said again, as if he needed confirmation. He reached out and ran his knuckles down her tear-dampened cheek.

She gripped his wrist and turned to kiss his knuckles. "You're alive."

"I love you, Sky. Please tell me you're staying. Please put my poor heart out of its misery."

Her eyes brimmed with fresh tears, and she let out a garbled laugh. "I love you, Struan, and, aye, I'll stay for as long as you want me to."

"Why, Sky? What made you decide to leave everything you know, your time, clan and family . . . for me?"

"I could no' bear the thought of my life without you, Struan. I almost lost you, and that is when I realized what I needed to do." She sighed. "I used to think I was no' cut out for adventure." She lifted her head to smile at him. "'Tis no longer true. Adventure suits me, and meeting you has been the greatest adventure of all—more than traveling through time, or escaping an enemy determined to take my life."

"You're the bravest, most audacious woman I have ever known, my love." He drew her closer.

"I'm glad you see me thus." She chuckled. "My place is by your side, Struan."

"Good, because I want forever with you." His entire being relaxed and settled. He rolled to his side to face her. "Tell me everything that happened between the battle with the Erskines and now."

She turned to him. He hadn't planned well, and lay on his wounded shoulder. It hurt, but he didn't move. He didn't dare break the spell he must be under, because he feared she might disappear. Tangling his fingers in her glorious hair, he leaned close and kissed her briefly. "The McGladreys said you took care of me at Moigh Hall. Then what?"

"We all kent . . . *knew* that your best chance for recovery lay in the future," she whispered. "Robley, Connor and I loaded you on a wagon, intending to visit . . . two of the Xs on Connor's map along the way, hoping one might provide us with the means to . . . you know."

"Aye, and did you find an open door?" He kissed her forehead and then the tip of her nose. He put his good arm around her waist. "You've lost weight, love."

"Aye. I've been under quite a bit of strain for the past fortnight." She nodded, her heart in her eyes. "That first day we traveled, you took a fever, and we never stopped at either spot. I insisted we travel with all haste straight to DúnConnell and my brother's keep. Katherine had medicines I hoped would heal you."

"Did her medicine help?"

"Nay. Katherine said you needed intravenous antibiotics, but we gave you what she had anyway. We hoped 'twould at least slow the infection." She sighed and snuggled closer. "Madame Giselle, Áine, happened to be at home in her cottage on my brother's land, and I begged for her help."

"Happened to be?" He smirked.

"Aye. She swore she had naught to do with anything that befell us." Sky placed her palm against his cheek. "She confirmed what Connor had guessed, that there are long-forgotten portals left open by the fae dotting the landscape on both sides of the Atlantic. She agreed to lend her aid, since she owed a debt to my mother. Áine gave us a crystal to open the way home for us. We talked about it, and decided the best thing to do was to return to the day we went back to the past." She brushed her lips against his before continuing.

"It worked. The rental car was still parked where we'd left it. We brought you straight to the hospital, gave them a story about a drunken brawl during an SCA reenactment event and told them you'd struck your head on a rock as you fell."

"Ah." He nodded. "Makes sense." He drew her closer. "Let's get something out of the way before the doctor or the McGladreys show up."

She grinned at him, her eyes sparkling. "Och, *mo rún*. You're far too weak for bed sport now."

He laughed, and happiness flooded through him. He'd believed he couldn't cheat death a second time, and he had—because of Sky. He'd also believed she'd reject him once she found out he was the bastard son of the earl of Sutherland, and he'd been wrong. The love of his life had returned to the future—to be with him. He grinned. "I wasn't going to suggest bed sport, princess."

"What then?" Her brow creased.

He found her hand, pressed his palm against hers and twined their fingers together. "Will you marry me, Sky Elizabeth, eldest daughter of the earl of Fife?" He kissed the tip of her nose. "Will you be mine to have and to hold for as long as we both shall live?"

She sniffed, made a choking sound and pressed herself closer. "Aye, Struan, son of the fourth earl of Sutherland. I will marry you, and I dinna wish to wait. Let us begin our future together as soon as may be arranged."

"All right. You'll get no argument from me, but I want you to know whatever you decide to do with your life, or whatever you want to make of yourself, I will support you."

She smiled through her tears. "There's something I need to tell you. My mother and sisters packed a good deal of gold and jewels along with the healing herbs and some of my personal belongings. I come to you with a good portion of my dowry."

"That's nice." He yawned. Money wasn't a concern. Perhaps they'd invest her dowry for their retirement and set aside some of the funds for their children's college education.

"Aye. I wrote my family a very long letter, which I gave to Robley to deliver. My cousin pointed out that we were all able to return to the past, and we found a way home. He suggested we visit from time to time. Might we?"

"After everything you've given up for me, how could I refuse you? Where you go, I will follow—now and forever."

Nodding through her tears, Sky rested her cheek on his chest. Profound peace and contentment settled over him like a soft blanket. With a smile on his face, Struan held the woman he loved in his arms. "I'm tired. All this emotional stuff has worn me out."

Sky laughed and sat up. "Take a nap. The McGladreys will be here soon. They're talking with Dr. Hamilton to arrange for your release so we can go home."

He tugged her back down. "Don't leave me."

"I won't, *mo anam*. Not ever. Sleep now—I'll be here when you wake."

"*Mo céile*, my wife," he mumbled, drifting. "I am the luckiest bastard on earth."

EPILOGUE

S ky opened the front door wide, taking in the brilliant crimsons and golds surrounding their valley, punctuated by the deep green of the pines and spruce. October had always been her favorite month, and not just because it was her birth month. She loved the transformation from summer to autumn, and here in Gordon Hollow, the colors were most spectacular. "Here they come, Struan," she called over her shoulder.

"Good. I'm hungry." He came to stand by the door with her, placing his hands on her shoulders.

She covered his hands with hers as they watched their family approach. Her heart wrenched. This would be her first birthday separated from her parents, siblings and relatives. She sighed.

"Are you all right, Sky? I know you're missing your family." He kissed her temple.

"I am." She leaned back into him. "'Tis . . . it's no' really so different though. Had I remained in the fifteenth century, married and moved to my husband's keep, I'd be feeling the same. I love the Gordons, Struan, and all of you are also my family."

The delicious smells emanating from their kitchen made her mouth water. With Lindsay's help, Struan had put together a feast in honor of her twenty-first birthday. Speaking of the Gordons, they were almost to the door now. Lindsay carried the birthday cake she'd baked for the occasion. Was that Brian by her side? Sure enough. She smiled, thinking about possible double dates in their future.

Sky waved at their approaching guests, and her engagement ring, forged by Struan's own hand, sparkled. He'd used a deep blue oval sapphire from her dowry. Two oval diamonds that he'd purchased for her were set on either side to frame the sapphire. He'd teased that since royalty always used sapphires or rubies for their wedding rings, he'd been honor bound to make her a ring worthy of a princess. She loved the ring, and the man.

"Come on in," Struan said. Michael, Lindsay, Gene and Marjorie entered.

Marjorie kissed his cheek and then Sky's. "Ethan and Carol will be late," she said. "They said not to wait. Little Gene is teething, and he's been fussy. They finally got him down for a nap, and don't want to wake him until absolutely necessary. Courtney and her husband should be here any minute."

"That will work. We're not going to eat for a while, anyway." Struan shot Brian a pointed look. "Nice of *you* to join us."

"I know, right?" Grinning, Brian took the container holding the cake from Lindsay's hands. "Where do you want me to put this?"

"Anywhere in the kitchen is fine," Sky said. "Make yourselves comfortable. What can I get everyone to drink?"

"Sky, you sit." Lindsay wagged her finger at her. "It's your birthday. We'll take care of everything."

"Oh," Marjorie gasped, staring at the wall where Struan had made room for her gift to him. "Your tapestry! It's absolutely stunning."

Struan took Sky's hand, and they joined his mother where she stood admiring Sky's handiwork.

"Did you make the frame, Struan?" Gene asked, coming up beside them.

"I did," he answered.

"You can almost see the water reflecting the sunlight," Marjorie said, reaching out to trace a golden thread gilding the waves of the lake. "Why, it's our lake, isn't it?"

"It is." Sky nodded, pride infusing her tone.

"Hmm." Lindsay studied the work of art. "Why that particular scene?"

Struan glanced sideways at her and squeezed her hand. Surely he was remembering the day by the lake where they'd made love for the first time. Her face heated, and she picked at a thread hanging from the bottom of her blouse.

"Umm," Lindsay murmured. "Never mind. I don't want to know."

"What?" Marjorie looked from him to Sky and then at Lindsay. "What am I missing?"

Gene put his arm around his wife's shoulders. "Young love, sweetheart."

Marjorie looked confused for a moment, and then her eyes widened. "Oh."

"Yeah, *oh*." Lindsay laughed.

"So, Sky," Michael said from his chair. "Have you decided what you want to do for the rest of your life? I mean, besides marrying my brother."

Sky glanced at Struan, and the look of pride shining in his eyes warmed her heart. He gave her a slight nod of encouragement.

"I have, but let's sit before I share my plans with you."

"Wait. I'll get beverages. Beer, Gene, Brian?" Struan busied himself with being a good host, and Gene helped. Once everyone was taken care of, Struan took his place on the couch beside her.

"Do we have to wait until everyone is here?" Marjorie asked, looking around the room.

"No, we can fill them in later." Struan put his arm around Sky's shoulders. "Go ahead, sweetheart."

She nodded. "Katherine sent me Meghan's high school and college diplomas, along with her transcripts."

"Why'd she do that?" Brian asked with a puzzled look.

"Lindsay, you're going to have to bring your boyfriend up to speed." Struan raised his brow. "For now, just listen."

Brian's brow creased, but he shut up.

"I want to enroll in nursing school. I wish to become a midwife like Erin."

"Perfect," Marjorie said, clapping her hands together.

"Does it bother you, doing all this under someone else's name?" Lindsay asked.

"Hmm, it's no' like I stole Meghan's identity. 'Twas given to me." Sky gazed at Struan. "I do wish to be married in my own name though. Mayhap once in a kirk, using Meghan's identity, and again using my true name."

Brian's eyes narrowed. "Are you in some kind of witness protection program or something?"

"Nay." Sky bit her lip. "I came here from the fifteenth century, and the McGladreys' daughter, who was taken to the past, is wed to my brother. It seems we have traded places."

Brian shot up from his chair. "Yeah, right. If you don't want to tell me, fine, but don't insult me."

Struan raised his brow at Lindsay.

"Come on, Brian," Lindsay said. "Let's go check on the horses."

Brian scowled Struan's way and stomped off with Lindsay.

"That ought to be an interesting conversation," Michael said with a smirk.

"Back to the weddings," Marjorie said, waving at her youngest son to be quiet. "How will you manage to marry in your true name?"

"Connor thinks he's found a man—a priest, actually—whom he believes came from the past. He's going to talk to him, see if he can't get him to admit where and when he's from. If things go well, Connor will ask him if he'd marry us. Mayhap it doesn't matter, but I want to take my vows as . . . me." She swallowed. "I want to marry Struan without having to deny my kin, my clan and my history."

She blinked several times, and Struan tightened his hold. "*We* know who you are and where you came from. I swear never to forget and to always honor your past."

Her eyes misting, she nodded.

"I hope you'll call me mother, Sky, because I already consider you my daughter," Marjorie said, moving to sit by Sky on the couch. Gene managed a nod, his eyes glistening.

"And as far as I'm concerned, you're my newest sister," Michael chimed in.

"Thank you." Sky swiped at her eyes. "I am most fortunate to have all of you in my life. I'm proud to be a part of clan Gordon." Her vision blurred as she looked around the room. She'd been blessed. First to have been born into her large, loving family, and then with the Gordons. Most of all, she'd been blessed with Struan. No longer did she resent her fae gifts, or fear having bairns of her own. No longer did she see herself as standing at the periphery of life, avoiding being noticed, or letting others make her decisions for her. Struan had given her everything she never thought she'd have.

A timer went off in the kitchen. Struan rose from his place beside her. "Time to set the table. How long do you think it'll take Lindsay to convince Brian we're not part of a witness protection program?" His family's laughter reverberated through their home. "Michael, come help me."

"On my way."

The front door opened, and the rest of their family crowded into their living room. Greetings and hugs ensued. Finally, Lindsay led a stunned-looking Brian back inside.

Brian frowned. "Does Andrew know?"

"He does." Struan nodded. "Let's eat before my efforts in the kitchen are ruined."

She and Struan had lots of helping hands to get dinner on the table, and finally they sat down at the feast-laden table, surrounded by loved ones.

She and Struan had it all: family, love and work they were passionate about. Sky sent up a prayer of thanks. Aye, she truly was a lucky woman, and she'd do everything in her power to hold on tight to the gifts she'd been given.

AUTHOR'S NOTE

The earldom of Mar has quite an intriguing history, as do all the politics of Scotland during the late medieval era. The fifteenth century was a brutal time, filled with treacherous, ruthless, power-grabbing and larger-than-life individuals. The history of the earldom is not in any way exceptional for that time.

Isabel Douglas was sister to the second earl of Douglas, who was also the earl of Mar. He died in battle without any legitimate heirs. Isabel inherited most of his land and became countess of Mar. She married Malcolm Drummond, brother-in-law to King Robert III. In 1404 Isabel's husband was murdered by Alexander Stewart, who then laid siege to Kildrummy Castle, the seat of the earldom of Mar. Alexander captured the castle, forced Isabel to marry him and to sign over all her land and titles. Isabel never had children, and she remained a captive in her own home until her death in 1408.

Alexander Stewart relinquished the title and estates of Mar in 1426 in exchange for a different title granted by King James I, the son of King Robert III. The estates and title then reverted to the crown. In 1435 the title of earl of Mar was claimed by Robert, Lord Erskine. However, the land that went with the title remained a contentious matter for the courts. King James I continued to hold the land under specifications of the previous reversion by Alexander Stewart, while Lord Erskine occupied Kildrummy Castle, had stewardship of the land, and held the title.

I write fiction. All the characters in the novels of Loch Moigh are products of my imagination. For the purposes of this story, I am glossing over the true history of the earldom of Mar and granting Robert, Lord Erskine, the title much earlier than when he made his claim. My antagonist, Oliver, Lord Erskine's grandson, is a completely fictional character. The hero in this tale, Struan, the illegitimate son of Kenneth, the fourth earl of Sutherland, is also entirely fictional.

There will be historians who will cry foul and point out the inaccuracies, and they will be correct. The historical aspects surrounding the earldom of Mar in this novel contain elements of truth, namely the legal claims and disputes regarding the land, while being entirely fictional when it comes to the timeline and the characters.

ACKNOWLEDGMENTS

As always, I must thank the folks at Montlake Romance for giving my books a home, and for assembling such a great team of developmental editors, line editors and copyeditors. I also want to thank my marvelous agent, Nalini Akolekar, for believing in my ability to spin a yarn or two, and for being in my corner.

I have to give a shout-out to Craig Johnson, of Arms & Armor, blacksmith extraordinaire, who patiently answered all my blacksmith-type questions. Any mistakes in my novel are my fault, not his. I also want to give a shout-out to organizations that keep the art of medieval warfare alive, including the Minnesota Sword Club and The Society for Creative Anachronism, Inc.

No one writes in a vacuum, and without my critique partners, Tamara Hughes and Wyndemere Coffey, I wouldn't be where I am today. Thank you!

ABOUT THE AUTHOR

Award-winning author Barbara Longley moved frequently throughout her childhood, but she quickly learned to entertain herself with stories. As an adult, she's lived in a commune in the Appalachians, taught on a Native American reservation, and traveled extensively from coast to coast. After her children were born, she decided to make the state of Minnesota her permanent home. Barbara holds a master's degree in special education and taught for many years. Today, she devotes herself to writing contemporary, mythical, and paranormal stories. Her titles include *Heart of the Druid Laird*; the Love from the Heartland series (*Far from Perfect*, *The Difference a Day Makes*, *A Change of Heart*, and *The Twisted Road to You*); and the other Novels of Loch Moigh, *True to the Highlander*, *The Highlander's Bargain*, and *The Highlander's Folly*.

46342079R00178

Made in the USA
San Bernardino, CA
04 March 2017